"You're a big one for speeches, Eli," she murmured.

"But when it comes right down to it, that's what you're all about, isn't it? Speeches."

He knew why she said it.

It gave both of them the excuse they wanted. His mouth came down hard over hers.

She met that kiss with all the fire and fury in her. It began as a point to be made. A battle and release. Almost a punishment.

And they took it deep, fast. They each had a little quiver full of erotic tricks they knew to drive each other to that precarious edge of control.

His hands threaded through her hair as she tipped her head back. That kiss was searching, tender, and then carnal as hell, driven by what felt like eons of unleashed, thwarted desire, and she felt herself dissolving into smoke.

In an instant, she was his in any way he wanted her. . . .

D0192449

By Julie Anne Long

JULIE ANNE LONG

WILD AT WHISKEY CREEK

A HELLCAT CANYON NOVEL

AVONBOOKS

An Imprint of HarperCollinsPublishers

WILD AT WHISKEY CREEK. Copyright © 2016 by Julie Anne Long. All rights reserved. Printed in the United States of America. No part of this book may be used or reproduced in any manner whatsoever without written permission except in the case of brief quotations embodied in critical articles and reviews. For information, address HarperCollins Publishers, 195 Broadway, New York, NY 10007.

First Avon Books mass market printing: December 2016

ISBN 978-0-06-239763-8

Avon Trademark Reg. U.S. Pat. Off. and in Other Countries, Marca Registrada, Hecho en U.S.A.
Avon, Avon Books, and the Avon logo are trademarks of Harper-Collins Publishers.
HarperCollins® is a registered trademark of HarperCollins Publishers.

16 17 18 19 20   QGM   10 9 8 7 6 5 4 3 2 1

To everyone brave enough to start over in a new place.
May you be as happy as Britt and J.T.

ACKNOWLEDGMENTS

My deepest gratitude to all the hardworking, lovely people at Avon Books for supporting my new contemporary venture, in particular to Tom Egner and his gifted art staff for the sassy, shiny, gorgeous cover; to Jessie Edwards for clever promotional support and cheerleading; and to brilliant editor, May Chen, for her incisive feedback and enthusiasm. My gratitude also to my agent, Steve Axelrod; Karen Crist for good-naturedly submitting to idea-bouncing sessions; and early readers like P.J. Ausdenmore and Janga Rohletter of the Romance Dish, who spread the word about how much you love the book. It means the world to me.

CHAPTER 1

You could turn over any given rock and find a more appealing collection of organisms than the folks gathered in the Plugged Nickel tonight, Eli thought. Or to put it another way, it was a pretty typical night at the Plugged Nickel.

Of course, they all looked as innocent as a black velvet painting of dogs playing poker. If he possessed X-ray vision, he knew he'd see the odd unregistered firearm strapped to a back, knives shoved into boots, drugs safely hidden in butt cracks or rushing through the pipes in the men's room. Much like actual dogs, they seemed to have heightened senses, at least for when the law was about to show up.

He hovered just inside the doorway and listened: *Clink, hiss, slam, crash.* The clink and hiss of bottle caps being yanked off, the bottles slammed on the bar for the customers, the empties hurled with gleeful violence into a big recycling bin. The mixed drinks here were strong, cheap, and careless—you could order the same one again and again, and it would never taste the same twice. The music was usually loud enough to vibrate the molars clean out of your mouth.

He hadn't been inside the place for several months. Carl, the Plugged Nickel's owner and bartender, had been uncharacteristically circumspect on the phone about why he might need Eli tonight. The Plugged Nickel generally didn't invite the law to visit, which its customers appreciated.

"Well, there was an argument between four guys. And now there's a poker game going on, Eli."

". . . And?" Eli could afford to be patient. Nothing was happening in Hellcat Canyon tonight. It was Tuesday, though bingo could get pretty cutthroat at the town hall, thanks to the rivalry between Elysian Acres and Heavenly Shores Mobile Estates. Given his clientele, Carl usually liked to police them himself, though a surprise visit from a deputy now and again kept them all from relaxing completely.

Carl cleared his throat. ". . . And I think the prize is a woman."

Eli frowned. Nothing made ugliness go down faster than a drunken fight over a woman. Especially in a place like the Plugged Nickel, which in its storied history had primarily distinguished itself as a haven for people who had nothing to lose.

"Guess I can pay you a visit," he'd told Carl, dryly.

He took a step deeper in and paused and leaned against the wall, getting the lay of the place. The Wall. That had been Eli's nickname in high school. Because he was big and quiet and you couldn't get anything or anyone past him on the football field. It had its advantages: it was how he'd honed a gift for swiftly noticing things—physical details and emotional nuances and minute anomalies, where Waldo was on a page or the perfect split-second gap on a football field to hurl a ball through to the receiver or how Glory Greenleaf's lashes were a sort of mahogany color at the very tips, where the sun got to them. His powers of observation were probably in his DNA. His dad had been a cop, too, and they kind of came with the territory. But life's vicissitudes had honed them.

He scanned the customers, mostly men, gathered at the scarred wood tables, and his eyes lingered on four guys seated at a table against the wall, heads close together. He knew three of them by name and reputation; the fourth was a stranger. Tension practically rose from them like steam.

And then he saw the real danger—in more ways than one—standing behind the bar.

His heart flipped over hard.

What the hell was Glory doing *here*?

He had a hunch this was why Carl had called him.

Her sheet of straight black hair was thrown carelessly over one shoulder; her chin was propped in her hands. Her soft old jeans molded the unmistakable curve of her behind. Her expression was complicated. A little amused. A little sad. A little wicked. A jaded, wistful quirk at the corner of her mouth, which, he knew, was where a dimple lurked. As if she'd set something in motion, an experiment, and hadn't abandoned all hope of being surprised, but she wasn't holding her breath.

Either she hadn't yet seen him or she was deliberately ignoring him.

His money was on the latter. Given she'd managed to do that for going on nearly a year now.

So while he practically sprained his neck with the effort required to keep his eyes aimed at those men and not at her, he was conscious of the other customers shifting and rustling, either turning or straining not to turn to look at him as he wound his way through to the four men. His presence had the kind of weight that disturbed the atmosphere.

He paused next to the poker players.

The card players slowly, simultaneously leaned back in their chairs and put their cards down. Clearly someone with a badge had told them more than once to keep their hands where he could see them and it was a reflex now.

The guy Eli had never seen before kept a grip on his cards and looked up at him.

It was a long way up. Eli towered.

This guy had sulky lips and movie-star cheekbones and a narrow white scar running from his cheekbone to his chin. But he was aging fast in a way that Eli recognized. It came from a hard life of doing bad things. He was wearing a leather vest, which struck Eli as frivolous, maybe even a little vain. Jeans, t-shirt, a gun, boots—what more did a guy need before he left the house in the morning?

"Evening Dale. Hey, Boomer. How's parole treating you?"

"Can't complain, Deputy," Boomer Clark said, polite as a boy scout. He was a blocky guy, a little dim, good-looking in a forgettable way, and an unpredictable drunk whose first impulse was to shed what he apparently viewed as the terrible burden of wearing clothes. Eli had once been compelled to pin a naked Boomer to the sidewalk on Jamboree Street and cuff him, which hadn't been easy since Boomer had been a wrestling champ in school. It was an intimacy Eli hoped never to repeat. Even if an audience *had* gathered and clapped at the conclusion, and the *Hellcat Canyon Chronicle* had printed a photo of the excitement, in which Eli looked triumphant if a trifle queasy and they'd pixelated Boomer's penis.

"Put in a garden this year, Eli," Dale Dawber volunteered. "Got some squash, beans, artichokes. If you need tomatoes, I've got 'em coming out of my ears. Even built a trellis to train them. Working on building a greenhouse. For the tomatoes," he hurriedly added.

"Good to hear your green thumb isn't going to waste."

Dale had produced a nice little crop of marijuana some time back. Law enforcement took issue, and Dale did some time.

"Heh." Dale smiled at that. Albeit a little cautiously.

"Ramon," Eli continued evenly. "How are things?"

Ramon Barros had gone to high school with Eli, and he knew Jonah. He said nothing. Ever since the thing with Eli had gone down, Ramon wouldn't say a damn word to Eli if he could avoid it. He did nod, though. He didn't have enough nerve to freeze him out completely.

A brief taut silence was interrupted by The Black Crows bursting out of the speakers. One of which was buzzing and was due to blow soon, Eli reckoned. Speakers didn't have a long tenure here at the Plugged Nickel.

"We haven't met." Eli turned to Leather Vest.

The guy stared at him. "Ezekiel."

Oh, brother. If his real name was actually Ezekiel, Eli would eat one of the pickled eggs that had sat on the bar since it opened in 1975.

"Your mama give you that biblical name in the hopes that you'd behave yourself?"

"Ha." Ezekiel's eyes were so dark it was hard to know where the pupil ended and the iris began.

The no-blinking thing was boring. For about a thousand reasons, Eli couldn't be intimidated.

"You all know you can't be betting in here, right?" Eli said it almost gently.

Not one of them was fooled by that tone.

They'd seen what Eli had done to Jonah Greenleaf, right here in the Plugged Nickel.

They all knew what Eli could do in general.

No one replied.

"Not playing for money. Are we, boys?" Ezekiel, or whatever the hell his name was, was all sly bonhomie.

The other three guys looked every which way except at Ezekiel, Eli, or Glory. Who, Eli was certain, was watching all of this raptly.

Eli hovered over them a moment longer, like a threatening weather system that could break any second.

"Well, I'll let you get back to your game. Now that I'm sure you're not betting. The Misty Cat Cavern might be interested in buying your extra tomatoes, Dale. The profits might be a little modest compared to your last crop, but what the hey."

"Heh. Thanks for the tip, Deputy," Dale said with more than a little relief. He seized his cards again.

Finally Eli moved over to the bar.

He leaned with his back against it, rested his elbows on it.

He didn't look her in the eye. Not yet.

He finally spoke.

"Your TV broke, Glory? You were watching that poker game like it's *Game of Thrones*."

For a moment—that moment so like the one after you trip over something and you don't know whether you'll be able to break your fall—he thought she might keep freezing him out. God knows he'd never known her to do anything by halves.

"Watching men act like idiots is about the only thing there is to do on a Tuesday night in Hellcat Canyon," she finally said.

"I hear knitting is another constructive way to pass the time."

Anybody strolling by would have thought this was a perfectly innocuous conversation.

But Eli's first memory of Glory Greenleaf was a blur and a splash: she'd hurtled past Eli and her brother Jonah on her plump five-year-old legs and thrown herself right into the swimming hole at Whiskey Creek just so she could say she'd done it first, just to impress her older brother and his friend, and just because it was something she hadn't yet done.

Glory didn't sit still for much, unless it was to play her guitar. Knitting would send her around the bend.

So that sentence was almost painfully intimate. It contained decades of memories.

And these were the first words they'd exchanged in months.

"Why?" she said finally. "You need a new Christmas sweater, Eli?"

When he was eleven, his aunt had sent him a Christmas sweater featuring three reindeer walking single file. He'd hated it until Glory pointed out that it looked like the reindeer were sniffing each other's butts. And then he'd worn it all the time.

Heartened, he finally turned around to look at her.

Damn. It was like spring on the heels of a bad winter, looking into her blue eyes.

She was smiling faintly, too.

"Maybe." He held her gaze.

Once he had talked to her more easily than almost anyone, Jonah included. But layer upon layer of unspoken things had created a nearly tangible barrier between them. Ironically, not unlike the glass that separates a prisoner from a visitor.

He suddenly felt just as much a prisoner as Jonah Greenleaf, trapped by his inability to say the words that would shatter that invisible barrier. He was trussed in a complicated knot of emotions, all of them volatile, none of them compatible.

And it was probably too late to learn eloquence. He'd spent a lifetime letting actions do most of the speaking for him.

Whereas Glory . . . Glory could sing a single word and make it sound like an entire story, full of nuance and ache. And she could write a song and then pull you into it when she performed, like it was a whole world unto itself. Eli had football trophies, a law degree, a gun, and a badge, but those felt like Muggle achievements compared to what she did, which was alchemy. She made it look easy. He knew it wasn't. Most people thought she was utterly fearless. He knew she wasn't. They'd grown up together, teasing and fighting and playing, but somewhere along the line he knew he'd be happy to just be Sir Walter Raleigh to her Queen Elizabeth. The person who laid his metaphorical cloak over mud puddles, making it safe for her to be her dazzling self.

He had a hunch it wouldn't matter. There were probably no right or safe words at the moment, even if he could come up with them.

Maybe there never would be.

He was proved correct when the faint smile dropped off her face and she turned from him abruptly. "Maybe you can use all that free time in your squad car to make yourself a new sweater, Eli. You know, in between getting hardened criminals off the street."

That sentence edged all around in little thorns.

A surge of impatience made his back teeth clamp down.

So be it.

He wasn't sorry about what he'd done to Jonah. Only that he'd had to do it.

"I just might do that," he said evenly. "Think I'd be good at it, in fact."

Once the very idea of Eli with knitting needles would have made her laugh.

Now her expression closed up again and she folded her arms across her chest. Then realized what she was doing and lowered them and plucked up a coaster from the bar and twiddled it in her fingers.

Her nails were cut short as usual and painted scarlet, and she'd striped them, for some reason, in silver. Glory did a lot of things just because. He knew the fingertips of her left hand were callused from holding down the strings on her Martin acoustic guitar. They'd probably been tough since she was twelve. Unlike nearly every other member of her family, Glory was willing to put up with a little pain in the service of something beautiful.

He remembered how those fingertips had felt sliding up the back of his neck in the dark.

The bands of muscle across his stomach tensed to withstand an echo of that shocking pleasure, and everything else that came after that.

He'd been able to see the stars up through the branches of the pine she stood against before he'd closed his eyes.

She'd closed hers first.

That was the moment he'd realized with epiphanic clarity that even when they'd seemed to be moving in entirely different directions—when he was a jock dating the cheerleader who was always on top of the pyramid, and Glory was dating that stoner idiot Mick Macklemore who'd had a really enviable GTO . . . even when Eli had left Hellcat Canyon for the police academy and law school and other girlfriends and she'd stayed behind working one crap job after another and was still with that dip Mick Macklemore—somehow it felt like they were still moving *toward* each other. If life was essentially a big Rubik's Cube, then every twist and turn, every meeting and parting, everything they'd ever said and done was necessary to get them to that moment at that party outside in the backyard up against that ponderosa pine.

She'd broken up with her boyfriend. He'd broken up with his girlfriend. He was returning to Hellcat Canyon for good. And she was finally leaving Hellcat Canyon for good.

Suddenly it was perfectly simple. The risk in making a move that could end their friendship suddenly seemed to evaporate in light of the fact that he might be losing her forever. And as they'd talked, they'd moved closer, and closer, and he'd reached up to pull a tiny leaf from her hair. That was a signal.

She knew it.

And she'd closed her eyes first.

As if she'd been waiting for that moment all along, too.

About two minutes later their tongues were twined and

his hands were down the back of her jeans and her hands were up the front of his shirt and hot on his skin and they were just about climbing each other when a loud, tipsy cluster of friends poured into the backyard.

They sprang apart, got swept off into different cliques, and then a half hour later Eli left to work the late shift and he couldn't find her to say good-bye.

Two nights later, he'd arrested Jonah Greenleaf for meth transportation about five feet from where they both stood now.

And BAM!

Glory had brought the full force of her stubbornness down, guillotining Eli out of her life.

She wouldn't return his calls. No one ever answered the door at their house.

She stopped showing up for open mics at the Misty Cat.

And as the months went on, he figured she'd finally left for San Francisco.

He was left to feel like a cut live wire, arcing and sparking. Haunted by that *click* of the cuffs as his own hands had trapped Jonah's familiar hands in them and by the expression on Glory's face when he dragged his best friend out of there. She'd been sitting across from Jonah, nursing a beer, because she didn't drink all that much.

But then . . . Eli had popped into the Misty Cat a month ago on an open mic night on a hunch when he was duty. And there she was on stage.

He'd tried calling her one more time.

No answer.

Fuck it. He knew she was hurt. He knew she was furious.

But so was he, and he had every right to be.

Maybe, in fact, more of a right than she did.

That stiffened his spine. He was here on business, so he might as well get on with it.

"Carl was a little concerned those four gentleman believe they're playing poker for your . . . let's get Victorian about it and say *favors*, Glory. Which could get ugly. Know anything about that?"

She stopped fidgeting with the coaster. "Huh." She sounded faintly surprised.

"Where do you suppose they got that notion?"

She shot him a sidelong glance, clearly contemplating hedging. Glory was stubborn as hell, but she also knew his nickname was the Wall for more than one reason. There really was no sense in trying to get around him.

She heaved a sigh. "Well, it's like this. They got to arguing over who could buy me a drink . . ."

This was a day in the life for Glory, for the most part. Men arguing over who got to do something for her.

". . . and for starters, I'm the bar-back tonight. I can't drink with them when I'm working, even if I wanted to."

"You're *working* here? You're working *here*?"

He shouldn't have betrayed any emotion at all.

Her chin went up. She met his eyes coolly. "Have to make a living somehow."

He only realized he was frowning when her gaze slid away from his.

An unworthy cinder of hope flared hot in him: Had she stayed because of him?

It was both the best thing and the worst thing he could hope for.

"Thought you were leaving town for good, Glory," he said shortly.

"Thought you were here at the Plugged Nickel on business, Eli," she countered tersely. "And what I do or don't do is none of your business."

It would have felt like a slap. But he knew her. And he heard the hurt threaded through the anger.

A silent stalemate ensued. Silent, that was, except for the staticky sound of "Iron Man" attempting to battle its way out of a fried speaker.

"Okay," he said evenly. "Did you *tell* those gentlemen you couldn't drink with them when you were on duty?"

"Mmm . . . Not in so many words. But I . . . well, I might have asked them to make their case in two sentences or less."

"Why did you . . . You made them answer *essay* questions?"

God help him, of all the things he ought to be feeling right now, he thought this was pretty damn funny. A bored Glory Greenleaf was a dangerous Glory Greenleaf.

"I didn't *make* them do anything," she pointed out quite reasonably, with a queenly little gesture of her hand. "Things were a little dull in here, and . . ." She shrugged with one shoulder. "I guess I got curious about what they'd say."

He hesitated. "What *did* they say?" Now *he* was curious.

"Turns out Boomer is a Capricorn who just read a good book about the Lord he wants to tell me about, and he got a cat named Daphne to look out for the gophers in his garden. Dale is excited about his succulents and he likes to tinker with vintage automobiles, I guess when he's not stealing them, and he says he'll take me for a ride in one on the back roads because he knows some great views. Ramon's uncle just kicked and left him a little money he wants to spend on me after he puts a new roof on his house."

He took this in, bemused. In truth, these little tidbits about guys he'd known for most of his professional life, usually on the adversarial end of it, were kind of touching. But then people had always seemed to want to tell Glory things. They laid them down trustingly, like little offerings, at her feet.

But only people who had the patience or nerve to let their vision adjust to the sparks she threw off caught glimpses of how bone-deep kind she was.

He realized he was smiling. All of it was so *her* and just hearing it made the world feel righter.

She dropped her eyes. Funny, even though the lighting in that bar was hardly optimal, he could have sworn she was blushing.

A beat of silence went by.

"What about Leather Vest?"

Her head shot up. "Oh, you mean Cheekbones?" she said breezily, and just like that, Eli's spine stiffened against a shocking rogue wave of black jealousy. "He's God's gift, and he told me in all seriousness that I should know from just looking at him that he's the best thing that will ever happen to me and he can show me fifty ways to have a good time, wink, wink. I guess he thought bravado would make him stand out a little from the crowd. The knife scar kind of highlights his bone structure, wouldn't you say?"

She met his eyes.

Challenging. Curious.

Glory being Glory.

"No," he said, slowly, to let her know he knew exactly why she'd said it. "That's not how I'd put it."

She held his gaze a moment longer, then turned away and rubbed a rag on the bar, which didn't need cleaning. The surface glowed her reflection back at her. That caressing motion made Eli restless.

"So . . . I guess it got a little out of hand there for a while," Glory conceded finally, ruefully.

If Glory had a coat of arms, it would say, "It Got a Little out of Hand There for a While." And right above that it would read, "I Got Curious."

In the middle would be an image of her holding a guitar over her head like Joan of Arc carrying her battle standard to war. Because Eli was certain that if the world could hear her sing and play, it would be hers to command.

"So what happened after the guys answered your essay questions?"

"I told them they all sounded so fascinating, I didn't know how a girl could choose, and if they were feeling competitive maybe they ought to play a game together. At least now they have an occupation and their hands are full of cards so they aren't arguing."

She sounded like a pre-school teacher who'd just passed out paste and construction paper to unruly toddlers.

"Glory . . . I'm pretty sure they still believe you're going to be the prize. Whether or not that was your intent."

She went still.

"Really?"

He almost rolled his eyes. He believed her. She might not be "his business," but that didn't mean he didn't still know her really, really well.

"Glory, do you remember when you were in the chemistry lab in high school, and you added the wrong chemical to the experiment, and it foamed all over and you had to stay after to clean it up and it took all night?"

A swift succession of emotions flashed over her face: surprise, wicked amusement, something like yearning. Maybe pain. She was realizing, maybe, that he had all the same memories she did, from different angles.

"I remember. It's actually called elephant toothpaste. I added the *right* chemical . . . if you want it to foam." Her mouth tipped up at the corner.

"Yeah, well, I think Leather Vest is like that little extra chemical in that mundane mix. Except I think he can blow up the lab. Don't play with that guy."

Damn. He shouldn't have issued it as an order.

She froze. Her face went dark. "You sure love to lay down the law, don't you, Eli? But you don't get a say in who I *play* with."

She shoved away from the bar as if she were pushing him bodily away and, with a flick of her hair over her shoulder, headed toward the back of the bar without another word.

"Dammit, Glory—"

Heads turned at his raised voice.

Glory was as good at exits as she was at entrances. The eyes of all those men followed the swish of her hips and the sway of her hair until she was gone.

Hell.

He knew how they felt.

And worse—or better—than that, he knew how *she* felt. He knew the weight of her whole self from the time he'd grabbed her by the belt loops just in time to keep her from skipping out into oncoming traffic when he was nine and she was seven.

Or from when he was eighteen and she was sixteen, the weight of her arm, which she'd slid to wrap around him when she'd found him outside alone on the day of his father's funeral, leaning against the back porch railing. His hand a visor over his eyes, as if he could hide the world from him and himself from the world. She'd tipped her head against his shoulder; there was no way she couldn't feel him shaking. She didn't say a word, though. He was everybody's rock, hers included—his mother's, his sister's. Everyone knew football heroes didn't cry.

She'd stayed with him until he could draw a steady breath again. And then she'd gone back into the house without a word.

In truth, her weight was no more a burden to him than wings were a burden to a bird.

His instinct right now was to lunge after her and pull her back by the belt loops again.

But she was right: he didn't have the right to do it. It would have been more of a capture than a rescue. An attempt to hold on to something that was doing its damnedest to pull away.

For a disorienting moment he felt utterly blank. As if the very laws of physics had changed.

And then he got a grip. Because she was right about another thing: he did love laws. He loved their structure and certainty and they were his refuge when life got a little too painful or messy or ambiguous.

And for God's sake, he had his pride. A lot of it. Well-earned.

That's what got him moving again. So he nodded to Carl, and Carl nodded back, and then Eli nodded once more to the poker players and accompanied it with a meaningful glare to drive his point home, and he went back out the way he came and got in his cruiser. He radioed his location to Deputy Owen Haggerty and told him everything was fine at the Plugged Nickel, which felt like such a lie.

Then he pressed his head back against his car seat.

Citizens were in a law-abiding mood tonight. The radio stayed quiet. His thoughts sure weren't. His stomach seemed to have tied itself into a cat's paw knot, one of the more complicated knots he and Jonah had learned in Boy Scouts. Jonah could get out of those. There was no getting out of handcuffs or a jail cell, though.

He sighed.

Fuck.

Eli looked out over the inky dark of the hills. The Plugged Nickel was roughly situated between Whiskey Creek and Coyote Creek. One was for pissing in, the other for swimming in, his dad had once said. Though he and Jonah had done both in both, grossing Glory out thoroughly.

It was so dark you'd have to stare for a long time to even make out the shapes of individual trees, though the hillside was carpeted with them. Imagining a life without Glory in it was a bit like that. No matter how hard he tried, he couldn't make out its outlines.

He breathed in again and swiped his hands down his face.

He'd decided to start his cruiser and back out, drive up Main Street, check on the storefronts, the usual.

Which was why he was faintly surprised to find himself flinging the door open and crunching off over the dirt and gravel into the dark, toward the back of the Plugged

Nickel, compelled by instinct and by a natural law that superseded all his logic and will and training. It was the same compulsion, he guessed, that had driven him to carve a set of initials on the Eternity Oak the day after his seventeenth birthday.

He wasn't much for superstition, but that was another moment where the need to do something had outweighed sense. And what he'd done then, if you believed local legend, was seal his fate.

CHAPTER 2

Glory stormed the length of the Plugged Nickel's dank rear hall until she got to the back door, which she shoved open as if it existed merely to spite her. She stepped out into the bracing slap of the night and let the door swing shut hard behind her.

That little bite in the air hadn't been there a week ago; summer was beginning to surrender to fall.

The *nerve* of time for moving forward when she was stuck here in Hellcat Canyon.

She leaned against the wall and closed her eyes and sighed and banged her head lightly against the wall. Once, twice. Her heart was going like a kick drum. Damn *damn*. Damn *damn*. Damn *damn*. Like that.

Just standing near Eli made her feel like a wire ran from her head to her toes and lit her up until she buzzed and crackled like the old neon sign out in front of the Plugged Nickel. The one that was bound to one day set the whole countryside on fire unless cheap-ass Carl sprang for a new one.

The ironies were many, and they were all a little hard to take.

For instance, wasn't it funny how a kiss a lifetime in the making could ruin her in moments?

And how every kiss from now on would be a footnote to that one?

Not to mention every man?

It was just her shitty luck that she hated him now.

Growing up, Eli had been . . . like the weather. Part of the texture of all of her days, one of the essential little currents that fed every part of her life, the way Coyote Creek nourished all the flora and fauna around here. But there was the Eli she'd grown up with, who would never do a thing to hurt her.

And then there was the Eli whose face was the deadly intent blank of a stranger's as he moved toward Jonah that day in the Plugged Nickel and . . .

She sucked in a sharp breath. Thinking about that day was like driving that narrow mountain road on I-5 up into Oregon at night in the pouring rain. You looked straight ahead, not down, not off into that infinite blackness, because you didn't know what it contained and you were better off not knowing.

So she didn't think about that day.

Or about Jonah.

And she hadn't talked to Eli since. She'd cut him right out.

Life as she'd known it had shattered so hard she could see its innards, see all the little pieces that could never be put together in the same way again. And that meant all of her best laid plans had been kind of blown to bits, too.

She'd suddenly needed a job again, stat. But she'd had to wheedle Carl into giving her this one, crappy as it was, given that she'd inadvertently singed a few bridges on what she'd thought would be her triumphant exit from town.

Here she was again, employee of the year, outside marinating in angst. She really wasn't proud of that. Pride itself was kind of a luxury, given her current circumstances, but she had a lot more of that than she did money, and it was the reason she wouldn't tell Eli why she was working here.

She wouldn't have been able to bear his pity.

Eli, who had always been her biggest champion. "Your happiness just contributes to the world's happiness, Glory," was how he'd put it once. "You have go for it."

She wondered if he was sorry he'd felt her up under that ponderosa pine now, and even now her body hummed, remembering.

She'd been about fourteen years old when she discovered suspended fourths and back-strums, magical ways to make a guitar chord sound huge and ethereal. She put them to use right away on a song it seemed she'd been holding inside for ages. She sang it to herself now, softly.

Oh, insecurity
Obsessed with sex
Obsessed with purity
Not the most compatible blend
Wide awake and wondering
In what way I'm blundering
For I sense that I am blundering again
Then a thought emerges, pulls your name
Like a banner through my head
I am comforted
You are my featherbed

It was a little literal, a little wry, a little melodramatic, wholly heartfelt. She'd called the song "Featherbed."

She might as well have called it "Eli."

She stopped singing. Music was like heat on an ache. Or a nice little hit of opium. Writing it, playing it, listening to it meant a few minutes of surcease these days. But once the song was over the truth settled right back in and hurt again, and she supposed—here was yet another irony—the point of hurting was so music could come into being in the first place.

"That's a pretty song."

She gave a start.

Oh hell. It was Leather Vest. Who had clearly followed her out the door. And apparently he'd all but tiptoed over here while she'd been singing.

That didn't bode well.

"Got a light?" he tried next. When she just stared. He brandished a cigarette.

She'd only called him Cheekbones to make Eli jealous. It had worked, that much was *very* clear, but there hadn't been much satisfaction in that. Leather Vest was definitely good-looking, but then, a lot of venomous snakes were pretty, too. Growing up in the country meant she could tell the venomous ones from the benign ones. He was the former.

"I don't smoke."

He'd planted himself with what felt like strategy between her and the back door of the Plugged Nickel. In front of them a few dozen yards away was an expanse of forest and Whiskey Creek, and over the hill from that was where she'd grown up, right now looking black and woolly with trees. Houses and cabins were tucked in there, but not a single light was on. It was going on two a.m. After all, even in the Whiskey Creek settlement, people had to sleep—or pass out—sometime.

Leather Vest put his cigarette away. "I had four queens."

"You telling me about your poker hand or what you did last weekend?"

It was a risky joke. But that was the mood she was in.

It took him a second to get it.

"Funny." He didn't sound amused. "I won tonight's poker game with that hand. Hey, you must be a little chilly . . ." The long thorough look he gave her settled on her skin like grease. ". . . in that top."

Fuck. It seemed Eli had been right about old Leather Vest.

Her top was white, had tiny frilly sleeves, laced up the front, fit like a glove, and showed just a little bit of tan midriff when she stretched up for things on high shelves. She did fill it out really well, if she did say so herself. She would be damned if this guy would make her feel cheap for that.

He moved in closer still. His slightly unwashed scent, sweat layered with beer and smoke, literally raised her hackles. He smelled like *bad* danger, not the interesting kind.

"Yeah. Too bad I didn't wear my leather vest over it." Her impulse was to do a quick dodge and feint and then dash around the other side of the building. But she was beginning to think this guy might actually enjoy a chase.

She was quick and she knew a lot about breaking types of holds and stomping on insteps and gouging eyes and where to hit a guy to get him to buckle over, moaning.

That was all thanks to Jonah and Eli, who had taught her all of that back when they could still all wrestle like puppies.

But this guy was wearing heavy motorcycle boots, so the instep thing wouldn't work. And these sinewy types could be surprisingly strong.

Maybe she *ought* to take up knitting. If only to get in the habit of carrying something long and sharp around with her.

Inside the Plugged Nickel Tom Petty was singing about American girls and she could feel vibrations against her butt, which was both reassuring and not. It meant there was life inside, but if she screamed, it was entirely possible no one would hear it. Out here in the deep dark sticks, they might mistake it for a fox or a coyote or maybe even a bigfoot.

"My car's right over there." Ezekiel gestured to an old Ford something deep in the "parking lot," an expanse of flattened dirt, entirely unlit, near where her own truck was parked. "Let's go heat each other up in the backseat."

"Thank you for the invitation, Ezekiel," she said brightly but firmly, "but I have to get back inside and finish my shift." She took a step away from the wall, toward the door.

His hand shot out and closed around her arm.

And he held her fast.

She slowly looked up at him. Absolutely speechless with outrage.

She tugged just a little.

That son of a bitch didn't let go.

Oh, poor Ezekiel. This wasn't his lucky night. She was in the mood to do some damage.

"I'm going to need you to take your hand off me. Now," she said very, very softly. It was very nearly a hiss.

"Aw, don't be like that." He used his grip on her arm to lever her back up against the wall. "In a few seconds you'll be *begging* for my hands all over you."

He was still standing too close for her to be able to get a knee up into his gonads.

But then he dumbfounded her by releasing her and turning his hand around to drag it down along her face in a caress. As if they were in a romantic comedy and he was the seductive hero.

She had a hunch this was a move he'd used with some success before.

She didn't breathe. She kept her eyes even with his black ones. And when his hand reached her chin she turned her head, ever so slightly into his hand, like a cat surrendering to pleasure.

"Yeah, *that's* it, baby," he murmured. "I'm going to rock your—"

CHOMP. She sank her teeth hard into the meat of his palm like a puma.

There was no way *his* scream couldn't be heard over the Tom Petty inside. It could have shattered windows.

He staggered back just a little, far enough for her to get her knee up, but just as she was about to deliver the coup de grace to his nuts, his eyes bulged, he made a hideous gargling noise and levitated about two feet off the ground.

It was a few seconds before she realized he was dangling from Eli's fist. The various metal elements on his uniform—his badge, his gun—glinted like stars against the dark and came into focus first. Above that, his face was stone and as cold as that moon.

He'd snagged a handful of the guy's vest and shirt and hoisted him like a sack of flour.

She spat on the ground, gasping. She tasted beer and smoke and salt from the peanuts Leather Vest had been scrabbling around in on the bar.

She wiped at her eyes, which were leaking tears of fury and sucked in a shuddering breath.

They didn't make alcohol in a high enough proof to rinse the taste of that guy's hand out of her mouth.

"She bit me!" Leather Vest wheezed.

Whiny asshole.

"Go inside, Glory." Eli's voice was calm as death, and she wouldn't have blamed Leather Vest if he'd wet himself right there.

She was still furious. "Let me take a whack at him first. He looks like the world's ugliest pinata hanging there from your hand."

"Go . . . inside."

She heard the words *the fuck* sandwiched in between the *Go* and *inside* clear as if he'd actually said them.

Her judgment might be a little awry but she wasn't stupid.

She almost but not quite did as ordered. She pushed the door open and stepped inside, but she stayed next to the door frame, leaving it open a few inches.

Eli's voice was almost conversational. "I can snap your spine like a twig and throw you down that embankment and everyone will think it was an accident. How many strikes you got on your record already, *Ezekiel*?"

Ezekiel didn't answer. Which was answer enough.

Eli raised his voice. "You wanna charge him with assault, Glory?"

Of course he knew she was listening. Just as he'd some-how known she was about to fuck up again. She won-dered just how much of her exchange with Leather Vest he'd overheard.

"She *bit* me! I . . . barely . . . touched her!" the guy wheezed out.

This was essentially true.

Eli loosened his hold and the guy's feet touched the ground.

"Don't charge him," Glory called. "But he should know I'm part gypsy and I just cursed his privates. If he ever touches a woman against her will ever again, they'll shrivel like raisins and fall off."

She had no idea where that came from.

"Colorful," Eli said neutrally after a moment.

She closed the door behind her.

Whatever Eli decided to do next, she didn't want to see it.

But doubtless it would be by the book. Eli did love him some rules. Even if it destroyed the lives of people he loved.

She sat down at one of the scarred wood tables inside the Plugged Nickel and waited for Eli to come in and give her hell.

She managed to lift a hand in a sort of general farewell as Carl shooed the rest of the stragglers out the door. One of the speakers was making an unnerving *zzzzt zzzzt* sort of noise, like a fly caught in a spider web. Carl shut the music off.

The ensuing silence practically rang. She was alone but for Carl.

"Don't bother getting up, Glory. I'll just put the chairs

up, Glory," Carl told her, oblivious to the little drama that had gone on outside. "Don't strain yourself, Glory. No need to help, Glory."

That was some fine sarcasm.

She was going to have to tell him she was quitting. No matter how much she needed a job, she could see now that she really couldn't work here. The ugliness would suck her under like quicksand and not even she was equal to it.

She watched the second hand jerk its way around the old neon Schlitz clock over the door about five or so times until Eli returned and settled in across from her.

She couldn't quite look up into his face yet. Not directly. She aimed her eyes somewhere past his shoulders, which meant aiming them some distance away, because his shoulders went on for yards, it seemed.

It wasn't as though he didn't know she was scrappy. He knew that if she was going to fight for anything or anyone, she always went all in, no holds barred.

But now that all the fury and adrenaline had ebbed, she was embarrassed. And ashamed. She didn't *want* to need Eli. But she'd wound up biting a guy in the back of a seedy dive in large part due to her own stubbornness. And Eli, who knew her better than anyone, had probably anticipated it even if she hadn't.

"His real name is Todd," he said finally. "He has priors."

The *of course he does* went without saying, so neither of them said it.

She didn't ask whether he was cuffed in the back of Eli's patrol car, or whether Eli had snapped him into a few pieces like he was made of Legos and hurled all the parts into the canyon. Probably not on the last one. After all, rules were rules. Eli did love him some rules.

She cleared her throat. "Thank you," she said stiffly.

Eli just gave a short nod.

She couldn't get a read on his mood, either. He was distracted and subdued, and he seemed full of the need to say something, but he wasn't saying it. For a number of reasons, Eli never used superfluous words.

But whatever he said was always worth hearing.

His hair used to flop down over his forehead. He'd been a little vain about it when he was a teenager. It was now buzzed no-nonsense short, which made the planes of his face—cheekbones like battlements; a right-angle jaw softened by the dimple in his chin; a nose with a slight bump, which she knew was from when he broke it trying to jump a big rock with his mountain bike back when he was twelve—seem even more uncompromising. He had this way of not blinking, and his eyes seemed silver in some lights and a sort of pale blue in others, and he had a way of fixing them on you that made you feel like the only important person in the world. It was like he could see right through to the contents of your soul, so you might as well yield your secrets.

She'd once found standing in the beam of his gaze the safest place in the world.

Useful quality in a cop.

He'd never been pretty. Not like her ex-boyfriend, Mick Macklemore, anyway.

Still, she never really wanted to look away from Eli.

His eyes dropped to the table, and she realized he was following the movement of her finger. She was tracing an old scar dug into the table. Someone had carved *FUC* into the veneer. She wondered whether they were some-one's initials or whether someone was rudely interrupted in the process of immortalizing the thing that she and Eli probably would have done to each other that night if they hadn't been interrupted, too.

She jumped when, behind her, Carl noisily clunked a chair up onto a table, just in case she'd missed his earlier sarcasm.

And still neither she nor Eli said a word.

And for a brief vertiginous moment, it was like they'd never even met. Like that table between them was as vast as the sea and they were on separate skiffs floating farther and farther apart.

"Anyway, Todd won't be bothering anyone around here anymore."

"Well, that's good news. I know how you love to get those bad guys off the street, Eli."

Eli's head went up slowly. And he stared at her in something like cold amazement.

But she couldn't help it. She wasn't even really sorry. Every time she tried to tamp the hurt and anger down, it popped out again, like Whac-A-Mole. She didn't know how or if that could ever change.

He stood up, slowly, resolutely.

She looked up at him. Way up.

She felt the collision of their gazes physically. A ping at the base of her spine that rocketed through her like the puck on the carnival strong-man machine.

For a moment he stared down at her. But all he finally said was "You should make better decisions, Glory."

And then he walked out the door.

CHAPTER 3

E li stripped off his uniform a piece at a time and chucked it into the washing machine and threw in two of those squishy little detergent pods instead of one, because psychologically that's what it took to get the scent of the Plugged Nickel out of his clothes.

He pivoted and frowned at his living room, which was the living room of the house he'd grown up in. Something seemed off.

And then he realized it was just a matter of contrasts. Glory was like an old rabbit ear antenna that tuned into his truest self. He felt funnier, freer, lighter around her. The whole world felt brighter.

And now the world had gone back to being a shade too dim.

Fuck it.

He scooped up the mail he'd dumped on the counter and sank down on the couch in his boxers to rifle through it: Bill, bill, discount coupon for a new restaurant in Hellcat Canyon, bill, bill, a shooting range coupon, an intriguing plump manila envelope from his mom in Sacramento, bill, bill, a postcard from his college ex-girlfriend, Courtney. He paused to peruse that one. Palm trees, big blue ocean, white sand beach. Admittedly a pretty appealing view. She'd taken a job in Miami and she'd wanted him to relocate with her. Plenty of law enforcement jobs there.

Instead, he'd broken up with her and had taken the job in Hellcat Canyon.

He turned it over and read:

Still think you're crazy not to come here.

He sighed and tossed it aside.

He slit open the envelope from his mom and pulled something out. He unwound a few miles of bubble wrap and finally found a silver frame around a newspaper clipping.

BARLOW EARNS COMMENDATION
Sheriff's Deputy Critical to Busting
NorCal Drug Trafficking Ring

Alongside the columns of text was a photo of him, caught by the news photographer mid-interview with a television reporter, all serious and strong jawed and buzz-cut. The caption read, "Deputy Eli Barlow of Hellcat Canyon was critical to the multi-agency law enforcement effort to take down a Northern California meth distribution network."

The article recapped everything that had gone down to lead up to the awards ceremony.

Jonah's name and photo were in that article, too.

Much smaller.

He was freshly buzz-cut, too.

But orange really wasn't Jonah's color.

"Jonah Greenleaf of Hellcat Canyon arraigned on charges of meth distribution" is what it said under his photo.

His mom had affixed a Post-it note to the back of the frame. It had a row of little tabby cat faces across the top. His mom was a sucker for anything with kitties on it. Funny, because she was one of the toughest people he knew.

So proud of you. Your dad would be, too.
Xoxo Mom

Every day he came home alive was a victory in his mom's eyes. Still, she'd love putting that commendation in the family Christmas letter.

She only lived a couple of hours away, but she still liked to send him little gifts, clippings and so forth, so he'd have something to find in the mail. A few weeks ago she'd sent him his grandmother's engagement ring with another little note: "In case you might want to give it to someone anytime soon." She might as well have added: "P.S. You're not getting any younger."

He remembered seeing that tasteful antique, a ruby flanked by two little diamonds on a gold band, on his mom's hand. His grandmother had been a tasteful antique herself, a patrician woman who had struggled to adjust to the idea of her Ivy League–educated daughter marrying Zachary Barlow, a small-town sheriff's deputy.

His grandmother had learned to love his dad, though. She had a heart as huge as Hellcat Canyon. Just like his mom.

Eli glanced down and saw that his knuckles were white. Maybe he was hanging on to a lot of things a little too tightly.

He opened the coffee table drawer, shoved the frame in, and slammed it shut.

Which is what he'd done with every photo of Jonah.

Except for one. It was on the side of the refrigerator, way in the back, where he could only see it if he was reaching into the cupboard and could mostly pretend it wasn't there. Glory was in that one.

If only he could slam all inconvenient emotions and memories into drawers and forget them.

Eli let his head fall back against the big plump macho leather couch—which was his one splurge when he was promoted to head deputy, though he was still getting used to how it looked in the middle of the family living room— and closed his eyes. And he released a sigh so deep and endless it was like he'd been holding it his entire life.

"It was *your* influence keeping Jonah on the straight and narrow, Eli. See what happened practically the minute you left Hellcat Canyon?"

That was his mother's way of trying to comfort him. His mother had never quite approved of his friendship with the Greenleafs.

Hell. She might actually be right.

Jonah had always thought rules got in the way of getting what he wanted, which was having a good time. He was forever looking for short cuts, for loopholes, for shades of gray. And sometimes this was fun and sometimes with this was trouble and often even the trouble was fun, and he'd never had a rudder because he didn't have a dad.

Eli was his father's son. But he'd also learned all on

his own that for him, rules *were* the short cut. Otherwise you unfailingly had to go back and learn something you'd skipped in an attempt to get what you wanted faster, or stop to clean up some mess you'd made on the way.

Or, like Jonah, take a plea bargain and go to prison for five years for helping to transport meth one town over.

It amounted to the same thing.

Jonah had been a very small part of a big operation.

But it had been the biggest betrayal of Eli's life. And even as he kind of understood how it all might have come about, the fury and hurt had been white-hot. Then cold and hard as granite.

His mom had never understand the appeal of the Greenleafs. Which for Eli was the loving chaos of their house. The defiance and resourcefulness and humor in the face of not-quite-poverty. How funny and quicksilver and kind and game for anything Jonah was, and how being with them had been like taking a hit of oxygen and was as colorful as Disneyland.

His mom may or may not have an inkling about his true feelings for Glory. She hadn't wanted him to take the Hellcat Canyon job instead of heading to Miami, that was for sure.

Eli pushed himself up off the couch abruptly and strode to the fridge, reached back and pulled that one remaining picture down from under its magnet. He took it and a Snapple back to the couch with him.

It was a shot taken in spring. He and Jonah, gangly, floppy-haired, shirtless, impossibly thin and long-limbed in their cutoff shorts. Eli never really felt the passage of years until he saw himself like that. They were both about eleven years old, their skin golden-brown and smooth, almost shining like metal in the sun because they were still so . . . *new*. They were washing the battered old Greenleaf car and Jonah was aiming the hose at Eli.

And there was Glory in pink shorts and a white shirt, about eight years old, her black hair all the way down to her butt. Glory never did have the patience for braids. She opted for one big ponytail in the summer, either behind her, like an actual pony, or to the side or up on her head, like a fountain. Most of the time her hair sailed out behind her, because she liked to flourish it, like a magician with a cape. Her mouth was wide open and her eyes had disappeared and her arms were crossed over her stomach because she was laughing so hard, so hard it was like she could hardly bear it. He used to tease her that he could see all the way to her tonsils.

That photo was taken right around the time he'd gotten in a nasty little argument with Mike Roderick on the playground over whose turn it was to use the red rubber ball at recess. Roderick had resorted to the sort of tactic guaranteed to chop Eli off at the knees. He'd mocked his stutter.

"Eli Barlow takes f-f-f-f-orever to get a word out!"

Eli was tall even then, but he'd frozen. Mute and paralyzed with shame.

And Glory had hurtled out of nowhere.

He'd snagged her by the collar before she could take a swing at Roderick, but her arms were windmilling. "I'd rather wait *forever* to hear him say *one word* than listen to you say anything, booger face!"

To his credit, Mike Roderick knew a little girl had just shamed him but good. He'd apologized.

Eli didn't stutter anymore. Mike Roderick was now on Hellcat Canyon's City Planning Commission, a fine upstanding citizen with two kids and a mortgage. The two of them were on perfectly cordial terms. But damned if Eli didn't look at him and still think "booger face."

Glory would fight to the death for people she cared about. She was a fighter, period.

Which is why it was so *strange* she was still in Hell-cat Canyon. And it seeded a traitorous little suspicion: Had the fight gone out of her? Had she decided to do the Greenleaf thing, which was nothing?

He jerked when his cell phone erupted in a ring.

He lunged to answer it. "Hey, Cam, what's up?"

Becky Cameron was a deputy in the nearby town of Black Oak who'd been married to a big sweetheart of a Samoan guy for twenty years, and she had three adorable giggly kids.

"You sound a little groggy. Were you sleeping, heart-throb?"

He cast his eyes ceiling-ward. For a time there, his image had been all over the news thanks to the meth ring bust—print and digital *and* television. His colleagues still gave him endless shit about it, mostly involving nicknames. "Heartthrob." "America's sweetheart." That sort of thing.

In other words, they were proud of him.

"Just worn out from a long day of saving Gotham City. You?"

"Not as awesome as you, precious. But listen, I wanted to tell you something in confidence. Totally off the record, just a rumor, but where there's smoke there's fire and so forth, otherwise I wouldn't be calling you now."

"Shoot."

"Word is that Davenport is retiring at the end of the year."

He was quiet for some time.

"Huh."

Which was Eli's way of saying, "Holy crap."

Davenport had been county sheriff for twenty years. The end of the year was a month and a half away. This was indeed monumental news.

Cam was a cousin of a cousin or something like that. She had her finger on the pulse.

"And Devlin is of course being talked about as his replacement."

Leigh Devlin was the obvious choice, since he was the current undersheriff. A good man, smart as hell, gruff. He'd worked with Eli's dad, and he'd been immeasurably kind to Eli's family after his dad was killed. It was Leigh Devlin Eli had turned to for advice when he'd decided not to take that football scholarship and instead become a sheriff's deputy.

And suddenly Eli knew exactly where Cam was going with this.

"Among others, Barlow, your name came up for undersheriff."

Yep. That confirmed it.

"You fall asleep on me, Fabio?"

"Fabio?"

"Hot guy on a lot of covers?" Cam tried.

"Okay, now you're really reaching. And now I know what you do in your spare time."

"Hey, at least I got a hobby. Who or what are you doing in your spare time?"

That question just made him feel bleak and surly, when what he wanted to do was savor the possibility of a triumph for a few moments longer.

"Shut up," he finally said, with typical eloquence.

She laughed.

Undersheriff. He savored that word in his mind.

Second in command in the whole county. That would mean no patrolling. Almost double the income.

And leaving Hellcat Canyon for good.

"So anyway, Barlow, I thought you might like some time to think about what you want to do, when it comes down. In case it does. Is that cool?"

"Yeah, of course. Thanks, Cam."

"I'm having a barbeque for my bae's birthday in a few weeks. You comin'?"

"Love to. Remind me, though. Send me an e-mail or text."

"'Kay. Night, lover boy."

He snorted and ended the call, then exhaled and leaned back against the couch again.

A slow smile spread over his face. Undersheriff. The title made it sound like he needed a cape.

And all that did was make him think of Glory and her hair, and Sir Walter Raleigh and the cloak, and how much better good news became when he shared it with her, and how she hated him right now for doing what was essentially his job.

And his job . . . well, like it or not, he was his job and his job was him.

His smile faded.

Damn. He was also really freaking lonely.

He wished he could fast forward to the wife, the kids, the two cats, and the mutt dog he'd always imagined. Truth be told, it had always been hard to picture Glory in that context. Even though she loved her sister's kids.

It was harder, though, to picture anyone else in it.

That was the paradox of his life. To be stretched out on a sort of Catherine wheel, pulled between equal and utterly opposing desires. And if you believed the legend of the Eternity Oak, he had only himself to blame.

But "martyr" had never been on the list of his ambitions.

He ran his thumb over her laughing face in that photo in his hand. As if he could dial back the past. That's not how time worked, though.

He took one last deep breath. He'd survived endings before. He could make destiny his bitch. And he would get over this.

And then he finally put that picture of Glory in the drawer with all the rest of them and slammed it shut.

CHAPTER 4

"Gary Shaw, that Sierra Property Management fella, the one that Britt Langley works for? I hear he's single."

Glory's drooping head shot up. She'd been inhaling coffee steam from a mug faded to a streaky yellow from countless journeys through the dishwasher. It was nine a.m. She'd spent the six previous hours mostly staring at her bedroom ceiling because her mind felt one way about Eli Barlow and her body felt another way entirely, and when her mind got tired, her libido took over. She'd flopped about in her bed like a pair of jeans in their old dryer. Irritable and yearning.

And she couldn't get the last words he'd said to her out of her head.

Now she was sitting at the kitchen table with her mother, the anticipated foreclosure notice on the table between them. Truth be told, in the annals of Greenleaf History, it wasn't the worst thing that had ever happened, or even the first time this had happened since this house was built in 1960. Still, miracles were not to be expected.

And seeing a foreclosure notice in person did tend to elevate adrenaline.

"I feel like the entire first part of a conversation took place inside your head, Mama. Why on earth are you talking about the Sierra Property Management guy?"

Her mother looked alert and fully groomed, complete with lipstick, even if her clothes were as faded with laundering as Glory's coffee mug. The radio, the one that had been in the family since before she was born and sat on the kitchen table between them, was on low.

"Baby girl, I'm just saying, that's the kind of guy who would make a perfect starter husband for you. He won't beat you, and if he tries you can outrun him. He'll kick in a few years and you'll still have your looks. He'll leave you with all his properties—you sell 'em, move on to a bigger city, where the men have more money, and pretty soon you got yourself, oh, an Audi. God didn't give you a face or boobies like the ones you got without a plan in mind."

She was only half joking. Charlotte Greenleaf was nothing if not a planner. Clearly the foreclosure notice had her thinking about Glory's future.

Gary Shaw was probably sixty-three if he was a day. Hollywood probably contained its share of hot sixty-three-year-olds, but Hellcat Canyon sure didn't. Every guy over sixty looked like Glenn Harwood, the owner of the Misty Cat Cavern, with a big comfortable stomach and a luxurious gray broom of a mustache.

Glory could have said, "I'm going to be a big rich rock star, Mama," but that sounded as improbable as marrying Gary Shaw at the moment.

She sighed. "Mama, do you ever listen to yourself? It's

like the women's movement never happened. And for the love of God, please don't ever say 'boobies' again."

"You think picking out a husband doesn't require any business savvy? I do my due diligence on a guy before I buy in, use my assets and experience to make the sale, and then I sit back and enjoy the rewards and take my lumps, as the case may be. How, I ask you, is that different from those rich guys like Getty? Society wants to judge me, so be it. What I do takes *nerve*, baby doll."

Glory was momentarily transfixed by this loopy rationale.

Then she zeroed in on the fatal flaw in this logic. "Getty never had to sleep next to Raymond Truxel."

Charlotte tried to glare at her daughter, but she'd never been able to hold on to mad too long. She grinned instead. It was the smile that hooked men every time: wry, bittersweet, dazzling because every man thought she harbored some secret sadness, which wasn't far wrong. "Every strategy has its risks."

Two husbands had come and gone since Henry "Hank" Greenleaf crashed his car into a freeway meridian and flipped it three times off an overpass when Glory was three years old and Jonah was six. Two husbands who had given Glory two stepsiblings—her sister, Michelle, who had three kids (who all had different fathers) and lived two towns away, and her younger brother, John-Mark. Truth was, Charlotte *wasn't* a great husband picker but she was, against all odds, an optimist who tended to see the best in people. That was both her nicest quality and her fatal flaw.

Hank's ashes went on the mantel and the 1963 Martin 000–18 he'd gotten in trade instead of a paycheck for doing some off-the-books house painting went in the corner of the living room, more a monument than an instrument, dusted but otherwise ignored until Glory got her hands on it in one of her "I wonder what would happen if . . ." moments.

It had been like letting the genie out of the bottle.

Writing songs was the closest she'd ever come to being able to impose some kind of order or meaning onto anarchic feelings, the ones that outright made you suffer from the beauty or awfulness of them.

Which was how she'd ended up writing something like five songs about Eli.

Five so *far*.

They didn't say the word *Eli* in the house anymore. They didn't say *Jonah*, either.

Not after Glory had refused to go with her mom to visit her brother in jail three times in a row.

Jonah had apparently been paying his own *and* her mom's mortgage with his ill-gotten gains.

All that money Glory saved toward leaving Hellcat Canyon had gone to keeping that roof over her mom's head.

And now that money was gone, and the silly bank still wanted to be paid.

"Pass me those cigarettes, sweet pea, will you?" Charlotte added.

Glory handed her the crunched pack of Camels next to the napkin holder. "You better take it easy on those since (a) we don't have much money for vices and (b) if you get a disease we can't afford to send you to a doctor."

"Don't tell me what to do, Glory Hallelujah, I'm still your mother." It was reflexive and distracted and she said

it over a Camel stuffed between her lips. "And I'm inde-
structible, child."

This probably wasn't far wrong.

Still, as a concession, her mother didn't actually light
the cigarette, and then she sighed and laid it down as if
she were surrendering arms. And smiled at her daughter.
It was absurd, but it made Glory feel loved. And just as
when she fought, when Glory loved, she went all in.

How could you want to hold on to something exactly as
much as you want to get away from it?

Her plans—which could be captioned as "get the hell
out of Hellcat Canyon and get famous"—had long been a
subliminal hum in the family. But no one she was related
to had ever really talked it about it, unless it was Jonah,
who'd allowed vaguely that she should "go for it." There
was simply no roadmap for success in the Greenleaf ge-
netic makeup, and no vocabulary for it, either. Not one
of them had ever before felt inclined toward a shred of
ambition beyond enjoying each day. They wouldn't dream
of leaving any more than the trees covering the hillside
would uproot and voluntarily hop a plane to New York
City. They were as indigenous to the place as the forests
and scrub covering the hills.

Unless, of course, you counted Jonah. Though the two
hours between Hellcat Canyon and the prison cell he occupied hardly counted.

It was Eli who had championed her.

On impulse Glory peeked in the big old ashtray where,
per household tradition, they emptied whatever spare
change happened to be in their pockets. Last time she'd
looked there was probably about five bucks in quarters
and dimes and nickels.

Just as she suspected: it was empty except for a Post-it note and two strawberry Starbursts, neither of which had been there earlier. Strawberry was her favorite flavor as it so happened.

She read the Post-it:

Glory—I had to donate the change in this ashtray to my car repair fund and I'll replace it when I can, but meanwhile, please enjoy these Starbursts.
   Xoxo John-Mark

She rolled her eyes. John-Mark earned just enough money to buy the beater car he drove to work and pay for the room he rented. Though the beater car was an endless money hog. At least John-Mark was trying to make an honest living.

Still, five bucks was five bucks.

"Guess John-Mark stopped by," Glory said dryly. She picked up the empty ashtray and shook it.

Her mom snorted. "I asked him to fix the gutters." And then she reached over and turned up the radio suddenly. "I like this song."

"Me, too."

The boppy hooks and thick harmonies of "In the Forest," a song by the improbably named band The Baby Owls, was so ubiquitous now she'd actually heard their neighbor, the nasty Mrs. Binkley, humming it as she ruthlessly clacked her big Edward Scissorhands trimmers over her hedges. Mrs. Binkley's yard was flawlessly, almost spitefully, groomed. It was a passive-aggressive response to years of living next door to the Greenleafs, whose yard was untamed at best, and featured a number

of pretty things growing in the wrong places, which rather
described the Greenleafs themselves.

> *This is the chorus*
> *Of we're lost in the forest*
> *You can never bore us*
> *Because we're lost in the forest*
> *Just try to ignore us*
> *While we're lost in the forest*
> *Going round and around and around*

It was a pretty stupid song, but then the lyrics of a lot of
great songs didn't bear up well under close examination.
Glory didn't hold that against it.

Her mom hummed softly along. Funny, but Glory
couldn't remember hearing her mom ever sing out loud.
Not even Christmas carols, and who could resist those?

"Maybe you could learn how to play it, Glory."

"Already did, Mom." It was an easy one. She'd even
given it her own bluesy spin, just for fun.

"Good for you, honey." But Charlotte said it absent-
mindedly. Her thoughts were back on their previous track.
"You know . . . you *might* actually meet a movie star. Like
Britt Langley did."

A cable TV series set during the Gold Rush—called,
appropriately, *The Rush*—had begun filming on location
in Hellcat Canyon, taking advantage of rugged vistas
and picturesque rivers and rocks and so forth. It starred
John Tennessee McCord, who had improbably swept Britt
Langley off her feet. Understandably, it had been the talk
of the town. And even YouTube.

"Heard she just quit waitressing down at the Misty Cat

to go to Los Angeles with John Tennessee McCord," her mom supplied. "Sort of a last-minute thing."

Her mom somehow got all the gossip. It circulated through Hellcat Canyon the way Whiskey and Coyote Creeks did. Charlotte Greenleaf was a social creature, and people liked to talk to her anyway.

Glory humored her. "Gosh. Maybe I will."

Britt was very pretty and well-spoken, and she'd always been quite nice to Glory, which patently wasn't true of a lot of women in town. She couldn't begrudge Britt either happiness or a movie star.

But Glory was pretty sure Britt Langley had never bitten a guy.

Or cursed his genitals.

And no movie star with a brain in his head would go out to the Plugged Nickel.

Damn. She needed to quit that job.

Her mom got up to refill her coffee. "You have any plans this weekend, sweet pea? You should be having some fun. Going on dates."

Glory almost snorted. "Don't worry, Mama. Pretty much every guy in Hellcat Canyon wants to go out with me. I'll pick one when I'm ready."

That statement was 100 percent correct, if one understood that "go out with her" meant "do her." And Glory knew the difference, by God, and no one was more particular while looking like a vixen.

Her mama liked bravado. "That's my girl," her mama encouraged absently, gazing out the window. Possible new husbands for herself probably scrolling like a stock market ticker through her brain.

The sun was up a little higher now and shining through

the sheer, faded yellow curtains. Like the radio, those curtains had been in the kitchen for as long as Glory could remember. The Greenleafs were like the Simpsons, she thought. *Their* kitchen curtains never changed, either. They were covered in little corncobs.

She'd begun to feel like she was sentenced to play a game of computer solitaire long after no moves were left. Or maybe she was lost in the forest, going around and around and around and around.

Maybe that song wasn't so stupid after all.

You should make better decisions, Glory.

Eli's tone when he'd said that. His expression. As if it was already too late for her. And maybe it was a matter of time before he had her facedown in cuffs, too.

Like he'd never kissed her.

Then whispered her name in a stunned voice.

Then kissed her again.

A great fresh bracing tide of pissed-off-ness propelled her out of her chair. "I'm going out for a bit, Mom."

She grabbed her jacket from the coat rack. She paused and pivoted. She'd almost forgotten.

She grabbed her stuffed tiger out of her bedroom and put it in the living room window, so it could have a view of the highway into town.

And she bolted out the door before her mother could ask questions.

She walked the whole way, down the unpaved road her family had lived on forever, which needed a coat of gravel now that fall was approaching, and gravel cost money. She knew every tree lining it; she even fondly, with an ache, remembered the ones that had toppled in storms. Every inch of it was the equivalent of a memory cell.

Down round the bend and through a narrow path trampled by decades of local feet and lined by big old pines was a shortcut to unused pasture lands surrounded by a splintered whitewashed fence. Every now and then someone mowed the grass in there so it didn't become too much of a fire hazard. In spring a thousand different wildflowers poked through that fence. When she was a kid, she'd pretended to be Queen Elizabeth and Eli had been Sir Walter Raleigh, and he'd laid down his jacket for her to walk across. She'd made a crown out of the wildflowers when she was Maid Marian, and she and Jonah and her siblings had pretended to be Robin Hood's merry band. Eli got to be Robin Hood. Jonah was Little John. They'd made that elm tree their headquarters, their fort, their castle.

Who knew Eli would actually grow up to be the Sheriff of Nottingham?

She paused on the rise and looked out toward the highway. Men in white painter's coveralls were clambering over the billboard on the highway, slapping up a new ad. The lip gloss ad was vanishing, which was kind of a shame, mostly because someone had drawn a pretty funny clown on it not too long ago, its butt up in the air, aimed at the big shiny lips. Glory was an admirer of subversiveness in its various subtle forms. Up above on the lip of the canyon was Hellcat Canyon's version of Olympus: a scattering of huge rustic summer homes, windows glinting like change you found in the street, belonging to tech millionaires and other people (none of whom Glory knew personally) who could buy a house and not live in it for huge swaths of the year.

As much as she itched to get out of town, every time it expanded into view as she emerged from the woods it was like hearing a familiar, beloved old song: meticulously maintained Gold Rush–era homes and storefronts glowing in dusty pastel shades unwound sinuously down tree and lamp-post-studded Main Street. More signs that fall was beginning to supplant summer: gerbera daisies and marigolds and sunflowers and mums, oranges and reds and golds, were now bursting from the little baskets hanging on hooks and the terra-cotta pots flanking storefront doorways. Hellcat Canyon was hardly a tourist destination, but rents were pretty modest and all of the businesses were small enough to survive any monkey wrenches the economy might throw. Some of the merchants, like Kayla Benoit who'd named her boutique after herself (and wasn't that just like Kayla, everyone said) and whose clothes weren't in Glory's budget (she preferred jeans and snug tops, anyway), even owned their buildings.

Glory traveled two blocks down Main and was halfway down Jamboree Street like a homing pigeon even before she realized she'd hooked that left. That wasn't her ultimate destination, but she decided she might as well check in with the mothership, aka Allegro Music, and she needed strings, anyway.

The big bulletin board on the side wall outside Allegro bristled with decades of staples, which was all that was left of flyers from bands and shows that had come and gone. But a new and blindingly pink flyer currently flanked drummer Monroe Porter's "lead singer wanted for death metal band" flyer. It was always there. When rain, dust, wind, and snow finally battered the last one into tatters, he put another one up. He'd done it for years. Hope did spring eternal. Especially in music stores.

"Good luck, Monroe," she muttered, because she really did wish him well. She might be queen of the open mic here in Hellcat Canyon, but it was harder than hell to pull a band together here in the sticks. Let alone a *reliable* band. Glory had played with Monroe once or twice, and he knew her usual open mic set pretty well, but she thought the *RAWWR RAWWR RAWWR* way death metal singers felt obliged to sing was really funny, which rather hurt Monroe's feelings. Different strokes was all. Over the years, she'd played a few gigs with rounded-up musicians in nearby towns like Black Oak and Whitney, but the nearest largish city was Sacramento, and that was nearly two hours away, and reliable transportation was another thing altogether. Currently she and her mom took turns driving their rattling old truck.

She peered at the bright pink flyer.

One Night Only!
THE BABY OWLS
Misty Cat Cavern
1 Main Street, Hellcat Canyon
Saturday, November 12th
Show starts at 8 p.m.

Glory gave a short laugh. "I'll be damned."

The flyer featured a photocopied image of three guys sporting woolly neo-lumberjack beards, heavy black hipster eyeglasses, and plaid flannel shirts. Their arms were crossed over their chests and they looked full of themselves, as rock stars ought to.

It just so happened that the Misty Cat Cavern was her original destination.

And then she froze.

Another inspiration had popped into her head like a quarter dropped in a slot machine.

And her heart picked up a beat.

Mesmerized by hope and her own chutzpah, she backed her way into Allegro Music, jangling the bells on the door.

"Glory, baby!"

The guy behind the counter reflexively thrust his hand out for high-fiving purposes but didn't lift his head: he was engrossed in some kind of delicate surgery. His anarchic gray-streaked black hair was restrained by a pair of goggles pushed back up on his broad, sweating forehead, and a variety of little tools were scattered around a prone, partially dismembered Alvarez acoustic guitar. Solder and sawdust perfumed the air.

She peered down at the patient.

"What happened to her?" she asked on a hush. The guitar looked like her. Something about the abalone inlay on her poor currently detached neck.

"Stolen from a guy's car in Placerville," Dion Espinoza said. "He finally found it on Craigslist—some other guy had bought it from some other guy, you know how it goes. When he finally got it back, it was in this shape. When I told him how much it would cost to repair it, he sold it to me cheap. Original tuning pegs had been switched out to these cheap things, the bridge plate has practically been pulled off, and I need to re-bore the holes since the headstock had a crack." He shook his head. "It's a beaut. Or was. This was a classic, man. It's criminal."

Guitarists from all over California brought abused or

aging instruments to Dion to be restored to their youthful sheen and vigor. Once or twice a year he built an extraordinary guitar on commission, and that's what actually kept his lights on. He was a master craftsman.

Mainly he kept the little store here in Hellcat Canyon because he liked living in the sticks and he liked to talk to music geeks all day long. Most local kids got their first music lessons from some long-suffering low-paid teacher in the warren of little offices in the back. Glory could hear the muffled constipated blats of a saxophone now. She was mostly self-taught, given that her mom thought shoes for her kids were a more important investment than music lessons, but she'd learned a lot by loitering in Dion's shop and pestering the good players who wandered in. Dion liked attitude and talent in anyone. He'd let her hang out as much as she wanted.

Dion delicately blew a particle of sawdust off the bridge plate. "I'll take that Martin off your hands when you're ready, Glory. It must be *such* a burden to you."

"Aww. Your selflessness is an example for us all, Dion."

He grinned. Glory's fifty-year-old Martin was worth about four thousand dollars, something Dion had told her in confidence and which she'd never told a soul. She would in fact sell her soul, if there were any takers, before she sold that guitar.

She idly spun the little rack of trade magazines next to the door: *Guitar Player*, *Rolling Stone*, *Mix*, *Spin*. And there they were again—on the cover of *Clang*:

**Wyatt "King" Congdon:
The Man with the Platinum Ear
Talks The Baby Owls, Future of Pop Music**

Wyatt Congdon was the legend who'd founded Stellium Records, and he was still viewed as the ultimate star maker, even in an industry changing by the second. More than once she'd entertained herself (and bored Eli and Jonah) with daydreams of meeting him. She could just *imagine* what that moment had been like for The Baby Owls.

Next she peered down at the contents of the locked, glassed-in case below the counter where Dion displayed smaller instruments—a few Hohner and Lee Oskar harmonicas, a pair of maracas and a güiro, a kazoo, a couple of cowbells. Sometimes he had an autographed photo or some other ephemera or quirky collectables.

Today a flash of red made her sink to her knees as if she was about to kiss the pope's ring.

"Dion . . . Is that . . . is that really an original forty-five of 'Hey Hey What Can I Do'?"

Technically, it was the forty-five single of Led Zeppelin's "The Immigrant Song," and "Hey Hey What Can I Do" was its B side. Both were brilliant, both were still all over classic-rock radio, and both would probably still be streaming in flying cars on road trips to Pluto in the year 2050, but "Hey Hey What Can I Do" had never appeared on any Led Zeppelin album, ever. Pretty much every serious music freak eventually learned that in a desperate quest to find it and own it.

She'd caught Eli air-drumming to it on the steering wheel of his old Fiero when she was fourteen and he was sixteen. He was parked outside the Greenleaf house, waiting for Jonah to come out, and his eyes were closed, his head was bobbing, his whole torso was swaying—in other words, he was doing what any sane human ought to do when they heard that song. He had a decent tenor but couldn't really keep it in key and his voice fractured into a honking bray on the high notes, *murdering* them.

It was funny as hell and touching, too, because it was so rare to see Eli just let go like that.

He'd almost gotten to the last verse when he noticed her standing on the porch, grinning like a jack-o'-lantern. Watching as raptly if she'd bought a ticket to do it.

He'd yelped and slapped the radio off.

"Like it's the radio's fault!" she hollered at him.

She'd had plans to never let him live that down.

YouTube wasn't a thing yet. The Greenleaf household was pretty low-tech, given that shoes and the mortgage got priority over gadgets, but she attributed her own resourcefulness to years of selective spending. She didn't even know what that song was called. So she'd sneaked Jonah's old tape recorder out of his room and waited under her covers at night with a transistor radio until she finally managed to trap it on cassette. It was absolutely in her wheelhouse, voice-wise: a little folksy, a little bluesy, pretty but gritty. Sexy, but then all Led Zeppelin songs were sexy. She didn't completely understand all the lyrics but she could wing it, she knew that she could let her voice flirt and lilt through the verse and she could really wail during the chorus.

A few weeks later she played that thirty-year-old song for Eli at his seventeenth birthday party. At twilight, beneath the huge liquidambar in the Greenleaf's shambling three-quarter-acre backyard, which wasn't much more than tamped dirt interspersed with lots of trees and a barbeque pit, she banged it out in front of about sixty teenagers. Which took balls. But then, she'd always had those.

As his friends tussled and flirted and danced and eddied around him, and Jonah pogoed around the backyard bellowing *"Ahhhhhhh! Yeeeeeah Yeah!"*—his Robert Plant imitation was definitely better than Eli's—Eli remained absolutely still. And he listened. Hard. And a tide of scarlet washed him from his collarbone to his hairline. But as she sang (a song which she realized years later was basically about a guy who was futilely in love with a hooker), the blush gave way to something like awe. Something very close to pain. Like he was stoically withstanding some internal crisis.

Twilight was dimming into night when she rounded in on that last verse, and his expression was now strangely resolute and peaceful. Like a guy who'd accepted some sentence fate had handed down.

She could feel the light of eyes on her skin all the way through to the end.

She finished with a flourish and held her guitar up high. Jonah threw his arms up and bellowed, "My baby sister, everybody!"

Later, she thought she recalled hearing clapping and cheering. But at the time, the only thing her senses took in was Eli.

He'd smiled at her slowly. And gave his head a slow shake. Like he simply couldn't believe the wonder of her.

And it was odd, in that it had started out as kind of a joke.

But if Eli had walked up to her and demanded she put into words what she was feeling right then and there, she would have had to use words like *I'd do anything for you* or *forever.*

She froze, guitar dangling from her hand. That was

the moment she understood that those feelings had been growing and growing out of sight, like the roots of that huge liquidambar tree in the Greenleaf front yard that had one day cracked the driveway right down the middle. And remained the bane of Mrs. Binkley to this day.

Then his girlfriend—Tiffany Margolies, who was brainless, which was probably why she didn't mind being on top of the cheerleading pyramid as she had absolutely nothing to lose if she toppled from up there to the ground onto her head—flounced over and looped her arms around Eli's neck from behind and the moment snapped like a spiderweb.

The very next morning, before school, Glory had gone and done something a lot of people would have considered rash.

And she'd never told a soul about it. Not one.

Though she was beginning to wonder if she'd pay for that rashness for the rest of her life.

Glory realized her hand was splayed against the glass case in the music store as if that whole night was trapped inside.

She forced herself to rise to her feet. She was happy Dion was focused on his guitar repair because her eyes were burning. Eli was everywhere. In everything.

It was so hard to imagine it any other way. Son of a bitch.

"Found that forty-five at the Our Lady of Mercy Thrift Shop," Dion told her. "Got it for a buck. It's in incredible condition."

It was a moment before she trusted herself to speak over the knot in her throat.

"I'm surprised they didn't pay *you* to take the devil's music off their hands."

The ladies in that thrift shop could be judgey. Dion was a sweetheart, but he looked like a big heathen with the enormous hair and the tattoos and his round belly taxing the elastic powers of his Pink Floyd t-shirt.

"There was a moment there when I thought my conscience was bothering me and I considered telling them what they had. But then I figured out that the twinge was just the burrito I had for lunch. I'll let you have it for twenty-five bucks."

"Highway robbery. I can get it cheaper on eBay."

Given that she'd had to root between the sofa cushions for the change she was using to buy a new pack of strings today, this was an entirely rhetorical observation.

"Cheeky wench," he said without rancor. He relished haggling and he had an encyclopedic knowledge of the value of music ephemera. He could not be taken. "Maybe five bucks cheaper, if that. I'll give the extra five bucks to the thrift shop to assuage my guilty conscience."

"Can't do it today. I'll take some strings, though."

"D'addario lights?"

"You complete me, Dion."

"**D**o you *see* it?"

Mrs. Wilberforce's voice was trembling with hushed outrage. She was wearing a scarf tied over row upon row of curlers, all wound round with iron-gray hair, and they looked like a crew of little Boy Scouts in sleeping bags. Eli figured she must be really incensed to call him before her hair was done. She was always stylishly turned out, in her seventy-year-old way. She was wearing white capri pants and little black ballet flats and sunglasses with gold initials at the temple. He was pretty sure they were Giorgio Armani.

Heavenly Shores Retirement Community was like a cross between Disney's It's a Small World ride and a miniature golf course: tidy streets of permanently parked mobile homes of varying vintages, all painted in some tasteful pastel shade, each one immaculate and personalized in some way—a picket fence here, a little pocket-sized yard exploding with petunias or roses or whimsical statuary there.

Law enforcement in Hellcat Canyon could swing between banal and deadly in a heartbeat, and Eli was hoping to burn off some residual Glory angst today by maybe chasing a bad guy. But he was so tired this morning that he found Heavenly Shores kind of soothing. A little like that time he'd stayed home from school sick and had taken a whopping dose of cough syrup and watched *Teletubbies*.

"Mrs. Wilberforce, forgive me, but what exactly are we looking at?"

"*That!* Just look at it. My rhododendrons! It's *murder!*"

The plant she was pointing at with a finger quivering in rage was indeed half brown on one side, as though it had been burned.

He didn't hold out a lot of hope for rehabilitation, at least.

"Yeah, that's a shame. Pretty flower."

"It *was* a pretty flower, you mean! That Carlotta Kilgore from Elysian Acres takes her beagle out for a walk in the morning and stops right there every morning so her dog can pee on it. Gives it a good soaking, as you can see. The same rhododendron. Every time. Death by dog pee! It's undignified for such a beautiful flower. And she *knows* it's part of my display. She knows that's what puts us over the top each year and why we win."

Carlotta Kilgore was another older lady, but she had a great mane of dyed black hair and her penchant for red lipstick and snug dresses hinted she might have been a siren back in the day, and maybe still was. The front of her own little mobile home in Elysian Acres featured a variety of statuary: gamboling forest creatures mingling with a variety of gnomes—a smiling lady gnome dancing with her skirts in her hands, a grinning bearded fellow with his hands planted on his hips, a cheerful waving fellow wielding an axe who had more than once given Eli a start when he drove through the community on his rounds late at night. Her yard was a huge hit with any and all visiting grandkids.

But the Heavenly Shores Mobile Estates Retirement Community had a rather cutthroat competition going with the Elysian Acres Mobile Estates over landscaping, and every year a grand prize was awarded by an allegedly impartial committee to both the finest landscaping and the community that showed the most creativity.

The contest got a little hairy. A lot of these retirees who bought these mobile homes had left behind high-level corporate jobs in finance and marketing and old habits died hard. The rest were just wily. They weren't afraid of a damn thing, not confrontation, not death, nothing.

And Eli knew their idea of morning was often about four a.m. The streets around Heavenly Shores practically teemed with track-suited dog-walkers around then.

"Have you ever actually seen Mrs. Kilgore do it?" he asked.

"No, but I *know*. That trollop wears White Shoulders, and when I step outside it's still hanging in the air like a pesticide."

Eli's own grandmother had worn White Shoulders; his mother had bought it for her every Christmas and Eli had a soft spot for it. But that was neither here nor there at the moment.

"I notice you don't have any obvious security devices outside your house. Maybe if you set up a web cam?"

"What's a web cam? A camera that drops a web down over a criminal when they're caught in the act?"

When she put it that way, Eli didn't know why a web cam shouldn't do exactly that. One day, probably. He could imagine a future in which cops cruised around each morning in recycling trucks, picking up little cocoons comprised of people who'd been netted in the act of peeing against sides of buildings or defacing bus benches with graffiti.

"If cameras could do that, Mrs. Wilberforce, I'd be out of a job. And we still live in a democracy. We're all entitled to be tried by a jury of our peers. Have you spoken to Mrs. Kilgore about it?"

"She denies it."

He could just *imagine* that conversation.

"Ask your grandson, Bill. Isn't Bill the one who likes computers?" He'd had many a long chat over the years with half the residents here. "The one who lives in San Francisco?"

The place Glory had been headed a few months ago.

How about that. He couldn't seem to get through more than a few minutes without at least a glancing thought of her. The problem was that everything he did, said, thought, or felt, could be followed right back to her, the way Whiskey Creek fed into the Hellcat River fed into the ocean.

"Oh yes, my Bill is brilliant!" Mrs. Wilberforce brightened immediately at the idea of her grandson. Eli had known she would. "What a good idea, Eli."

"He'll know how to set you up with a security system or a camera that you see on your computer. But while a dog peeing on your rhododendron is impolite and certainly isn't neighborly, I'm afraid it isn't strictly illegal, and proving intent might be a bit tricky."

"I've half a mind to pee on *her* flowers."

He sighed. "I really hope you don't, Mrs. Wilberforce."

They both shot straight up in the air and twirled about 180 degrees when a god-awful sound, a cross between a leaf blower and chainsaw, swelled and in an instant was deafening.

Eli crouched when he landed and put his hand reflexively on his gun. If they were being strafed by enemy planes, there wasn't much he'd be able to do about it, but at least he could say he'd gone down fighting.

A rotund elderly gentleman in plaid pants and a jaunty matching cap was rounding the corner on a mobility scooter that had clearly been souped up in some fashion. His enormous rectangular glasses magnified his eyes to the size of ping-pong balls.

They went even bigger when they saw Eli and he quite clearly mouthed the words *oh shit*, did a sharp left turn, and went back the way he came.

He cut the engine, and merciful silence reigned again.

Mrs. Wilberforce had started talking before it was completely quiet. ". . . that damn scooter of his with a lawn mower motor or something. I think he can do fifteen miles an hour on that thing."

It was illegal as all hell, but Eli frankly thought he'd be

tempted to soup up his scooter, too, if the day came when he couldn't get around easily on two legs.

He'd be obliged to give that guy a ticket, if he could catch him.

And he had a feeling the old guy wouldn't go down easy.

He sighed. The gang here at Heavenly Shores was as much of a handful as the gang down at the Plugged Nickel.

"I don't know how he can stand the sound of that thing," he said.

"He turns his hearing aid off," said Mrs. Wilberforce.

"Well, you have my advice, Mrs. Wilberforce, with regards to your rhododendrons. Let's hope we resolve it peacefully. Always good to see you. I should be getting on my . . ."

A tall, slim woman with long, streaky honey-gold hair was walking toward them, an overnight bag slung over her shoulder, worry and amusement and affection all over her face. She was definitely out of context here at Heavenly Shores. Quite possibly she was a mirage. Given how tired he was, it wouldn't surprise him.

"Grandma, why are you talking to the handsome police officer in your curlers? Did you pull off a heist again?"

And Mrs. Wilberforce pulled the willowy beauty into a hug and a both-cheeks kiss.

"Oh, Eli. This is my granddaughter, Bethany. She's in town working on that television show they're filming nearby. She'll be staying with me."

The wind caught and tossed Bethany's mane of streaky gold and brown and she swept it out of her face with a musical laugh.

Eli had learned to be a little leery of girls whose names ended with an "any" sound. Melanie and Tiffany and

Brittany and the like. He'd dated a few in high school and they were all as astonishingly high maintenance and as temperamental as the rust-bucket Fiero he'd bought dirt cheap in high school and that he and Jonah had tinkered with over many a summer weekend.

"Eli Barlow isn't married, either, Bethany," Mrs. Wilberforce continued. "And he's the *sheriff*, too."

Oh, for God's sake. And now he deplored that willingness to say anything at all. Surely occasional circumspection was less dangerous than, say, skipping a blood pressure pill.

"Deputy sheriff," he clarified, modestly.

"In charge of *all* the deputies around here! All of them. And he was on the news. On *TV*," Mrs. Wilberforce clarified, as if being on TV were all the credentials someone needed. "He's a hero!"

Bethany gave a short laugh and sparkled ruefully up at Eli. "I'm so sorry. It's how my grandmother classifies the world—married or not married." But her words were all warm affection. "I've been hired as a freelance makeup artist on *The Rush*. Have to make those guys looks authentically dirty."

That was a flirtatious line if Eli had ever heard one.

And it had been a while since he'd heard one.

He took the hand she extended. Her nails had those neat little square white tips and it was very soft and probably lotioned and scented. She had that natural yet thoroughly groomed look which annoyed a guy when he had to live with it because it took forever to achieve but which he generally admired when he saw the end result.

He was certain the fingertips of her left hand were just as soft as the ones on the right, not callused.

In an instant he was under that tree again, and Glory's eyes were soft and amazed, and her fingers combed up his neck as he went in for a deeper kiss.

He hadn't known Glory had any surrender in her at all until her body softened to fit his, as if she was a missing piece of him.

Eli suddenly envied the ability to turn things on and off, the way the guy on the scooter had switched off his hearing aid. Things like his feelings and his libido and his memory. He'd only use them when it was safe.

He let go of Bethany's hand, freshly reminded of how very much he enjoyed touching women. And of last night's resolve to move on.

"I just want you to be as happy as I was, Bethany, sweetie." Mrs. Wilberforce was regarding this meeting with proud satisfaction and a little glimmer of hope.

"Gramps was one of a kind." Bethany slung an arm around her grandmother and gave her a half hug.

"Bet Eli could give him a run for his money."

Mrs. Wilberforce actually nudged Eli with her sharp little elbow.

He was six feet five inches and in many ways hard as nails, and there was a gun hanging at his hip, but Mrs. Wilberforce might actually make him blush.

The melting-chocolate eyes of Bethany sparkled up at him, reminding him that he *was* actually (1) a catch, (2) a red-blooded man who had more than a few moves, none of which he'd deployed since he'd had Glory Greenleaf pressed up against a ponderosa pine, and (3) his resolve of the previous night. Every journey began with the first step, as they say.

"I can show you a little bit of the town if you like,

Bethany," he offered. "I know every bit of it like the back of my hand. Grew up here. I have a few free hours tomorrow, if you'd like to join me."

Within the hour everyone in town would know he'd just offered to take out Bethany.

"That sounds wonderful, Deputy Barlow. I have a few days before I need to be on *The Rush* set full-time, so my schedule is wide-open."

That sounded a bit like innuendo, too.

He smiled at her as Mrs. Wilberforce beamed triumphantly. "Excellent. Call me Eli."

CHAPTER 5

Legend had it the Misty Cat Cavern got its current name because the previous owner, Earl Holloway, ordered a neon sign over the phone while he was falling-down drunk. He'd *meant* to call the place the Aristocrat Tavern, and he'd pitched a fit when the sign came but he couldn't afford another, so he hung the one he got and the name stuck. The place had begun its life in the Gold Rush as a saloon with a whorehouse upstairs, and it hadn't changed much since then, architecturally, anyway. It was said a certain former resident, a prostitute named Naughty Nellie, who was murdered by a jealous miner, had allegedly never left. Some claimed to have seen her spectral face in the upstairs window in the wee hours of the morning, but then, most people who were anywhere near the Misty Cat in the wee hours of the morning were probably pretty drunk.

Poor Nellie couldn't seem to leave Hellcat Canyon, either. *At least* I'm *still alive*, Glory pep-talked herself. And she had a plan.

The Misty Cat was now a wildly popular restaurant, and Glenn and Sherrie Harwood had owned it going on two decades now. The food wasn't fancy but it was pretty flawless and always satisfying, the place was almost always packed, and you left feeling hugged, if only metaphorically. And thanks to some mysterious magical conspiracy between the ceiling height and the aged redwood and the depth of the place, the acoustics were marvelous. Glory had been a regular at the Misty Cat's open mic nights ever since she was old enough to get in the door with her real ID. (In a small town, there really was no way to get away with a fake ID.) Its famed acoustics were why college and indie bands like The Baby Owls often detoured there on their way to bigger venues up and down California and Nevada and Oregon.

Glory timed her arrival at the Misty Cat for the lull, if one could call it that, between the breakfast and lunch rushes. She pushed open the door and the bells hanging from the handle leaped and jangled frantically.

Everything looked and smelled the way it usually did: the big white board over the grill read "TRY THE GLENNBURGER! SEVEN SECRET INGREDIENTS!" And Giorgio was behind the grill. He was downright soothing to watch when you were hungover after a late night: the slapping, scraping, clanging, and sizzling were like a sort of noisy industrial ballet. He had a certain charisma, maybe even hotness, if you liked your guys irritable and taciturn and enigmatic. Glory didn't. He didn't really hold too many mysteries for her. He'd grown up in Coyote Creek and had more relatives in jail than she did, and she'd gone all through school with him. And he rented the tiny flat upstairs at Allegro Music extra cheap (as well it should be, given that it was right over kids learning how to play trumpets and guitars and whatnot), and she'd once

seen him shuffling off to the bathroom with his tooth-
brush and shaving kit tucked under his armpit when his
own toilet had backed up.

Sherrie's crimson hair was heading toward Glory like a
beacon born aloft. It was the color she'd been born with,
only more so, courtesy of a box she usually picked up at
Costco or Walmart, whoever had her shade on sale that
week, and her complexion was cured brown by decades
of hot mountain summers. Usually the only thing brighter
than her hair was her smile, which Glory basked in now,
though today it was a contest between her smile and the
orange and fuchsia striped shirt she was wearing. She and
Glenn had four kids and Glory had gone to school with
most of them, too.

"Well, hello, hon! Haven't seen you in a while. We've
missed you at the open mics! Did you phone in a to-go
order?" Sherrie seemed genuinely delighted to see Glory.

"Um . . . no. No, I didn't, actually." In a flash everything
at stake made her palms go damp.

"Oh . . . do you want a table, then? You can have a seat
right over there, if you want. See where that pink flyer
is?" Sherrie waved a hand.

It was a Baby Owls flyer.

That clinched it for Glory. She squared her shoulders.
"Actually, Sherrie . . . I came in to see if you might be
hiring. I heard you might be short a waitress, since Britt
is moving on."

What ensued in the wake of that sentence was a sort of
cosmic record scratch.

Sherrie's smile congealed.

Giorgio froze, spatula mid-air. He looked absurdly like
a swarthy marching band conductor.

The only thing moving was the ceiling fan. Glory could see its reflection in the laminated gleam of the menus Sherrie was clutching.

"Oh!" Sherrie said brightly, finally. "Well!"

And that was all she said. Her smile didn't shift at all.

But Glory could practically hear her brain gears whirring like the blades of the fan overhead.

And she didn't say a word.

Glory cleared her throat again. "I didn't know whether you'd hired anyone yet, so I thought I'd, you know, just, inquire . . ."

Sherrie had apparently come to some silent accord with herself, because she re-animated. "Well, hon, let me . . . let me just go and get you an application. We'll need to get your particulars from you."

Glory had a hunch she was stalling. Glenn was probably back there in the Misty Cat's little office, and they were probably going to have a confab.

Sherrie pivoted and slipped behind the counter and disappeared into the depths of the kitchen.

Glory sat down at the empty table Sherrie had gestured to and looked around. At one table a guy was twirling his final French fry into a pool of ketchup, his face the picture of dreamy, gustatory satisfaction. At another table a pair of guys in heavy work boots, hardhats slung over the backs of their chairs, those huge, tough work gloves hanging out of their back pockets, were laughing over something on one guy's phone. One of them glanced up and saw her, and she lifted a hand. Bill Cranford, one of Jonah's old friends from high school.

And that was how it normally was in the Misty Cat. Half the time you'd know at least half the people in the place, and they all knew a little too much about you, too. Same was true of Hellcat Canyon itself. The blessing and curse of small towns everywhere.

Giorgio was glowering at her as if she was the health department. He knew Glory pretty well, and he clearly anticipated she would be a disruptive force in his orderly world if she got a job here.

"You can glare at me all you want, Giorgio. I saw your pee-pee when you ran through the sprinklers at my cousin's house when you were five years old."

Giorgio lowered the spatula, impressed by this opening gambit.

"Piglet panties," he said pointedly, after a moment.

Well, damn.

She had indeed split her pants when she was in kindergarten and the whole class had seen her underpants, which were covered with little Winnie the Poohs and Piglets and Eeyores. Honestly, she could hardly blame them for calling her Piglet Panties. She was only glad no one had thought to call her Pooh panties.

"Well played," Glory allowed.

He actually flashed her a little smile and saluted her with the spatula.

Mutual blackmail sorted out, she resumed looking about the place as if she hadn't done it a hundred times before. Old pickaxes and sieves hung on the walls, now decorations where they'd once been tools in someone's hands. Daguerreotypes of scruffy guys, some of whom struck it rich, some of whom never made it out alive. A few women were pictured, too, hardy souls, camp followers, a few prostitutes who made excellent marriages, and a few, like Nellie, a victim of the primal lawlessness of that time.

Glenn Harwood emerged from the kitchen wiping his hands on a towel. He was tall and big boned and soft bellied, and he had a bushy head of hair, all gray, as was his formidable mustache.

"Let's sit over here, kiddo, and have a chat," he said briskly.

He'd coached her softball team when she was in grade school, and then he'd coached soccer in high school. His daughter Eden, who ran the flower shop and had hair a few shades lighter than her mom's, was the same age as Glory. In Glenn's eyes Glory was probably forever nine years old. He would probably call her kiddo until the day he or she died, whoever went first.

Thing was, he also knew her pretty well. And he knew her family lineage going back a long, long way.

"So, Glenn. Did Sherrie send you out here to talk me out of wanting a job?"

He grinned. "There. Right there is why she likes you. She says it's because you're smart and you have strong opinions, and if that doesn't describe my Sherrie I don't know what does."

Glory smiled cautiously.

"Strong, ceaseless, unsolicited opinions," Glenn expounded.

That was also true. For example, "You'd probably be able to bend over and do your own filing if you'd just unclench and let that stick slide out, Mr. Torkelson" was Glory's exit line at her last job. Mr. Torkelson was a mortgage broker who had hired her to "sit quietly" and answer phones and file papers even when the phone didn't ring and there wasn't a scrap of paper in sight. "I'm not paying you for your opinions," he'd said when she pointed out that maybe this didn't make a whole lot of sense. It was just that the kind of routine required by the jobs she was qualified for was a recipe for personal misery, and she'd do nearly anything to alleviate it, which is probably how four men ended up thinking they were playing poker for her favors at the Plugged Nickel.

"Some people are more comfortable issuing orders than taking them, let's just say," Glenn added.

"I can be flexible." Even she wasn't convinced when she said that.

He snorted. "Flexible the way a slingshot is flexible."

She started to laugh at that, but she cut it short. She was in the business of persuading him to give her a job.

The Baby Owls flyer suddenly slipped from the wall. Glenn grabbed it before it could go sailing onto the floor. He looked down at it.

"The Baby Owls," he groused. "Stupidest name I ever heard. Owlets! Baby owls are called *owlets*. Sweet Jesus."

"I think it's meant to be ironic." She was amused.

He snorted. "Ironic. Irony is for wimps. Their album is called *Hoot Are You?*, did you know that? A takeoff on 'Who Are You,' by The Who. Whatever happened to just smashing your guitar when you're finished with your set? But my little granddaughter Annelise loves that damn song, though, so . . . I worked something out with their manager. Who is a bit of a tool, between you and me."

"'In the Forest' is a good song, at least," Glory said stoutly. She knew how hard it was to write a good song, let alone an earworm kind of song. She slipped the flyer from Glenn's hand and carefully patted it back upon the wall in solidarity with bands everywhere.

"Well, if anyone would know a good song, you would," Glenn said sincerely.

It was a nice little vote of confidence and it warmed her heart.

But that didn't have much to do with the quest at hand. And her musical talent really didn't have much of a relationship to carrying plates to tables.

Glenn smiled at her. "Kiddo, being a waitress involves a lot of being pleasant to people all day long. And a lot of being patient. And a lot of not saying what you actually think. And a lot of putting up with every manner of behavior—rude, sexist, drunk, you name it. Even when you think they're ordering something that will make them fatter than they ought to be or will raise their blood pressure, or if they try to grab your ass."

When he put it that way, it did sound well-nigh impossible.

She took this in, mulling. "Well, I can handle an unruly audience. And you've met most of my relatives over the years. Rude, sexist, and drunk are in my wheelhouse."

He laughed.

"And I can be . . . I can be pleasant." She issued that word gingerly. She wasn't certain she'd ever been anything so banal as "pleasant."

Glenn grinned at her. "Kiddo, you're delightful, and I mean that sincerely. I like you. You're talented. You are one of a kind. You are never dull. But that ain't the same as pleasant."

Ouch.

Perversely, she liked Glenn for saying things like that. He was stern and he loved his kids, all of whom seemed to be thriving, and he didn't take crap from anyone. And she liked being *known*.

Which made her double determined to win him over. Because she did very much like winning, period, no matter what the game was.

She also had another agenda, but that would be the next battle in this particular war, and she had to win this one first.

"Maybe your customers would enjoy a colorful wait- ress. Liven up the place."

This amused him, too. "Maybe so. Maybe so. Let's try a little exercise. Say I'm a customer and I very plainly order rye toast. You write it down on a tag. You bring me rye toast. I tell you I didn't order the rye toast, I ordered sourdough—you must have heard me wrong and could you please scurry off and get it right away and what the hell is wrong with your *ears*, you air-headed woman?"

She could feel her stomach muscles tightening as he spoke, even though this was all hypothetical.

There wasn't a soul in the world who would get away with talking to Glory like that.

Glenn knew it.

She drew in a breath, and released it slowly. "Well, who are we talking to? Man or a woman?"

"Say it's a woman."

"I say, well, I'm so sorry. I brought you rye toast because I read an article that Angelina Jolie eats it for breakfast, and something about your eyes reminded me of her, and I guess I must have gotten confused."

Glenn stroked his mustache. "Damn." He was im- pressed.

Glory leaned back in her chair a little cockily and folded her arms. "Try another one on me."

"What if it was a man?"

"I'd say, well, I read somewhere that rye helps build

muscle and when I saw your forearm, I thought, this guy
looks strong, the kind of guy who knows how to really
use tools and lift heavy things, and so I just sort of de-
faulted to rye."

Glenn snorted. "It *would* take a strong man to shovel
his way out of that pile of bullshit."

She laughed.

"And we'd have guys volunteering to lift you and carry
you on out of here, you talk like that. Riots starting up."

She shrugged idly with one shoulder. Guys wanting to
do things for and to her was just another day. "Doesn't
mean they get to. One thing I know for certain? People
like to be noticed. Whether they're making smart choices
for breakfast or reading a good book or their shirt brings
out their eyes or whatever. And even if they know it's
B.S., they often just appreciate the attempt."

Eli was so good at this sort of thing, the noticing of
little details. Of course, he used it to catch criminals, too.

Glenn's eyes widened a little, impressed again. Then
they narrowed, and they sat in silence for a moment.

Then he gave his fingers a drum. And then lowered his
voice to something approximating gentle.

"What are you still doing here, anyway, young lady?"

Her heart lurched.

"In . . . the Misty Cat?" Her voice was a little frayed.
"Now?"

Because she was pretty sure she knew what he meant.

"In Hellcat Canyon. In general."

Glory gave a short, nervous laugh. "You know an interview isn't going well if it ends with your interviewer
wanting you to get the hell out of town."

But Glenn had heard her play. And she'd seen him stand
absolutely motionless every time she'd played that Linda

Ronstadt song "Long, Long Time." And she'd seen his eyes get shiny.

Glenn wasn't as crusty as he looked.

So at most every open mic she played, she included it in the set, just for him.

Glenn had seen every manner of college band stop in at the Misty Cat to play over the last decade. At least one band a month with a decent following, sometimes more. He loved music, and he had his own singular tastes and a strong sense of musical history.

And Glenn thought she was quite simply amazing.

"Weren't you headed to San Francisco?"

She thought about what to say. "It's . . . a long story."

He could probably fill in the blanks. Everyone in town knew about the drama with Jonah.

Glenn was quiet a moment. "Sherrie wishes she had a whole record of you singing so she could listen to it in the bathtub. She does a whole girly thing with candles and bubbles and a glass of wine." Glenn waved his hand in Sherrie's direction.

"That's sweet. One day soon, hopefully, I'll have one for her."

She'd never recorded a demo. She didn't have the kind of laptop you could record things onto. Because she couldn't yet *afford* the kind of laptop you could record things onto. She just sang into Jonah's old tape recorder with her guitar. Admittedly, however, she loved the way that sounded: intimate, every rustle in the room and exhale of breath audible and somehow part of every song, and every now and then birdsong, or a door slamming, found its way onto the recording, too, and sounded somehow right.

She took a deep breath, ready to really sell Glenn on her.

"Okay, let's look at all the pros. You've known me for a long time, so no surprises. What you see is what you get. I have a good memory, so I'll never forget an order. I can think on my feet. I've never been late for anything in my whole life, and you know that, because I was at every softball practice right on the dot. I have, um . . . excellent balance, so I won't be dropping things, and I like to move fast. Giorgio and I have an understanding."

She shot Giorgio a look.

He ducked his head and applied himself to scraping the grill.

"I can *make* people like me. I'll do a good job."

"You've got a way with a crowd, I'll hand you that," Glenn mused.

Sherrie swept by with a wet towel to bus a table and smiled encouragingly at Glory.

Glenn was thoughtful and quiet for a moment, studying her.

"You know, speaking of Sherrie's notions, Glory, I built her a koi pond. She has some idea about meditating next to it." He shook his head as if this was a hopelessly eccentric thing to do, but Glory knew how proud he was of Sherrie and how indulgent he was of any notion she might have. "You know what I learned when I was reading up on building koi ponds? If the pond is too small, those beautiful big fish suffer something fierce."

Glory stared at him.

Her throat knotted.

And she thought about the tigers.

When she was little, she'd loved tigers as passionately as she'd loved horses. She'd draw pictures of them to hang on her walls. And then one day three of the grades at her school had gone on a field trip to the zoo. She'd been so excited to go.

But then she'd seen the tigers pacing in their cages . . . back and forth . . . back and forth.

She found a bench and sat down. And she'd put her face in her hands and just wept. She didn't know why, for certain, but she felt a sort of desperate, panicky sorrow for the tigers.

It was so incredibly unlike her that Jonah had been concerned and embarrassed all at once, astonished to see his scrappy sister transform into an astonishing baby. He'd been frantic in his attempt to shush her.

But Eli had given her the napkins from his ice cream cone to wipe her eyes, and then he'd sat next to her on the bench and arranged his arm across the back. She'd pressed her skinny little shoulder blades against it and he'd pressed back with his arm, so that no one except them knew they were both taking and giving comfort.

"It's not right, Eli," was the best she could do by way of explaining. "It's not how it's supposed to be."

She could still remember how he smelled that day. Like a boy, earthy and grassy and sweaty and wild. He didn't say much. Back then he stuttered when he got excited. So Eli mostly listened.

He got the stutter under control over the years. Eli always got everything under control.

"I know." She could feel him suffering on her behalf. "That won't be you, Glory."

Only Eli understood it had nothing at all to do with her being afraid of the tigers and everything to do with those cages. Those cages and the tigers' beauty.

A year after that, he'd given her a little stuffed tiger for her birthday. It was kind of a secret between the two of them. And she'd gotten in the habit of moving her tiger around the house every day, just so the tiger knew it *could* move, and then the habit stuck.

It occurred to her that Glenn might actually be working toward issuing a no. Because he was no pushover. He knew for a fact that she was a risky choice as waitress, that he needed a good one, that he wanted someone to stick around for a long time, because he was a smart businessman. And he knew, like she did, that she didn't belong here in Hellcat Canyon forever.

She was also a Greenleaf. Possibly the only Greenleaf who had saved every penny she'd made or found since she was twelve years old. Nevertheless.

Glenn sighed. "Be here tomorrow at eleven for the lunch rush. We'll throw you in at the deep end, see how that goes."

She exhaled in exultant relief. "I *love* the deep end."

"I know you do, kiddo. I know you do." He sounded sort of amused and resigned. As if he already knew how it would all turn out but he was willing to watch the show.

They shook hands on it firmly, and he pushed away from the chair, casting one final glare at the flyer.

"Owlets," he muttered again irritably on his way back to the kitchen.

"Bye, sprinklers!" Glory called to Giorgio as she left.

She tried not to skip, but she indulged in one on the way back up the street.

Halfway home she paused to admire the billboard. The men had finished slapping it up, and it was now shining on the highway.

HOOT ARE YOU?
The new album by The Baby Owls

There they all were, beards and flannel and glasses, only probably about fifteen feet taller than real life.

That was a good omen for certain. She figured she needed to at least put in a full day's work before she hit Glenn up for the second part of her plan.

CHAPTER 6

Eli pulled out of the parking lot of Heavenly Shores, bemused by the mazelike turns his job often took. He'd arrived to address a pissed-upon rhododendron; he'd departed with a date with a hot blonde.

Not the worst day he'd ever had.

He made a left down Main Street and waved at Eden Harwood, who was just arranging little tasteful buckets of flowers in front of her store while her black-and-white tuxedo cat, Peace and Love, wound around her ankles, and he found himself singing softly. "This is the chorus, of we're lost in the for—"

Holy *shit*!

Was that a *Porsche*?

Hard to tell exactly *what* it was when it was doing what amounted to light speed. It was basically a blue smudge on wheels.

Eli switched on his lights, cranked the wheel hard to the left and floored it until he was practically on that Porsche's bumper.

The Porsche slowed obediently, then practically slinked over to the verge side with such ease and grace Eli wouldn't be surprised if it rubbed itself on a tree with self-satisfaction like a cat, and despite himself, he admired how that thing handled. If the driver was hammered or otherwise pharmacologically impaired, he probably wouldn't be able to maneuver a speeding vehicle with that kind of delicacy. Or who knows? Maybe Google had finally invented a self-driving Porsche and set it loose on California back roads. A few Bay Area tech moguls and other outrageously wealthy types owned cabins up along the ridge, and this could be one of them.

It certainly didn't have that fine coat of red dust that all stalwart Hellcat Canyon vehicles acquired after a few days spent here. It was beautiful and rare and too fast for this place.

All that thought did was remind him of Glory.

Maybe he ought to get a rubber band to wear around his wrist every time he thought of her.

Maybe all he had to do was train his thoughts in a different direction the way Dale Dawber trained his tomatoes up their stakes.

There were so few deputies in Hellcat Canyon they often went out alone, so he radioed his location to Owen Haggerty, standard procedure in case things got hairy, got out of his cruiser, and crunched over the graveled road to the verge.

The Porsche's window was already lowered.

Eli bent down. "License and registration, please."

The guy behind the wheel whipped off his sunglasses. "Was I going too fast?" He sounded contrite. "I didn't see a speed limit posted."

"Yeah, I imagine it's challenging to read a speed limit sign when you're roaring past it at seventy miles an hour down the middle of a small-town street," Eli said evenly. "Must have just looked like a blur."

The guy just grinned at him, at peace with the world, utterly certain of his place in it. He radiated self-satisfaction. His teeth were flawless uniform rectangles and so brilliant Eli was glad he'd kept his mirrored sunglasses on, because he didn't need deeper squint lines. Those were definitely not Hellcat Canyon teeth. They were Los Angeles teeth.

And if that guy in the Plugged Nickel last night was what passed for dangerously handsome in Hellcat Canyon, this guy might as well be from another dimension. His face had the prismatic elegance—all hollows and angles and whatnot—of the guys who posed in their underwear on billboards.

Suddenly Eli knew exactly who this was before he even glanced at the license.

Millions of people around the world knew who this was.

"I clocked you at seventy and it's thirty-five miles an hour through the main part of town. There are only a couple of stoplights, but we like to think they're there for a reason. We probably have more than enough deer and squirrels in Hellcat Canyon but we still don't like to see them turned into pancakes. We figure they got a right to go about their business, same as all of us. And at speeds like that, you can take pedestrians out, and well, we're all kind of fond of the people who live here, too."

Franco Francone's smile faded gradually, evenly, as Eli spoke, as if he actually kept it on a dimmer.

Eli was aware that his tone was approaching parodic, that he sounded like a sardonic folksy kindergarten teacher, that he was doing it on purpose.

But frankly, it pissed him off that he needed to actually say any of this to a grown man. Especially to this one.

"You know who I am." More a statement than a question. "I'm Franco Francone."

Eli stifled a sigh. The "don't you know who I am?" would never work in a million years on Eli. And he'd really hoped Franco Francone was above that.

"Yep," he said neutrally.

Francone eyed Eli thoughtfully, almost encouragingly, as though he was a fellow actor who had delivered the wrong line in front of an audience of hundreds and trying to decide whether they could save the scene.

And then Eli took off his sunglasses, because he wanted Francone to remember his face and to read implacability in his eyes.

Eli did occasionally let people off with a warning. A few weeks ago, a seventeen-year-old girl had forgotten to turn the headlights of her dad's old pickup back on after she pulled out of a brightly lit gas station, for instance, and had sobbed in distress over her mistake. Or a clearly terrified teenage boy who'd been feeling his oats speeding just a little in his dad's old Camry when he'd been pulled over, and Eli figured he could still be sufficiently and permanently unnerved into driving the speed limit by a big granite-faced law enforcement officer. Or a harried mom with a car full of rambunctious kids having the sort of bad day that culminated in accidentally running a stop sign, then remembering to stop ten feet into the intersection. He was experienced enough to deploy discretion.

But he was going to give Franco Francone a ticket. Because Franco Francone deserved a ticket and he could afford it, and he was a grown-ass man and he'd known exactly what he was doing. Franco could wreck this Porsche and buy another one. Franco Francone could probably wreck his own face and buy another one.

There passed a moment of mutual alpha-male staring. But Eli had the badge and the gun and his penis size was more than adequate, even if he wasn't famous and didn't own a Porsche.

He was also aware that he might be behaving like a slightly bigger dick than usual.

He was man enough to own up to the realization that a breezy, self-satisfied person can only make you irritable if you're not precisely content with your current life circumstances.

He couldn't shake a peculiar sense of premonition—an ominous one—and it had to do with Mr. Francone. Not the sort that told him who might have stuffed drugs down his pants five seconds before Eli appeared. This was something else. Like he was picking up the sound of an advancing army from a long, long way off.

"I enjoyed your show, Mr. Francone," he offered. Every-so-slightly conciliatory. "Used to watch it with my dad."

He and his dad had actually enjoyed making fun of the law enforcement inaccuracies in *Blood Brothers*, the wildly popular cop show that had starred Franco Francone and John Tennessee McCord. To be fair, they were pretty scarce, though the show had taken some wild liberties with procedures. For the most part, it was a well-written drama, even if the pithy exchanges and one-liners made his dad snort.

He was surprised there was enough innocence left in him to be disappointed that the guy who had played such a heroic cop on *Blood Brothers* was so cavalier about the law.

"Glad to hear it." Francone had likely heard this a million times in his life, but he managed to make it sound more or less gracious.

"You here on business?" Eli was writing the particulars on what was going to be a very expensive ticket.

"Have a three-episode arc in *The Rush*. Filming on location nearby."

Eli wasn't entirely positive he knew what an arc was, but he could hazard a guess. "Oh yeah. I've met J.T. McCord. Good guy, J.T. Just met a makeup artist named Bethany. Her grandmother lives at the Heavenly Shores Mobile Estates here."

"Mobile Estates, huh? So quaint. I don't often find myself in small towns. Usually it's L.A., New York, Paris, London. The odd tropical island."

Eli didn't know if the guy was joking or bragging. He frankly didn't care.

"More deer than Kardashians in Hellcat Canyon, Mr. Francone. They don't often look both ways before they cross the street, and a deer could do some major damage to this beautiful machine. Not to mention those sharp sunglasses. And that would be a damn shame, wouldn't it?"

"Sure," Francone said tautly. After a moment's pause, during which he'd probably entertained and discarded various other sardonic things he wanted to say.

"Thirty-five," Eli said again, pleasantly. "That's the downtown speed limit. I'll hold you to that during your visit with us. Which I hope is otherwise enjoyable."

He ripped the ticket from his pad and held it out. It fluttered in the breeze for another second.

And then Francone's hand extended slowly.

Giving Eli a chance to change his mind.

Finally, he took it gingerly.

And when he had it in his hands, he looked down at it, as if to ascertain it was real.

Then looked slowly up at Eli again.

There was another little moment of silence. Quite stunned on Francone's part.

"Must be tough, working in a small town," Francone said thoughtfully, finally.

If this was meant to be a dig, it didn't come close to penetrating Eli's hide.

"Tough is relative," Eli said evenly.

Franco sighed, as if a favorite child had disappointed him. "Maybe I'll see you around, Deputy."

"Maybe. I'll be easier to spot if you drive the speed limit. You give my regards to J.T."

He gave the Porsche roof a pat and headed back to his cruiser.

He was pretty sure he and Franco Francone weren't going to be friends.

Glory reported to the Misty Cat at five minutes to eleven o'clock the next morning, wearing a pair of jeans and a snug, short-sleeved flowery blouse she'd picked up for a song (not literally, though if she could trade songs for things, all her problems would be solved) at Walmart a few years back.

Sherrie intercepted her at the door. "Good morning, hon. Don't you look pretty! Now turn around."

For one wild moment she thought Sherrie was telling her to get out, and for one wild moment, Glory was tempted to take off at a run down the street.

And then she realized Sherrie was brandishing a barrette. "We need to get your wonderful mop up and out of the way so it doesn't wind up in the food. No one likes to floss *while* they're eating. If you turn around I can put it up for you."

"Oh, let *me* do her hair!"

Casey Carson from The Truth and Beauty had just crossed the street. She was the local expert on all things fashionable, and she could do anything you wanted to any hair on your body, whether it was cut swingy layers, blow it silky straight, wax it into a heart shape, pluck it into submission, bleach it, ombre it, or tease and pin and spray it into a two-foot high red-carpet updo. Glory visited Supercuts about twice a year for a competent but no-frills trim since her budget didn't quite run to Casey's expertise. But they liked each other. Casey was a strapping golden blonde and her sunny confidence was like a major C chord to Glory's major G.

"Morning, Casey!" Sherrie handed her the barrette. "Send Glory back inside when you're done with her. I'll go see if Giorgio has your to-go order ready yet."

Casey pulled Glory onto the sidewalk, turned her by the shoulders, whipped out a brush, and used it to drag Glory's hair back from her forehead. Glory felt her eyebrows go back, too.

"Easy there, Casey."

"Sorry, hon. Sherrie said to be quick. I'll just do a French braid," she announced. "Fancy but not complicated. Always wanted to get my hands on your hair! Just didn't think it would be outside the Misty Cat. You taking Britt's old job? What happened to your San Francisco plans?"

"Let's . . . just say I experienced a little setback. Resulting in a slight delay."

She saw Casey's reflection shrug in the Misty Cat's window. "I like to think of setbacks as trampolines. They eventually bounce you up a little higher than before."

Glory was arrested by this image.

And then she immediately started thinking of all the things that rhymed with *trampoline*.

"I think you gave me an idea for a song, Casey."

"Well, if Rihanna can sing about umbrellas and Sia can sing about chandeliers, there's no reason you can't sing about trampolines."

Glory laughed. "You gonna stop in for the open mic night? I haven't done one in a while. I have a new song I might spring on everyone."

"Oh yeah, I'll be there. There's that chamber of commerce reception right before it, too. Free booze! I'm going to try to get in to see The Baby Owls, too, aren't you?"

"Oh yeah. I'll be at The Baby Owls show, for sure." Glory surreptitiously crossed her fingers about that one.

Casey spun her around again. "Okay, every last one of your hairs is strapped in there and you look great. Good luck!"

Glory's hands went up to her head in a sort of exploratory alarm. Her eyebrows felt an inch or two closer to her hairline. Casey was pretty strong from hefting blow dryers and ripping wax from bodies and that braid was as tight as a trucker's hitch.

Glory figured that she'd just have to get used to it the way a horse has to get used to a bit.

Casey gave Glory an affectionate little shove back into the Misty Cat, and Sherrie intercepted her as if she were a baton, looped a chummy arm around her shoulders and steered her about the restaurant, narrating Glory's duties like a Universal Studios tour guide. She pointed out the difference between the caf and decaf pots of coffee, introduced the little creamer pots as if they were celebrities, demonstrated how to stuff the little jellies and butters neatly into their caddies as though it was an E-ticket ride, and there was a whole part of the tour involving lemon slices and straws and napkins and tabasco and so forth. It was pretty clear Sherrie had given this spiel a few dozen times over the years to various waiters and waitresses. She barely stopped to breathe. Glory hoped for her own sake and Sherrie's she wouldn't have to give it again to some other waitress tomorrow.

Glenn signaled Sherrie with an eyebrow wag and Sherrie gave a nod and wrapped things up. "Take their drink orders first. Bring 'em water only if they ask. The specials today are eggs Benedict, which comes with potatoes and white, whole wheat, rye, or sourdough toast, and the turkey club, which comes with a salad or fries—and tell them the specials right after you say hi like they're your long lost best friend and dazzle 'em with a smile. Oh, and push the pumpkin muffins. They're delicious and Glenn made a big batch of 'em. You think you can handle it?"

"I will!" Glory vowed, momentarily infected by Sherrie's zeal. "I can!"

"Okay, you take that side of the restaurant, I'll take the other, I'll be in charge of seating, and if you have any questions, ask me on the fly. Here's your order pad, hon. And . . . go!"

She gave her a little nudge toward a table occupied by one person, which seemed like the perfect way to dip a toe in. Fueled by a peculiar mix of hope, dread, brio, and truth be told, a little thrill at the novelty of it all, Glory strode over.

The world went slo-mo as she registered who was sitting at that table.

Hell's. Teeth.

Or, to quote a song Mikey McShane had played at an open mic not too long ago: "fuck small towns."

Mrs. Adler hadn't changed much in about eight years: she was petite, linear as an exclamation point, her face oblong and weathered to a glossy walnut brown, her inky black hair bobbed precisely at her shoulders and sliced in the straightest imaginable line across her forehead. Her eyes were huge and round and dark, like a colon turned sideways. She was the human equivalent of a diagrammed sentence. Glory never could decide if she'd morphed into an English teacher because of how she looked or if her looks had given her no choice.

"Well. Myyyy *goodness*. Miss Glory Greenleaf." Her eyes glinted sardonically up at Glory. "As I live and breathe. It's been quite a while. I thought you were . . . now how did you put it on that last day of class? 'Getting the hell out of this stuffy, dusty hellhole'? Which is why you didn't have to care whether you got an A or a C on your English final? And why you found diagramming sentences such a ridiculous pastime?"

Alas, this was all true. She *had* said this. Glory kind of wanted to go back in time and smack herself, even if the sentiments held true. And Glory had given enough thought about diagramming sentences to be able to use them as a metaphor. And that was about it.

She tried a smile, but her mouth was having none of it. She finally managed to peel her top lip up off her teeth a little. "Hi, Mrs. Adler. *What* a great memory you have. I guess all that stuff I said . . . was a figure of speech."

Which she recognized immediately was the wrong thing to say to an English teacher.

"Ah. A figure of speech, was it? So you *didn't* mean to imply that the town resembles a hole in hell, one which is coated in dust, populated by prigs, suggesting that it's a very unpleasant place indeed?"

The way forward was littered with little landmines, representing all the things she desperately wanted to say. Glory counted to five in her head before she opened her mouth.

"I guess I have an impassioned way of expressing myself."

She was pleased with that answer, but all this did was make Mrs. Adler go silent and grim. This was in part what had maddened Mrs. Adler about Glory. Glory was clearly intelligent and articulate and did indeed express herself colorfully, and Mrs. Adler could count on one hand the students she'd known who bothered to use the word *impassioned* in a sentence. But Glory had always balked against doing things when she failed to see their point. Diagramming sentences, for instance.

"And you said all that in front of the whole class, no less."

"Guess I can't resist an audience. Ha ha. Let me tell you about our specials, Mrs. Adler. Eggs Benedict is the breakfast special, and we're serving that all day. And the turkey club is the lunch special. Only $6.99!"

"Weren't eggs Benedict the special just *last* week?" Mrs. Adler countered, shrewdly.

Crap. This was turning out to be right up there with all

the dreams she'd had about showing up to school naked or all of her teeth suddenly falling out into her hand.

But she was *not* about to flail incompetently in front of her former English teacher.

"The eggs Benedict here is truly special *every* day, but you can get them for a little less today. You'll have enough money left over for . . ." She shot a sneaky glance at the whiteboard over the grill. ". . . a pumpkin muffin. And if the eggs Benedict is *special*," she riffed, "well, the pumpkin muffins are *spectacular*."

Sherrie breezed by with her arms full of plates, but she still managed to give Glory a surreptitious thumbs-up and a nod.

Mrs. Adler was eyeing Glory with those huge dark eyes that missed nothing and loathed everything about overly spirited students. "I want the turkey club, Miss Greenleaf. But hold the turkey, lettuce, tomato, and cheese. Bacon very crispy."

Glory processed this like a word problem. "So . . . what you want is a triple-decker toasted bacon sandwich pinned together by a toothpick?"

The worried look Sherrie shot her on her way back to the kitchen was confirmation that she'd failed to keep incredulity entirely from her tone.

"That's exactly what I want, Miss Greenleaf. If only you'd paid that much attention to detail in class, young lady, you'd have gone far indeed. At least as far as the next town over."

Oh. *Well* done, Mrs. Adler. Perversely, she appreciated skillful sarcasm when she heard it.

"Aren't you going to ask me what I'd like on the side?" Mrs. Adler prompted sweetly.

Why, you bitch, Glory thought admiringly.

Glory knew it would make Mrs. Adler's decade to hear Glory say "do you want fries with that?"

They stared each other down.

"I'll bring you a pumpkin muffin, Mrs. Adler," she said finally. "They're good for . . . sweetening things up."

She pivoted immediately lest she say the "you bitch" part out loud instead of in her head, scribbled the order on the tag, and headed over to Giorgio. She hovered there by the grill a second, distracted and soothed by *sounds*: the rhythmic swish of the flour sifter in Glenn's hand, the clink of silverware and glasses, the jingle of the bells on the door.

The jingle of the bells on the door.

Followed by more jingling of the bells.

She whipped about. A veritable flood of customers was pouring in. The lunch rush was officially on.

"One customer down," Sherrie murmured to her in passing. "Keep moving, hon. Daydream later. If things get too hairy, Glenn can help out on tables. But speaking of hairy . . ." She gestured with her chin. "I had to seat him on your side. But if things are a little weird between you, I'll take that table."

When she heard the word *him* Glory's thoughts immediately leaped to Eli. It was interesting that the pronoun *him* now seemed to be his alone. But Sherrie couldn't possibly know anything about that.

She realized too late who the him in question was. She tried to turn around before he got a look at her face, but it was too late.

"Glory?"

And the fact that the braid was tugging her eyebrows

up into arches probably made her look surprised to see him, too.

She sighed. "Hi, Mick."

He was staring at her in frozen, wounded, puppy-eyed shock.

In high school, Mick had been considered quite the catch, what with the long hair and leather jacket and the GTO and arm tattoos, only one of which was misspelled. (It said "Piece." He'd meant it to read "Peace.") He was sweet and a little dim and while a pretty good kisser, he went at sex the same way he went at Dance Dance Revolution. Or reading the instructions for how to assemble an IKEA desk. As if he was following steps in order to get to the next level. The same ones. Every. Single. Time.

And he was no bad boy. Glory knew from real bad boys now thanks to her stint at the Plugged Nickel. She'd pass on those, thank you very much.

He'd wept when she'd kindly but firmly ended their on-again, off-again relationship for good. And then he'd asked for reasons. She'd demurred. And then he'd begged and whined and wept and insisted until she blurted out all of the reasons, with a lot more detail and less delicacy than she probably could have.

She'd just been so *certain* he'd been just as bored as she was.

It wasn't her first lesson in realizing that stasis was as good as it got for some people. That some people liked never changing at all. She supposed that explained a lot of her family.

And Mick didn't grow, because he noticed nothing. He existed with the placidity of a potted plant. There was nothing fundamentally wrong with this. Once upon a time this hadn't seemed important. But she now knew what a luxury being truly known was.

He was sitting with Megan Forster, whom she also knew from high school.

"Hey, Megan," she said. "Good job on the eyeliner."

Eight years out of high school and Megan was still Goth, at least from the neck up. She was wearing office attire from the neck down. Seems even Megan had a grown-up job now.

"Hey, Glory. Thanks. Um, Mick and I are together now." She said this sympathetically, with a head tilt. As if Glory would understandably be torn up about the news, but that the feminine sisterhood would compel the two of them to be mature about it.

"Gosh. Congratulations, you two. Let me tell you about our speci—"

"I thought you were leaving for San Francisco, Glory. And that's why you broke up with me."

Mick's voice was pitched about an octave higher than usual. Glory knew that pitch. Any second now his bottom lip would start trembling.

Glory's eyes darted toward Sherrie, who was absorbed in conversation with another customer. She lowered her voice. "Come on, Mick. I had a list of reasons. Remember? You *made* me tell you. Don't make me do it again," she warned, with stern desperation. "Speaking of lists of things, have you looked at the menu? I recommend the pumpkin muffin."

The pumpkin muffin was becoming her little go-to refuge. A little island in a stormy waitressing sea.

"But you said you were *leaving*," he repeated. The word *leaving* wobbled a little.

She pushed a menu gently into his hands, and his fingers reflexively curled over it like a drowning spider offered a twig.

"He'll have the pumpkin muffin," Megan said patiently, clearly confident of her place in Mick's life and obviously accustomed to his sensitivity. She knew how hard Glory had dumped him, and she liked having a project. "I'd like a pumpkin muffin, too."

"Good choice." Glory was relieved. A take-charge woman was just what Mick needed. "Anything to drink, Mick?"

"I've already swallowed a gallon of my own tears," he said, an accusing throb in his voice. "I couldn't drink another drop ever again."

"I can get you a Sprite," Glory said through gritted teeth.

"He'll have decaf," Megan said placidly. "I'll have an Earl Grey."

"Coming right up!" She spun about and all but sprinted to Giorgio with this order. That was it. The thrill officially gone from the newness of this job. And there were a lot more tables to go.

She squared her shoulders, took a deep breath, and—

Well.

Well. Well. Well.

An improbably good-looking man, one she'd never seen before in her life, was seated at a four-person table near the front entrance, his back to the wall.

He was a little too pristine, maybe—she liked to be able to imagine a scar or two on a guy, or see some evidence he'd taken a risk in his life. This guy looked as though someone rushed to shove a mattress underneath him every time he tripped. His shirt was a sort of green linen, simple, sexy, and entirely lintless, his face was a sculptural wonder, and his deep-set eyes were soulful and dark.

She put a little swing in her hips on her way over to him.

He leaned slowly back in his chair and smoldered at her appreciatively with those eyes.

And then smiled slowly.

She smiled in return. She was great at flirting, and this was the kind of guy who wouldn't take it seriously, given that women probably *only* communicated with him by flirting.

"Good morning. I'm Glory. I'll be your waitress. Are you ready to order, or would you like a moment?"

He studied her a moment. "Glory," he mused. "Is that actually your name, or the word men exhale when they get a look at you?"

"It's both. Though that's not the only adjective that comes up."

He nodded, thoughtfully, as if that was the answer he'd been looking for. "It's a perfect fit."

"Right back at ya, mister."

He grinned. "Man, I'd love to know where the Misty Cat Cavern here in the middle of nowhere California gets their waitresses. Because every time I come in here I'm knocked out."

"Gosh, there's absolutely *nothing* women love more than being lumped in with other women. May I take your order?"

"Forgive me, Glory. Anyone can see you're one of a kind."

"Mercifully enough, that's true. Are you ready to order?"

He grinned again. His teeth were startlingly uniform and as white as that reflective strip down the middle of the highway.

He had the most recent iPhone, lined up there next to his utensils. It kept buzzing little notes and messages in at steady intervals. Popular guy. He glanced down, then returned his attention to her.

"Is Glory your real name?"

"Yes. Why, did you think it was my Roller Derby handle?"

"Mine is Franco Francone."

She froze. Holy Shit.

He was *indeed* Franco Francone.

The Franco Francone.

He was a little thinner in real life. A little older-looking than he was on television and the internet and so forth. But there was really no question.

"Now *that* name sounds made up, Mr. Francone." That was pure deviltry on her part.

She knew exactly who Franco Francone was. She wanted to see what he would do if he thought she didn't.

His handsome face went a little darker in bemusement. "What *is* it with this town? You'd think it was Brigadoon. That cop, for instance . . ."

That cop? What cop? Her heart lurched. The word *cop* also meant "Eli" to her, though technically he was a sheriff's deputy.

But Francone didn't finish that intriguing sentence. Glory gave a guilty start when Sherrie shot her a worried warning look as she escorted a pair of people through the restaurant to sit at the counter in what happened to be the last empty seats in the restaurant. Sherrie was probably belatedly realizing the complications that could ensue if she left Glory Greenleaf to attend to someone who looked like Franco Francone.

"What can I get for you, Mr. Francone?"

"Your phone number, for starters."

"Wow." She gave a short laugh. "Talk about *cheesy*."

Oh crap. Sherrie flashed her a distinctly quelling look on her way back to a table against the wall. "That is, the Denver omelet is *cheesy*, and I recommend the pumpkin muff . . ."

Suddenly her brain was full of white noise. Just like when the cable went out because they hadn't paid the bill.

Eli was standing in the doorway.

CHAPTER 7

He was wearing a pair of soft old jeans, and the way they hung on his hips and clung to his thighs made her stomach muscles contract from yearning.

A lightweight gray t-shirt hugged his shoulders and hung a little loosely at his narrow waist, and her hands twitched, as if they could slide over those delicious quadrants of muscle she'd discovered there the night they'd nearly banged each other against a tree.

But . . . something was different about him. Something seemed a bit . . . off.

And then she realized it was because something besides the jeans and t-shirt were clinging to him.

A blonde.

To be fair, she wasn't so much clinging to him as chummily looping a hand through his crooked elbow and pointing at some Gold Rush ephemera hanging on the wall of the Misty Cat.

He lowered his head a little solicitously to hear what she was saying.

He hadn't seen Glory yet.

Glory realized her breathing had gone shallow. She

couldn't take her eyes off that slim tan hand on Eli's arm. As if some terrible species of arachnid had landed on him and she couldn't find her voice to warn him about it.

Finally that hand dropped away.

God knew Glory had seen blondes hanging off Eli all through high school. She'd seen him making out with various blondes over the years, too. Just as he'd seen her with Mick, racing around in Mick's car, making out with Mick at school dances.

How long had this blonde been in the picture?

Glory was innately competitive.

But what she was feeling now wasn't mere competition. It felt a little more primal.

She hadn't anticipated that one kiss would somehow alter her own body chemistry permanently to think "mine!" every time some woman touched Eli.

Whether or not she wanted him.

And then she realized she was now completely ignoring Franco Francone.

"I have a Porsche," Francone said suddenly. Clearly wanting her attention again.

"What's a Porsche?" she said absently, with wicked and quite faux innocence. Without looking at him. She suppressed a smile, imagining steam coming out of his ears.

Eli heard her voice. His head whipped around.

He went absolutely motionless when he saw her. He must have in fact gone rigid, because the blonde took her hand from his arm and looked up at him quizzically.

Finally he smiled slowly and crookedly, as if he couldn't help it.

Glory's heart seemed to sort of obsequiously roll over on its back.

"What's that name tag for, Glory?" Eli said finally. "I would have thought a warning label would be more appropriate. Something like, 'contents under pressure' or 'handle at your own risk.'"

She would *not* blush.

"Ha. This is my job. People need to be able to call me something when they want refills on their coffee. Hence—" She wagged a finger to and fro at the name tag.

There was a beat of silence.

"You're working *here* now?" His eyebrows dove.

There ensued a strange little moment where he was clearly trying to get a grip on a number of conflicting emotions, one of them amusement, another confusion before the blandly non-judgmental expression he was clearly aiming for was able to settle in.

"I can be a waitress," she said defensively.

He pressed his lips together.

She was becoming less and less certain that this was true. Given that the rich pageant of her personal history kept coming in the door.

"I'm so sorry," Eli said suddenly, remembering the blonde. "I'm being rude. Bethany Walker, this is Glory Greenleaf. Glory, this is Bethany Walker. Her grandmother is Mrs. Wilberforce."

"Mrs. Wilberforce at Heavenly Shores? With the rhododendrons and the grand prizes?" How had this come about?

"Yep, that's her, Glory! Gosh, I love small towns," Bethany gushed. "Everyone knows everything about everybody."

"Yeah," Glory said flatly. "That's what's so great about them."

Bethany was willowy and delicate featured, and she had big, brown, friendly eyes, like a cocker spaniel's, skillfully mascaraed lashes, and the most symmetrical eyebrows Glory had ever seen. She thrust out a hand to shake, and Glory took it. Her manicure was flawless.

Her handbag was quite stylish, a floppy orange leather number that spoke volumes to Glory's color-loving heart, and her hair was about fifteen exquisitely nuanced shades of blond, only about one of which was natural, if Glory had to guess. Casey Carson would know.

"I'm one of the freelance makeup artists on *The Rush*," Bethany volunteered. "I'll be staying here in town while they film a few scenes on location."

Eli was still staring at Glory. And then his face transformed, as if he'd finally figured out what was bugging him.

"What's . . . going on with your hair?"

"It's just a braid. Jeez," she added. Like a ten-year-old.

"You look about ten years old. And a little alarmed."

That would be due to the upraised eyebrows.

"That's not what *I* was thinking at *all*," Franco volunteered from over her shoulder. "And I'm ready to order, Glory."

Glory turned a smile toward Franco. "Oh my goodness. My apologies, Mr. Francone."

"No worries, Glory. I'm happy to wait for you. Or wait *on* you. Or even open the passenger side door of my Porsche for you."

He grinned to let her know he knew this was smarmy as hell. She grinned back.

She turned back to Eli and his . . . "date." Even in her head she put that word in quotes. As if she could make it less real that way. Though it was pretty clear that's what this was.

She was surprised to see that Eli's face had gone thunderous and almost pensive. It was a familiar expression. She realized it was very similar to the one he'd been wearing when he'd threatened to break Leather Vest in half.

She suspected, exultantly, it had to do with Franco Francone.

Then again, she wasn't entirely certain it had to do with *her* and Franco Francone.

Only one way to find out.

"Look, Eli," she said, "we don't have any available tables, so . . ." She shrugged. Which she hoped he'd interpret as "scram."

Very bad waitressing, admonished a little voice in her head that sounded a bit like Mrs. Adler but was surely her conscience. Her bad waitressing got even worse when she turned her back on them without waiting for an answer, pivoted toward Franco, froze . . . and then smoothly, slowly pivoted back toward Eli and Bethany with a fresh and evil inspiration.

"Mr. Francone, would you mind terribly sharing your table? It's just . . . this is Deputy Sheriff Barlow. He's the top lawman in town. And I know your last show was all about law enforcement, and since Bethany works on the show you're filming now, well . . . you'll all have a lot to talk about, I imagine. You'd really be helping us out." Us being the Misty Cat. She illustrated this with a general wave of her arms.

She gave him her best smile, all vixeny sparkle.

She'd just put all of them in an interesting—for her—and probably untenable position.

Francone would look like a jerk if he said no, given that he had a nice comfortable four-person table to himself. And he seemed rather invested in impressing her.

She knew full well how Eli felt about *Blood Brothers*.

And Bethany was an underling on that show. It was both a chance to schmooze and to be seen with *the* Franco Francone.

"Mr. Francone and I have met," Eli said.

Boy. That sentence was forged on an anvil and coated in icicles.

Fascinating. When would this have happened?

Franco frowned faintly, studying Eli. And as recognition dawned, he came slowly to his feet. An observer might have interpreted that gesture as gentlemanly.

But Glory knew it was really just one guy demonstrating to another guy just how tall he was.

Eli had him by an inch, maybe a little less.

But Francone was well aware that every eye in the place had watched him rise, because he had a sense of drama. He was so handsome it was nearly otherworldly. As if someone had strolled in wearing a Franco Francone costume.

And Eli, by contrast, was very *of* this world. Like Hellcat Canyon itself. The *actual* canyon. Big and glowering, rugged and a little bit dangerous.

Franco Francone extended his hand. Eli took it.

Glory suspected a little macho hand-crushing was going on.

"A pleasure to meet you, Bethany," Francone added graciously, when he took his hand back. "I imagine I'll see you on set for a few days. And what should I call you, Deputy, when you're off duty?"

"Deputy works."

Glory happened to know that nearly everyone in town called him Eli when he was off duty. Often when he was on duty, too.

"The deputy here gave me a ticket for speeding," Franco told Glory. "That's how we met."

"Eli is *such* a stickler," Glory said sympathetically. "He loves enforcing laws more than anything in the whole wide world."

Eli shot her a look that made her feel nine years old again. "Mr. Francone was doing warp speed down Main Street."

"Oh, *can* you do warp speed in a Porsche?" She turned sparkling fascination toward Franco.

"You can do a lot of things in a Porsche, Glory."

She smiled at him. Franco smiled back at her, then looked away reluctantly. "Please, do join me, top lawman in town and makeup artist on *The Rush*."

Bethany shot a look at Eli that looked like part apology, part plea. Glory could practically see the thought bubble over Bethany's head: *But it's Franco Francone!*

Eli shrugged, smiled at her, and pulled out her chair. Bethany slid into it, gazing back at him like he was Sir Walter Raleigh and he'd just flung his cloak over a puddle for Queen Elizabeth.

Glory wanted to pinch her hard, which seemed unreasonable. Or blurt, "Sure, he has nice manners, but have you seen him throw someone to the ground and cuff them?"

And a pointed little silence ensued. Glory ought to be taking everyone's drink orders, but she kind of wanted to see what would happen next first.

Eli and Francone looked about as happy as the Road-runner and Wile E. Coyote sitting together.

Bethany cleared her throat. "When I met Eli, he was wearing his uniform." Bethany made *uniform* sound like *crown*. "I know it's cliché, but there's something about a man in uniform, wouldn't you say, Glory?"

"There's something, all right."

Eli and Franco didn't appear to hear this exchange. They were as silent as two boxers in opposite corners of the ring.

"Eli has a very nice, big, comfortable truck," Bethany said into the silence stoutly, perhaps worried Eli might feel less than manly because he didn't have a Porsche. "It's very powerful. Took those hills and curves like they were nothing at all." This last sentence was delivered with a sly little smile and a sidelong look at Eli.

Well. Glory's own flirting chops were highly honed, and she always took a sort of professional interest in witnessing someone else's technique. This Bethany might be a little loose.

Judging from the glimmer in his eyes and the sideways glance, Eli appreciated the innuendo.

Then again, it was possible he'd already explored Bethany's hills and curves.

The very idea made Glory tense everywhere, which oddly made her braid pull tighter, which just made her feel irrationally as testy as a pit bull staked to the ground on a short chain.

"Mr. Francone," Bethany said politely, "we just spent an hour in it driving around and looking at the sights of the town and listening to music, and it's such a charming location for a show like *The Rush*. I thought it was

adorable when that John Cougar Mellencamp song about
small towns came on. Eli, what's that song called?"

"'Small Town,'" Glory and Eli said simultaneously.
Without looking at each other.

Glory was awfully tempted to add, "Duh."

They both hated that song, as it so happened.

"It was like Kismet," Bethany expounded.

"You believe in Kismet, huh?" Glory said neutrally.

She knew Eli was wildly suspicious of words like *Kismet*
and *Scorpio* and *aura* and the like. He liked things to be
defined, not theoretical. That tendency had gotten even
more pronounced after his dad was killed. And Glory
knew it was one of the reasons he found refuge in the law.

Crap. An ache started up, for all the things she knew
about Eli. For all the ways he was strong and for all the
ways he was vulnerable.

"Sure, Kismet's a lovely concept, don't you think?"
Bethany persisted. "I never thought I'd run into a handsome, charming cop in the middle of my grandmother's
retirement community. Or have breakfast with *the* Franco
Francone. Let alone work on his TV show. Today is absolutely my lucky day."

She was skillfully distributing flattery equally between
Eli and Franco in the manner of sycophants and underlings everywhere. *The* Franco Francone gave a subtle,
courtly nod, as if Bethany had just handed him the salt.
Gushing was probably his version of small talk.

Eli was the one Bethany wanted to *do*, Glory thought.
If she had to pick one or the other. She knew that with a
woman's instinct.

Franco idly picked up the little salt shaker. "I picked up
a local station in my Porsche right after the deputy here

pulled me over." He made *Porsche* and *the deputy* sound italicized. "They were playing some girly song from the nineties . . . 'You Suck'?"

He said this directly to Eli.

Eli's head went up slowly and he fixed Franco with an interested stare.

"It's by the Murmurs. I like the Murmurs," Glory said hurriedly. "Discovered them on YouTube. Don't hear them too often these days."

"What's your favorite song, Francone? 'I Can't Drive 55'?" Eli's tone was jocular. Eli's eyes weren't.

"Funny," Franco said, not sounding amused. "But no. I'm actually kind of partial to an old Ian Hunter song . . . 'Bastard.'"

Eli unwrapped his silverware from his paper napkin as carefully as if he was cleaning his gun.

"'Bastard,' huh? That song always reminds me of that Three Days Grace song. 'I Hate Everything About You.'"

Those two songs were in fact almost nothing alike, Glory knew.

This might be the most unusual pissing contest she'd ever witnessed.

Or, more specifically, instigated.

She sincerely hoped there wasn't a rock song called "Beat You to a Pulp." Because things could get messy in here.

Glory felt a hand on her elbow and gave a guilty start.

It was Sherrie.

"Mr. Francone," Sherrie said to Franco, "I see you've met our Glory. Glory, honey, your back has been to the restaurant for a while, so you may not have noticed that we have quite a number of other customers."

That was admirably dry, given that the place was packed and heads were craning for waitstaff. None of them had quite figured out that Glory was a waitress, given than she hadn't moved in a while.

"Maybe the braid is cutting off circulation in her head," Eli suggested. "Maybe it's making it harder for her to think on her feet."

"Is that why you keep your hair so short, Eli? To take some of the weight off your brain, let a few thoughts get through?"

"You guys are so funny," Bethany said somewhat uncertainly.

"Always good to see you, Eli," Sherrie said warmly. Having delivered her other subtler yet pointed message to her new employee, she moved off again to attend to some of the hungry customers.

"Last time I saw you in a braid, Glory," Eli persisted thoughtfully, "you were about eight years old. You got it caught in the door hinges of your classroom at school on your way out to recess and they had to call the janitor to get you out. We could hear you screaming bloody murder from across the school."

This was true. Glory had always taken her hair very seriously. As seriously as Samson.

He could probably pull a memory of her out for every occasion. Damn him.

"She told them the hinges were a hazard and they ought to change them. Stomped her foot and everything. Glory always has very strong, understandable, if occasionally completely misguided feelings on issues."

Well, well, well. Eli had been setting up a point.

Glory's temper officially dialed up to a simmer.

She locked eyes with Eli.

"Speaking of hair, it's been a little odd getting used to Eli with short hair. You should have seen him with a blow dryer when he was younger," she said chummily to Franco and Bethany. "It was his crowning glory. What was it your grandma called you, again? Started with a 'B'? Something to do with a shampoo?"

Eli's eyes narrowed in warning.

"Breck Girl?" Franco supplied, blithely.

"Yeah. That was it," Glory said slowly. "She said he had hair like a Breck Girl."

Eli received this stonily.

"Gosh! These are charming stories," Bethany said sweetly. "Did you know Christie Brinkley was a Breck Girl?"

"Hear that, Eli? You're in good company," Glory said. "Christie Brinkley."

"She's even more gorgeous in person," Franco said offhandedly. "Speaking of gorgeous people, Glory here reminds me of a young Charlotte Rampling. Or maybe Katharine Ross. Bobbie Gentry, too, to pull a name out of the musical past. She had a kind of sultry thing going on."

He was reminding them that they were in the presence of someone who had been in the presence of Christie Brinkley. And possibly Charlotte Rampling, whoever that was.

"Very flattering," Glory said graciously. She was pretty sure Franco was the only one at the table who knew who those first two women were. "You know, I'm a musician, Mr. Francone, and I actually play a Bobbie Gentry song in my set. You should come by open mic here at the Misty Cat tonight. It's about the only thing to do in town at night, unless you like bingo."

"A musician, eh? I'll do that, Glory," Franco promised.

Bethany was listening to all of this closely. Her fingers crept toward her cell phone. She was clearly dying for a selfie with a major star.

Francone gave his head a little shake: no.

Bethany's hands went back to her silverware.

And just then Eli stretched luxuriously, and his shoulders and pecs moved in a very interesting way beneath his t-shirt, and Glory's head felt light and irritability and frustration were like burrs over her skin.

"Have to keep my hair short and streamlined these days," Eli said. "I can catch the bad guys faster that way."

He actually winked at Bethany.

She'd never seen Eli wink in his life. Growing up they'd all tacitly agreed that winking was lame and strictly the province of elderly perverted uncles and the like.

Bethany laughed softly and she touched Eli's arm again.

Glory remembered that big, brown arm braced against the tree when she looked up into his face that night. And then his hands sliding down against her skin into her jeans, and somehow he'd shown her about two dozen new degrees of bliss with just his mouth. All inside of about two minutes.

And it was all Glory could do not to reach over and take Bethany's hand from him and press it gently and firmly down on the table as if she were correcting a grabby toddler or training a puppy. *No, Bethany. Bad, Bethany. Down, Bethany.*

"We're going to need a minute to look at the menu, if that's all right, Glory?" Eli said mildly.

Even with *the* Franco Francone sitting there and complimenting her with the names of actresses she'd never heard of, the word *we* was like nails raked right over Glory's heart.

This was entirely unexpected. Why *shouldn't* Eli date? Why shouldn't Eli be happy with this clearly normal, very pretty, if probably a bit slutty, blonde, who probably had perfectly manageable relatives and wasn't holding a poisonous grudge against him?

She turned abruptly away from him. "Mr. Francone, what can I bring you?"

"Umm . . . the keys to your heart, of course, Glory. And an egg white omelet. Have to stay in fighting trim so I can fight bad guys on TV and get photographed on the red carpet."

He didn't wink, but he did grin at her again as if she were in on the joke.

She laughed musically, perhaps even a little maniacally, and whipped around so fast Eli was forced to duck like a ninja to avoid being lashed by her braid.

She might get to like that braid, after all.

Sherrie took that table from her immediately with these diplomatic words: "Hon, I think the dynamic there is a little too tricky for your first day on the job. Maybe another day."

As if *that* was ever going to be a regular threesome.

Glory wasn't certain whether to be grateful or sorry Sherrie took that table away.

She tried to keep an eye on things there, but the rest of the tables managed to keep Glory scrambling, and then Eli and Bethany and then Franco were gone before she knew it, though she sincerely doubted they'd departed together.

She wished she could take a moment to decide how she felt.

Glenn pulled her aside during something of a lull around two o'clock. "Sherrie and I thought you might like to discuss your first day of work. Why don't you sit right here, kiddo. We'll keep it short."

Uh-oh.

"Is this a good cop, bad cop, kind of thing?" she tried.

Which made her think about Eli and Franco Francone. Although that was more hot cop, hot fake cop.

"Ha ha." Glenn's laugh sounded insincere.

In other words, yes.

She settled in across from Glenn and Sherrie and folded her hands in front of her like a defendant preparing for castigation.

Sherrie began breezily enough. "Let's start with the pluses. You only brought the wrong order to the wrong table once. Only one cheese omelet congealed up on the counter and one French dip got cold. You didn't drop anything. You sold six of the muffins, which is excellent. You didn't get into any tussles with Giorgio. You got here on time. No one complained about hair in their food."

Glory began to feel like a first grader who was about to get a star on her chart for participation.

"Now . . . let's talk about room for improvement."

Naturally, this was Glenn's portion of the program.

"You probably shouldn't seat a taciturn sheriff's deputy who just gave a speeding ticket to a movie star on location with said movie star. Eli's face was so scowly half the time I'm pretty sure he scared a few people from walking in. I could swear I saw a whole crowd back up when they got a look at him sitting in the window. And he wasn't even in his uniform."

Glory perked up. "Was it?" she said eagerly. "I mean," she hastened to add, "I should have thought that through. I'm sorry. I just didn't want anyone to have to wait, and it seemed to make sense at the time."

"And Eli kept watching you," Glenn added, shrewdly.

Glory's heart skipped a beat. "He was probably just wondering where his order was."

"Sure, sure," Glenn said noncommittally. "He's a big guy. Needs his food."

He and Sherrie exchanged a speed-of-lightning glance that Glory wouldn't quite interpret.

"But wait, there's more," Glenn added dryly. "We like to apportion equal amounts of time to all of our customers. Even the ones who aren't as good-looking as Sherrie thinks that actor kid Francone is."

"Isn't he, though?" Sherrie asked, laying a hand on Glory's arm. "Those eyes! That tush! Such a nice boy, too. Very friendly."

This was almost funny. *Friendly* and *boy* were such homely little words for Franco, but then, Sherrie had an egalitarian spirit and wasn't easily wowed.

"I swear to you, I didn't really start it. He was flirting with *me*." She sounded like a ten-year-old again.

"Of course he was, hon," Sherrie said, soothingly. "But just because *you're* good at something, too, doesn't mean you need to deploy it full on all the time."

Glory tried and failed not to grin at that.

"And I'm *just* not certain how much . . . oh, *substance* he has," Sherrie mused.

Glory crinkled her brow. This was odd. Sherrie wasn't the sort to editorialize aloud about her customers.

But Glenn wasn't finished. It was as though he had a bullet-point list in his head, rather like the one she'd been carrying around about Mick Macklemore before she dumped him. "Mrs. Adler said you brought her a pumpkin muffin in a, and I quote, 'passive-aggressive attempt' to imply that she ought to be sweeter. Though she did enjoy the muffin."

Damn. Mrs. Adler was smart. And of course she was a fink.

"At least it was . . . passive-aggressive?" Glory offered weakly after a moment. "Not *aggressive*-aggressive?"

Glenn snorted. "I'll allow she's a tough old stick—none of my kids loved having her as a teacher—but you can't imply anything of the sort while you're waiting on her, Glory. While our customers are here they should feel like beloved long-lost relatives. A couple more things—you need to get the food out to the tables as fast as possible. Customers shouldn't be able to lift off the cheese melted on their omelet tops in a single solid lukewarm sheet. Giorgio takes it personally when that happens. And customers shouldn't have to get neck cramps searching the restaurant for the person who's supposed to take their orders."

Glory was silent. Bravado was slowly hissing out of her and she began to feel like she was sinking, as sure as though the ground beneath her chair was made of mud.

She wanted to give a crap. She truly did. Glenn and Sherrie were lovely people who had hired her against their own good judgment, and they loved this business and it was a wonderful business. Glory loved playing music here, and she loved the history and the food.

But she was bad at this and she didn't want to do it and she *had* to, and for that reason it felt less like a blessing than a sentence, which made her feel deeply ungrateful, which made her feel something close to wretched.

Why couldn't she, from the bottom of her soul, want a job that came with either a rule book or a defined set of steps? Like lawyer or deputy or hairstylist or grill cook?

Sherrie must have seen something in her face.

"You can do it, sweetheart," Sherrie said stoutly, giving her a motherly pat. "And you won't need to do it forever. *You* are going to be a superstar! And . . ." She shot another look at Glenn that Glory couldn't quite interpret. "Mr. Francone asked me to pass this to you."

Sherrie pushed over a napkin.

Ten digits were written across it. Glory took it gingerly. "I'll be damned."

A movie star had just given her his phone number.

Or one of his phone numbers.

"Handle that with care, peaches," Sherrie said sounding sincere. "We'll see you here tomorrow for the breakfast shift. Say about seven-thirty? I'll open up and we'll do a little more training in the morning. You can follow me around for a bit. You'll get the hang of it. I know you will. "

Gory didn't *want* to get the hang of it. But she would have to.

"Thanks, Sherrie," she said humbly.

She carefully folded that napkin and put it in her pocket, where it all but pulsed.

She wasn't sure what, if anything, she intended to do about it. She'd at least made a good impression on one person. Doubtless Franco Francone was just passing through to work on *The Rush* and wouldn't mind having someone to do while he was here.

"And you'll play at the open mic right after the chamber of commerce reception tonight? Eden's going to let

Annelise stay for a few songs. She loves music. And she thinks you hung the moon."

This was lovely to hear, too. Truthfully, all she really wanted was to be loved for what she did best, for her best self. "Definitely. Annelise is a sweetheart. Yes. I'll be there."

Sherrie slid her chair back and headed toward the kitchen, and Glenn got up almost reflexively to follow his wife. It was touching, the way he always warmly tracked her with his eyes, as if she was magnetic north. *That* was the proverbial match made in heaven.

She wondered what her mother's life would have been like if Hank Greenleaf hadn't driven off an overpass.

Glory steeled her nerves. The timing was hardly perfect but it was now or never.

"Wait . . . Glenn, can I ask you about something?"

He turned in surprise, then settled back into his chair and arched his brows in a question.

She crossed her fingers in her lap for luck. She took a deep breath.

"Out with it, kiddo."

"I was wondering if I could open for The Baby Owls. Maybe play a thirty-minute set or so."

He froze. He appeared to be speechless.

Then he gave his head a little shake, as if he was re-tuning his hearing. "Just to be clear, Glory. You've been on the job one day—one hardly very distinguished day, I might add—and you're asking me for a *favor*?"

She hesitated. Then she nodded. Because, well, what else could she do?

He was apparently so astonished by this that the astonishment looped around past outrage and landed on amusement. "You've got brass ones, kiddo."

But they both already knew this.

"When I'm famous, Glenn, I'll return triumphantly and bring tons of business to the Misty Cat. I'll film my documentary here. I'll record my legendary live album here."

He gave a short laugh. He fell into a moment of what looked like mulling. Then he sighed hugely.

"Have to tell you, I actually think it's a great idea. I'd flat out say no to anyone else, but you're damn great at what you do and I think more people should have a chance to hear you. The crowd won't be huge but they can funnel word out to their friends if you make an impact. And there's no reason *I* can think of that we can't kick things off earlier, say, give you about thirty, forty-five minutes. But I'll need to text their manager and get his go-ahead, since you'll basically be taking advantage of The Baby Owls' audience. I might have mentioned that he's kind of a tool, or whatever word you young ones are using to describe insufferable jerks these days."

Glory's heart was doing a happy, hopeful, staccato beat. "*Douche* works. Or *prick*."

"I'll try both of those out next chance I get, but not to his face. He keeps sending me lists of things the band wants available when they get here. Organic this and gluten-free that. And Scotch. Apparently those pretentious owlets drink Glenlivet. They're from Oregon, for God's sake. They were probably bottle-fed on craft beer. They'll get what they get."

Glenn would probably get them at least the Glenlivet, Glory thought. No amount of bluster could disguise the fact that he was a pretty nice guy.

The Misty Cat's business did not depend on whatever bands happened to cycle through here. Though they did do a rather brisk business in beer sales on band nights, and the publicity didn't hurt at all, and Glenn liked money as much as the next guy.

"But I'll text him for you, Glory. And I'll tell him you're amazing and a good fit for their music and that you'll do The Baby Owls' proud. I'll let you know what he says."

She exhaled at length. And where misery had deflated her, relief did the opposite. She felt aloft and as illuminated with hope as that billboard of the The Baby Owls out on the highway.

"Thanks, Glenn. I really appreciate it. I know I probably don't deserve it."

"Glory Hallelujah, life doesn't always portion things out according to what you deserve. It's not a tit-for-tat situation. A lot of times it's just dumb luck and timing."

And with that uplifting bit of philosophy, he got up from the chair. "See you tomorrow morning, bright and early."

CHAPTER 8

Kismet.

The word popped into Eli's head again as he steered his cruiser past the big wooden sign shaped like a big hand facing palm out hanging from chains on Main Street.

Yeah, he *really* wasn't crazy about that word. It belonged between the pages of the kinds of books Greta sold at the New Age Store. She read palms (hence the big sign) and tarot cards behind a velvet curtain in the back of the shop, and the carpets and walls of the place were permeated with sweet, exotic incense smoke funk. She held monthly lectures on things like "feng shui" or "chakras" or other topics that to him sounded like the names of Brazilian percussion instruments. She did a pretty booming business, though, and he liked her. She was more pragmatic than airy and she adhered to her convictions, however loopy, which he admired.

Thing was, *Kismet* implied that there was some sort of larger, ultimate plan and he was at the mercy of it. He'd never much liked being at the mercy of anything. He did not like ambiguity.

It was hard to deny, however, that he was at the mercy of a number of things at the moment.

Because maybe Kismet was in play when he and Glory were interrupted at that party just when he'd had his hands down her pants and she'd had hers up his shirt.

And maybe the reason they were interrupted was because Franco Francone was about to roll into town.

And maybe that was why Glory had stayed in Hellcat Canyon. Because of Kismet.

Because he still didn't know what the hell she was still doing here. He did, however, now clearly understand that his instinctive, irrational dislike of Francone had been a premonition of what it would be like to see him standing next to Glory. Like they were members of the same species. They both had that sort of charisma that went beyond just being exceptionally good-looking. The kind of charisma that had a whiff of destiny about it and all but lit them up like sun through stained glass.

Eli knew he could raise a blush, not to mention nipples, by just standing close to a woman and letting his eyes imply how he could make her body feel. His height, his quiet, innate sensuality and authority, all of that suggested great reservoirs of secret hotness, or so he'd been told. He liked to think it was true.

And he'd felt Glory's body melt into his, and he'd had the minutest hint of how explosively good it would be with her. Unlike anything he'd ever experienced.

Everything on his body tightened then. His grip tightened on his steering wheel lest he drive off the road.

But he'd always wondered whether he might be too sort of earthbound for her. Always.

And he'd never anticipated he might have to actually

witness a guy like Francone take her away when the time came. A guy who actually felt like competition, which, if he was being honest, he'd known that that idiot Mick Macklemore patently never was.

At least . . . she was still angry at him. Which seemed an odd thing to be optimistic about, but where there was anger, there was often both hurt . . . and heat. And where there was hurt and heat, there was hope.

Maybe.

His male ego was pretty sure that if he could get her into bed, he'd win hands down. Hold her in a lust thrall. Because they had that kind of chemistry.

But . . . dammit all anyway . . . he would never do that to her. Or, frankly, if he was being truthful . . . to himself.

Fuck the need to do everything the right way.

It was honestly the only way he knew how to do things.

The only way he knew how to live with himself.

He hooked a left down Jamboree Street, where Allegro Music was—and where he'd tackled a drunk naked Boomer Clark—and waved at Dion Espinoza, who was out culling old tattered flyers from the bulletin board in front of his store.

Bethany hadn't seemed to notice that she was present at The World's Most Uncomfortable Lunch. On the contrary: the fact that he was indirectly the reason she got to sit with Franco Francone (oh, wait, he thought sardonically, *the* Franco Francone) was apparently a point in his favor, and she'd glowed all through the meal, even if Francone had frostily retreated into his phone halfway through lunch as Sherrie took over the table and had departed before they did.

Francone was clearly rationing whatever charm he possessed and he wasn't going to waste it on either of them.

Bethany was easy company and she pronounced him a good listener, which made him feel a little guilty, since he hadn't been listening so much as letting her words pour in his ear like talk radio. Although he now knew more than he really needed to know about "contouring." She'd asked intelligent questions about Hellcat Canyon and she was enthusiastic about her job and he was charmed by both of those things and by the simplicity of her happiness. She'd laughed at nearly everything he said, which made him feel more suave than he knew himself to be, and all her innuendos and little touches made it abundantly clear she found him very attractive. It was undeniably pretty pleasant. Maybe not invigorating. But a guy could do worse than pretty pleasant.

He'd dropped her off back with her grandma at Heavenly Shores and told her he hoped he'd see her again, and he made his escape before he felt obliged to make a concrete plan. He was back in his uniform and his cruiser by three o'clock. Looking for crime was oddly the first time all day he'd begun to relax.

He hooked a right back onto Main again. He waved at Greta, who was in her window arranging a stack of books—something about "manifesting," he could see from the shiny gold letters on their covers—and Lloyd Sunnergren, who was chalking the word *SALE!* on an easel board out in front of his feed store, then headed up toward the Angel's Nest, the big, lacy lilac colored Victorian bed-and-breakfast. From there he could see the The Baby Owls billboard out on the highway, and he imagined seeing Glory up there one day.

He took the on ramp out onto the highway. A few hundred feet later he was surprised to see that instead of fifty-five the speed limit on the side of the sign now read

TITS

And a boy of about twelve years old was shinnying down the pole with a can of green spray paint in his hand.

Eli pulled his cruiser sharply over to the shoulder and grabbed his loudspeaker microphone.

"Hold it right there!"

The kid glanced over his shoulder and then nearly shot skyward out of his jeans in fright. His legs scrabbled futilely on the gravel for a moment, like Fred Flintstone in his Stone Age car, and then he got traction and bolted straight for the bushes in the median.

Eli scrambled out of his cruiser and bolted after him.

The little bastard was fast and low to the ground and Eli felt like he was chasing a damn squirrel. But Eli also had longer legs, he was pissed now, and no one knew better than him how to tackle. He lunged and grabbed a fistful of striped shirt.

The kid thrashed frantically. "Help! Police!"

"I *am* the police, you knucklehead! Stop wiggling!"

The kid's legs were going like egg beaters. Eli twisted in time to avoid taking a heel in the nuts. He made a grab for the kid's spray paint and swore again when he came away with a hand sprayed green.

Some days there was just no dignity in this job.

He finally got a look at the kid.

"Aidan? Aidan *Parker*? Knock it off. Hold still, for fuck's sake, or I'll spray paint *tits* on you."

This made the little jerk laugh a little and he went limp.

Eli wasn't about to let go of him. He kept a grip on his arm.

"Deputy Barlow, please don't tell my dad!"

"Don't tell your dad you risked your life and limb to spray paint *tits* on a speed limit sign? Yeah, I think he's gonna want to know."

Eli already had his phone out. He told Siri to call Parker's Hardware and conveyed the info tersely over the phone to Aidan's dad.

Not more than seven minutes later Aidan's father came screeching up behind Eli in a red Ford F-150. He was already yelling on his way out of the truck.

Aidan's dad owned the hardware store in town. He'd just inherited it from *his* dad, who'd inherited from his dad, and so forth on down to about 1930 when it first opened.

"*Why*, Aidan? Are you out of your mind? You could have been killed! Why in God's name did you risk your life to spray paint *that* word?"

"What else would I spray paint? *Math*? And I can't *draw*."

This was twelve-year-old logic at its finest.

Eli had a hunch math was a sore point in the Parker household.

"Why do you have to spray paint anything at *all*?"

Doug and Eli exchanged looks. Honestly, from about Aidan's age on it was pretty much the only thing on a guy's mind, and they both knew that. That word, and its various titillating cousins. It emerged in all kinds of inconvenient ways. Eli himself had gotten in trouble for drawing a penis in pencil on a desk when he was twelve.

He wouldn't have gotten caught except Jonah couldn't stop laughing.

"I thought it through," Aidan protested. "None of the other things I thought of would fit."

Doug Parker sighed a sigh that tapered into a moan. "This is what you have to look forward to, Eli, if you have kids."

"Can't wait," Eli said dryly.

But the notion made him feel restless again. He thought it might be kind of fun to have a kid who was rascally enough to spray paint a sign, as long as he only tried it once.

"We'll pay for the sign or any damage, Eli. More specifically, Aidan will pay for the sign out of his allowance, and he'll be working his butt off this sum—"

Eli's phone buzzed. His heart gave a little lurch.

It was Leigh Devlin.

"Hang on, Doug. It's the big boss. I gotta take this."

He strode about fifteen paces down the gravel verge out of earshot of Doug's harangue and answered the call from Leigh Devlin.

"Sir. How are you?"

"Excellent. How are things there, Eli?"

"Scintillating. Just checking out a . . . ." If he mentioned it to Leigh, he'd be obliged to write Aidan up, and he hadn't decided whether to do that yet. ". . . rumor about a homeless encampment up at Coyote Creek." Which he was about to do.

"Listen, I was hoping you'd come up here to county for a meeting sometime in the next few weeks. Don't want to go into it over the phone, but let's just say it involves your ideas regarding your future career direction. Thought we could have lunch after we meet. Amy would love to see you, too, I know. You interested?"

Amy was Leigh's wife.

"Of course. It would be my pleasure, sir."

"Great. Pull together any insights you might have about law enforcement in the county and ideas about where you'd like to see yourself in a few years. I'll have my assistant mail you a few dates, you pick one, get back to me?"

"Sounds perfect."

Devlin ended the call.

Eli was still a moment, staring down at the phone.

Then he glanced back up the road.

He wasn't certain whether he'd miss hollering at twelve-year-old vandals when he was *undersheriff.*

If he was undersheriff.

But damned if that didn't provide a little extra glow to this challenging day.

He started to smile.

And then his smile faded.

And hell, maybe *that* was Kismet. He'd be working closer to Sacramento. Which is where Bethany Walker lived. That didn't provide quite the "ping" in his gut he thought Kismet ought to.

"Hey, Doug," he called to Parker, who was still lecturing his now thoroughly penitent son. "If Aidan does a little litter clean up and helps clean that sign, I'll let him off with just a warn—GODDAMMIT, FRANCONE!"

The blue Porsche was roaring by him at around seventy.

The nerve of that motherfucker.

He could have sworn he saw Francone's arm waving gaily at him out the window.

"Wow. If he can talk like that, why can't I?" Aidan Parker said reasonably enough to his dad.

"You gotta earn it, son," Doug Parker said.

When Glory returned to the Misty Cat that night with her guitar, fresh from a nap and smelling sweet from a shower, her hair fluffy and washed and unfettered, the open mic sign-up chalkboard read as usual:

Open Mic Night!

And first name on it, in bright pink chalk, was *Glory Hallelujah Greenleaf.* Because she'd signed it just before she left the Misty Cat for the day. Just one of the many privileges of being an employee. That, and she'd had Giorgio make her a Glennburger on her break.

But there was already another name on the board.

It drooped drunkenly southward beneath hers: *Mick Macklemore.*

Oh, shit.

Glory froze and rotated, peering cautiously about the room. *What* the hell was he up to?

She'd once tried to teach Mick to play guitar, because what could be hotter than a hot bad-boy guitar-playing boyfriend with a GTO? But once he discovered that holding down the string kind of hurt his fingers, he'd pronounced it much too hard.

"I want to *know* how to play, not *learn* how to play," he'd explained earnestly.

Nor could he sing a note. But neither of those things had ever really stopped anyone from signing up for open mic night.

Glenn had already hit most of the lights so that it had gone from a cheery chamber-of-commerce-reception glare to moody and shadowy rock and roll. Which meant it was pretty dark in the body of the restaurant.

She peered cautiously around. She was somewhat relieved that Mick was nowhere in sight. Unless he was in the bathroom or had slinked into the poolroom. Maybe he was just going around drunkenly writing his name on things. He'd gotten a label maker for Christmas once, and he'd labeled everything in his bedroom just because he could. His lamp had said "lamp" on it.

Some stragglers from the chamber of commerce mixer were laughing a little too loudly and polishing off their little glasses of wine near the counter. These were adults who had jobs with defined trajectories, jobs that required staff and storefronts and college degrees or training programs upon which you got some sort of certificate (or so Glory imagined). In other words, careers that didn't hinge on playing open mics, working random jobs, and dumb luck.

Eyeing them, she felt a little like a child who'd already gone to bed peering into the dining room on Thanksgiving, where all the adults were sitting. She spotted Eden Harwood, Glenn and Sherrie's daughter who was a florist, that good-looking lawyer Griffin Campbell, and Casey Carson, who was talking to Lydia Flynn, who owned the wonderful little bakery. And—was that *Bethany*? Her flawless golden blow-out was pretty unmistakable. Maybe she was on hand representing the movie crew. Or maybe she'd caught word of the free wine and invited herself, and really, who could blame her?

Glory felt removed from them, and she knew a sharp

little twinge of loneliness that evolved into the tremendous honesty of relief. Because having storefronts and certificates and the like just wasn't the life for her. She supposed in some ways she was neither adult nor child. She was that other creature: the Musician. If she was a tarot card, she'd be the Wizard, she decided. And one day she was going to be an industry unto herself. With not just staff, but an *entourage*. And a freaking billboard out on the highway.

She aimed her guitar case carefully, like the prow on a ship, and began to weave through the tables toward the stage, when a voice hailed her from a dark corner.

"Glory. Join me for a minute?"

She turned.

Franco Francone was ensconced at a table, his feet up on one chair, his arms spread across the back of another. He looked like a lounging pasha, which was very difficult to do in the Misty Cat given that the tables were all at least thirty years old, needed to be de-gummed with a spackling knife at least once a month (whoever lost the coin toss did that, Sherrie had explained), and were carved with almost as many initials as the Eternity Oak. That ancient, dangerous tree up by Full Moon Falls. Dangerous because legend had it if you carved your initials and your sweetheart's in it, you were bound for life, for better or worse.

She smiled and cautiously sat down at a table next to him. Not committing to sitting *with* him, necessarily. And studied him again, with something like quiet amazement.

It wasn't Franco Francone's fault that he looked the way he looked. Devastating and so forth. But she wasn't born yesterday. This was a guy who was probably used to getting whatever he wanted, at least when it came to women. She'd taken that napkin containing those ten magic numbers and tucked it into her nightstand drawer and she still wasn't sure she'd use them.

She didn't particularly care for his nonchalance. But maybe it was because she was accustomed to men stammering or blustering to get her attention, and she knew how to work with that. He was something else altogether.

"I have to be on in five minutes. You often drink alone, Mr. Francone?"

"Call me Franco. And I'm not alone anymore, am I?" He raised the beer in a toast to her. "I considered asking you whether it hurt when you fell from heaven, but I decided that I didn't think you were an angel. Though a devil might have taken advantage of my phone number."

"You guessed correctly, but you really should diversify your come-ons. The whole falling from heaven thing is so 1995. From what I understand. I think I was in second or third grade."

He grinned lopsidedly. "Ouch," he said mildly, not sounding the least bit offended. "You probably won't believe me, but I'm not always this smooth when it comes to talking to women I like."

"You don't know me well enough to *like* me."

"I know you're not intimidated by me. And I like that as well as at least a dozen other things about you. Hence, I feel the word *like* is appropriate here."

He wasn't completely correct about the first part. He didn't know that Glory often used sass when things scared her a little. And she cranked sass to eleven when things scared her a lot.

"A dozen, huh? Most men single out just the two."

No one but Eli fully understood that she did indeed get scared. That she just powered through it.

Francone laughed. "Okay. I like what you just said. I like your laugh. I like your sass. I *love* your blue eyes, so that's two more things. I like your swagger. I like that you're a surprise and a little out of context in a town like this. I like that I suspect you're nobody's fool. I kind of like that you're either hard to get or playing it."

He stopped.

It was, indeed, a flattering list. But a lot of it was just what she chose to show the world. Not who she really was.

"I might not have gotten 'A's' in math, Franco, but even I know that wasn't twelve things."

She was a little uneasy now, because she was starting to believe Franco Francone—*the* Franco Francone—wasn't just flirting. He actually genuinely wanted something from her. Even if it was just to do her while he was on location.

On the one hand, it was like a window had suddenly opened between her life here and the one she wanted, and in he'd flown, like an exotic bird. The way sailors long at sea knew they were close to land when shore birds started visiting their ships. That longed-for sign of land.

And given that she hadn't done anyone for going on a year, she suspected burning off a little steam in the sack wouldn't kill her.

So tremendously odd, then, that someone like him should at the moment feel more like a consolation prize. A TV dinner, when she wanted Thanksgiving.

Or like a substitute. For something real.

Someone laughed from over in the adult area. Coincidentally, it sounded like Bethany. Glory's spine stiffened.

"Substitute." Now, that was a killer song by The Who. Maybe she should consider adding it to her set.

And all at once it occurred to her she could create a whole story arc using songs, the way Eli and Franco had sniped at each other with song titles.

And suddenly she was thinking of that, instead of Franco.

If Franco Francone was serious, he could damn well do a little more work to prove it, she decided.

"Franco, I'll leave you here to think up the rest of those reasons. I have to get up on stage. Glenn runs a tight ship."

"I hope you're good, Glory Greenleaf."

She stood. "I'm never good," she assured him over her shoulder. "But I am *always* amazing."

She put a little more swing into her hips on her way toward the stage. Because ambivalence about a guy had never stopped her from enjoying his admiration.

She gave a start when a guy slumped over a table sat bolt upright like a jack-in-the-box.

It proved to be Mick.

"I bought a kajoo." He brandished it. "At the mushic store. Gonna play it."

Boy, was he hammered.

"*Good* for you, Mick. Music is very healing. And it's called a *kazoo*. With a 'Z.'"

She crossed the floor away from him, past Marvin Wade, who was poised at the edge of his seat, tense as a harp string. He would start doing his languid swirly dance the minute the music started unless she ordered him to sit.

She pulled her guitar out of its case, buckled her capo on, draped the strap around her neck, and settled it against her rib cage.

And now she felt complete. It was her version of a space suit. The guitar was what she wore into orbit.

Right on schedule, Glenn swooped over and twisted the mic stand up to his height.

"Ladies and gentlemen of the chamber of commerce, please feel free to stick around for open mic night. I know many of you know how talented our own Glory Greenleaf is, and some of you are about to find out. Give it up for Glooooory Greenleaf!"

The applause sounded sincere, and surprisingly polite. Glory peered out into the dark. There were about fifty people all told still present, which constituted a down-right remarkable crowd for an open mic night. No one drunkenly shouted "Show us your tits!" which was a refreshing change of pace.

Glory re-adjusted the mic, mulling on the fly what her set might be. And then she knew just how she was going to do it.

"Now, I know my little friend Annelise Harwood has to get home to bed, so these first two are for her."

"That's me! They're for me!"

Annelise hopped up and down in excitement next to her grandma Sherrie.

And then Glory plucked out and bent those first funky, bluesy notes of "Son of a Preacher Man." She gave the strum a little extra chop, a little more funk, shaping the song into something with a little more edge. She moved her hips and shoulders with the rhythm, and it was infectious: it got heads bobbing and shoulders moving. The audience knew they were about to get rocked.

That moment when the mic picked up the first note she sang and filled the room with it, immersing her in her own sinuous, smoky-edged voice: it never lost its thrill. She'd heard comparisons to Dusty Springfield, but her tone was grittier and bigger; she could do Janis Joplin justice, but her voice was more velvet than gravel. Above all, it was absolutely her plaything. She could caress notes, flirt with them, send them wailing into the stratosphere, and pull them right back down again.

The applause was protracted and sincere and loud, maybe a little surprised, when she brought the song to an end. And then she segued effortlessly into another classic, "Me and Bobby McGee," and delivered it with soul and yearning. There were quite a few *Wooooos* when she'd finished it. Not all of them drunken.

So far, two songs about men. About ache, nostalgia, loss. She was building a mood, and she could feel the audience surrendering to it without realizing it.

She was going to take them deeper still.

Down, down to a hush with those first deceptively simple, softly plucked, notes of Bobbie Gentry's "Ode to Billy Joe." Just like she'd told Franco Francone earlier today.

The audience was almost entirely motionless. Like children being told a spooky bedtime story.

When she'd first heard that song as a little girl, it had almost frightened her; its offhand mystery seemed very adult and oblique, but beautiful and transfixing in its simplicity. It was the kind of song that got under your skin.

And now she sang that haunted little Southern Gothic story like she'd lived it, the supple, husked velvet of her voice delivering those potent lines almost matter-of-factly. She saw the audience leaning forward, into her voice, into the song. Listening to every word as if for the first time, because she made it sound and feel new. She hoped it was new for some of them.

It ended. "Thank you," she said quietly.

And the applause was even louder now, and someone whistled. Feet were stomping.

And now she was going to take them deeper still.

Because tonight's theme, she'd decided, was going to be love and pain, in all their infinitely subtle gradations, because frankly she needed it. The audience might not be big but she wanted to break each and every one of their hearts and make most of them cry. She could do it, too.

So she picked out the first notes of Fleetwood Mac's "Songbird."

There was no freaking way a warm-blooded human could hear that song sung competently and not get a little wet-eyed. Or at least battle a throat lump.

But Glory's voice slid into it, caressed each separate note as if they were treasures she'd collected, and turned it into a sensual, aching hymn, a sort of thanksgiving born of sorrow.

And she knew by the absolute lush stillness in the room that she was killing all of them. They were all sincerely suffering in the best possible way.

It was artful sadism.

It was bliss.

She was, for this half hour at least, in her milieu, and it was freedom.

She'd played that song the night they'd taken Eli's dad's ashes down to Whiskey Creek. He'd wanted to be cast there at sunset, to join the Hellcat River and be taken out to the Pacific Ocean, so that's what they did. Then they'd built a bonfire. And then she'd played that song and sung.

Eli had sat on the opposite side of the fire, arms wrapped around his legs, his cheek resting on his knees, flickering in and out of her vision. His girlfriend's arms wrapped around him from behind.

Tonight she was conscious of Franco Francone out there listening to her in his dark corner.

And Eli out there in his cruiser, catching the bad guys, laying his life on the line, a job that could be dull as hell or whimsical and then, ten minutes later, him dead on the verge of the highway, like his dad.

She didn't know how anyone got that brave.

Maybe he was making his first foray into attempting a peaceful future that didn't include any Greenleafs, what with Bethany Walker and all.

Eli deserved peace.

Did he deserve it at the cost of *hers*?

She was going to run over her allotted time by about a minute, but she was going to sweetly torture this audience with one last song tonight, one of her own, and she'd tenderized them so thoroughly that she knew it would sink into their bones.

She tuned her low E down to D. And then she thumbed out a soft heartbeat on that string. She kept it going for a bit. Lulling them.

"This one is new," she said into the mic. "And it's mine. It's called 'Permanently Blue.'"

Remember when you said
Every star overhead
Reminded you of me
Because their light was always shining
Even when we couldn't see

Now your summer sweetness
Tastes like ashes in my mouth
Every now and then the truth will out

I could stand with my arms out
And never quite reach you
Color my skies
Permanently blue

It was a softly shimmering dirge, interesting and pretty and a little unnerving. The verse was about innocence, then betrayal and loss; the chorus rose in weary, futile yearning. Very nearly a muffled wail.

It was, of course, about Eli.

Writing that song, structuring it, was one way she'd kept sane between the time he'd kissed her and after, when he'd hauled one of the people she—and he—loved best in the world off in handcuffs.

A really effing great song, if she did say so herself.

And while she sang it, the audience gave her the tribute of their stillness—no reflexive cell phone checking, no throat clearing, no fidgeting. They were in it with her. In thrall.

Marvin Wade, who had taken a few too many of the wrong drugs—or the right ones, depending upon how one viewed it—in the seventies drifted out of his chair and began gently twirling around the floor like an unleashed balloon caught in a draft. She didn't tell him to stop this time. Because Marvin was kind of lost in the forest, going around and around and around and around, and it kind of seemed right.

That familiar rise and fall
The rhythm of each day

Cauterized and frozen
Gently held at bay

Now your summer sweetness
Tastes like ashes in my mouth
Every now and then the truth will out

She held the last note delicately, letting it trail off into a wisp of crystal-pure sound.

And she was still.

Someone sighed audibly, and she could swear a few beer coasters were being used to dab eyes.

"Thank you," she said simply. "That's it for now."

The audience erupted in joyous noise, including some foot stomping and *Wooooing*, and a few people managed those two-finger whistles that Glory always wished she could do but never could, no matter how Jonah and Eli tried to teach her.

Glenn swooped in for the mic and she do-si-do'd him as she went to put her guitar back in its case. "Just brilliant," he murmured to her in passing. To the audience he said, "Glory Greenleaf, everybody! Wasn't she *wonderful*? Thank you, Glory! You are a gift to us all. Next up . . . um . . . Mick Macklemore, apparently?" Glenn shot a worried glance at Glory.

She shrugged.

Some polite yet skeptical pattering of hands ensued. They were still in a lovely haze of musical goodwill and had high hopes that the fine entertainment would continue.

Mick staggered from his table, dodged the still-twirling Marvin—the music never really ended in Marvin's head—

walked toward the stage, and crashed shins first into it. It was pretty clear he wanted to take that step up onto it, but he was much too drunk and he was clearly puzzled about how to go about it. He tried it again with the same result. Finally, he sat carefully down on the edge of the stage, tipped over onto his side, pushed himself up onto his hands and knees, then used the microphone stand to haul himself upright, as though he was climbing a rope. The mic protested with a few squeals of feedback.

Drunk musicians. Nothing everyone here hadn't seen before.

He swayed like a dandelion in a gentle breeze.

"Okay, quiet everyone. Quiet," he ordered. Even though everyone was staring in mute fascination. "Thish ish *important*."

He belched softly into his fist. Then he gave an inaugural toot on the kazoo. *Honk.* As if tuning it up or testing to see if it still worked.

"Great chops, man!" some wit hollered.

"Okay. Okay," Mick said into the mic. "This is called 'She'sh Wrong.' Anna one anna two anna three anna four!"

He blew out a blues riff on the kazoo: *BA DA DA DA DUN!*

"Booooo!" someone assessed correctly.

Glory hovered next to the stage, riveted in a "look at that train wreck" sort of way.

Foreboding was prickling her scalp.

Mick tooted the blues riff again: *BA DA DA DAA DA DUN!*

And then he growled boozily into the microphone while thumping his foot against the stage.

Lemme tell you a story
(BA DA DA DAA DA DUN)
About a girl named Glory
(BA DA DA DAA DA DUN)
She says I'm a dud in bed
(BA DA DA DAA DA DUN)
But she's GREAT AT GIVING HEA—

Glory dove for the microphone like she was sliding into home and yanked it away from him, and Glenn seized it from her and ferried it way out of Mick's reach like a burning torch.

Deprived of the microphone, Mick performed a rude illustrative gesture using the kazoo as a prop instead.

"YUCK, dude!" a discerning person hollered.

Glory was actually amazed Mick had managed a rhyme.

"Oooooooooh, *man!*" Someone in the audience was clearly gleefully horrorstruck.

"YOU SUCK, MICK!" someone else yelled. Either in support of Glory or by way of editorial review. Both were fine with her.

"*YOU* SUCK!" Mick predictably snarled by way of reply to the invisible critic.

He staggered off the stage toward the voice and collided with the still gently whirling Marvin Wade, sending him spiraling precariously out of his orbit and crashing into a guy gingerly balancing two half pints of beer in his hands. They both went down hard in an explosion of glass, beer raining down after them, just as Mick threw a wild punch toward his insulter, so wild that it spun him about 180 degrees and the punch landed on the wrong guy, who toppled flailing backward in his chair into the guy next to him, who shoved him upward into the guy Mick *meant* to punch, who shot to his feet and shoved him roughly off, got hit in the face for his effort, and in seconds all was pandemonium.

CHAPTER 9

When Eli picked up the phone at the sheriff's station he thought Glenn was shouting "MAYDAY! MAYDAY!"

Then he realized it was "MELEE!"

This became clearer when he heard what sounded like breaking glass and furniture crashing and a little feminine shriek of fright.

"My kajoo!" someone bellowed. "You motherfucker! You stepped on my kajoo!"

"Get here!" Glenn shouted to Eli, and he ended the call.

Good God. How could a chamber of commerce mixer devolve into a *brawl*?

Oh wait: it was open mic night, too, that was how.

Glory was there.

He could extrapolate from there.

The citizens of Hellcat Canyon were treated to the rare sight of three sheriff's deputies cruisers roaring down Main Street, sirens wailing and lights blazing.

And when the deputies leaped out of their cruisers, they could hear grunting and thumping and the odd crash from outside the Misty Cat before they even entered.

Eli pushed the door open and they all burst in together.

It was still dimly lit for open mic night and the floor was as warm with bodies, some rolling on the floor, a few pinned and taking what amounted to bitch slaps, a few others locked in what looked like grappling, drunken tangos. Hardly a world-class group of fighters, but they were drunk and angry and they had projectiles to hand if they really wanted to go Wild West in here.

And then—Dear God—he saw Glory was in the middle of it trying to pull some guy off what looked like Marvin Wade, who was flat on the floor. She had the guy by one arm and was tugging, leaning back on her heels, like some kind of waterskier. She looked up, then her eyes flicked past him and she dropped the arm she was tugging.

"Eli! *Look out!*"

He spun around.

Mick Macklemore had hoisted a squat bar stool and Eli saw its four legs coming at him sideways. He knew in an instant that it was too late to duck completely. He was going to get nailed good.

Then Glory hurdled Marvin Wade's prone form, cocked her arm, and hurled a punch at Mick's jaw.

His head snapped back and he flailed, skidding in spilled beer and landing on his ass. The stool rolled away from him and landed with a thud. Glory set it upright and gave it a pat.

Eli was on top of Mick in an instant and got him in cuffs.

Eli and Scotty waded into the rest of the idiots fighting and got them separated and shaken and scolded into submission then cuffed and lined up like bad children on a bench in the front of the Misty Cat, ready to load them into cruisers or release them on their own recognizance, once they got all their statements.

Eli was going to let his deputies take care of the paperwork part.

He searched the shocked crowd—who knew open mic night at the Misty Cat was so exciting?—and saw Glory sitting on the stage, her head in her hands, surveying the wreckage with a sort of glum, philosophical resignation.

He took a seat next to her. She glanced up at him ruefully.

They didn't speak for a moment.

"I just hope they all make bail before the next open mic, because there goes my audience if not," she said dryly.

He smiled at that. "How'd it all start?"

She sighed. "Mick got drunk and apparently wrote a dirty song about me on kazoo."

Dear God.

This was deeply horrible and about the funniest thing he'd ever heard.

"Mick wrote a dirty song about you? On *kazoo*?"

"I managed to grab the mic from him before he got to the worst part of the song. Then someone yelled 'you suck!' at him, and Mick went in there swinging. And it all kind of escalated from there. That's the capsule version of it anyway."

She looked up at him. He'd had to bite the inside of his cheek to keep from laughing, and she saw that his eyes were watering, and hers flashed wickedly for an instant.

"Guess he took the breakup kind of hard," Glory said with great, great irony.

"Yeah, well, to be fair . . . you're kind of hard to forget."

She looked up at him sharply.

And then she smiled softly, and as he looked into that familiar blue of her eyes, just for a moment his whole being was a song.

They sat for a moment in silence.

"Hey," she said suddenly. "Why is your hand half green?"

"Oh." He held it up. "I caught Aidan Parker right after he'd spray painted *tits* on the road sign out on the highway. Couldn't get the paint all the way off."

"Huh. *Actual* tits, or the word *tits*?"

"The word."

She tilted her head. "Wow. That's even harder."

He laughed. "Let me see *your* hand."

She hesitated a moment. So funny that this was now fraught with meaning, this simple, casual touch. He held his breath.

And then she gave her hand to him.

He took it gently. Held it as though she'd handed him a baby squirrel that had fallen from a nest.

She had beautiful hands, long and slim fingered, from their tough tips and short, striped nails to their tender palms. She had a little scar on one wrist. She'd burned herself toasting marshmallows when she was about twelve, as he recalled.

"I count all five fingers." His voice was kind of husky.

Her voice was a hush. "Doesn't hurt. I know how to throw a punch."

"Yeah. You sure do."

Neither of them said *but you really shouldn't*. It probably wouldn't have made a difference.

They both became aware that he was still holding her hand. They'd gone very still together, even as the place was still recovering from the uproar.

He ran his thumb lightly over her fingers, tracing each knuckle in turn, gently, slowly.

It was officially a caress.

A statement.

And her head lifted slowly to look into his eyes.

And there was no reason to keep holding on to her. But he didn't want to let her go.

And she didn't pull away.

"Punch with the knuckles on the outside," she said softly, finally. "Use the first two knuckles. The way you and Jon . . ."

She stopped.

Froze.

Realizing what she was about to say.

The way you and Jonah taught me, she almost said.

She looked up at him. A hunted, furious sort of yearning look flickered across her face.

"Anything else hurt, Glory?" He risked, softly.

He knew what the answer was.

Only everything.

He could have said *same here*.

Suddenly, from seemingly out of nowhere, fucking Franco Francone emerged from the remainder of the milling crowd, strolled across the stage, and sat down in the middle of it right next to Glory, as if he owned the damn place. As if he owned *her*. As if he was the rock star. And he looked like a rock star: tall and whip lean, black shirt open at the throat worn over a pair of jeans, some kind of leather necklace thing around his neck, very expensive-looking boots that the jerks in Oasis or what have you probably wore.

Glory gently pulled her hand away from Eli.

Folded it in her lap.

Eli'd stirred up the old pain and it was going to stay stirred and there was nothing he could do about it at the moment.

"Evening, Deputy," Francone drawled. "Glory . . . what can I say? You were glorious."

"Where the hell were you, Francone, when she was in the middle of that fight?"

Francone's head jerked toward Eli. They locked gazes for a moment of raw, mutual, undisguised dislike.

Glory watched this warily, shocked.

It was very unlike Eli to be so very blatant. And rude.

"I was in the poolroom, Deputy. The guy went up there with a *kazoo*, for God's sake. No sane person would stick around for that. And I had to go hide my tears after she sang the *hell* out of 'Songbird.' By the time I came out to check out the ruckus it was pretty much over."

Eli swiveled his head toward Glory. "You sang 'Songbird'?"

He hadn't meant to make it sound like an accusation.

Glory held his gaze a moment. And then she shrugged with one shoulder. "Seemed like that kind of night. Felt like I . . . felt like I needed it."

The last time he'd heard her sing that was the night they'd taken his father's ashes down to the creek.

He often thought the only reason he hadn't lost it that night was because that song, and the way Glory sang it, had done the crying for him.

And finally, as the three of them sat there, Eli was able to put his finger on one of the things that bothered him about Franco Francone: it was the sheer indolence of the man. As if Glory wasn't something he needed to fight for or earn or live up to.

As if he quite simply had the right to her just by virtue of who he was.

Eli stood up from the stage abruptly, driven by some sharp knot in his gut. He took a few steps back from the two of them.

"Eli!" And to his surprise, Bethany half jogged half skipped over to him and looped a friendly arm through his.

"Hey!" He smiled down at her. "I didn't know you were here! Are you all right?"

"I was here for the chamber of commerce thing earlier—I got an informal invitation, and I'm kind of representing the crew on *The Rush*, and I stayed for Glory's show. I was hiding behind the counter with my hands over my head."

"Sensible," he complimented her.

That was for Glory's benefit.

Glory fixed him with a dark look.

"But I popped out to watch when you guys came in to break it up. That was so impressive, watching you be a cop and wrestle all the bad guys into handcuffs and stuff."

"Yeah. Wrestling people into handcuffs is what he does best," Glory said laconically.

Fuck it. He ignored that.

"I've never incited a riot," Bethany said. "That was very rock and roll of you, Glory."

Glory wished she could have replied "It was a first for me, too," but she wasn't entirely certain that was true.

"Thanks" was what she settled upon, finally.

"Franco should have gotten in there," Bethany added. "He's amazing at martial arts. Those fight scenes in *Blood Brothers* were amazing. And didn't you give a demonstration on *Ellen* once? I have a friend who helps choreograph fights for TV and movies. It's very cool."

"I don't usually like to get into the middle of fights for the hell of it," Franco said easily. "Not anymore, anyway. I pretty much reserve my fighting for the camera."

"And then when you're done fighting on camera someone like Bethany fixes your mascara for you?" Eli asked mildly.

Whoa!

Glory shot Eli a worried look, astounded.

And the look those two exchanged then was enough to make the hairs stand up on the back of her neck.

One fight with her in the middle of it was enough for the evening.

Bethany seemed to miss all the undertones and undercurrents, but then, she wasn't precisely listening for them. "Well, it's not so much mascara as it is a sort of clear gel, Eli," she said brightly. "At least that's what I usually use for guys. Makes their lashes more distinct. Glory, you have a little bit of . . ."

And then Bethany's pretty face was right up in Glory's face, and she was squinting her doe eyes and chummily removing a bit of schmutz from below Glory's eyes.

She'd probably been splashed with beer. She was definitely sweating a little from trying to pull that guy off poor Wade.

Who was off to the side, holding ice to his face. Sherrie was fussing over him.

Bethany laughed. "Sorry. Force of habit. Most so-called waterproof mascara is actually only water *resistant*. Not everyone knows that. But I just have to tell you . . . you're so talented, Glory. It was absolutely beautiful and you made me cry, but you see? No running." She pointed to her own eyes. "I can't believe you haven't been discovered yet."

"I agree it *is* a wonder," Glory said ironically.

Glenn bustled over, looking mostly unruffled. It wasn't the first melee the Misty Cat had seen over its storied history, not by a long shot, and probably wouldn't be its last. Most of the damage could just be swept up off the floor.

"Hey, kiddo. We haven't had a fight in here in a long time, so I guess we were overdue. You gonna help clean up some of this mess? Mop's in the back."

Life, such as hers was, went on. She was probably lucky he didn't fire her for being drunken Mick's muse.

"Sure," she said glumly. "Of course."

Glenn pivoted around and raised his arms up into the air like Moses accepting the commandments. "OUT! Unless you're a deputy or one of my employees or the deputies need to talk to you, time to get on out! Good night and thanks for coming!"

Glory looked back at Eli.

Eli's head was ducked close to Bethany's, the better to hear what she was saying. They were walking as they talked, drifting closer and closer to the door. What on earth did they talk about? Eli probably did a lot of listening.

But it wasn't hard to see why Eli would like Bethany. Not only was she both genuinely nice and hot, she was probably pretty soothing company. And, as she'd said, she'd never incited a riot, thereby making his job a little harder to do.

Her head felt peculiarly light.

And then she realized she'd tightened every muscle in

her body as she watched Eli with Bethany. As if she was literally bracing for or about to withstand a knife attack.

Franco slid gracefully forward and took Eli's place next to her. He was close enough to her now that she could smell him. And he smelled clean and expensive and exotic.

She sincerely doubted *she* smelled anywhere near as good at the moment. Unless he considered a splash of Sierra Nevada Pale Ale an aphrodisiac.

He seemed to be considering what to say. He leaned forward and folded his hands on his knees.

"Glory . . . you're astonishingly talented. I was just blown away. I'm not just saying that, even though it would be like me to just say that."

"Thank you," she said carefully. After a moment. She cast a sidelong look at him, reluctant to give him her full attention. For some reason, it seemed critical to keep Eli and Bethany in her sights. "That means a good deal."

"Listen," Franco said suddenly. "I want to take you out to dinner. I want to discover more reasons to like you."

She pivoted toward him, for some reason stung. "Some invitation, Franco. I might be no angel but I sure as hell don't jump just because a hot actor 'wants' me to." She put *wants* in air quotes.

He blinked.

She immediately regretted the outburst.

He regarded her for one assessing moment, and then his mouth quirked wryly.

"You're absolutely right, Glory. I apologize. You've had a rough night, and I could have done and should have done that with more grace. I was just trying to be macho, like that cop. He really doesn't like me, does he?"

"Deputy," she corrected. "And nope. He really doesn't."

Franco gave a short, humorless laugh at that.

"You're just . . . very different guys," she tried to explain. "Oil and water."

"I'll say," Franco muttered.

Franco swung his legs, and the heels of his boots thumped the stage.

"Okay. I get why you wouldn't believe me when I say this, and why it sounds like a line, but I genuinely want to know you. I suspect you don't have a boring bone in your admittedly very appealing body. Is it okay if I point out that last part?"

She sighed. She turned to look at him full on. He was worth looking at, for sure.

He was amusing, she'd hand him that. She could field his kind of flirtation until the cows came home.

"Just . . . take this." He held out a card. "All my contact info is on it."

She hesitated. It felt oddly portentous.

Then, because there was really no reason not to take it, she did. Gingerly. And looked down at it.

And in a dizzying flash she could imagine the kinds of people he might know, the connections in entertainment that fanned out from him like spokes on a wheel.

She stole a glance toward the door. Eli was now conferring with the rest of the deputies; he seemed to be issuing orders. They'd apparently stuffed all the various handcuffed guys into their cruisers, Mick included.

Bethany was hovering off to the side. As though she was waiting for him.

And then, suddenly, he was out the door. And out of sight.

And so was Bethany.

Glenn shut the door behind them.

The sound of that closed door seemed to echo unduly in the now mostly empty restaurant.

Glory stared at it.

She took a deep breath and exhaled slowly. "I'm really sorry I snapped at you," she said to Franco.

He shrugged. "Hey, I deal with *actresses* all the time. That was nothing." He made the word *actresses* sound like *live ammunition*. "You got your cell phone on you?"

"Nope." She didn't volunteer that it was because she didn't currently have a cell phone. She and her mother had trimmed everything but the bare essentials from the budget.

"Text me if you want to have dinner with a 'hot actor.'" He used air quotes, too.

She smiled at that, albeit crookedly.

Her heavy heart seemed to be holding down the other side of that smile.

He smiled back at her. And damn, but he was a gorgeous devil. He really knew it, too, and was pretty happy and content about it. His looks were like his Porsche: something he possessed that made most of his days much more pleasant than everyone else's days.

They continued gazing at each other, and for a wild moment, she thought he intended to kiss her.

For a wild moment, she thought she might not mind.

But not for the right reasons. Which were: She wanted a distraction from being herself. She wanted to be reminded that she was wanted.

But Franco apparently had more discretion than that. "See you at The Baby Owls' show, regardless?" he said lightly.

"Sure," she said.

"Good night, Glory Hallelujah Greenleaf." He leaped off the stage and headed out that door just as Glenn appeared and put the mop in her hand.

"I'll pay you overtime," he wheedled, by way of persuasion, and really how could she resist, when he put it that way?

CHAPTER 10

Glory lay awake for much of the night, staring at the ceiling and punished herself by reviewing the highlights of her week.
So far she'd:

Bitten a guy and cursed his genitals
Quit one job at which she sucked
Gotten a new and better job at which
    she also sucked
Incited a pissing contest involving classic
    rocks songs between a deputy sheriff
    and a famous actor
Indirectly caused a riot
Inadvertently launched the musical career
    of her ex-boyfriend
Decked her ex-boyfriend
Gotten hit on by a famous actor

And all of these were witnessed by Eli. Who had, earlier in the week, suggested she ought to make better decisions. She fell asleep feeling sodden with failure, but she awoke feeling charged with penitent purpose and sprang from bed. First, she reflexively moved her tiger to a spot in her bedroom window. Where it could look out toward the highway.

And after a very short shower—water and the energy to heat it cost money, after all—she pulled on jeans and a boring long-sleeved berry-colored t-shirt. And twisted her hair up into some sort of demure Gibson Girl–esque hairdo and secured it with a barrette.

There! It was symbolic. Maybe reining in all that hair would help keep potential chaos at bay. And she could drive to work today, so she wouldn't risk jostling it loose. She stared a moment longer. And then she felt too fettered and muted and she panicked, so she added a pair of dangly silver teardrop-shaped earrings that ended with a small sparkly blue stone. Quite pretty, and quite fake. That was a little better.

It was barely past dawn and her mom was still asleep. She went to make a pot of coffee and found a sad, saggy, empty bag of beans in the freezer.

She made a feral sound in her throat.

There was a note in the middle of the kitchen table.

> Glo—
> Borrowed the truck to go pick up some lumber to fix the gutters. And I drank the last of the coffee. Also I used the last of the detergent. And I drank your Diet Coke.
>
> P.S. I left a six pack of Mickey's big mouth in the fridge to get cold! Don't drink them! I'll be back for them tonight.

P.P.S. Okay, you can drink one. ONE! Just ONE. You got that? One.

P.P.P.S. I heard you caused a riot at the Misty Cat last night. Good one!

P.P.P.P.S. If you love me, you'll put any extra ten-dollar bills you might have lying around right HERE.

Below *here* he'd drawn a big, currency-sized rectangle.

P.P.P.P.P.S. Just ONE (1) !!!!!
Your loving bro,
John-Mark

Glory studied the note.

Then she slipped a pen from the little soup can pencil holder next to the telephone and carefully drew a hand with an extended middle finger in the rectangle. She added a smiley face to it so that it looked like a friendly cartoon character. She signed it.

Xoxo Your loving sister

She hauled her weary, shame-soaked, heart-achey but somewhat animated-by-hope butt down to the Misty Cat on foot, taking her favorite route, down along Whiskey Creek, through the pasture and over the fence, down to the dirt road. The big elm was officially wearing fall colors; and it would do its annual total striptease pretty soon, dumping piles of flame-colored leaves at its base. A few were already sprinkled around the trunk.

She pulled her jacket tighter around her. It was a little

chilly, which reminded her that they were coming up on winter soon. And winter meant heating bills.

Or burning their furniture in the fireplace.

Ha.

Two interesting glimmers of potential remained, however: The possibility of playing an opening set for The Baby Owls. And the fact that a hot, if older, actor wanted to take her out to dinner and possibly do her. So she held on to those things and managed to massage her mood into something a little more optimistic.

Which required her not to think about what Eli might have done with Bethany after they'd vanished out the door last night.

The Misty Cat's doors were still locked so she knocked. They were opened by a brisk, be-aproned Sherrie, her hair as bright as the fall-colored leaves in the early light.

Sherrie and Glenn had raised four kids into respectable adults. One son was even a surgeon. They were no strangers to drama or upheaval or even bar fights.

Sherrie was a balm, the very personification of equanimity. "You had quite the lively night last night, didn't you, Glory hon? Let's see if we can have a more soothing, or at least less eventful, day. Why don't you follow me around a bit and you can pick up, well, let's call 'em little *nuances* of service." She paused to peer critically at Glory. "You look like you could use a cup of coffee."

"John-Mark drank the last of ours."

"Young men that age are like termites. They'll eat and drink you out of house and home if you let 'em. Go pour yourself a cup. I have a few little things to take care of in the office and then I'll bring our order pads out and we'll unlock the doors and let in the madding crowd. Tomorrow I'll have *you* do the morning prep," she said brightly, as though Glory was in store for a treat.

Sherrie vanished into the back of the restaurant, where a little windowless lockable room served as an office.

Glory liked the Misty Cat first thing in the morning. The slight damp brought out its wonderfully old smell, redolent with history, and the dusty tree-filtered light threw pine branch patterns on the floor. The blinds were all the way open, a nod to the fact that that brutal summer heat was already ebbing. She poured herself a cup of coffee and watched Giorgio fire up the shining grill, set up little bins of diced ham and peppers and mushrooms and various cheeses, and inventory his various supplies and utensils, making rattling and clanking and jingling sounds.

"Morning, Sprinklers," she finally said to him.

"Great set last night," he said.

She was shocked. Given that he rationed words like a miser. No one really knew what Giorgio's daily word quota was.

"Gosh! Um, thanks."

"I meant Mick's."

"Ha," she amended blackly.

He hid a small smile and continued with his setup.

She sipped at her coffee, then spotted the counter stool Mick had almost beaned Eli with. It was old and plump and upholstered in red vinyl. On impulse and instinct, she thumped it with her fist, and it yielded a surprisingly satisfying sound. Boy, it would have done some damage if Mick had managed to connect, though Eli's skull was pretty thick.

She thought about Eli and the sweet, golden-haired

Bethany trailing him out the door last night. And like exhaust from a car, what emerged were the first few lines of Fleetwood Mac's "Go Your Own Way." And she accompanied herself on the stool because she freaking *loved* how the drums came into that song.

Before she realized it, she was rounding on the second verse and really jamming on the red vinyl with her hands.

So it was a moment or two before she realized that the noises from the grill had stopped.

She looked up.

Giorgio was glaring at her in blackest amazement.

He held her gaze for a moment. Just to let his censure settle in.

"Don't," he pronounced tautly, enunciating every letter. He was clearly incredulous he would have to say that at all.

She obeyed. There really was no question who the more valuable employee was.

Sherrie returned with their order pads, a damp towel, and a broom and assigned Glory the task of giving the floor one last sweep and the tables one last wipe. This was part of "morning prep."

Glory caught a glimpse of her puffy hairdo and martyred expression in the reflection of the table she was cleaning and almost laughed. She looked a bit like Cinderella. Which perversely cheered her up. Because in the end, even when her dress was in tatters and she'd lost one of her completely impractical shoes, even Cinderella caught a break. And after the week she'd had, she was due for one, she figured.

"It's *pornography*!" Carlotta Kilgore was incensed.

"Wellll . . ." Eli said. "I'm not sure I'd call it that, precisely."

Revenge is what he would call it. For walking a beagle in the wrong place, over and over. And he'd also call it hilarious. But he wasn't going to say that.

His eyes were burning with the sheer unnatural effort it took to hold back the laughter. But it was his job to be sympathetic and impartial, and damned if he wasn't good at his job.

"That woman *knew* we were having the press out today to Elysian Acres. The paper came around to photograph our displays this morning. Do you know how many photos they took of this? Around a hundred before you got here! The shame!"

Eli had shooed the "press," a couple of giggling college interns with the *Hellcat Canyon Chronicle* snapping photos with their phones, away from the crime scene. But he supposed it didn't hurt to have a lot of documentation. So he took his own photos, just to be sure.

He might even make one of them his screen saver.

The irony, on the other hand, was almost too much. Because the last thing he'd done last night was answer a call about a riot. And it was kind of the first thing he was doing today, too, in the crisp cool of the early morning, here at Elysian Acres.

Well, it was more on the order of an orgy than a riot.

"If it's any consolation, Mrs. Kilgore, I'm pretty sure the *Hellcat Canyon Chronicle* can't legally publish photos of . . . of this kind of activity."

"This kind of activity" was a bit like Caligula, re-imagined by Disney.

Some of her gnome statues appeared to be humping the rabbit statues. The deer statues were humping each other. Another gnome was tipped over on its back, an empty bottle of Jägermeister next to its upraised hand. Another gnome was flat on its back at the feet of the cheerful lady gnome who was doing a cancan. He was clearly getting an up-skirt peek. On Carlotta's stone bench, a boy gnome's face was propped against a girl gnome's crotch. The girl gnome was grinning broadly up at the sky. Near the front stoop, the little kneeling lady gnome had her face pressed against the groin of the bearded gnome whose hands were triumphantly resting on his hips.

"I understand why you're upset, but they all seem to be . . . um . . . intact."

Even if they're not virgins anymore, he was so, so tempted to say.

"And it's difficult to prove consent or lack thereof," he added. "Seeing as how they're statues."

She glared at him.

"They all appear to be enjoying themselves. They're all smiling, anyway. Except the rabbits. Though it's often hard to tell what rabbits are thinking, in general."

"You think this is funny, Eli!"

He surrendered to his, slightly ornery, bordering on anarchic mood. "Hell yeah, I think it's funny."

"Eli!" she was reproachful.

"C'mon, Mrs. Kilgore. Where do you think baby gnome statues come from? One reckless night at a gnome party just like this one."

He was lucky the corner of her mouth twitched at that one and her eyes lit up.

He was going to lose it in a minute.

Last night he'd said good-bye to Bethany after the Misty Cat melee rather abruptly once he got out the door of the Misty Cat, but then, he had a legitimate excuse: squad cars filled with unruly drunks to be processed down at the station. Not to mention a head full of unruly thoughts.

And now two moments from last night replayed in his head, like jammed slides in a projector. Glory pulling her hand from him. Glory reaching out to take Franco Francone's card. Glory pulling her hand from him. Glory reaching out to take Franco Francone's card. Like that. *Kachunk. Kachunk. Kachunk. Kachunk.*

It was getting harder and harder to think of Kismet as bullshit when he'd been interrupted *yet again* when he happened to be touching Glory. And just when he'd been so *close* to melting that wall between them.

Fucking Franco Francone.

"You can get fingerprints off the statues, can't you?" Mrs. Kilgore was gazing up at him.

"I'm afraid you might be confusing Hellcat Canyon with *CSI: NY*, Mrs. Kilgore. And I have a hunch they're all covered in each other's fingerprints. That was *some* gnome party."

She snorted at that. "Nevertheless, this means war."

Eli sighed. That was all he needed. The War of the Mobile Estates. He could see it now: the mobility scooter cavalry, infantry swinging walking sticks with tennis balls on the bottoms, a front line of briskly fit grandmas shot-putting brownies and oatmeal cookies, backed up by a few columns of the world's gassiest grandpas.

Hell, maybe he'd get another commendation for intervening in that.

Maybe he could avoid it altogether if he became undersheriff and moved from Hellcat Canyon.

The irony here was that he knew how to fight—dirty, clean, martial arts, you name it. He could tackle like a tank and shoot the hearts out of targets; he knew how to deftly, methodically grill a suspect to yield up sordid truths or soothe a frightened burglary victim. But none of that was a match for a stubborn Glory Greenleaf. It wasn't enough to be himself anymore, because that's who she was mad at. And with her, he didn't know what else to be.

She wasn't the only one who was hurt and angry. But he was the only one getting shut out.

And that, frankly, was making him even angrier. And the quagmire of emotions he felt about the whole thing, the ones he never could seem to transmute into the right words, had now cranked up to something past a simmer.

It was also starting to feel a little like gamesmanship.

Still, being played was marginally better than the notion that she might be ambivalent. That she might need to flip a mental coin between the humble deputy who'd slammed her beloved brother to the floor and hauled him off in handcuffs and the hot, too-slick-for-his-own-good actor, who might just be the conduit to superstardom and the end of open mic nights at the Misty Cat.

He scowled at that grinning stone gnome with his hands on his hips. The one who appeared to be getting a blow job. At the moment, he envied that gnome for being made out of stone. And for the other thing, too.

"I have a granddaughter, too, you know," Mrs. Kilgore added, suddenly, competitively. "She's very pretty."

Eli stifled a sigh. He was completely unsurprised that everyone knew his business.

Quick as a wink, Mrs. Kilgore swiped a photo up on her phone and pointed it at him.

Carlotta Kilgore's granddaughter looked a lot like

her—pretty, sultry with masses of wavy brown hair. She was pouting to show off her new lipstick, if Eli had to guess at the story behind the photo. Which was iridescent and red. She was doing one of those sideways peace signs, and what was the deal with those? Whatever happened to just letting your face speak for itself?

One granddaughter at a time was about all he could handle, at the moment, thank you very much.

"Thank you for sharing. You must be very proud of her," he said gently.

Mrs. Kilgore glowed. *That* would be how he'd halt the advancing armies of elders in its tracks: he'd flatter all their grandchildren, and then they would melt into puddles.

"I have to get a move on, Mrs. Kilgore, but I'll write up this incident and I'll make sure the *Hellcat Canyon Chronicle* quotes me on the fact that even whimsical vandalism is a crime. And, um . . . gang . . . warfare is in particular frowned upon by law enforcement officials."

He hiked a brow and fixed her with a good shot of his steely-gray gaze to make sure Mrs. Kilgore and her sprinkling beagle understood this.

"Okay, Eli," she said, humbly. "Thank you."

He got back in his cruiser. And when he shut the door behind him, it was a little too quiet in there. His thoughts were not his friends these days. And when he was still, that ever-present tightness in his gut made itself known.

And then suddenly a text chimed in.

It was from Bethany.

Hey Eli! I wondered if you'd like to go with me to see The Baby Owls at the Misty Cat , if you're free?

She'd included an emoji of a bird and a cat.

Hs smiled faintly. It was breezy. Like Bethany.

There was no way Glory wouldn't be at that show.

Then again, there was probably no way Francone wouldn't be there, either.

And there was really no reason why he should deny himself the company of a pretty woman, or an acoustic show by a band he liked. It was time to get re-acquainted with his resolve.

He texted back:

I'd love to, thanks.

Glory trailed Sherrie for most of the breakfast shift, watching how she made everyone feel like a beloved member of the Misty Cat Family, how she deftly extricated herself from conversations with her customers in order to make sure everyone got quick service but didn't feel slighted, how she timed the delivery of food orders, and Glory knew she was watching a master. She thought she did a pretty good job of pretending to be fascinated, but she doubted Sherrie was entirely fooled.

Sherrie finally set Glory loose to take tables on her own at the beginning of the lunch rush, which proved mostly uneventful. She knew about half the people she waited on but she'd never kissed, worked for, or insulted any of them, either inadvertently or otherwise, so by about two o'clock she was about ready to exhale in relief as she waited on her final customer.

He was an older guy, and her tired eyes rather enjoyed the contrasts of him: silver hair brushed backward off his forehead, bright blue eyes, a suspiciously even golden tan and a coral-colored collared shirt sporting a little logo of a guy on the back of a horse swinging a mallet over his head, which reminded her incongruously of Giorgio wielding his spatula at the grill. The shirt was in fact perilously close to pink, a color no man she knew personally would be caught dead in, but which pro golfers and wealthy car dealers and the like could pull off. He'd added a slim gold chain to his neck. She was always kind of touched when men decided on a piece of jewelry. Did he think his outfit wasn't complete without it? Or did he just like shiny things?

"Good morning, sir. I'm Glory. Are you ready to order?"

She had a hunch he'd like the *sir*. Worth at least about fifty more cents in her tip.

"Well, Morning Glory, yes I am." He beamed at her with laser-white teeth. Yep, salesman, if she had to guess. They always found out your name fast and used it repeatedly. "I'll have a decaf coffee, the egg-white omelet, and rye toast, no butter, aaaand . . . do you think I could get a side of dressed greens instead of potatoes?"

He was what you'd call fit. Probably scared into that condition by a first heart attack some years back, judging from his breakfast order. And not bad-looking, in a weathered old Clint Eastwood-y way.

"This is a respectable establishment, sir. All our greens are dressed." She winked despite the fact that she and Eli had agreed some time ago that winks were lame. He probably winked all the time at Bethany, anyway, who would laugh inordinately, because she wanted to do him, if she hadn't already.

But heck, this guy looked like a big tipper.

He smiled again. But then the smile faded and a little

furrow appeared between his eyes. "You look familiar, young lady."

Uh-oh.

Or yay!

Depending upon the circumstances.

"Are you by any chance related to Charlie Tilden?" he asked.

Glory was startled. This was the first time a stranger had *ever* asked her this question.

"Um . . . she's my mom. She goes by Charlotte Greenleaf, now."

He blinked. Then he gave a short, rueful laugh and leaned back in his chair. "So she married Greenleaf, huh?" he mused dryly.

Glory was a little uneasy. "Yeah. But he passed away when I was very little. Then she married Raymond Truxel and Bill Horton, but she went back to *Greenleaf*."

The guy was quiet a moment. "I'm sorry to hear about Hank," he said, sounding sincere. "Don't know the other schmoes. You look a *lot* like her."

Funny way to put it. Alas, her mother's last two husbands, her sister's and her brother John-Mark's fathers, rather did fit that description.

"People sometimes still mistake us for sisters. Self-preservation runs in the family."

He chuckled. But he wasn't so much looking *at* her as through her, mistily. As if she was some kind of window to the past.

"Charlie—your mom—had a job at the produce market on Crestview," he mused. "Had a smile for everyone and the prettiest eyes I've ever seen. *What* a color. A lot like yours, doll. And such a great laugh. Sorry if I'm embarrassing you, but when you're my age, you'll understand these fits of nostalgia. I haven't been back to Hellcat Canyon or the Misty Cat in a while. Burgers still good?"

"You're never too young for nostalgia, believe me. And nothing beats the Glennburger."

"Good to know some things never change."

"I'll be back with your coffee stat, sir, and the rest of it right after that."

He hadn't introduced himself. If he wanted to get a message to her mom, he'd probably volunteer it. He spent the rest of his lunch on his phone, and he nodded when she brought his food over to him. She overheard things like "points" and "Umpqua Bank" and "the foundation is shot."

And the next thing she knew she saw him out at the curb, climbing into the most gorgeous blue Lexus, as rare as Porsches in Hellcat Canyon, still on the phone.

He'd left her a 25 percent tip, though. Pretty nice of him, considering she hadn't even asked if he'd wanted a refill.

She pocketed it and watched him pull away from the curb. Someone had once told her it was completely silent inside a Lexus, as quiet as a house sealed up, even when it was moving. In the old Ford she and her mom shared, you could hear every rattle, hum, bump, whine, and roar of all its parts, not to mention the world outside, when it moved. It had the road-hugging responsiveness of a covered wagon.

Maybe it wouldn't be too much of a sacrifice to go for a ride in Franco Francone's Porsche. Francone had another ride in mind, too, though. She wasn't that naïve.

She gave a start when she picked up Glenn in her peripheral version, bearing down upon her with grim purpose written all over his face.

Uh-oh.

"Glory, can I have a word before you head out?"

"Sure. Of course."

He pulled her gently aside, and lowered his voice ever so slightly. "So, kiddo, I heard from the manager of The Baby Owls."

"And . . ."

She kind of guessed from his expression. He wordlessly handed her his phone, which was open to a text.

Who the fuck is Glory Greenbean? I've never heard of her. No. No openers. The Owls get the full two hours and we'll have someone on-site recording it.

She should have guessed Glenn wasn't one to rip the Band-Aid off slowly.

She couldn't look up just yet.

She hadn't realized how very much she'd been counting on that until all the colors of the day seemed to desaturate at once.

"A douche, right?" Glenn said grimly. "I'm sorry you had to see this, but I thought I should show you. I did try."

But she could tell he was genuinely both disappointed and angry on her behalf.

"Yeah. You did the right thing. I'm glad I saw this so I know what you're dealing with. And I know it must have been a little awkward to ask that guy for a favor and I really appreciate it. Good use of the 'D' word, just now."

He smiled wryly. And a little sadly.

She couldn't move, though. It was like someone had

yanked her batteries out. She hadn't realized how very, very much she'd been counting on that. It had just seemed so . . . what was Bethany's word? *Kismet.*

So much for Kismet.

"I don't think Sherrie will be crazy about my new vocabulary, though. I really am sorry, kiddo. Your time is gonna come."

He seemed unaware that he'd just quoted the title of a Led Zeppelin song to her, one of her favorites, one that she could play the crap out of.

She was struggling with this philosophy at the moment, however. If her family history was any indication, her time was not gonna come. She'd keep going around and around and *arrrgh that effing song*!

"Oh! One more thing." He reached into his pocket. "A customer found this on top of his French toast."

Glenn held out her dangly silver earring.

He dropped it into her palm.

"He made a joke about a prize inside the Cracker Jacks. He's not litigious, but you might want to pocket both of them, eh? Maybe wear those little post earrings next time? Or none."

She sighed, feeling a little more like Samson denuded of his hair.

By the time she got out the door of the Misty Cat, the cumulative roughness of the week was still clogging her own carburetor. She couldn't shake an edgy sort of sadness, something that was perilously close to defeat, and she'd never accepted defeat in her entire life. So as she walked down the street toward home, she put just a little more swing into her hips. A little more swagger to remind herself that life itself could be a song and she could be the rhythm section. And that maybe this was just the minor-key bridge part of the song.

And then she pulled the pins out of her hair and gave it a shake and let the air move through it.

Tight clothes, loose hair. That's how she felt most herself.

She began singing softly to herself.

Tight clothes, loose hair
Seems I can find trouble
   anywhere

Hard Work
Big Tips
Hot night
Soft Lips

Needed a little work, but it was going to be fun. She could feel it: she'd turn it into a boogie, an anthem for girls everywhere who worked go-nowhere jobs and rocked the clothes they bought at Walmart and who might never ride in a Lexus, who had rough edges, big hearts, and big dreams and made a mark on the people in their worlds.

The song had started to nudge that little cloud squatting over her mood. And when that glutton for affection known as Peace and Love, a tuxedo cat who lived with Eden and Annelise Harwood at the flower shop, flung himself upside down on the sidewalk in front of her with a delighted chirp, she paused to pet him.

The shop bell jingled, and Annelise Harwood, Eden's daughter and Sherrie and Glenn's granddaughter, slipped out. Her strawberry blond hair was up on her head in a high spray of a ponytail and wrapped in a scrunchy that had little black-and-white cats printed all over it.

"Oh my gosh! Glory! Glory! Hi, Glory! Hi!"

"Hey, sweetie, how *are* you?" She held out her fist and Annelise bumped it with her own little fist with great gusto.

"I'm *great*. Glory, oh my gosh, my grandma gave me a guitar because I love to hear you sing, just a little one. The guitar is. She says you're as good as Janis. The only Janis I know is the receptionist at Dr. Mulgrew's office. I've never heard her sing. She always gives me a green sucker, though."

Annelise ducked down to help Glory pet the cat.

"Hey, green is my favorite flavor of sucker, too," she told Annelise. "And a guitar is the best kind of present! Your grandma is so smart. I think she knew you'd love it because she loves you. I think the Janis your grandma was talking about was a singer called Janis Joplin who was a famous singer back when your grandma was a little girl. And ooooh, my goodness, Annelise, she had a big, big voice, like nothing you ever heard. And she could make you feel so many things, so strong and happy or heartbroken, but in a delicious way. And everyone knew who she was and felt like they knew her, so they called her Janis. That song about Bobby McGee? That's by Janis."

Annelise was listening to this as raptly as if it was a bedtime story.

"That's just like you, then!" Annelise said brightly, oblivious to the grandeur of the compliment. "Everyone calls you Glory."

"Well," Glory said, touched and honored down to the soles of her feet.

Peace and Love was in hog heaven, getting both his back and front scratched simultaneously, and he was purring all over.

"The song about Bobby McGee, Glory. That's my favorite. And the one about the preacher's son. And the one about Billy Joe. I like songs about boys." She giggled here. "I wrote a song about a boy. Wanna hear it?"

"Damn straight, you bet I want to hear it." She could have added *practically all my songs are about one boy in particular, because boys are a pain and a wonder*, but if Annelise stuck with the guitar as she grew up, she'd probably figure that out on her own.

"Okay, Okay, hang on, I have to do it right." Annelise stood up.

Then she pulled the scrunchy out of her neat ponytail and Glory watched, amused, as she shook it out thoroughly.

She planted her feet apart and put one hand on her hip and whipped her hair back over her shoulder in a brilliant, saucy imitation of Glory.

Glory was absolutely riveted by the tribute.

And then, using her fist as a microphone, Annelise soulfully sang, with great brio and surprising tunefulness:

It's sunny outside and it's not fair
That I'm not allowed to go out there
Until I clean my room
But Gregory is riding his bike
And Gregory is climbing a tree
And I'm so sad that Gregory
Is doing all of that without me

Glory laughed with real pleasure, then applauded. "Dang me, Annelise, if that wasn't *awesome*! You're a natural! I loved it! Is Gregory a boy in your class?"

Annelise squirmed happily. "Nope. I just thought it sounded kind of grown-up, and it's fun to say. My mom says the handsomest man ever in movies was named Gregory."

"*Gregory* does have some good syllables. It's almost like a whole song in a single word, isn't it?"

"It *totally* is. I don't know any Gregorys. I like Jaden in my class, but he likes Carlie," she said sadly. "So do Caden and Aidan. Carlie is really pretty. But Joe likes me."

"Joe sounds promising," Glory said stoutly. "If he likes you, he must be pretty smart. A lot of things rhyme with Joe, too. You know you're pretty, too, right?"

"I know," she said so happily and innocently that Glory's heart squeezed. "Except my friend Ella saw Joe pick his nose once and then eat the booger."

"Well, that's a bit disappointing. But I've seen guys do worse. We can put chords to your song if you want. You bring your guitar on down to the Misty Cat and I'll teach you a few when I get off work sometime this week."

Annelise's hands went to her face in flabbergasted delight. She'd painted each of her nails a different color, and she'd painted little silver stripes down them. Just like Glory's. It gave Glory a little glow.

"Oh my *gosh*, would you *really*?"

"I'd love to, Annelise."

She forgot her whole crappy week for just a second while she basked in the glow of the happiness of a little girl who looked up to her.

"Are you going to go see The Baby Owls at the Misty

Cat tomorrow, Glory? My mom says I can! At least for a little while. Maybe I can stay up past my bedtime for a little while, too."

Ouch. The Baby Owls mention was like a surprising little jab in a fresh wound. It inconveniently reminded her of the ignominy of the previous few days, and how much of a peon she truly was.

"Well, sure. I like The Baby Owls! I'll be working with your grandma and grandpa during their show so I guess I'll see you there."

Suddenly Eden Harwood pushed open her shop door. A petal was caught in her hair, and Glory smiled. Hazards of her business. With her long green apron and soft red-gold hair, she kind of looked like a rose.

"Annelise, what on earth are you doing out here? I *know* you haven't finished your math homework."

Annelise gave a guilty start. "Gotta go! Bye, Glory!" She waved and skipped backward. "I'll come over to the Misty Cat for a lesson soon, 'kay? Bye!"

"Bye, you two!" Glory called.

As the door to the flower shop swung closed, Eden scooped Annelise in with one arm around her shoulders as if re-claiming her. And though her voice was lowered, Glory distinctly heard, before the door swung shut, "What were you doing out there talking with the likes of Glory Greenleaf?"

Glory blinked.

The *likes* of her?

The likes of her?

She gave a short, stunned laugh.

What in God's name did that mean? Although she was pretty sure she knew. Given that her last name was *Greenleaf*, and all.

She'd never dreamed Eden ever thought that way, though. Given how pragmatic Sherrie and Glenn were.

But after the week she'd had, that offhand comment made her feel as if everything that made her a human who could think or feel or speak or sing had been scooped out, leaving her hollow and raw as an empty tooth socket. A stray breeze might have tooted a note out of her.

Like a kazoo.

And suddenly she had a hunch what she was going to do when she got home.

CHAPTER 11

The call came into Eli around eight-thirty p.m. From Mrs. Elmore Sims of the Heavenly Shores Retirement Community, who said she heard "loud rhythmic thunking noises off in the distance." And it probably wasn't gunfire, though one never knew, but how was a person to get any sleep when there were loud rhythmic thunking noises off in the distance?

For all the people who sported hearing aids at Heavenly Acres, it seemed just as many had ears like bloodhounds.

So Eli drove out to Heavenly Acres, stepped outside his car.

And listened.

THUNK.

A few seconds later:

THUNK.

About five seconds passed this time.

THUNK.

The thunks were slightly different in timbre each time.

It definitely wasn't gunfire. Or the sound of construction. It was about a mile off, maybe, though sound at night could be deceptive and bounce off things and carry.

What the hell *was* it?

Never a dull moment on his job.

There wasn't much else happening, so he rolled down his window and cruised the streets at a low speed, listening, in search of the sound, and it grew louder as he took that turn up toward the hills behind the Angel's Nest Bed and Breakfast.

And he saw a figure standing on the hillside below the billboard of The Baby Owls.

"*What* the . . ."

It was Glory. He knew that from the hair hanging down her back, flying up in the wind, like she was a witch in a fairy tale.

A hammered witch, that was.

Four empty Mickey's big mouth bottles glowed in a neat row near her.

He pulled up as close as he could get to her in his cruiser.

She didn't even turn around. He cut the engine.

And rolled down the window.

"Hi, Glory."

"Well, *hello*, Eli." She didn't look at him. She squinted one eye like Popeye, then pulled her arm back. She had a fist-sized rock in her hand and she seemed to be drawing a bead on the billboard of The Baby Owls.

What the hell was she *doing*?

"Hey, Glory. How about you put that rock down and climb in the car. We can have a chat."

She turned toward him.

He patted the front seat.

"Nope. I still got some rocks left. Because *I* at least like to finish . . ." She hurled that rock. She still had quite an arm. ". . . what I start."

Oh boy. That sounded like an innuendo or an accusation. He should proceed with caution here.

"Thing is, Glory, I got a call wondering about a, and I quote, 'loud thunking sound' from a nervous lady at Heavenly Shores. I followed the sound out here to you. Technically I can charge you with disorderliness or disturbing the peace."

"Yeah, that sounds like the *likes* of me all right," Glory muttered. "Disorderly and *disturbing*," she said darkly, pulling her arm back again. "And charging me sure sounds like the likes of you."

He sighed. "C'mon, Glory. Dammit. Put that rock down. Don't throw that thing."

The irony was that she had assembled a little pile of rocks, which were neatly lined up next to her, and he suspected that when she'd finished throwing that collection, she'd be done. If that didn't sum up Glory, he didn't know what did.

She turned around and she lowered her throwing arm, but she didn't let go of the rock just yet.

He'd never known her to do anything violent, per se, to anyone else unless it was in defense of someone she loved. Or herself, of course, he thought, remembering that she'd bitten old Leather Vest.

But she was in a mood tonight he could truthfully say he'd never witnessed. It was a dark, ironic mood.

"Okay, I'm gonna ask you something I never thought I'd ask anyone. Why are you throwing rocks at a billboard, Glory?"

She didn't answer for a moment. "Felt mean. Felt like throwing something. Thought I might like to throw something at their smug . . . fluffy . . . faces."

She spun and hurled that rock like a minor league pitcher. *BAM*.

It didn't really answer his question.

"I see," he said carefully. "Alcohol improve your aim any?"

He saw her mouth twitch up at the corner. Albeit sardonically. "Not so's I've noticed. Can't throw hard enough to make a hole in that thing, anyway, though I'd love to. I've been aiming for that middle guy's glasses. You know I've got good aim."

"I do know that."

"Remember that time I got the window out of that abandoned house three miles up Whiskey Creek in one throw?"

"Still kick your butt at horseshoes, though."

"As if," she muttered. She hurled the rock in her hand, missed, and bent down to pick up another one.

"Hey, I thought I heard you were going out with that Hollywood guy tonight."

He hadn't actually heard that. He was fishing. And he knew full well that was not a professional question, and it was off topic. But she might just be drunk enough to answer it, and he didn't get to where he was today without knowing an opening when he saw it.

"Franco?" she said so airily and affectionately Eli's back molars immediately ground together. He was amazed he didn't emit sparks. "Nope. Not tonight. Gave me his card, though. Wants to take me to dinner."

She hurled another one and missed entirely. "Crap," she said softly. And picked up another rock. "What about you and Blondie McBlonderson, Eli? You got a *thing* going there?"

He gave a short, stunned laugh. But he was suddenly encouraged. "Bethany?"

"Yeah. If you say so. You like her?"

He hesitated. "Yeah," he said truthfully.

Glory didn't reply. But she'd frozen with the rock in her hand, like an Olympic shot-putter.

"Hey, Glory? Why don't you take a break and sit down beside me for a second?"

She turned to look at him assessingly. Rock still clutched.

"Just as friends. Not gonna cuff you."

He pushed the cruiser's passenger side door open. Tipped his head toward his shoulder beckoningly.

She narrowed her eyes at him, assessing the truth of this.

And she set the rock down neatly in the pile as if that was where it belonged and climbed into his car, pulling the door shut behind her.

They sat there quietly for a moment.

It was suddenly just them and the night. And the crickets starting up.

And if he'd been asked for his definition of heaven right then and there, damned if he wouldn't say Glory, and the night, and the crickets starting up.

"Comfy seat," she murmured finally, sounding surprised. She fumbled around next to it, then adjusted it and leaned way way back, making herself at home.

He adjusted his in the same way.

Now they were both leaning back and staring at The Baby Owls billboard as if it was a drive-in movie. There was a splotch on the middle guys' glasses that hadn't been there before. She *did* have good aim.

"Want to tell me the reason you felt mean enough to throw rocks at a billboard? I know you've had a rough week. Enough to make anyone want to throw things."

She didn't answer for quite some time.

"You must think throwing rocks at a billboard is ridiculous," she said finally.

"Well, yeah. But I might change my mind when I hear your reason."

She quirked her mouth. And sighed. "Mostly . . . it's something Eden Harwood said." She said it with a hint of bleakness he'd never before heard in her voice, which made his heart feel wrung like a washrag.

This was about the last thing he'd expected her to say. Primarily because Eden Harwood and Glory Greenleaf, while both perfectly lovely women, were as different as two women could get, and he didn't think they spoke to each other at all.

"Something Eden Harwood said to you? Or about you?"

"Yeah."

"Want to start from the beginning?"

She tucked a wayward hair behind her ear, and took a deep breath. "Well, I asked Glenn if I could open for The Baby Owls." She glanced at him swiftly.

"Damn. That's a *great* idea." He realized he had his fingers crossed for her, worried about the second half of her sentence.

"But their manager told Glenn something like 'who the fuck is Glory Greenbean?' So in other words, nope."

He was instantly incensed on her behalf. "Guy sounds like an asshole." That could explain her choice of targets tonight.

She almost smiled at that. "Glenn thinks so. So I was a

little bummed about that. And when I got off work at the Misty Cat for the day and was walking down Main Street, I stopped to pet the little black-and-white cat outside the flower shop—"

"Peace and Love?"

"Yeah, Peace and Love. And you know little Annelise Harwood, right? She's just a doll, that little girl, isn't she?" She turned questioning eyes up at Eli. All at once his thoughts careened off track, and he could imagine a little girl with Glory's eyes and cheekbones and his chin dimple running up to him when he came home at night.

"Mmmhmm," he said faintly, shocked.

"Well, she came out of the flower shop, and we started talking. She sang me a song she wrote about a boy—it was a great song, Eli, heartfelt and super funny—and I told her that if she came into the Misty Cat I'd sit with her and we could put chords to it. I taught myself and I could teach her. Don't you think?" She sounded almost defiant.

"Sure. Of course you could," he said, a little startled.

"And then Eden came outside to see who Annelise was talking to. And you know, I've known Eden Harwood for practically my whole life. But you should have seen how she . . . how she *looked* at me. I guess she thought I would spray *Greenleaf* over Annelise like I'm some kind of skunk."

She was trying to be flippant. But her voice cracked on the last word.

Eli closed his eyes. That crack in her voice might as well have been the sound of his own heart breaking.

"And she said . . . she said . . . She doesn't want her daughter hanging around with the 'likes of me.' The '*likes* of me.' That's funny, isn't it? Like there's a whole army of me invading the town like the zombies on *The Walking Dead*. The likes of me. The likes of me." She gave a short, dark laugh. "I might be a little drunk."

And he couldn't say a word. He was speechless from just imagining how that must have hurt.

"She's one to talk, right, Eli? Getting knocked up and no one knows who the daddy is and she won't say. I for one would never judge a person for that. Look at my *own* sister, Michelle. But everyone knows the Harwoods. 'Good people.' That's what they all say. People divide you up like that, don't they, early on? Good people and bad people. And that's all you get to be, forever. Unless you leave Hellcat Canyon. And if you can't leave, then you're kinda fucked."

He sat with this a moment, thinking it through. She wasn't, unfortunately, completely wrong.

"You want my opinion?" he said finally.

"Sure," she said dryly. "Lay it on me, Eli."

"Okay," he began. "Maybe Eden's extra protective of her little girl *because* she's a single mom. She's got a lot to lose now. I think I have a sense for what it was like for my mom when my dad died and there was just me and my sister and her. Your mom probably felt the same way when your dad died, when he was gone. We don't know what kind of hurts are in Eden's past because she isn't telling. And maybe she feels like *she* was a bad girl. Like she made her mistakes. None of us gets a road-map when we're born. Maybe it all feels precarious to her, and . . . I don't know what I'm saying. I guess I'm mostly saying I'm sorry she hurt you, Glory, and I wish she hadn't."

Glory was clearly mulling this. And then she sighed.

"I can kind of see it," she said finally, softly. "I might have done the same thing, if Annelise was my little girl. It's just Eden got me on a bad day in a bad week. But hell, maybe she's right. Maybe I'm just a late bloomer and the badness will come out later, after husband number six or jail term three."

"You better get started on both. You've got a lot of catching up to do."

She snorted.

"You want to know what I think, Glory? None of that will ever happen to you. Ever. You've been surrounded your whole life by people who indulged every impulse they ever had, whether it was good or bad or smart or stupid. They don't stop to think about how consequences ripple out, like when a rock is chucked into the Whiskey Creek. Or how it might affect you. But you . . . you think things through."

That was risky. She had a huge blind spot when it came to her family, but he just couldn't seem to give up trying to show her what was in it.

She'd frozen as if he'd caught her in the act of something.

And then all at once something occurred to him. "Wait . . . that's why you're still here, isn't it? Who needs the money?"

He was furious on her behalf but he did a brilliant job of not showing it.

She didn't answer for a moment. "I gave the money I saved to Mom. She needed help with the mortgage. Because . . ."

He groaned and closed his eyes. Fucking Jonah. Jonah must have been paying the mortgage. How could someone they both loved, and who loved them, *do* something like that?

"Good God, Glory," he said weakly.

If he'd known that would happen to her, would he have done it any other way?

He couldn't speak. He probably didn't know the answer.

"Hey, Eli?" she whispered.

"Yeah?"

"What do *you* think of the *likes* of me?" She sounded half teasing, half tentative. "Do you think I'm a bad girl?"

"Are you asking me a serious question?"

"Kinda. No. I mean. Yes. Okay, yes I am. I'm asking you a serious question. Though I might be a little drunk," she half warned, half explained, again, in the manner of drunk people since time immemorial.

"Hmmm . . . What do I think of the likes of you . . . I think someone had to be the linchpin in your family and you decided that person was going to be you. But you took that on and you held it together and *that* is who you are. And I think, sometimes, you like it when people think you're bad. Because that way they can't get to you. The way roses like to think they're badass for growing thorns, when really . . . they're fragile. But they're always worth risking a little bloodshed. And they can't hurt you if you know how to handle them. Or . . . or . . . where to touch them."

She'd gone so still it was as though she'd stopped breathing. And then she turned to him.

And her expression about yanked his heart right out of his chest like a lasso.

He surreptitiously drew in a long, long breath to replace the one she'd just stolen.

Suddenly, swiftly, gracefully, she slid into his lap, straddling him, and looped her arms around his neck.

Not quite what he'd expected.

"It's possible I didn't think *this* through," she murmured. After a moment.

During which he didn't take a single breath.

The blood his brain needed for forming words rapidly defected to his nether regions and his hands were now sliding up beneath her shirt of their own accord, because what sane man wouldn't do that?

Oh God.

The place where their groins met was about a thousand degrees. His brain might as well be pudding. Everything else on him was hard and getting harder by the second.

And for a moment they just breathed. And he could feel, almost could taste her breath, and then his lips brushed against hers, and the soft give of them almost did him in.

Someone moaned softly.

Maybe they both did.

Oh, dear God. He swallowed and tipped his forehead against hers.

"Glory . . . I'm on duty and I'm an off . . . off . . . icer . . . of the law . . ."

He stopped his hands from traveling upward any farther than her waist with a control that felt wildly unnatural, bordering on the absurd. The silk of her skin was the most decadent thing his senses had ever known.

She shifted a little again, quite deliberately. Lust drove a spike right down through him. He heard the catch in her throat, too. He wanted to shove his hands down into the tempting gap in the waistband of her jeans and cup her cool smooth ass and grind her against him, his mouth on hers, until they both came explosively and loudly, like rabid, sex-starved teenagers. He suspected it would take mere seconds, even through their clothes, the way he was feeling now.

Sweat actually began to bead his temples.

"That's not your gun, Eli," she whispered.

An inordinate amount of time seemed to pass before he could get a sound out.

"Nope." His voice was about two octaves lower and his answer was more a gasp than a word.

And for a few seconds they didn't say a thing.

He had what he'd always wanted: Glory in his arms. But what kind of man would he be if he took advantage of her right now, when she was drunk and hurting?

A smart one! his penis informed him.

His brain and his very soul knew, damn them anyway, better.

"Glory." His voice was a rasp. He cleared it. His breathing was ragged, but he got the words out. "You've had a shitty day and you're hurting and you want to feel better and God knows sex will accomplish that and God knows I want that, too. But I just . . . I know you'll hate me and yourself for it tomorrow. These aren't the right reasons."

He could feel her stop breathing because his hands were still on her.

Her eyes narrowed assessingly.

And then she spoke. "I think you're *scared*." She all but hissed it.

He froze. It was the last thing he expected to hear, about the worst thing anyone could say to him, and the best way to light his temper on fire.

Glory knew how to fight dirty.

"Watch it, Glory." His tone was all even, flat warning.

As far as she was concerned he'd just layered more hurt and rejection over her hurt and rejection.

"You're scared. Of losing control. Of being *baaaaad*," she mocked. "Of people *thinking* you might be bad. You do all that thinking so you don't have to ever take a chance. I mean, you've got your laws, officer, to tell you what to do and what not to do. What else do you need? Chicken."

"Glory, you don't know what the *hell*—"

In a single abrupt movement she flung herself off his lap and shouldered the door of his car open and all but toppled from the car. She staggered a bit to get her footing, her arms pinwheeling, and it might have been funny if he hadn't been so furious. She stalked off into the dark walking backward.

"Don't you dare follow me, *deputy sheriff*," she growled.

Glory would make her way home safely. Her temper would singe everything in her path.

But he was going to follow her surreptitiously anyway, just to make sure.

"Wouldn't dream of it! Tell Mr. Hollywood I said hi!" he shouted after her.

"HE HAS A *NAME*."

"What is it? JACK Q. ASS?" he yelled after her.

"Yeah, and the 'Q' stands for CUTE!" she bellowed with a stomp of her foot and a melodramatic flail of her arms.

"Jesus, what are you, *nine years old*?"

Which was basically the pot calling the kettle black at this point.

He heard her blackly mutter something in reply he probably didn't want to hear.

"Fuck fuck FUCK." His words reverberated all through

his empty car and the third *FUCK* about shredded his throat from the volume as he pulled his door shut.

He'd gone from feeling hypnotized by lust to feeling blackly livid and faintly ridiculous, sitting here alone in the car with a huge erection. He'd get the emotional bends at this rate.

He flung himself back in his seat and gave a dark, ironic laugh.

She was so damn smart, and boy did she know him, in all his strengths and vulnerabilities: his reasons for shutting down hot front-seat sex *weren't* all noble. She'd closed in on a truth he'd prefer to hide even from himself, because he didn't know how to master it.

He *was* afraid . . . of not being enough for her. And of having her and then losing her to someone like Francone, and frankly . . . he didn't know how he'd get over that.

But how could he ever tell her something like that?

And he'd probably just driven her into Francone's arms.

This was his punishment for carving their initials on the damn Eternity Oak all those years ago. *See, Glory?* He wished he could shout after her. This is what happens when you don't think things through. This ceaseless existential torment. The never-satisfied boner. A yearning that felt like your insides were being steadily stretched on a rack.

He felt like he'd said some of the right things. But he could never seem to say *the* right thing.

And maybe the only way to win this game was to simply stop playing it.

And as he stared at that bulletin board of The Baby Owls, three guys who got a wondrous break, the kind of break Glory deserved, too, his radio crackled into life.

"Got another call, Eli, from Cora Ludlow at Heavenly Shores. She thought she heard a loud argument. Someone was shouting the F word."

That was almost funny.

"Be right there," he said evenly.

Since he was already right there, he got out and walked about a hundred paces upward, into the pines, down into a clearing, and fixed his eyes on one spot.

And when a shadow appeared, and Glory stepped into the rectangle cast by the porch light and disappeared into her house, he exhaled and turned back to this car. Despite everything, nothing would be okay again if she wasn't.

CHAPTER 12

She woke up because the place between her nose and upper lip was strangely hot. She opened one eye and discovered it was because her blinds were haphazardly closed and the sun was lasering down on her in that spot.

She opened her other eye and then shut them again with a groan. She'd had worse hangovers, hangovers that felt like tympani, but not for quite some time. This one felt like a huge cotton ball packed around her brain, somewhat muffling her ability to think.

Alas, things started to come back to her a little too quickly.

The Baby Owls show was tonight, and she was due to work an afternoon shift.

And from there, everything else from last night sifted back.

She flung a melodramatic arm over her eyes and she groaned in abject humiliation.

Eli had declined the opportunity to drunkenly hump her in the front seat of his cruiser, and then she had yelled at him.

Correction: He'd wanted to hump her, he'd just opted to do the right thing instead.

Last night it had scalded her pride. This morning, dear mother of God, was she ever grateful nothing had happened, because he was right.

But why did he *always* have to be right?

And witness to her most ignominious moments?

Good night's work, all in all, Greenleaf, she told herself.

She crawled out of bed, turned her tiger toward the wall so it wouldn't have to look at her, then climbed back in.

Then again, it was entirely possible he was getting his needs met by Blondie McBlonderson.

Or would be soon. Given that Glory had gotten him hot and hard and then departed in a huff.

And why shouldn't Eli enjoy a less . . . eventful . . . woman? She couldn't picture Bethany hurling things at billboards, because, let's face it, how many sane women would?

And for that matter . . . why shouldn't *she* explore the possibilities presented by a gorgeous actor with a Porsche?

As this train of thought was hardly soothing, she finally dragged her sorry butt out of her bedroom and made for the kitchen, yawning and calling "Mom?"

No answer. Her mom was already out and about.

Fortunately, at some point her mom had bought more coffee. The budget-stretching kind that tasted like burned sawdust and came in a can that might as well read "ACME" on the side.

She troweled about two cups' worth into the French press and put on the kettle. That ought to clear the cotton out of her head.

She peered blearily around the kitchen and her gaze stopped at the kitchen table.

She wasn't surprised to see a note from John-Mark there. She was only surprised he hadn't pinned it there with a dagger. She could see a black row of exclamation points from where she stood.

She peered down at it.

You drank FOUR of my Mickey's??????!!!!!!!!!!! I said one! ONE!

He'd drawn a little angry face, with hair sticking straight up all over the head, bushy eyebrows, and fangs, for some reason.

P.S. My car needs a whole new carburetor! Doesn't that suck? Help. $$$$$$$$
  P.P.S. Because fangs are fun to draw, that's why.
  P.P.P.S. I took Dad #3's old leaf blower and I'm going to try to pawn it. Will replace. We'll just have to re-learn how to use a rake. I think they have classes at The Learning Annex.

Below it he'd drawn a rectangle and labeled it:

Carburetor donation/good karma fund.

She studied the note, mulling just the right response, and then very neatly wrote under his rectangle.

One? I thought you said four.
  Xoxo your sister Glory

Now that, *that* was funny. She grinned, picturing his face when he read that.

Her smile faded. He wasn't going to get squat for that leaf blower. And John-Mark needed that car to get to work and the absence of an exclamation point after *help* told her he was maybe a little scared.

Which scared her, too.

Because scared people get desperate.

Then again, bless him, John-Mark had less imagination and more patience than Jonah, he was willing to work a little harder, and he probably had less pride, too. His friends were primarily dorks, and some of them even had brains.

But that little dull headache between her eyes throbbed a little harder, and that's because her shoulder muscles had bunched up as befit . . . what had Eli called her? The linchpin. As if he'd actually known this for some time, and maybe wasn't crazy about it. As if maybe it was something that bothered him a little. Somehow she'd always thought of her family as a single heaving, entropic entity, not in terms of who played what part.

But he was right: it's not like her mom was helpless.

But she was the one who had stepped up to hold it together. At the cost of her own dreams and her own self.

She sucked in a breath. Encroaching on her awareness again was that steep drop and murky darkness. She knew it had to do with Jonah, and she had a hunch the blackness included every emotion, the way black included every color.

One of them, and she could feel it in the band tightening across her gut, was big anger.

She didn't want to feel it.

She headed for her jacket instead, hanging on the hook

just inside the front entry. She fished in the jacket pocket and found two wilted dollars and laid them on John-Mark's rectangle.

And then she took her "coffee," such as it was, back to her bedroom and pulled her guitar out of its case. She pulled it into her arms for a brief little good-morning cuddle, then leaned back in her bed and sighed and strummed a C major. The vitamin B6 of chords. Big and bright. She was trying to wake herself up.

She followed that with a friskily arpeggiated G major.

She decided she'd teach Annelise those two chords. And just in case Eden decided to unclench and sent Annelise over, she'd bring her guitar with her to work today.

She played the C and the G again. And if she wanted to, she could lay an endless variety of melodies over those two chords. But they weren't what she needed right now.

She'd have to fish around until she found the chords that both fit and would purge her complicated mood, the ones that would coax out just the right words for just the right song, because she could feel that a song wanted out.

She leaped to the opposite end of the mood spectrum and strummed an almost comically gloomy D minor add 9. Then fingerpicked it. Beautiful, dirgey little chord. Monroe Porter and his death-metal friends would have sighed in pleasure.

"That's a pretty tune, baby doll," her mother called, her keys jingling as she let herself into the house. "A little like 'Greensleeves.'"

This was so patently ridiculous and wrong it cheered Glory up perversely.

She got up and closed the door to her room.

She sat down on the floor again, leaned back against the old double bed, the one she thought she would have left behind a year ago, stared out the window at that old tree she'd stood under when she'd sung "Hey Hey What Can I Do" to Eli on his birthday, and at her stuffed tiger, whose striped butt was facing her and whose face was pointed out the window in the direction of the highway.

She was just going to have to sit still for a bit and *feel*, no matter how uncomfortable she currently found that prospect.

He had said such beautiful things last night. Eli had learned early on to speak with truth and economy thanks to his stutter. She knew he never believed he was eloquent. Glory knew better.

Tentatively, she laid her fingers on the strings, in the shape of a D major sus 2. And trailed her fingers down them; more of a caress than a strum. It was wistful but not dark. Portentous, in that it promised something soaring. Restrained, but could be built into something, built and built in layers like the tide coming in.

That familiar little tingle told her. Yeah, *now* she was feeling it.

She went to a G major with the added D.

With her foot she tapped a rhythm that was very nearly martial. And just sang whatever came into her head.

Are you afraid to touch me, darlin'?
Are you afraid you'll burn?
You'll have to get in line, darlin'
You'll have to wait your turn

Yeah everybody wants me, darlin'
But one day you'll finally learn
I only ever wanted you

Because, baby, I'm a badass rose
Baby, I'm the kind that grows
Stronger when it storms
And weaker in your arms
I might cut you, make you bleed
But I'm all you'll ever need
Don't give up on me
Oh, don't give up on me

Damn.

She laid the guitar aside gingerly, as if it were a chainsaw she'd just turned off. She had a knot in her throat.

Those last few lines had come out of nowhere. Odd how the song had swung from taunting, sexy bravado to something like a plea.

But then her guitar had always felt like the divining rod that helped her get to the truth.

And maybe it had just revealed something she needed to know.

CHAPTER 13

"Don't smack anybody if they grab your ass, Glory. Leave the corporal punishment to me." Glenn was running down a list of The Baby Owls show agenda items and this, apparently was on it.

"You think someone will grab my *ass*?" Swell.

Glenn had rounded up the troops to brief them on how "An Evening with The Baby Owls" (pretentious as hell, Glory thought—they were hardly rock's elder statesmen—but the manager insisted that all mentions of the event, including the notice in the *Hellcat Canyon Chronicle* online and any local radio announcements, refer to it that way). The crew for the evening—Glenn, Sherrie, Glory, Giorgio, and Truck Donegal—were sitting together inside the Misty Cat like an earnest prayer circle.

"We've never had a big show yet where some jerk hasn't tried to fondle a waitress. So yes. I do think someone will try to grab your ass. And the more beer they drink—we're going to sell gallons—the more they'll try it. Though some of these indie band types are cheap bastards. It's the rockers that drink the most. Remember when Blue Room came through and did an acoustic set years ago, Sherrie?"

"We completely ran out of beer. Made a mint. We had quite a Christmas that year," she said mistily.

Blue Room was enormously successful now. Glory was a fan.

Glenn had enlisted Truck Donegal to check IDs at the door. He was a huge guy with a square, handsome face, and he looked dumb and not averse to cracking the occasional skull, which wasn't far wrong. But thanks to a little inspiration from John Tennessee McCord and to the astonishment of everyone, he'd become a pretty successful entrepreneur, and his fundamental, considerably more decent self, was shining through more and more.

Giorgio was in charge of sound equipment, of all the microphones and the mixing board and any other equipment the band might need, though Glenn had learned they were bringing their own sound guy. Glenn was emcee and waiter; Glory and Sherrie would be the waitresses.

A long line of The Baby Owls fans were queued outside the Misty Cat, which had room for about two hundred when packed to capacity for a show. Glory craned her head. It was a veritable sea of plaid flannel and knit caps and hipster spectacles and big woolly hipster beards. The influx of faux lumberjacks (Fauxmberjacks?) and their dates (Lumberjills? Limberjills?) meant there wasn't a spare parking space on the entire block.

Ping! An epiphany struck. "They look like owls! Like baby owls! Those round glasses above those woolly beards . . . They look like owls in a nest!" Glory breathed.

"Ooooohhhhh," everyone said simultaneously, as they all stood up to look.

"Anyway," Glenn continued meaningfully, and they all sat down hard again. "Sherrie already knows the dodge-

the-ass-grabbers drill, and Glory, point out any culprits to me and I'll have a stern word." Glenn was like a grizzly bear when it came to people he cared about. "Truck will escort the customer out, if such action is warranted. *No taking matters into your own hands.* It could get hairy and we know how to handle this. Got it?"

"Got it," she said humbly. In other words, no throwing her own punches, regardless of how good she was at throwing punches.

Truck Donegal nodded along, too. He'd actually heckled Glory once or twice at open mic nights, but that was practically part of the drill and she could handle that, no sweat. He was a peer of Jonah's and Eli's and he privately considered Glory sort of like that YouTube video of the little cat who hadn't hesitated to smack the crap out of an alligator on its snout, driving it back into the water.

He'd also long known that messing with Glory would mean messing with Eli or Jonah or both.

"And in case things get truly hairy," Glenn continued, "I understand Deputy Barlow will be here. With a date." He glanced at Sherrie, who nodded. "He'll be off duty, but of course it's always useful to have someone present who can get someone in a full nelson as quick as a wink."

Ooof. Her *heart* felt like it had just taken a punch.

Of course everyone knew Eli's business. Small towns.

But was Eli making a point by bringing Bethany?

Or was he bringing Bethany as insurance against Glory straddling him out of the blue? Given that it must seem rather hard to predict what Glory would do lately.

She could feel a flush begin to paint her from her collarbone upward.

Why *shouldn't* he be able to just enjoy The Baby Owls

concert? She could hardly object to his presence. Then again, why couldn't he do it alone?

"We'll put Eli and his date in the little V.I.P. Section," Glenn continued. The "V.I.P. section" was basically a roped-off section near the counter, complete with some of those comfy stools, one of which Mick Macklemore had nearly brained Eli with. "We'll bring those folks in through the back. Eden and Annelise will be there. And your friend Franco Francone called ahead, Glory, to see if we could hold a spot for him, too."

Well. It was shaping up to be an interesting evening. "What makes him *my* friend?"

"I saw that fella preening onstage next to you after the brawl the other night. He gave you his digits on a napkin. He's got himself a crush, kiddo," Glenn confirmed.

"He's the sort that can't go three seconds without attention from a good-looking woman," Glory asserted.

"Maybe so. But tag, you're it."

Franco Francone wasn't giving up, which was interesting. His presence would go some way toward ameliorating the fact that Eli would be on a "date." She'd never realized how much she hated that word.

"Okay," Glenn said with finality. He leaned back and looked at the clock. "Aaaaaand . . . Break! Truck, get the doors!"

Truck threw open the doors and they began funneling in the crowd.

Within a half hour, the Misty Cat was teeming and actual conversation would only be held either mouth to ear or shouted from a position of inches away. Glory was kept hopping, but she did manage to see a few of her friends get in, like Casey Carson and Kayla Benoit, Monroe Porter, the death-metal drummer, and Marvin Wade, who had come to dance, of course.

And the drunker everyone got, the louder it got.

She was collecting money from a bearded guy, who looked like the type to get affectionately handsy when he was drunk, and handing off his beer when she saw Franco Francone slip in through the back hallway, ushered in by Glenn. She only had time to toss him a quick wave, which he intercepted with one of his white grins.

No sign of Eli yet.

And fifteen minutes before showtime, there was absolutely no sign of the band.

Fifteen minutes *after* showtime there was still no sign of the band.

Twenty minutes after showtime, when there was still no sign of the band, was when the crowd really started to get restive. In a very peculiar way.

"HOO! HOO! HOO! HOO! HOO!"

Glenn grabbed Glory's arm and pulled her aside. "What the *hell* are they doing?"

"They're *hooting.*" Glory had read up on The Baby Owls in the internet version of *Clang* magazine. "Apparently that's what they do at The Baby Owls' shows. You know, like owls do."

Glenn's eyes nearly disappeared into his head from rolling.

"How far does this owl thing go? If they riot will they roost in my rafters? Will they crap on my floor? Will they catch rodents and spit out the bones? Not that I have any rodents," he hastily added. "Where the hell *is* that damn band?"

And then suddenly his eyes widened and he seized his phone like a gunslinger. It must have buzzed. "Finally have a text."

He jammed his reading glasses up onto his face. "It says, 'Our bus broke down on I-5 in Bulgaria.'" He was still shouting at Glory.

She frowned. ". . . the hell?" They had a Nevada City in this part of California, which was rather confusing, but not a Bulgaria.

He scrolled. "Got another one. Oh wait. Not Bulgaria. 'Bumfuck.' Their bus broke down in Bumfuck. Autocorrect."

Bumfuck more or less accurately described huge swaths of forested Northern California, at least according to city folk. The Baby Owls were going to have to get more specific.

Another text came in. "Ah. They've determined that they're just outside Prentiss."

"Prentiss!" Glory was aghast. "They'll be lucky if anyone drives by that patch of highway this time of night. Anyone who can haul a bunch of guys and their instruments, anyway. I'm amazed their texts are getting through at all."

Prentiss was about an hour away, give or take. They could conceivably still make it to the show and play at least an hour, forty-five minutes.

"HOO! HOO! HOO! HOO! *HOO!*" The audience seemed to be getting more vehement.

"No one's going to pick them up if they try hitchhiking. They look like they live in caves, with those beards. All they're missing are axes to complete the murderous look," Glenn fussed. Then he brightened. "Oh, look, there's Eli. Maybe he can help."

Glory's heart lurched. Eli had two or three inches on

most of the guys in the crowd, so he was painfully easy to see. He was taking golden-haired Bethany's coat from her and draping it gallantly over the bar stool in the V.I.P. Section. Glory wondered if he'd spotted Franco Francone yet.

Franco's presence ought to just about make Eli's night. Then again, maybe he'd be too captivated by his "date" to notice him.

Glenn shot an arm up and waved until he caught Eli's eye. Then he beckoned him over with a sweep of his hand. Glory was prepared to dart in another direction, but she really couldn't see a way into the crowd at the moment. She was trapped by a sea of drinkers.

"Evening, Glenn," Eli said, voice raised. "Great crowd."

And then he saw her.

He paused a beat.

"Glory," he said neutrally, by way of greeting. One would never dream she'd tried to mount him in his squad car last night.

"Eli," she tried to say just as neutrally. She wasn't nearly as good as inscrutability as he was. Her face was hot as a struck match head. She hoped he couldn't see it in the dark.

Glenn put a chummy hand in the middle of Eli's shoulder blades. "I know you're not on duty tonight, Deputy, but do you think you can make a few calls to your professional buddies, see if they can find a band down on I-5 near Prentiss, help them get here? Their bus broke down and their cell reception is spotty."

"So that's what's going on?" Eli scanned the place, reminding Glory of the Terminator. Eli really could read a room.

And then suddenly, Eli froze. Went absolutely still, like a spaniel pointing.

If Glory hadn't known better, she would have thought an invisible lightbulb had clicked on over his head.

He pivoted back toward them slowly.

"I thought I saw your guitar in back, Glory, when I came through."

He fixed her with a gaze so laser focused with meaning it instantly told her this wasn't an idle observation.

"It is."

Suddenly, in the swarming dark of the crowd, she could see Bethany's golden, smooth head bobbing its way steadily toward them. She was wearing a darling off the shoulder red shirt, and the exposed shoulder was the kind of smooth, polished tan only money could buy.

"And that's Franco Francone sitting on a stool over there," Eli added, almost as a question. As if inventorying all the things that would mean something to Glory here in the Misty Cat at the moment.

"Yep. He's sure hard to miss, isn't he?" she said blithely, just as Bethany's arm looped through Eli's from behind.

"Hi, Glory!" Bethany beamed at Glory.

"Hi, Bethany!" Glory said brightly. She tried a smile, but she had a feeling she only managed to curl up part of her lip, which probably made her look either like Elvis or a rabid terrier.

Bethany looked startled. As well she might.

"Gotta go help Sherrie keep the customers drunk," Glory said abruptly as she dove back toward the tables.

After last night, Eli really wasn't feeling particularly charitable toward Glory. He'd resolved to have a perfectly pleasant if un-extraordinary evening with Bethany.

Seeing Francone's flawless mug and lanky·body parked on a stool as he entered the Misty Cat had done nothing but solidify his resolve.

But as he watched the crowd swallow Glory up now, damned if there wasn't that tug in his chest. As if that maddening woman kept his heart on a tether wrapped permanently around her wrist.

And it suddenly felt odd to have another arm looped through his. As though a new and unnecessary body part had been grafted onto his.

He smiled down at Bethany because it seemed the polite thing to do, and she smiled back, and that was nice.

Nevertheless. He watched the space where he'd last seen Glory.

And . . . there was something he had to do.

"Can I use your office to make a phone call, Glenn? I'll see what I can do about that band."

Eli could still hear muffled *HOO HOO HOO HOOing* through the door of Glenn's office. He punched Deputy Owen Haggerty's number into his phone. His heart was thudding steadily but hard, as if he was the one who was about to go onstage. As if he was about to commit a crime.

"Hey, Eli. Aren't you on a *date*?"

Jesus. Everyone in town knew everything about everyone.

"Yeah," he said shortly. "Listen, Haggerty? Will you call Deputy Becky Cameron over in Black Oak? A worried friend just reported a pack of guys with huge beards and tattoos and axes out on the highway near Prentiss. Parked in a bus. Out on I-5. Maybe send armed backup. Drugs might be involved."

Not a bit of that statement was inaccurate. So help him.

There was no way a band didn't have axes on them, for instance.

The six-string kind, that was.

And in this part of California, it was hard to know whether possessors of big bushy beards were ironic hipsters or meth-making neck-tattooed thugs. Cops in his part of the state were unlikely to give them the benefit of the doubt. And God help The Baby Owls if they had any drugs on their bus. Which, rock and roll being what it was, they probably did.

Ah, well.

Odds were pretty good that band was in for a long night, and it wouldn't be anywhere near the Misty Cat. At least they'd be in out of the cold, if they had drugs on them. In a nice cozy sheriff station somewhere.

He ended the call.

Guilt pinged him, but only faintly. He felt something more like steely, unapologetic resolve. Life for a band on the road was grueling. Success was hard to come by and was in large part a crap shoot. But they were already on a billboard out on the highway and on Conan and Kimmel and radios and Spotify everywhere.

He might not be Franco Francone, but he could do this for Glory. At least this much.

He could let her do the rest.

And he could go try to enjoy his night with his date.

And if he knew Glory—and boy did he—he was positive he knew what she would do next.

Glory handed out beers to and took money from the astonishingly thirsty—and solvent, judging from all the cash shoved at her—crowd. She craned her head, but she could see that Eli hadn't emerged from Glenn's office yet. But every now and then a woman returning from the bathroom would glance toward Franco and do a violent double take and nearly trip over her own feet.

Glory could almost see the moment she decided that there was no way that guy was actually *the* Franco Francone. That maybe she should drink a little less.

Finally Glory was able to pay him a swift visit. "Anything I can get for you, Franco?"

"You already know what I want, Glorious."

"If you also want a Sierra Nevada Porter, I can make *that* wish come true right away."

He grinned at her. Another woman strolling by caught the reflected dazzle from his teeth and walked straight into a wall.

"Oof," she said. Rubbing her forehead.

Glory winced.

"Is the porter any good?" Franco hadn't even noticed.

"Sure. I like it."

"Then the porter it is. What's up with the missing band?"

"Bus broke down."

"Bummer." And then he glanced up and froze. And his face darkened so abruptly Glory spun around.

Eli was standing right behind her. "Francone," he said flatly.

"Deputy," Franco drawled.

The air pulsed with so much dislike Glory was tempted to wave her arms about to dissipate it.

Nobody said a word for an absurd moment.

"Think the band is going to make it, Eli?" she said evenly.

He hesitated. "I did what I could," he said carefully. "I'd say give it ten minutes. Then go talk to Glenn."

He was looking just past her shoulder. As if he couldn't bear to look at her full on, with Francone standing right next to her.

She didn't know what had happened in that office, but she had a hunch that Eli had come to her rescue again.

And her heart leaped.

But then he just kept walking away, shouldering his way toward the end of the counter, where Bethany's face turned up toward his like a flower, and he ducked his head to talk to her.

That pose. It was so masculine and solicitous and possessive. So . . . *claiming*. And Glory felt instantly nauseous.

So maybe he'd made an emphatic decision in that office, too.

Whatever. She could cope.

"What did he mean by 'give it ten minutes'?" Franco's mood hadn't quite rebounded from eye contact with Eli yet.

"I'm not sure," Glory said tautly.

That wasn't quite true. She knew exactly what it meant. She gave it seven minutes.

Glenn was particularly easy to find tonight. He was the big gray-haired guy who looked ready to pull his hair out.

She planted herself in front of him and put her hand on his arm to stop him. "Glenn. This crowd is going to leave if the band they came to see doesn't show up. Figure at least two more beers in each of them, on average, that's another, what, thousand bucks for the restaurant at least? Giorgio can pinch hit as a cocktail waiter if you need him. Let me play."

He gave his mustache a quick chew and scanned the crowd.

Then turned to her abruptly. "Can you get it together and be on stage in five minutes?"

"Less," she said instantly.

"Do it," he said swiftly.

"Yes!" She punched the air and gave a little hop then spun around and located Giorgio, grabbed him by the arm and held him fast. She ignored his dumbstruck glare and rattled off orders. "Giorgio, can you grab me that short padded stool next to the counter? The one that Mick almost brained the sheriff with? And that box the olive oil came in today. The empty one. Bring them up to the stage and mic them. I'm gonna play."

"You're going to mic the *stool* and the *box*?"

"Yep. You'll see. Oh, and grab the big flour sifter, too."

Someone in the crowd jostled him right into her. "WHAT? I thought you said *flour sifter.*"

"I did. GO GO GO!"

Bless his surly little heart, he was off like a shot.

She knew *exactly* what she was doing. It was so much easier to give orders than follow everybody else's.

She saw Glenn talking to Sherrie, who gave her the thumbs-up as she retrieved her guitar from its case. She slung it over her neck and strapped on the harmonica, adjusting it as she walked through the hall just like a rock star emerging from an arena's backstage labyrinth.

She arrived on stage to find that Giorgio had mic'd the box and stool expertly. He settled the flour sifter down on top of the box with a flourish. He offered her a high five as he walked off, too.

And then she took a deep breath. And she stepped into the spotlight and planted herself in front of the mic.

The crowd noticed pretty quickly. "Hoot the fuck are you?" someone hollered immediately.

"'Freebird'!" someone else yelled. Predictably. The Lynyrd Skynyrd request had cycled back around and was now considered wittily ironic. She probably *should* do a version of 'Freebird' one day.

"Show us your tits!" came from another guy in the crowd.

"LANGUAGE!" Glenn bellowed from some place in the restaurant.

But this was all as standard as "Check, one, two" in any unruly club audience. She'd even heard women shout that at guys. She could handle it, piece of cake.

"Don't you mean my *hoot*ers?" she said idly. "And by the way, sweetheart? No fucking way am I showing them to *you*."

This got a laugh. "Preach it, girl!" some woman shouted approvingly. Very good. Laughing was good. She needed to act as if she *owned* this crowd right from the beginning or she was sunk.

Her hands were trembling. That moment between silence and her first note was like diving into a beautiful ice-cold sea every time. The dive was terrifying, but once she plunged in the waters were positively holy. Once she was in, she was a freaking porpoise.

"And besides, hooter guy . . ." she said offhandedly, continuing the conversation, as it were, as she fine-tuned her E string ". . . in a minute, dude, you're going to want to show me *your* tits. In fact, you'll want to do anything I tell you to do. I will own you."

This got a *WOOOOO!* You had to show a crowd who was boss. It was like the cat slapping an alligator on the snout.

"You're hot!" someone drunkenly yelled.

"Don't you mean *HOOT*?" she shot back.

"No, I meant HOT," he countered, sounding wounded.

"You speak the truth, son," Glory agreed placidly into the mic, and they laughed again. "Hey, any drummers out there? Monroe, Monroe Porter, you out there?"

Drummers, she knew from experience, always carried around sticks. They were forever percussing everything. They really couldn't help themselves.

"I'LL DRUM YOU, BABY!" some fool hollered. Sherrie and Glenn were making a mint.

Oh brother. "What does that even mean?" she laughed. "Someone bring that guy a beer! He's obviously not drunk enough yet."

More laughter and *WOOOOOs!*

The crowd shifted and undulated like a ball pit and Monroe Porter squirted through and sprinted up to the stage. He was, as she'd predicted, carrying sticks. She leaned into him to tell him what she wanted him to do.

His face lit up. "Dude!" He approved. "I can totally do that. I know most of your set."

He climbed up next to her.

"Glory, you ready?" The voice was right in her ear. She jumped. She hadn't even noticed Glenn sidling up.

She nodded.

Glenn seized the mic stand and pulled it toward him.

"QUIET!" he bellowed.

The audience was so amazed to be yelled at that silence fell immediately.

"Ladies and gentlemen . . . The Baby Owls' bus broke down on the highway, and we're doing our best to get them here. Got our best people on it."

"BOOOOOOO! SSSSSSS! HOO! HOO! HOO! HOO!"

"*QUIET*. You're about to be grateful for that little mechanical malfunction because, ladies and gentlemen, you now get to listen to . . . GLORY GREENLEAF!"

He set the mic stand back in front of her and strolled off with a murmured "knock 'em dead, kiddo."

CHAPTER 14

But his announcement was met by a scattering of polite applause. *Pat pat pat pat.* Not even any heckling. Which was almost worse than no applause at all. Someone belched. A woman giggled. She heard someone who sounded a lot like Casey Carson yell a delighted "Go, Glory!"

She peered into the restless dark, which was interrupted only by cell phone screens and glints of eyeglasses aimed at her. She felt a bit like a lone camper who sees the yellow eyes of wolves in the dark.

She'd decided on her first song, and there was no way that at least half this crowd full of music geeks wouldn't recognize it once she started: it was a legendary song from a legendary band from a legendary record. If she nailed it, she'd have them eating out of her hand.

If she botched a single note, it would sound like a bad parody and she'd be lucky if they didn't start hurling beer bottles at her.

They ought to just mic her heart. It was about ready to kick its way out of her chest.

She gave her head a shampoo commercial shake, threw

her shoulders back, and smiled as if she was about to spring the best secret on the crowd, then put her lips on her harmonica and blew those first notes of Led Zeppelin's "Your Time Is Gonna Come."

That lonesome, pure, winding lick seemed to fly right up into the rafters and then pour out of the Misty Cat's walls.

There was an audible rustle of leather and flannel and denim as the crowd shifted, leaned forward.

Some guy shouted a muffled *yes!*

Someone else exhaled an impressed "Damn!"

And, oh yeah: she *nailed* that intro.

She brought her head down hard to signal Monroe, who brought his sticks down on that plump stool just as she laid into the first chord, then arpeggiated it, funking it up just a little more than the original, getting heads out there nodding.

Her voice soared and ached, singing the story of a lying cheating lover, howling the pain of it, soulfully threatening retribution.

The first *WOOOOO!* hit around the third line of the verse. The audience was *in*. She could almost feel that click, like two continents colliding to form a new one.

And when she got a little carried away, she demanded, "Sing it with me!"

Only actual rock stars had the all-fired balls to withstand the shame if the audience decided that nope, they would not be singing it with her, even after she entreated.

But they *actually did*.

She felt literally intoxicated. Helium filled. Soaring and unfettered for the first time in eons, maybe ever. Because *this* was her milieu.

A few guys actually attempted to flick their lighters. Glenn was prepared for this and he waded through the crowd and yanked them from hands before the sprinklers could go off.

And then she cued Monroe to cut the song, and slammed it to a finish.

"WOOOOOOOOOO! WOOOOO!"

She heard hands slamming together emphatically. Tables slapped. Two-fingered whistles.

Not one single "Hoot."

*Ex*cellent.

She was well on the way to mesmerizing them into believing they'd come to see *her.*

"This next one . . . is for my friend Franco," she said slyly. "And his good buddy Deputy Eli Barlow."

And she got everyone's feet stomping with Janis Joplin's "Mercedes Benz."

That was going to drive Eli *nuts.* Particularly the line about her friends all driving Porsches.

She could see Franco laughed, his white teeth flashing. He gave her the thumbs-up. And as for Eli, over there next to Blondie McBlonderson, he was shaking his head, his lips pressed together. She knew he was struggling not to smile at her pure audacity.

The crowd showed their love for that one, too, with lots of whoops and loud applause, but she had to keep it moving, and she pretty much had to stick to a set that Monroe knew. She briefly considered maybe throwing a little Florence + the Machine or Adele or Brandi Carlile in there, but the risk of sounding like a wedding singer, or worse, a karaoke singer was too great with more contemporary songs. Keeping the set a little retro, putting her own unique stamp on songs—that was the way to go. She'd do big songs, a few iconic ones, ones that moved a crowd pretty much no matter what, almost no matter the arrangement.

So she mesmerized them with a haunted, smoky version of Bobbie Gentry's "Ode to Billy Joe." A soulful, angst-filled, foot-stomping, ringing version of Neil Diamond's "Holly Holy" shook the rafters and again had them singing with her, like it was a revival meeting and she was a faith healer and they'd all come to be cured of heartbreak, and everyone was wall to wall goose bumps.

The opening notes of R.E.M.'s "South Central Rain" were greeted with cheers, and she sped the tempo up and rocked it a bit harder than the original, and turned that one word chorus—Sorry!—into a howl of shame and rue. A sultry countrified blues version of The Baby Owls' "In the Forest" resulting in a nearly unmanageable chorus of hoots was clearly a mistake, but she pulled it back from the owls' nest with a witty, yet poignant version of Guns N' Roses'"Sweet Child O' Mine." She played that famous opening lick on the harmonica, and just about delighted the pants off the crowd, who threw their fists in the air with the chorus.

And this was when Marvin Wade finally fought his way to the front to do his swirly dance, and she didn't even tell him to sit down, because she was twirling right along with him in her heart.

She paused to breathe, to take a sip of some water that had magically appeared near her—probably Giorgio had slipped it in there—and said, "This one is for my friend, Annelise."

She pointed to Annelise, who was standing with her

mom, who was actually grinning, and Annelise hopped up and down in excitement.

And she launched into "Me and Bobby McGee," and played a rocking harmonica line intro. By the time that song was over, everyone was singing as if they were a bunch of hammered kids around a campfire.

And that's when she noticed, as if in slow motion, Blondie McBlonderson lean her head cozily against Eli's huge shoulder.

And Eli's arm appeared to be draped behind her.

Maybe not *quite* around her.

And Glory held perfectly still.

Momentarily dumbstruck. As in, like she'd literally been struck and was literally briefly mute.

Granted, it was hardly a cuddle. But Bethany could smell him, probably. Could feel how hard his arm was, right through her body. Could extrapolate from there how hard and hot the rest of his body was.

And just like that, the very devil took Glory.

Her sense of drama told her to remain still a heartbeat or so longer.

Long enough for the audience to go still, too. Long enough for everyone to start wondering, but not long enough for them to begin rustling. Long enough for her to infect them with portent.

Then she crooned the opening words of Three Dog Night's famous song: "Eli's Comin'."

Two words. They sailed out there in the Misty Cat and filled the whole room, and she pulled out that last syllable into a crystal-pure note that soared like a warning, sung in a way that made it sound like it was much too late to save yourself. Eli was comin'.

And he was going to destroy your heart.

It was a singer's song—emotional, even histrionic, crazy high notes, room to growl and scream for vocal acrobatics. It was hard and fast and had a killer hook—and Monroe about beat holes in the box and the bar stool.

And she sang the whole damn thing *straight* to Eli. Did not take her eyes off him.

She KILLED that song.

When she brought it to an abrupt end, the crowd screamed approval.

She didn't pause to bask. Although she did notice that Eli slowly removed his arm from behind Bethany and crossed both of his arms over his chest, almost like bandoliers. And his face was expressionless.

She was on a mission now, whether it was worthy or not, though if pressed, she'd have to go with not. She didn't care: it was untold relief to pour out her frustration and fury and angst and lust, turn it into the kind of fuel that made an audience wild. She segued into "Featherbed," the song she'd been singing out behind the Plugged Nickel just before she bit a guy, the first song she ever wrote about Eli. Its huge, ringing ethereal chords were the perfect fit right there in the set, and when she was done, the audience cheered it as if it was an FM radio classic. She half suspected they'd cheer if she burped into the mic right now, but she wasn't about to split hairs.

"Thank you! *That* was one of my own. And speaking of something of your *own* . . ."

She segued right into the chiming chords of Fleetwood Mac's "Go Your Own Way."

And maybe it was a little on-the-nose lyrics wise. But suddenly, without realizing it, she was both wooing and waging war with song tonight. And maybe it was unfair, but she didn't care.

Monroe slammed into it on the stool just like she had when she'd annoyed Giorgio with it the other day, squeezed the flour sifter and used it as an ersatz cowbell during the verses, alternating that with the box and the stool, and it was just brilliant.

And then suddenly Glenn loomed in her peripheral vision and flashed five fingers at her.

Five minutes.

And then she had a reckless inspiration.

Under cover of ecstatic *woooooing* she bent down to Monroe and said "this one's new . . . Think . . . it's kind of like . . . She patted out the rhythm for him quickly. "Almost a bolero. Kinda like Led Zep's 'Kashmir.'"

"You start. I'll get it," Monroe said. He was glowing with success, and his dyed black hair was plastered to his head with sweat.

She trailed her fingers over that D sus 2, then the G, and with the anticipation of that haunting, martial intro, her hips moved into the rhythm, showing them all how that song was going to make them feel.

Monroe kicked in after a few bars. He used his hands, humping out a muffled rhythm on the box, turning it into a sort of tabla. And he had it exactly right.

The audience was instantly captivated. It only got better when she opened her mouth to sing.

Are you afraid to touch me, darlin'?
Are you afraid you'll burn?
You'll have to get in line, darlin'
You'll have to wait your turn

Yeah everybody wants me, darlin'
But one day you'll finally learn
I only ever wanted you

Because, baby, I'm a badass rose
Baby, I'm the kind that grows
Stronger when it storms
And weaker in your arms
I might cut you, make you bleed
But I'm all you'll ever need
Don't give up on me
Oh, don't give up on me

And as she drove it toward that verse crescendo, every last one of the men in there imagined what it would be like to feel their hips moving over hers.

And all the women were infused with a sense of their own power.

And Eli was still as a stone, and his arms were still crossed. As if to protect that soft underbelly that she was going for.

By the second verse, the dark in front of her was lit by cell phones that were all up and aimed *at* her, to capture this song and this moment. A few guys attempted to stand on chairs and tables and were quickly all but swatted down by Glenn and Truck Donegal.

The last verse she sang mostly a cappella, accompanied by the softest of heartbeat pats on her guitar.

Are you afraid to love me, baby?
A little scared of pain
Cuz love is kind of messy, baby

And heartbreak leaves a stain
If you'd rather wake up with a stranger
than open up a vein
I guess that's how it goes
Baby, I'm a badass rose

And when that last note of the song rang by itself, she knew every pair of lungs in the place had stopped moving.

So they could savor that last note until it vanished into the ether.

She remained motionless.

Frozen, as if she'd cast a spell on herself.

And then she leaned once more into the mic.

"I'm Glory Greenleaf. *That's* who the fuck I am. Thank you. Good night."

Just in case The Baby Owls' management was listening, or something.

A sort of pandemonium ensued.

But not, thankfully, the kind with thrown fists and stools.

Cheers and stomping revealed an audience that was well and truly drunk with beer and glorious entertainment, high on music in a way that hadn't anticipated. A happy, happy crowd.

She grinned and raised her guitar briefly overhead like a prizefighter and let the cheers rain down on her as if they could soak into her skin, right down into her soul, wash out every ache she'd ever had.

Wash out how it felt to have Eli standing there next to another woman, who would ride home with him in the dark, and maybe he would kiss her, and maybe he would even make love to her, but the whole time, the *whole* time Glory was sure he'd be thinking about her so hard it would be a wonder he didn't cry out her name.

It wasn't fair but life wasn't fair and love might as well be war and music was hers to use any way she wanted.

And then Glenn grabbed the mic from her and practically elbowed her out of the way.

So much for mystique. But zoning and noise laws were what they were.

"Thank you, Glory Greenleaf! Wasn't she fantastic? Thank you all for coming! Now get out!"

The crowd laughed merrily. Everyone thought Glenn was a character.

But he meant business.

A kid fought his way up to the front.

"That was awesome, man. Glory! Do you have a CD I can buy? Will you sign my boobs?"

He hiked up his shirt.

Jesus. He was pretty hairy.

But earnest.

"I don't have a Sharpie on me, but—" she started.

Another guy popped up. He had a huge beard and a zealous gleam in his eyes.

"You were *incredible*. You remind me sort of Adele meets Grace Slick meets PJ Harvey meets—"

"GET OUT, young man. Shoo!" Glenn waved his arms at them like they were bears getting into the garbage.

They scrambled backward and turned and jogged for the exits.

So much for savoring the afterglow.

But she understood. There were noise laws and there was at least one lawman on the premises.

"I can't thank you enough, Monroe. You were *brilliant*." She high-fived him.

They were both incredibly sweaty. His Motörhead shirt was glued to him.

"You, too, Glory. I loved it. Hey, I'd stick around to talk some more, but gotta strike while the iron's hot. You know how it is."

She rolled her eyes, but she fist-bumped him.

He grinned and leaped off the stage. Given that he was a newly anointed rock star for the evening. A cluster of girls were around him almost immediately, chattering happily.

She hoped Monroe got lucky tonight. He might not ever find the perfect death-metal singer here in Hellcat Canyon, but getting laid might help take the edge off the disappointment, and she knew how precious dreams were.

"OUT!" Glenn bellowed into the mic, and the final stragglers finally massed and scurried out. "Drive safely, people. We want you to get home alive. And if you drive drunk our deputies will get you immediately."

Glory reflexively reached down into her case for her red bandanna to begin wiping down her strings.

"Here." Glenn pressed something into her hand. It looked like a stack of order pads.

"What's this? You're giving me *homework*?"

Talk about anticlimactic.

"We passed these around while you were playing, told people to look up your Facebook page and write down their e-mail addresses. They're yours to keep."

She flipped through them. She had maybe a couple hundred names here. For a musician, it was almost as good as currency.

She looked up at him mistily.

It was such a lovely thing to do and in all the excitement she hadn't thought to do it.

"Boy, you must really want to get rid of me, Glenn."

"The sooner the better, sweetheart," he said, but he smiled. "One last thing." He pushed something else into her hand. It was actual currency.

"It's two hundred bucks, in fives and tens and ones. Don't spend it all it once place." He patted her and bustled off, waving away her drop-jawed gratitude.

Two hundred bucks! That was officially the most she'd ever made playing music.

She'd give Monroe and Giorgio some of it, for sure.

She rolled it tightly and jammed it deep into the pocket of her jeans.

She looked up sharply, suddenly, as alert as if someone had flicked her in the back of her head.

Eli was moving steadily through the crowd, making his way toward her at an unnervingly purposeful, stalking gunslinger pace.

He stopped finally.

So, briefly, did her heart.

His face was extraordinary. Tense and brilliant with some emotion that was hard to identify, but which wasn't the least bit mild, and was probably a little dangerous.

Her heart jabbed hard in her chest. She'd never anticipated a verdict more.

"Subtle," he said finally.

The most dryly ironic single word she'd ever heard.

She just held his hard gaze with a little faint smile.

As though she'd won a round of a duel.

"Glory, you were *amazing*! Wasn't she amazing, Eli?" Bethany had apparently ducked into the bathroom, and now she bounced up behind him and looped her arm through his. "I was dying to see The Baby Owls, but you felt so much like the real thing I didn't miss them at *all*."

The real thing.

Those words sort of vibrated in the air.

Glory couldn't face Eli's hard, questioning look, or his taut jaw anymore. The line of tension between them was charged, and the air was full of lightning, and if that line snapped, dangerous sparks could fly everywhere.

She dropped her gaze and gathered her hair in her fist and used it to fan the back of her neck.

"You need me to blow on it back there?"

Her head shot up. Franco Francone had bounded up next to her on the stage.

Eli turned on his heel and walked straight for the door, pushed it open, and was gone.

Glory watched that extraordinary reaction with a certain unworthy satisfaction.

And more than a little uneasiness.

Bethany looked startled.

Then she spun and all but loped after Eli, her hair bright in the dark light. "Bye, Glory. Wonderful show," she called.

Glenn and Giorgio and Sherrie were swooping about, gathering bottles and re-arranging tables like pros. The place would be spotless again by morning.

Glory dropped her hair. Once again, her eyes were on the door.

"You're a star, Glory," Franco said. "And at this point in my career, I know a star when I see one."

"Kind of you to say so," she said to Franco. Uncharacteristically humble. But she now realized she was tired.

She studied Franco. And thought about Eli taking Bethany home in his big truck. And anarchy stirred in her soul. She wondered if she ought to just make out with

Franco in the dark in his fancy car. The way she once made out with guys at parties in high school until she and Mick Macklemore had become a thing. And then maybe she ought to shut off her brain and let her body decide for her if she wanted more.

Because Eli had been right: sex was a great way to make yourself feel better. It was a little like alcohol, though, in that it had the power to make you feel pretty horrible if you did the wrong kind of imbibing.

She looked at Franco and thought all of this.

Trouble was, it seemed inconceivable that she had ever kissed anyone casually. Or without consequence.

Now, thanks to Eli, she knew what a kiss could be. What it could mean. How it could make and ruin a life in just a few moments.

"Need a ride home?" Franco said softly.

Giorgio loped onto the stage and started briskly breaking down the mics. He paused and intercepted a glance from her. He went still. And he must have read something in her face.

"I'm parked out front. You still need a ride home, Glory?"

She was surprised. They'd of course never discussed any kind of ride.

"Yeah, thanks, Giorgio." She turned to Franco. "Thanks for the offer, but I told Giorgio I'd catch a ride with him. He's scared of the dark."

She couldn't resist that one.

Giorgio muttered something that sounded like "Piglet panties" under his breath and shook his head as he stalked off with the mic stand.

But people could surprise you.

In the half light of the Misty Cat, up here on stage, Franco sure looked like he ought to be the romantic hero in her story.

But then, that's why he was paid to be on TV.

The real thing. Those words came back to her.

Franco was reading her face while she was reading his, apparently, because he leaned toward her and said softly, as if confiding a secret, "You should give me a chance, Glory. You won't regret it." He gave her a quick cheek kiss, more a mischievous peck than anything, then gracefully made his exit with a flap-of-his-hand farewell. Out the back, like a star.

Glenn hollered from across the Misty Cat, "You're exempt from the mopping tonight, kiddo. See you in the morning!"

CHAPTER 15

"Bye, Glory! Thank you! I mean, Thank you, Hellcat Canyon! Good *night*!" Annelise paused in the doorway of the Misty Cat with a hand planted saucily on one hip and blew her a kiss.

Glory laughed and blew one back.

Eden Harwood, whether she wanted it or not, was going to have her hands full with that little girl. She was blazing smart and quirky, and the lucky little thing was surrounded by people who loved her.

She didn't know how it had happened—maybe Eden had unbent all on her own, which given how many times Glory had said the "F" word in the throes of concert adrenaline last night seemed unlikely. Maybe Annelise badgered her into it—because how could anyone say no to that face?—but Annelise had shown up with her mini guitar today after Glory's shift.

And together she and Annelise had turned "Gregory" into an actual whole song, with actual chords. She'd eventually like to teach them to Annelise one by one. Today, however, was all about G.

Glory knew Annelise was going to go home and drive her mom nuts by strumming G all night.

As she sat on the edge of the Misty Cat stage and rested her chin on the soothing curve of her guitar, Glory thought about what Eli had said about Eden being a single mom, with hurts and secrets of her own.

Eli, who noticed so much by virtue of being quiet and observant and just, dammit all, by being good.

Given Annelise's age and given the fact that music was pouring out of her and given the bands that not infrequently cycled in and out of Hellcat Canyon, Glory had a hunch who her dad might be and how that might have happened.

But that was Eden's journey, and she had her own reasons for keeping that entirely to herself.

On a whim, Glory tuned her low E a whole step down to D and strummed it. *Ahhhhhh*. She could feel that chord right between her ribs. That little primal thrum of a bottom D was like therapy.

She picked out a snatch of Fleetwood Mac's "Never Going Back Again."

She wondered if that's how Eli thought of her.

She'd awakened to close to two hundred new likes on her Facebook page and wiggly camera phone video posted to it by one of the concertgoers, who had tagged The Baby Owls, thus opening her up to the possibility of hundreds of thousands of views.

She still looked and sounded amazing in that video, and she could critique a dozen things about it, but it was simplicity itself, that performance, with the stripped-down rawness of something like The White Stripes.

And she'd drawn in a shuddery little breath. Finally, things were moving forward. It was just one gig and one wobbly video, but it was infinitely more and infinitely better and more than she'd had yesterday.

She'd made the *Hellcat Canyon Chronicle*:

**Local Musician Brings Down House
After The Baby Owls Fly the Coop**

And the tagline was "Crowd Sings Hallelujah for Glory Greenleaf."

Glenn had framed it and hung it on the wall where The Baby Owls flyer used to be.

Below that article online was another article:

**The Baby Owls Guitarist Busted
for Possession of One Tiny
Marijuana Cigarette**

It was pretty clear they let college interns write the headlines, because the headline just dripped with reproachfulness.

The article went on to describe how the band had been surrounded by the California Highway Patrol and sheriff's deputies with guns drawn on I-5 outside of Prentiss, and their bus had been searched pretty thoroughly. Marijuana smoke tended to cling to bushy beards and apparently the fact that they all reeked of it was probable cause.

Rough night for The Baby Owls, all in all.

Glory was mildly sympathetic. That's rock and roll, as they said. Most musicians didn't get through entire careers without at least a few headlines like those. They'd get off with a fine, no doubt.

She had a sneaking suspicion Eli had a little something to do with it. Whatever phone call he'd made in that back room, it hadn't resulted in tenderly sympathetic law enforcement personnel bent on rescuing the owlets.

He'd been bent on rescuing her.

Now that Annelise's sparkling self had gone out the door, she understood that, despite last night's triumph, there was a sense of tense disquiet about the day. A waiting feeling. She wasn't certain she'd taken a full, deep breath today.

Portentously, a shadow fell over her hand.

She looked up.

"Hi, Glory. Your boss said I could find you here."

It was Bethany.

Glory stared up at her, examining her for any evidence of having been kissed senseless or otherwise sexually satisfied last night.

Bethany gave her head a little self-conscious toss and her hair spilled over her shoulder like a butterscotch and saffron tassel.

"Hi. Bethany, right?" Glory scrunched her brow a little.

That was indeed bitchy and very unlike her. She was sorry and not sorry.

"Yeah. Bethany. I think Glory is such a cool name. It's like you were born to be a rock star."

"Yep."

She was aware she was being obnoxious, and she didn't much like herself for it, but if there was one advantage to being a rock star it was that no one would be surprised if you showed a little attitude.

Bethany was working up to something, she was pretty sure.

"Your gig was *amazing*. I've never seen a woman jam on a harmonica like that. I guess I always thought of it as a sort of a guy's instrument."

"Yeah, the mouth organ is a masculine instrument, all right."

She watched unblinkingly and guiltless as perfectly nice Bethany slowly turned scarlet.

"Ha ha," Bethany said uncertainly.

Glory was beginning to enjoy herself in an entirely unworthy way.

She wrapped her hands around her knees and stared up into Bethany's brown doe eyes and waited for the next thing Bethany intended to say. Like a chess prodigy deciding upon which strategy she intended to use to decimate her opponent.

"You and Eli grew up together, didn't you? You're kind of like a sister to him? You guys seem to know quite a bit about each other."

This was either a fishing expedition, a very subtle declaration of war, or actual innocence on Bethany's part.

Whatever it was, the "sister" thing was pretty unpleasant to hear.

"Is that what he told you?"

She didn't think he'd say that. Eli wasn't one to tell a lie. Not even a placating white lie to the woman he'd just started to date.

And the undertone of the relationship between her and Eli was so deafening to Glory that it seemed inconceivable that Bethany couldn't hear it. It was, in fact, kind of like that low D tuning. It thrummed through every word they said to each other; it thrummed in the silences, too.

"It's just you guys seem to have grown up together and you seem comfortable with each other. What with all the, um, teasing, and so forth."

Maybe Bethany was just quite nice and not terribly complicated because life never hacked chunks out of her and so she thinks, poor fool, that what she sees is what she gets.

"Yeah. I've known Eli my whole life," she admitted finally.

She wasn't going to cop to "comfortable." Comfortable was the last thing they were these days.

"ANYways . . ." Bethany bravely continued. "You probably know his birthday is coming up," she said brightly. "Of course he's a Scorpio. No surprises there, am I right?"

Glory greeted this sentence with a pitying, incredulous stare designed to make Bethany feel like a whimsical fool.

She privately thought the same thing. Boy, if there ever was a Scorpio, he was it. Still waters run deep, the stare, the sizzling, the whole nine yards.

Bethany soldiered on, still faintly pink.

"Soooo . . . I kind of wanted to get him a present. You know, something small, but not something dorky or jokey. I thought maybe I'd ask you for ideas. Wasn't sure who else to ask. I've only gone out with him twice, but we're going out again tomorrow, and . . ." She lifted a shoulder in a shrug, and tucked a strand of hair behind her ear. "It'll be our third date, kind of."

Glory's stomach suddenly and violently cramped into a pretzel knot.

Everyone knew that the third date was supposed to be the sex date.

And Bethany didn't strike Glory as at all prudish. She looked like a girl unopposed to having a good time.

Glory looked up into Bethany's face and for a moment didn't see her. Her own had gone bizarrely hot, and the backs of her hands fuzzed over in heat. Somehow knowing that it hadn't happened yet, and knowing when it would, was worse. The notion of Eli sleeping with Bethany—his hands in her blond hair, his mouth touching hers—made her want to lift open the top of her head and shot-put her brain far, far away from her, somewhere her imagination couldn't torture her.

It was as excruciating a moment as she'd ever experienced.

But it was a valuable moment. Because the shock of it burrowed like a bullet down through all the various strata of hurt and anger and finally struck an unshakeable bedrock truth that made all the hurt and anger pointless.

She sat with that truth for a silent moment.

And all at once she knew what to say to Bethany.

"Is twenty-five bucks too much to spend on a gift?"

"Of course not." Bethany sounded surprised. "That's about what I had in mind."

Of course not. Glory and her mother could have heated hour-long Kitchen Table Summits over how they could spend twenty-five extra dollars if any should show up.

And in a flash Glory kind of understood why Jonah might had done what he had done. Because that chasm between wanting and having was sometimes unbearable. It took a strong person to patiently build a bridge across it, stick by stick. Jonah wasn't that person.

It took someone like Eli.

"I know what you should get him," she told Bethany.

Eli's entire body was clean scrubbed and he smelled like a crisp Irish spring, which he knew because he'd given his pits a good sniff. He'd trimmed up his privates and inspected his nose hairs and shaved his face until it glowed. His house got the same treatment: it now smelled like bleach, Lemon Pledge, and the Air Wick candle he'd chucked into his basket at the supermarket, and he could see himself in the surface of his coffee table. He'd thrown out all the expired food in the refrigerator, replaced it with a few grown-up things like wine, cheese, and a head of broccoli so that he didn't look so much a bachelor, and he'd pummeled his sofa and bed pillows into plumpness and changed his sheets to the high-thread-count ones his mom had given him last Christmas and which he hadn't seen the point in, because weren't sheets *sheets*? They were pretty soft, granted.

Eli of course knew what traditionally happened on a third date.

And so he did all this stuff ritualistically, as if in so doing he could summon the desire.

But he'd slept badly last night.

He'd kissed Bethany when he'd dropped her off last night after The Baby Owls show. A brush of his lips against hers. Which probably puzzled the crap out of her. She was the kind of woman men would normally love to paw.

He'd done it to be polite.

And then he'd asked her out to dinner tonight, in both defiance of how he felt and retaliation for last night's show, and as an apology to Bethany for not wanting to paw her. Bethany didn't know any of this, of course. She just knew she was going out to dinner at a nice restaurant with a sheriff's deputy.

Because he'd left the Misty Cat feeling as though Glory had essentially whaled on his soul like a cowbell.

He was still reverberating, feeling bruised, and swinging between the poles of quietly, coldly furious about it and . . . damn, but it was also just so *funny*. It was so . . . Glory. She'd been spectacular. And awful. And brilliantly, capriciously punishing. He'd been so proud it was nearly painful, watching her take wing like that. And he'd been horny as fuck.

That incredible new song. "Badass Rose." What did it mean? Had she just used the image for inspiration, or was she trying to tell him something she just couldn't say out loud?

He just didn't know what she *wanted*.

If the game was simply torture: mission accomplished.

But enough was enough.

And the smoothly tan, sweet-smelling, very pretty woman now sitting across from him at Cafe Elegante was sophisticated enough to know what should happen on a third date, too. And judging from all the little touches she'd been sneaking in—a hand laid on his arm to ask if she could change the radio station in the truck, another lingering touch that transformed into a light caress when she was pointing out the billboard of The Baby Owls on the highway, a lingering look and a small smile at the stoplights—she was into it.

"What I'd really like to do is work on a, say *Pirates of the Caribbean* type of movie," she was saying. "Something like that. Something where I can really transform a person into someone else entirely, rather than just prep their face for camera work. I'm fortunate to have a steady job right now, though. I'm hoping *The Rush* gets picked up for more seasons."

That would mean she'd be around more, but neither of them pointed that out.

"Say I'm an actor, getting ready for a scene. What would you do to my face?" he asked.

She tipped her head and studied him. "Well, we'd start with moisturizer, of course."

Of course? Did he look like a catcher's mitt? "Sure. Of course," he repeated dryly.

"And your eyebrows—" Suddenly she leaned forward and she reached across and lay her finger like a sextant over his brow bone.

His eyes crossed involuntarily. Her fingers smelled like some light floral lotion.

"Everything beyond my finger toward your temple would have to go. Yank."

She was touching his face. Which seemed awfully intimate, if not innately sexy at the moment.

He'd never thought minutely about his eyebrows before. Occasionally a few hairs would spring up between them but the unibrow never seemed to threaten. The Barlows weren't an inherently hairy people.

She took her finger away as the waiter sauntered over with a basket containing a variety of hot little bread rolls.

"Tossed a couple extra in there for you, Deputy Barlow. The ones with seeds that you like."

Bethany reached for a roll speckled with little seeds and leaned toward him confidingly, her eyes sparkling. "In this town, it's like *you're* a celebrity. Everyone knows you're a cop. Do you shake them down for protection money?"

He smiled. "Yeah, I get paid in bread rolls and special tables by the window. The bread here is great, by the way. They make it in SON OF A *BITCH*."

Bethany jumped and her roll shot straight up in the air, landed three feet away, and rolled across the floor.

That *$!#! blue Porsche had whipped by going at least sixty miles per hour.

It was all he could do not to chase the guy and rip his bumper off with his teeth.

He whipped his head back toward Bethany.

"Oh God. I'm so sorry about that, Bethany. Cop instincts. Francone. That guy is a menace."

Someone at a table down the way toed the roll back toward them, as if he'd friskily invited them to play soccer.

The waiter gracefully strolling down the aisle swooped upon it and took it away as though flying bread rolls were only to be expected.

Bethany shook her head. "Franco and his Porsche."

"Yeah," Eli said blackly. "Franco and his *Porsche*."

"You know, I still can't believe I'm actually working with Franco Francone and John Tennessee McCord. Can't believe I call him *Franco*. 'Franco, hold still and let me pluck your eyebrows.'"

"I can think of a few other things you can call him."

She smiled at that. "Let's talk about you. Did you always want to be a cop?"

Damn.

A seemingly simple question, and the kind he ought to expect on dates. But he dreaded it. Because he didn't like to lie. And leaving stuff out sometimes felt like a lie.

He considered his answer. The easy thing to say would be "yes." Not, "no. I was going to college on a football scholarship and my dad was shot and killed during a routine traffic stop and then I suddenly felt like I needed to be a cop. It was like I could undo that injustice every day one person at a time, but of course that'll never happen because people will keep on being people. But I love what I do and I'm good at it."

And then he'd have to talk about his dad.

He understood fully, now more than ever, what a luxury it was to simply be *known*. Not only for the details of his life, but all the subtle parts of it, too. Being with someone who *knew* you was like unbuttoning that top button of your pants the minute you got home from work.

He missed Glory so much right now it felt like the air was being squeezed out of his lungs.

He missed Jonah, too.

That asshole.

And a date with a pretty woman shouldn't feel like a slog.

He settled upon "It was kind of my calling" to keep things light. "How about you? Did you always want to learn how to, um . . . contour?"

Good God, how his colleagues would mock him for knowing that word. But she'd used it again as they were driving here. She'd pointed out Rebecca Corday's bus bench ads and said, "nice contouring."

She laughed. "I just always liked to play with makeup, and I love fashion and the idea of transforming people into maybe not their best selves, but . . . like an HD version of themselves. It's been a dream come true, this job on *The Rush*. Some actors won't give makeup artists the time of day. But the cast has been very kind. Franco and Mr. McCord are respectful and pretty amusing. I'd always heard Franco was kind of a womanizer but he's been a gentleman."

Of course he was. Francone might be a lightweight whose authority stemmed from excellent DNA, family connections, and the good luck to fall into a hit television show years ago, but Eli didn't make the mistake of thinking Francone was stupid. Bethany was quite hot by any guy's standards, but Franco knew women and he had taste, and he wanted Glory, because he recognized something rare when he saw it.

"Next time you're applying mascara—oh wait, clear gel, I remember—to Franco or however you get him ready for the camera, try telling him that hot women like guys who drive the speed limit."

Bethany laughed and laid a hand flirtatiously on his forearm again. "I'll tell you a secret: he still breaks out. At his age. He's probably about forty. It took me an extra half *hour* to disguise a zit he had near his temple. And in the age of HD, every tiny flaw shows up on camera."

News of this flaw gave Eli a very unworthy surge of satisfaction, even though he was certain he probably wouldn't survive HD's scrutiny without a good spackling. "You should get hazard pay for hiding Francone's zits. Wonder where our wine is?"

He lifted his water glass and took a sip.

"I talked to your friend Glory a little today at the Misty Cat. She's nice, isn't she?"

He nearly did a spit take. *"Nice?"*

He didn't think anyone had ever ascribed such a pallid word to Glory before.

"Yeah. I think Franco said he was going out with her tonight. Maybe he was rushing her home just now to get her in the sack. He seems to really be into her."

Eli put his glass down so hard that Bethany jumped and her roll shot out of her hands again.

It landed with a soft thud on his side of the table.

He retrieved it and gently put it on the little plate next to her.

And said nothing.

In a minute Bethany was going to think he was some kind of Neanderthal who had trouble with his motor skills.

Suddenly he couldn't come up with words. Any words. Let alone idle, light, sparkling words. For the life of him he couldn't remember what he'd ever said to the Tiffanys and Brittanys in high school between making out with them in his Fiero.

Probably because there hadn't been much talking.

He remembered a conversation he'd had with Glory once. "Why are flies called flies?" she'd said once. "A lot of things fly. Were they the first things to fly?" He liked how being with her was like roaming a building with infinite corridors and atriums. You never knew where you would wind up.

"I can get more rolls," he said finally. "I have connections."

"We still have plenty," Bethany said with a game smile.

He helped himself to one, drove the knife almost violently down through it to split it.

Maybe it was all metaphorical, and exactly as it should be: Glory racing at high speed in one direction in a movie star's Porsche.

Eli remaining in place, in a restaurant he'd been to a dozen times before. So many times he knew which curtain hanging in which window had a tiny burn hole from some diner's wayward cigarette, back when people actually smoked in restaurants.

The waiter interrupted the silence by bringing over the

wine. And after the sniffing and sipping had taken place, he poured and then vanished.

Eli raised his glass. "To wonderful company."

"To wonderful company." Bethany, sounding relieved, clinked her glass against his, and then sipped and settled it down again.

A little silence fell.

Her long slim fingers absently played with the stem of her glass. She stroked it up and then down. Up and then down.

Maybe doing warm-ups for later.

He was aware, however, that he'd fallen awkwardly— perhaps even darkly—silent again.

It was a physical struggle not to peer out the window in the direction of that Porsche. If he was a cartoon character, his head would transform into a giant magnet and suck the car back down the road.

He smiled at Bethany instead.

"Okay, Eli," Bethany said brightly. "So, I happen to know it's your birthday this week. And we can't let your birthday go by and not acknowledge it at *all*."

He groaned good-naturedly.

She laughed. "I promise I won't ask the waiters to sing." She pushed a little flat square package over to him, tastefully wrapped in brown parchment paper and tied with a wide, sheer orange chiffon ribbon. Minimalist and pretty.

"It's just a silly little thing. And I mainly did it because I like wrapping things."

"It's pretty," he said.

"The gift is actually on the inside," Bethany teased dryly. But as she said it, she fingered the top button on her dress. Whether she knew it or not, it turned her sentence into an innuendo.

She was a nice person, Bethany was. And a big flirt. But he had a feeling that she'd be cool with a fling, or whatever they decided to do.

And it occurred to him that once you really just let go and were halfway on your way to having sex—maybe the clothes were mostly off or on their way there, the bra was unhooked, that sort of things—you could forget nearly anyone or anything.

Problem was, he had a feeling that everything he'd ever felt and never said aloud was too close to the surface, kicked up like some kind of monstrous, spinning dirt devil, bigger by the minute. It had been growing for days now. It was playing havoc with his internal equilibrium.

Something had to give. A few minutes of shattering oblivion might just be the ticket.

"Let's see what's on the inside." He tugged the ribbon open, and slid a finger beneath the tape.

He found a little cardboard box with a lid.

He glanced over at her and she lifted her eyebrows encouragingly.

He sneaked a glance at their outside edges. Not a stray hair there. He'd notice that from now on in every person he met, he was pretty sure, dammit. And yet every little detail about a person told a story, and as a cop, he was sort of glad he knew about eyebrows now.

He pried up the box lid and parted some tastefully beige tissue paper.

He gave a little laugh. "It's . . . I'll be damned!" He lifted out an old forty-five RPM record of Led Zeppelin's "The Immigrant Song."

"Your local music store had it. Do you like it?"

He smiled. "Yeah! Very cool." He turned it over to the flip side. "So thoughtful of you. Thank . . ."

He was suddenly as airless as if he'd been gut-punched.

And as he stared down at the name of that song on the flipside, it was like sunlight blasted through his every cell. Joy and fury and grief and yearning were suddenly one hybrid emotion as he was being dragged backward roughly through time.

He couldn't look up at Bethany. Not yet.

He breathed in.

Breathed out.

He was going to have to finish his sentence.

But he was pretty sure he couldn't finish this date.

He finally lifted his head.

". . . you," he finally managed.

New restaurants in Hellcat Canyon weren't precisely on Glory's radar, since her radar only picked up things she could afford, and eating out wasn't one of those things lately.

Cafe Cinnabar managed to be shiny and cozy and modern. One wall was painted a glossy deep green. Another was a glossy cayenne. Another, butter-yellow. She was certain the food would be farm-to-table and served in little vertical stacks centered on white plates, like framed modern art. It was almost too hip for Hellcat Canyon, but rent in town was cheap and the place was small enough to actually make a go of it. She wished them luck.

Getting here had been fun. It was interesting to see Hellcat Canyon go by in a blur through the window of a Porsche. Kind of like an impressionistic painting of a small town.

"So Glory Hallelujah Greenleaf . . . what made you

decide to go out with me?" Franco asked when they were settled in and the wine had arrived.

"Maybe I've just been mulling pros and cons all this time."

Maybe she was doing it so she wouldn't have to think about Eli and Bethany on their third date.

"You? I have a hunch you would have given me a flat out yes or no from the beginning. Unless you wanted to toy with me a bit. Or there was some other consideration."

"I've been known to toy." Which wasn't a complete lie.

Franco smiled. "Have some more wine."

She'd already downed a half glass with almost unseemly haste. It was fantastic wine, nuanced and expensive, and ought to be savored. But she'd all but belted it back after she'd seen Eli's truck parked outside Cafe Elegante.

Her senior ball date, Mick Macklemore, had taken her to Cafe Elegante for dinner lo these many years ago. There were little white eyelet half-curtains on skinny rods in the windows and cane-backed chairs and votive candles in frosted glass holders. It was romantic and charming and unsurprising and the food was very good. It was where you took dates you wanted to impress. At least in Hellcat Canyon.

After seeing Eli's truck, getting a handle on her mood was going to be like stuffing a porcupine into a burlap sack. A few barbs were bound to escape, and Franco was sitting in their path.

"I don't get any looser when I'm drunk," she warned Franco. "In fact, I've been known to throw things."

"I'll just bet you do," he said with relish.

"How did you hear about this place?" Glory twisted slightly in her chair to look around at the tasteful little original paintings on the butter-yellow wall. They were all for sale.

"I have people who find things out for me." He waved a hand airily. "It opened not too long ago. And it met your criteria."

Which was "nothing fancy, some place where I can wear jeans."

It was tremendously odd to recite *criteria* to a gorgeous, famous man. And then have him do her bidding.

A little silence fell. She twisted her wineglass in her fingers.

"Anyone ever tell you that you're beautiful?" Franco said.

She stared at him. "Seriously?" she said finally.

"Well, yeah."

"Of course. C'mon, Hollywood, I'm expecting better patter from you."

He grinned. "Okay. Beautiful and a handful?"

"I gave up a whole night of watching repeats of *Wheel of Fortune* with my mom for this," she teased, but she was aware her teasing was getting edgy.

She imagined Eli pulling out a chair for Bethany. Maybe putting his hand on the middle of her back in a gentlemanly way. Smiling in that way he did when he was really listening, so that you knew he actually cared what you were saying.

"You could watch repeats of *Blood Brothers* instead. I get a nice little check every time you do."

"I certainly could, except it's on local television stations earlier in the day so the retired ladies at Heavenly Shores can watch it."

He gave a startled laugh. "Ouch."

She sighed, ashamed of herself. "I'm sorry, Franco. That was ungracious. I might be a little nervous and it just comes out that way. I'll try to be nicer."

This was true, but Franco didn't have much to do with her nerves, or that hollowed out feeling in her gut. Like her stomach had taken an elevator down two floors below the earth's surface.

"I like surprises, Glory Hallelujah Greenleaf. So don't apologize. Bring it on."

"So what's *your* criteria for a date, Franco? Something pretty to look at across a table while you enjoy a good meal?"

"Of course. Isn't that everybody's?"

She gave a short laugh. "But what do you usually like to talk about on dates?"

"Well, myself, mostly," he said, with self-deprecating irony.

She smiled. "But don't you get bored staring at pretty things who just listen to you talk about yourself?" She was genuinely curious. "Couldn't you just get a mirror, like a parakeet?"

Franco's eyes widened, startled. He looked undecided as to whether to laugh or scowl at this.

His expression finally settled into something like reluctant amusement. Maybe even admiration.

"I'll admit it's lost some of its shine, finally. And yet it was once so reliably pleasant."

"Hard to know what to do next, isn't it, when the things that used to work for you don't work anymore."

"Yep," he said. "Usually I get over those kinds of humps by buying another Porsche," he said blithely. "Hey, did you know I went to Harvard?"

She furrowed her brow. "No. I'm also not quite sure what to do with this information."

He smiled at that, too. As if she kept presenting him with little surprises. "I'm bragging, I guess. Because I want you to think I'm smart, because I think you probably are."

"Soooo . . . if I'm understanding this correctly, your implication is that college is where you go to get smart? Or . . . wait! Is college where they hand out talent? Kinda like the Tin Man getting a heart from the Wizard?"

He leaned back in his chair and stared at her. "Damn, woman. You are *hard* on me. Okay, when you put it that way, no. I guess not."

"If you want me to think you're smart, Franco, just say smart, insightful things," she said relentlessly. "Your daddy pull some strings to get you into Harvard?"

He shook his head. "Man, you do have my number. I had to get passing grades, though. And I had to work for the roles I got. I'm not a *complete* slacker."

"Ohhh, passing grades," she teased. "Be still my heart."

He grinned. "What did *your* report cards look like?"

"Well, I've never gone to college. But my last report card was 'A,' 'B,' 'A–,' 'A,' 'D,' 'C.' I wrote a song using just those chords. D minor, of course, because the D was a bummer. That was for P.E. I hated those polyester shorts we had to wear because they itched and made me sweat, and wearing a uniform always makes me kind of uneasy. I kept getting docked points for 'forgetting' . . ." She put that in air quotes. " . . . to bring them."

Franco smiled all the way through this. "You're not one of those people who think it's more virtuous to struggle for success, are you? That you have to do penance in order to deserve it?"

"No," she said vehemently. "There's no virtue in struggle, believe me. I think there's virtue in working toward a goal, sure. You just have to play the hand you're dealt the best you can."

"Completely agree. It's not like my picnic has been completely ant-free, you know. I never did win an Emmy."

Boy. Some people's problems.

Then again, it was a problem she hoped to have one day—worrying about whether she was going to win that Grammy. And she could certainly sympathize with wanting what she didn't currently have.

"The Emmy could still happen, right, for your role in *The Rush*? Or some other show?"

"Sure. But J.T. McCord got one and I didn't. I can't turn back time and get it before he did."

Men.

"Well, tenacity is sexy."

"*Tenacity* is a pretty good word for someone who never went to college."

"What makes you think there's a relationship between college and vocabulary? Maybe I just read a lot."

"Yeah? So do I, as it so happens. Can't really read you, though."

That was an interesting observation. She studied him with a faint smile.

He smiled back at her. He seemed to have realized he'd finally said something that officially intrigued her. "Did you know I'm pretty good friends with Wyatt Congdon?"

Glory's lungs seized up.

She lowered her wineglass carefully.

"Was . . . *that* a smart, insightful thing to say?" Franco said mildly.

She couldn't speak yet. She surreptitiously released a shuddering breath.

"You do know who Wyatt Congdon is," he pressed.

"Of course. If you're a musician, you know who Wyatt Congdon is," she said quietly. "Come on."

"He's actually my godfather. He's got an estate in Napa. Beautiful . . . you should see it. Lawns like velvet carpets. Vineyards. Soft rolling hills. Spectacular sunsets, just unreal. Hot tubs and saunas. He's flying up to it next week from Los Angeles. He'll be there off and on through Thanksgiving, give or take a few meetings in New York."

Kismet. Maybe it *was* a thing. Maybe this was why Franco Francone had blown into her life. Shouldn't she feel more elated, though?

"Napa's just a couple of hours away," she said faintly.

"Yeah. He invited me to go up there the week before Thanksgiving. And he said to bring anyone I might want to bring."

She was pretty sure she knew where this was going.

"I'd like you to come with me. If you want to," he added.

Yep. And there it was.

A rather loud silence ensued.

"That's a very kind invitation," she said as formally as someone accepting the collection plate at church.

"I expect you'll want some time to mull," he teased.

"If that's all right with you."

The waitress brought over a charming appetizer, unrecognizable as food, frilled with some sort of green vegetable, floating in a shallow pool of some artfully scribbled dark sauce.

It was delicious and she didn't let on that she didn't quite know what it was as she ate it.

"So . . . you know I think you're hot, Glory," Franco said after a moment, putting his fork down. "And I think you're smart in an original way, and original in a smart way. And I'm a little in awe of people who have talents that I don't have, especially ones that can make me forget where I am on the planet for a moment. Because when you have enough money to get nearly anything you want, that kind of experience is hard to come by."

A silence beat by.

This didn't feel like conversation. It felt like negotiation. Or persuasion.

"I'm leaving this quiet space so you can now lavish *me* with compliments, if you so desire," he said, lightly.

"You ever been in love?" she said suddenly.

"Whoa." She couldn't tell whether she'd shocked him or impressed him with that question.

She half expected his head to start swiveling for the exits.

"C'mon. Don't be a chicken. Consider it an essay question. You keep saying *words*—names, and places and so forth—but it doesn't tell me much about what you actually *think*."

Franco laid his hands on the tablecloth. She suspected she was making him uncomfortable but that he didn't precisely hate it. "They don't like us to think in Hollywood," he joked.

"I asked you that because sometimes if you startle people they'll say the truth before they get around to . . ."

"Obfuscating?"

"Why, yes. Excellent word for an actor, Hollywood."

"Good old-fashioned psychology. That tactic. Obfuscating."

"Is it?"

So, he either didn't know how to answer the question she'd asked. Or he didn't want to.

Eli never would have dodged that question. Even if it scared him. He was a thinker. He liked a challenge. And he didn't play games.

Mostly she knew that if *she* asked the question, he would try to answer it.

Thing was . . . she'd never have the courage to outright ask him. Because his answer to that question was the only one that mattered.

She wondered if Bethany had given him his birthday present yet.

It was so strange to sit here, suffering because he was on a date, while at the same time hoping he was doing okay with the small talk and wasn't uncomfortable because she knew how he sometimes suffered over stuff like that.

"I know *you* have," Franco said after a moment. He sounded hesitant. Faintly resentful, but a little curious, too.

"I've what?" she said, almost forgetting the thread for the moment.

"Been in love."

She was startled. "How do you know?"

"I actually *listened* to your songs."

"Ah."

Now, *that* was a smart and insightful thing to say. It disarmed her and shut her up.

"Don't need to be in love to enjoy having sex," Franco pointed out, quite accurately, after a moment of her being quiet.

"True enough."

"I'm *really* good at it." But he was teasing.

"All the practice, I bet, with all those pretty things."

The corner of his mouth quirked, and he shrugged a shoulder. "Good way to get your mind off something or . . . someone," he expounded. "Sex."

"Like the fact that J.T. won an Emmy before you did?"

He gave a short, pained laugh. "Ah, look. Our entrees are here."

CHAPTER 16

Franco had dropped her off at about nine p.m., kissed her chastely (on the cheek she turned to him as if she was some kind of nun, which might mark the first occasion Mrs. Binkley, who was peering through her curtains, had seen a Greenleaf chastely kiss anyone, let alone in a Porsche), and he told her to meet him at nine in the morning at Cafe Cinnabar on Friday if she wanted to go to Wyatt Congdon's Napa Estate that weekend.

And to pack light.

The implication being that clothes would be pretty superfluous.

And that the weekend would be anything other than chaste.

She hadn't told anyone she'd gone out with Franco. She particularly hadn't wanted to get her mom's hope up about Glory being snatched up by a movie star just like Britt Langley.

She mulled over the notion of Kismet the next day during the morning shift as she delivered wrong orders to the wrong tables 50 percent of the time, probably because the decision she faced occupied about 50 percent of her brain. Things certainly seemed to be going her way (if not Giorgio's, or her bosses' ways, at least not today) with the success of The Baby Owls concert and the two hundred bucks and her burgeoning Facebook page and the famous actor waving Wyatt Congdon and his estate at her. *Estate.* What on earth made something an "estate?" Was there a castle? She should look that up.

But she'd always imagined that Kismet would feel more like, say, The Moody Blues' "Nights in White Satin" sounded. Destined and seductive and easy and *right*, as though a path was just unfurling a bit at a time right in front of her.

Instead a sense of tense anticipation remained. Of something unfinished.

She found herself wondering about Eli's Kismet.

And what he'd done when he'd opened that birthday gift from Bethany. If he'd shown her gratitude, third-date style.

She pocketed her tips, grateful that her customers had bothered to leave them, and headed home from work on foot, welcoming the steep, sinewy walk up Main Street, the greetings from various animals (Peace and Love the cat, and Hamburger, Lloyd Sunnergren's big hairy dog), and the waves through windows, and even as she loved it she knew she could leave it behind in a heartbeat in order to be who she was.

And she headed out on that familiar route, up the hill, up and up, across the pasture, through the fence, past the tree—

She leaped backward and clapped her hand over her heart.

Eli was leaning against the pasture rail. Still as a tree.

In jeans and an old pale blue t-shirt.

She couldn't get a word out for quite a few seconds.

He didn't say a thing. The sun struck what looked like silver sparks from his eyes.

"Jesus, Eli, you nearly scared the *life* out of me."

He didn't answer her. Just studied her thoughtfully.

And then he moved. Subtly.

Time seemed to elongate strangely as he moved toward her. Slow, measured, stalking steps. Someone, perhaps, preparing for battle.

And then she saw what was in his hand.

Her heartbeat kicked up a notch.

Yep. Bethany had given him the present.

He stopped about three feet in front of her. Looked at her, as if for the first, maybe the last, time.

"What is this, Glory?" His voice was strange. Taut and abstracted. The question sounded less like a question than a warning.

"Um . . . It . . . it looks like an old forty-five record." Her voice a little gravelly.

He took another step toward her. "But what *is* it?"

She took a step backward.

Putting the tree behind her. Which might have been unwise. Because that gave her nowhere else to go. And it might have been their castle and their fort when they were younger, but it sure wasn't going to help her now.

"It's a record. Eli, I'm not sure what you—"

"What. Does it. Mean?" He laid those words down like bricks. The tone suggested she had until the count of three to tell him.

She'd only half understood before why she'd told Bethany to buy him that record. She had a hunch that it would be like a little grenade thrown into their date. That it would tear his walls down.

But she was suddenly scared to death of what she'd done. Because she hadn't considered that by tearing his walls down, hers would come down, too, and it was going to hurt like a motherfucker, and now she was panicking.

"I don't know what you want me to say, Eli. It's a rec—"

And the words rushed out of him.

"My seventeenth birthday. You were wearing a denim skirt and a white top with little flowers on it, and you'd made a barrette out of three old guitar picks and you'd clipped it right here." He pointed to his temple. "The sun was just going down, and your hair was lit from behind, and it almost looked like you were wearing a sort of . . . of . . . crown of coals."

His words were almost breathless, shaped in ache and fury. Like he'd held them in forever.

She was stunned. "Eli . . ."

"You sang *this* song." He held it up, accusingly, like it was something she'd stolen. "This song. 'Hey Hey What Can I Do.' In front of a bunch of kids who were older than you. You sang the *hell* out of my favorite song in the world. And it was the funniest, most beautiful, bravest, most *badass* thing and it was almost more than I could do to listen to it, because I wanted to, like, *wear* that song. I stood there thinking . . . does she know? Does she know she's turning her real self inside out for the world to see? Does she know how amazing she is? I almost wanted to cover you up, because it was so raw and so *you*, and I know how deep it goes when you *feel* things, Glory, and I never want anyone to hurt you, then or now. So I stood there thinking all of this. And it turned me inside out, too. I was almost . . . *angry*. Because back then, I liked to think I was tough and nothing could shake me, but it turns out your voice finds all those sore, scared places inside me and reminds me that I'm only human after all. That all I've done is hidden them, even from myself. But you managed to make even those things, the things that hurt, beautiful. And I . . ."

He stopped abruptly. His breath was coming in a raw rush now.

Her heart was jackhammering. She was awestruck. And thrilled. And terrified. Because she knew she was in the presence of a profound beginning or a bad ending. Maybe both.

"And then I . . ." he tried again.

He caught himself.

He didn't seem to want to commit to finishing that sentence.

She was motionless.

A breeze whipped a strand of her hair across her face and she left it. She wanted those words, those beautiful, terrifying words, possibly the most words she'd ever heard him say in a row, maybe, to ring by themselves.

She'd set this in motion. And all at once she wasn't certain she had the courage to see it through, even though she liked to think of herself as a badass.

"So stop lying, Glory. Just . . . stop it." He sounded end-of-his-rope weary. His voice cracked and maddened. "I know you must have told Bethany to buy this for me when she asked for suggestions. I think you *know* what this means to me. I think I know what it means to you. And I think I know why you did it. But I need you to tell me."

Birds sang a lovely liquid melody as they stood there, feet apart, and she didn't say a word.

They both just breathed. She wasn't sure what to say.

She was, in fact, afraid to tell him the truth. She wanted to say something lyrical, something mature.

Instead out came the thing that had tortured her.

"Did you sleep with her?"

"NO I DIDN'T SLEEP WITH HER."

Her hair nearly blew back with the force of his emotion. He sounded both tortured and amused and blackly furious.

He swept a hand back over his own head. Forgetting his hair was too short for that gesture to be satisfying anymore.

And their eyes locked.

"I was going to," he added cruelly, evenly. "I wanted to. I wanted to want to."

He went silent again.

They were still a peculiar distance apart. As if they were both open flames.

"What about Francone? You sleep with him? I bet he shouts his own name when he comes."

She flinched. Despite herself, she kind of liked to hear Eli talk dirty.

She'd revealed her hand. It was her turn to demand answers. "Why are you such a *jerk* about him, Eli? I've never seen you like this. Everybody speeds sometimes. He's a perfectly nice guy who happens to have a glamorous job. A perfectly nice, absolutely gorgeous guy with endless supplies of money who actually asked me to go to Napa with him to meet Wyatt Congdon."

His head jerked back as if she'd shoved a torch into his face.

"Yeah, that's right," she repeated slowly. "*That* Wyatt 'King' Congdon."

Eli was white about the mouth. He knew exactly who

Wyatt Congdon was. Glory had mentioned him once or twice or a hundred times over the decades.

"I'm a jerk about him," he said slowly, almost abstract-edly as if he could hardly believe he needed to explain it, "because I think you think you might decide he's good enough for you. Just because of who he is. And that's a guy who would *never* be able to appreciate how rare you are in a million years. Or how to *be there*. No matter what he says. He doesn't know how. It's . . . just not how he's made. But if that's who you want to be . . ."

A million conflicting emotions knotted her throat.

"You sure it's not because you think he can give me something you can't, Eli?" she said softly.

He flinched. That was a bull's-eye. He recovered pretty quickly.

"What's that, Glory? A communicable disease?"

"You'd have to get laid to get one of those in the first place," she shot back.

Damned if Eli didn't smile faintly. Crap! She'd forgotten he was the law, after all, and good at getting confessions. She'd also just as good as admitted she hadn't slept with Franco Francone. He'd probably led her right into that confession.

No one had ever known her like he had.

They didn't talk for a moment. The first initial burst of fury was spent.

And all the while a bird sang its fool head off.

"Okay," he said. Quietly. With great finality. As if he'd finally run this mess through the powerfully efficient fil-ters of his mind. "I think we're talking about two things. So let's talk about them. Let's finally fucking talk about it. You start."

She was supposed to be the eloquent one. But suddenly

tears flooded her eyes. And the first words out of her mouth were "I hate you."

He gave a short humorless laugh. "That's one way to start."

Her furious tears blurred him and she swiped them away violently and sniffed. But they kept coming.

He didn't move. He gave her nothing. He just waited.

And waited.

For the dam to break. Because he knew it was about to.

And then it did. And the words were a furious, raw torrent that nearly shredded her throat.

"It was *Jonah*, Eli. Jonah. I saw his face when he realized what was about to happen to him. When he saw that it was you. And then when he got up and tried to talk to you . . . you were his friend, his best friend, and he never could hide his feelings, you know? You fucking tackled him, because you know how to do *that* so well, tackled him hard. And then sort of grabbed him and flipped him around like he was *nothing*. And yanked his arms behind him and I could *see* that it hurt him and you clamped the cuffs on him. Like he was some *animal*. Like he was just some *scum*. Like you'd never hung out in the driveway with both of your heads under the hood of your Fiero, or played Horse on the playground until the sun went down and our moms had to holler themselves hoarse over and over at us to come home, or laid out on the rocks in the sun after we swam and talked about how much we hated 'Wind Beneath My Wings' and how we all wanted at least three kids. He can't *have* any of that stuff now. You marched him out of there like he was a fucking *trophy*."

Eli was white now. "I cuffed him because he is a criminal." His voice was hoarse and furious.

"He was your *best friend*."

"EXACTLY!"

He bellowed it. She was surprised his frustrated anguish didn't dislodge the squirrels from the trees and send them crashing down.

She didn't flinch.

She did blink.

It occurred to her she'd *never* seen Eli this angry. And that maybe she should be worried.

But she was falling apart, messily, endlessly, recklessly. She couldn't seem to care. Her voice was a broken thing. "It's just . . . I love him, Eli. And my family is all I've *got*, Eli."

He closed his eyes and his head went back. He shook his head slowly in an agony of disbelief.

"Glory . . . sweetheart . . . that's not true. Good God, you idiot . . . That's *never* been true."

He startled her by hooking his forefingers into her belt loops and pulling her flush against his body. As if he wanted to literally impress something upon her. As if he could transfer all his strength and certainty to her. His mouth was inches from hers.

"Listen to me. What Jonah did? He might as well have said straight to my face, 'Eli, I think your whole life is a joke. Your father's death. Everything you stand for and live for. A joke.' He knew how I felt about my dad. He knew how hard I worked to be what I am now. He knew what I gave up to do it. But he decided to get involved with that meth ring anyway, Glory. He spit right on everything I am. Call it desperate, call it lazy, call it Jonah. I guess I still love him like a brother, but you just don't *do* that to people you love. And you know what I can't forgive him for? He did it to you, too. *He did it to you.* It's okay for you to be furious at me, Glory, because maybe I deserve some of that. But he did it to you. And that . . . that about killed me."

He'd ripped away one layer of defense, and she saw it: he was right. And now that she was holding on to Eli, or he was holding on to her, it finally seemed safe to turn and look head-on into that dark drop that had been dogging her for ages now. But it wasn't as dark anymore. Eli had gone and blasted the light right into it.

And she knew what to call all those emotions writhing together there: staggering hurt. Fury. Shame. Betrayal. Grief. All of a big, black, entangled, pulsing piece. And it wasn't just for herself or her family or Jonah, who had unthinkably betrayed her. But for Eli. Who'd been forced to break his own heart and hers by arresting his best friend.

It was just so much easier to blame Eli. To put her burdens on the strongest person she knew because he could bear it, even as he was bearing it now. To avoid her own pain by avoiding him.

"Oh, Eli. I know he did. I'm sorry. I know. I do know."

He closed his eyes briefly and nodded, as if this was everything he'd so long wanted to hear. She could feel some of his tension leave his body. But he wasn't done.

"And you want to know what still sometimes keeps me up at night, Glory? You're right. I humiliated him. I *did* want to humiliate him. I wanted to shame him but good. I was so furious and hurt, there were nights it sometimes felt I couldn't live with what I'd done. But he did what he did, and my job is what it is. And I would *do it again*. My whole world came down, too. I wanted him to feel *every* moment of shame for that."

She just let the tears fall. Eli blurred in her vision.

They were so close she could feel his every breath swaying against her chest.

"Do *you* think I'm a joke, Glory?" he said tautly, finally. Softly.

She took in a shuddering breath.

"No, Eli. Never." Her voice cracked. "Never."

Her hand went up to touch his cheek. To apologize, to soothe. She thought better of it. Not sure he'd welcome it.

He inhaled at length, and then let it out slowly, like a man taking his first free breath in months.

And then he freed one hand from her belt loop and tenderly drew a fingertip beneath her eyes. First one, then the other.

His fingertip came away shining with her tears.

"So if you think it didn't *kill* me, too, well, you're wrong." His voice broke. "I know you kept Jonah in your blind spot because you didn't want to feel that kind of hurt. Here's what I know: you're equal to it. You're equal to anything you want to take on. Whether it's big, big hurt, or the big, big success you're meant for. Remember how much you felt watching the tigers pacing back and forth in their cage that day at the zoo? *That's* what it's like for me to watch you stay here in Hellcat Canyon. Like you said that day, it's not right. It's just not right. I'm not Francone. I'm not the person with the golden ticket out of here. You need to figure that out for yourself. But don't let Jonah or *anyone* stop you, Glory."

She knew by "anyone" he was talking about himself.

She tipped her forehead against his chest and heaved a sigh.

His heart thumped against her forehead. Her favorite rhythm in the world.

And then she tipped her head back and looked up at him, and his eyes were a little wet, too.

She tentatively, softly, touched a finger to his mouth, softly traced it. She was aware only then of how well she knew the shape of it, how she could have drawn it with her eyes closed.

"You're a big one for speeches, Eli," she murmured. "But that's what you're all about, isn't it? Speeches."

She knew he knew why she said it. It gave both of them the excuse they wanted.

His mouth came down hard over hers.

She met that kiss with all the fire and fury in her.

It began as a point to be made. A battle and release. Almost a punishment.

And they took it deep, fast. They each had a little quiver full of erotic tricks they knew to drive each other to that precarious edge of control. But as his hands threaded through her hair, she tipped her head back into the cradle of them, that kiss was searching, tender, and then carnal as hell, driven by what felt like eons of thwarted desire finally unleashed, and she felt herself dissolving into smoke. In an instant, she was his in any way he wanted her.

Lust ripped control right out of their grasp. His mouth never left hers as he reached for her zipper and yanked it down, and she got hold of the top button of his jeans and all but tore at them, and all the rest of his buttons slid cooperatively open.

Practical blue boxers were tented by a huge hard cock and she slid her hands inside, dragged them over the hot, pulsing length.

He hissed an oath of pleasure.

He pulled her jeans down a little, to her hips, and with

nearly brutal and unbearably delicious efficiency slid his hand down the front of them, and she gasped, arching into his touch.

In a bit of deftly executed sexual jujitsu he swiped another hand swiftly down her front and click! Her bra popped open. He tugged her shirt from her jeans and slipped his hands down the back, scooping her up to press against his hard cock, his mouth against her throat, his hips moving to grind against her in torturously slow, deliberate exquisite rhythm, as the kiss grew wild and searching, a clash of teeth, the twining of tongues. He moaned her name.

It became purposeful as she moved with him, seeking her own pleasure. Rocking and grinding. It hurt a little, but it was exquisite. She ducked her head against his throat, and reached for the waistband on his boxers to tug them all the way down . . . but she hesitated.

And he covered her hand with his.

And then . . . they both went still. Utterly, carefully, still.

She wasn't sure what had happened, but some well of pure sense she didn't know she possessed had risen up and stopped her.

She could still feel the sway of his breath against her body.

"*Now* do you understand what we're playing with here?" He whispered this close to her lips. It was almost an apology.

"Yep," she said dryly. Her voice was a thread. "It's all pretty clear."

He exhaled.

She looked up at him. She thought she would never

forget his expression for as long as she lived: the tenderness and ferocity and pride, the ache. He smoothed a hair that had lashed itself across her lips behind her ear.

"So no more games," he said softly. "When you're certain, when you really know who and what you want, come to me. And ask for it. Ask for *me*. In a real and true way. Not because you're pissed off or hurt or sad or horny or lonely. But just. Because. It's me. And, Glory . . . it'll be the best thing that ever happens to you." His mouth tipped at the corner in a cocky smile.

"Big talk, Eli."

She was half teasing. Half broken.

"You think I'm lying?" He whispered right into her ear and then touched his tongue there again.

She didn't say a word. She shivered from the pleasure rippling through her, and her body protested at the sheer lunacy of letting this pleasure machine named Eli get away.

"Look in my eyes, Glory. Do you think I ever lie about anything?"

She looked into his eyes. "Nope," she said, quite sincerely.

Reluctantly, slowly, simultaneously, as if in some tacit agreement, they took their hands from each other's bodies; they stepped back and put distance between them.

The world seemed strange. Her head was still spinning. She felt like an astronaut rudely ejected from her shuttle while she was up in space.

He buttoned his jeans.

Funny how watching him get dressed in some ways felt more intimate than sliding her hands into his underwear.

She re-arranged her own wanton disarray. Dragged her

fingers through her hair in a probably futile attempt to straighten it.

He drew in a long breath, and it was like he was drinking in the sight of her.

"Just . . . be sure, Glory."

She knew he meant for his sake and for hers.

He didn't kiss her good-bye. He did pause to pick up the forty-five single of "Hey Hey What Can I Do," which he'd dropped.

It was unscathed.

"I'll be keeping this," he said.

He turned around and walked away, off toward the home he'd lived in for as long as she could remember.

And suddenly it was like every memory she'd ever had of Eli, at every age, in every season, walking away was superimposed on that big man walking away from her now.

She put her hands up to her hot face. Her body was ringing like a suspended fourth chord, but her whole soul felt scraped raw and ached like an open wound.

A cleansed wound, maybe.

But it still hurt like hell.

She sank into a crouch and pretty soon she was weeping again, for the enormity of everything, for the beauty of it, for her fear of the unknown, and for the big decision she'd have to make on her own. Without Eli or anyone.

One way or the other, it looked like she was going to lose something.

And finally she swiped at her eyes. And sighed. Boy, she was going to look like hell when she got home.

Finally she stood, exhausted as if she'd run the length of Hellcat Canyon and back.

And perhaps naturally, she began singing softly to herself. A sort of stop-start near waltz of a melody. The song of someone gasping for breath. Maybe out of fury. Maybe because he'd exhausted himself with lovemaking.

Too much crying today
Too much hurt
Too much truth
Too much dirt

Too much love
Too much fury
Too many things
We try to bury

It was raw, and had beauty and ache and promise, and it needed work. Like everything else in her life.

CHAPTER 17

When she got home, that big blue Lexus she'd seen outside of the Misty Cat was parked in front of their little house. The one the tan Clint Eastwood-y older guy had climbed into. It was looked wildly out of context against the untamed shrubbery, and it was almost the width of their house.

She stared. Then squeezed her eyes closed and opened them again.

Nope, still there.

Mrs. Binkley was in her garden, pretending to dead-head some flowers but in truth enjoying her usual front-row view of the Greenleaf drama.

"I think your mama has taken to entertaining gentleman callers. Times being what they are for you Greenleafs."

"Bite me, Mrs. Binkley," Glory said almost ritualistically. With the solemn reflexiveness of a churchgoer uttering "And also with you."

"He's been there for *hours*," Mrs. Binkley added, standing on her toes expressly to see Glory's expression when she told her this.

Shit shit *shit*.

She didn't even bother to try to hide her angst over this news.

Glory hovered indecisively on the porch.

First she checked her own reflection in the sideview mirror of the Lexus, just to see if she looked as though she'd been ravished in the woods and then wept for a half hour.

And that was exactly what she looked like.

She was altogether rather pink, a bit chafed from wild kissing, and her hair was just a degree more subdued than Medusa's. Her eyes were pink, too. That she could at least blame on allergies.

So she was forced to some grooming in the sideview mirror while Mrs. Binkley watched, evilly amused.

Finally she put her hand on the knob of their house gingerly, as though it was suddenly electrified.

She had an entirely heretical thought: What if Mrs. Binkley was actually *right*? And her mother was making a little money on the side?

There was no way. There was just no way. She knew her mother too well.

And then . . . she heard her mother laugh, a big, delighted, genuine laugh.

The rumble of an amused masculine voice rushed alongside it.

Glory went still.

She knew her mother's social laugh from her real one.

This was the real one. A little stab of happiness stole her breath.

She was realizing she hadn't heard her mother laugh quite like that in a long time.

She went toward it almost reflexively, as if she were going toward the light, and turned the knob before she knew it.

Her mom was sitting on the sofa, and the Lexus guy was sitting across from her in the armchair.

"Glory, honey! Come on in and sit down and meet my old friend Gary Shaw. He went to school with your uncle Bill. Turns out we know practically all the same people. I remember him coming into the supermarket before I met your daddy. He was driving by the house because he buys up foreclosed properties and I was out in the yard, and he recognized me, and before you know it . . ."

She and Gary Shaw laughed together giddily, even though this wasn't exactly funny. Especially the bit about foreclosed properties.

"Maybe I should have told you, Charlie. I confess I met your daughter a few days back down at the Misty Cat. I just got so caught up in catching up with you, it didn't come up."

Their faces were lit up in that way people have when they've been laughing and talking for hours. They were in a little haze of happiness and peace, and the sunlight through the windows cast them in a little amber glow.

They were each holding a little highball glass tinkling with ice.

Her mom hadn't gotten those glasses down, or poured any celebratory booze in the house, in God knows how long. Booze cost money, and her mom hid it well in case John-Mark had any ideas about helping himself to it.

Glory sat down gingerly on the edge of the armchair.

Unwilling to commit to whatever this scenario was just yet.

Her mother laughed. "Oh, honey. It's okay. Don't look so shell-shocked. Turns out Britt Langley has done favors for us both. She resigned her job showing properties for Gary because she's going to draw cartoons from home, or something like that, and Gary thinks I'm just the person to fill her shoes. It'll be fun to have a job! And he's interested in buying the house from the bank and renting it back to us."

"Sure," Glory said cautiously, ironically, after a moment. "Jobs are fun."

She probably shouldn't have sounded so incredulous.

It was just that this was so out of the *blue*. This sudden lifting of a terrible burden from all of them. It would take some getting used to walking without it. Maybe an hour or two.

"Job doesn't pay much," Gary said cheerfully. "And I call at unreasonable hours. Just ask Britt."

Glory sat motionless in absolute bemusement.

She knew the difference between her mother trying to charm someone and her mother genuinely enjoying herself. She understood all at once that she hadn't seen the second in ages.

She was radiant. She was lovely.

And Glory felt unaccountably selfish for not noticing that her mom had been suffering in grace.

And as for Gary Shaw, sitting in that old worn brown-and-yellow print armchair, well, he looked as though he'd come home.

Glory ended up taking her tiger to bed with her that night, like a needy toddler. A full moon was making its presence known, and it lit part of her ceiling, which she watched as if it were an old familiar movie. And in some ways it was.

A castle. A bearded wizard blowing bubbles. A monster pushing a grocery cart. That big old elm tree surrounded by the worn white pasture fence. The face of a lion. A treble clef. A plate full of nachos. Glory had picked out all of these things in the stucco pattern of her ceiling at night since she was a little girl. When she lay still, when the light was right, she could find them all again.

Tonight, she wished the ceiling was an oracle. Maybe if she peered hard enough, her future would emerge from the pattern. She'd see future Glory, stepping into a limousine, waving at adoring fans as she swept into the Grammy Awards. Or future Glory, playing an open mic night to an audience full of hecklers on her fiftieth birthday, simply because she hadn't taken that one chance, that one, sudden, surreal opportunity, to go with *the* Franco Francone to meet *the* Wyatt "King" Congdon.

And in all likelihood sleep with *the* Franco Francone.

Judging from the internet search she'd done, approximately a gajillion women would be happy to do just that for no reason other than, for crying out loud, because just look at the guy.

She finally sighed gustily and threw off her covers and slid out of bed, and then, just to give herself something to do, she picked up her tiger and put him next to her African Violet so he could have a little taste of the jungle.

She snorted at herself. And she sat back on her bed and looked at her tiger.

Gary Shaw had taken her mom out to dinner at the

fancy French place in Black Oak. And she'd heard her mom come home a little tipsy a few hours ago, and she'd sung.

Out loud.

For the first time Glory could remember.

She sang all around the house, that damn song by The Baby Owls. Really got into it.

And for the first time ever Glory thought maybe some of the music in her must have come from her mom. Her voice was pretty and expressive and joyous. Her mom's gift, Glory realized, was to love and be loved, and she was happiest when she was in a relationship.

And as Glory sat there staring at her old tiger in the moonlight, she all at once understood why she'd never heard her mom sing around the house before. Because like a bird with a blanket thrown over its cage, her mom hadn't seen the point in it.

And from there, the realizations came in a cascade.

Glory understood that she was, in fact, despite ongoing appearances to the contrary, inherently lucky. *Really* lucky.

Because she'd seen examples of big, big real love her whole life. She'd seen the before and after of it. How it felt to live with it, and how life looked and felt when suddenly, in a heartbeat or a gunshot, it was gone.

She was lucky she'd seen her mom talking to Gary Shaw today and to suddenly realize that even while her mother had managed all these years without her dad, Hank Greenleaf, and even though she'd taken a chance at happiness with two other men since him, the whole time a big part of her had remained unlit, like the dark side of the Moon.

Who knew someone like Gary Shaw could walk in and change everything? But he had.

She was even lucky to know how Eli's shoulders felt shuddering beneath her arm on the day of his dad's funeral.

And how his mother's haunted face had looked that night at the bonfire.

And to see Jonah facedown in handcuffs.

And to feel Jonah gone out of their lives.

All the laughter. And fights. And summer days and summer nights.

All of those things had taught her about love. And how being loved like that, being part of a big panorama of love like that, that was the reason she'd ever felt free to pick up a guitar and write her songs and be exactly who she was.

Above all, she was lucky a certain bullheaded man would always, always do the right thing by her, no matter the cost to him. Because instead of grabbing her by the belt loops and pulling her back and banging her deliciously senseless in the woods, which is what she wanted just about more than anything and would probably have made her his slave, he'd let her go so she could make a decision that could very well break his heart all over again.

She doubted Eli was sleeping tonight.

She was pretty sure Franco Francone, however, was sleeping like a baby.

She smiled, at peace.

When she thought of her whole life like this—as an improbable, ceaseless cavalcade of blessings, not as something that pivoted on a single dire choice to sleep with a hot actor or not, she knew what to do.

She got back into bed and slept hard after that.

Franco sauntered into Cafe Cinnabar ten minutes after she'd arrived and slid into the chair across from her.

She'd been nursing an excellent cup of coffee and enjoying being entirely alone in a newish place.

"I don't see any luggage, Glory," he said by way of greeting. "Unless all you've got in that purse is a bikini and some lip balm. In which case, congratulations. You've nailed precisely the dress code."

Glory smiled tautly. And said nothing. Yet.

Her heartbeat had started to ratchet up.

"Heated pool. Heated hot tub. Heated *everything*," he expounded. "You can fashion a sarong out of a satin sheet when we go down to dinner."

She still didn't speak.

"I bet you rock a bikini."

"I do," she said sadly, finally. "I really do."

Once she said the words she couldn't unsay them. And part of her was floating over her body, observing the surreality of the moment. Because a lot of people, 90 percent of them women, would think she was out of her mind.

"I can't go."

He leaned back in his chair slowly.

A little silence fell.

"Do . . . you have to work?" He was clearly pretty puzzled. "You can't get off work?"

"No. That's not it."

There was a little silence as he studied her. She saw it plain as day when she saw the realization strike.

"It's the deputy. That fucking deputy," he said with a sort of grim, ironic astonishment.

"Funny. That's kind of how I think of him, too."

He leaned back in his chair hard again. And stared at her incredulously.

And then the amazement evolved into something like patience. As if he was about to school her.

"Glory . . . maybe you haven't figured this out yet, because you've been here in this small town, there's always going to be some guy. For a woman like you? Always. But there's not always going to be a chance to meet Wyatt Congdon. You can labor in a charming backwater for the rest of your life never really getting anywhere or anything apart from a few cheers from a few drunks, or you can meet Congdon and rise into the stratosphere like . . ." He snapped his fingers.

"'Wyatt Congdon,'" she repeated slowly. "See, you're just saying words again now, Franco."

His face flared with astonishment. "Two words that can change your life *forever*."

Glory was about to school *him*.

"Here's the thing about the guy in question. He would never hold something I want more than anything in the world over me to get something *he* wanted. Because that would make a whore of both of us. He wants me for *me*. He wants me to want him for *him*. And ironically enough, it's not sexy to feel like a whore."

Franco's head went back sharply, as surely as if she'd shoved an epee at him. *En garde.*

He was quiet for some time. Outside, there was Hellcat Canyon as she always knew it. It seemed somehow surreal that she should be having this kind of conversation with this man while nothing outside changed.

"You really think anyone in the entertainment business doesn't whore themselves at some point?" he tried, a little subdued.

"I'm not speaking in general and you know it. What I'm saying is that you want to have sex with me, and you think waving Wyatt Congdon at me will increase the odds of it. You're just too fucking lazy to win me over with your own charms."

"Whoa." His eyes actually widened.

"Am I wrong?" she pressed. It was probably rash, but now she had the momentum of a point to make. And she was pissed, quite frankly.

"No one has *ever* spoken to me like that before." He sounded more impressed than angry. He was definitely both, though.

Though when the shock wore off, it was hard to know which of those emotions would settle in for keeps.

"Well, maybe J.T.," he added, dryly. Almost to himself.

J.T. must be John Tennessee McCord.

Another tense little silence ensued.

"Listen, Glory . . ." Franco was frustrated. It was pretty clear this was a new corner for him, and he didn't know how to argue his way out of it. He also wasn't used to not getting what he wanted. "You can believe me or not believe me . . . but there's really no implied obligation here. I want a chance to *know* you. I want to spend time with you."

"Sure. But you probably think it would be the least I could do. The polite thing." She was sardonic now.

"Sleep with me on an overnight trip to Napa? Well, yeah. If you're a stickler for etiquette." He was joking. Mostly.

She gave a short laugh. "You are hot, Franco, and you know it. You're sexy and you know it. You're smart, and you know it. You're good at your job. But I'm not sure you know anything else about yourself. Because if you do, you don't seem to want to show it."

He visibly tensed. He wasn't crazy about being summed up that way by her, that was for sure. "What the hell could you possibly know about me or the world?"

She could handle pissed-off men, though. Piece of cake. "Probably nothing. In the scheme of things. But thanks for suggesting I might be just that ignorant."

He made an exasperated sound and dragged both of his hands back through his gorgeous curly hair.

"Glory . . . I know you'll probably think this a line, and I probably only have myself to blame for that. But . . . I honestly can't stop thinking about you. Not entirely sure why. It's the music, the attitude, the way you laugh. I do want to *know* you, and not just in the biblical sense."

She believed him. It happened that way sometimes. Even to movie stars, she supposed.

And while it was hard to truly feel sympathy for a guy who'd had it so easy—or seemed to, she amended in her head, because appearances could in fact be deceiving—she did understand having it easy might get in the way of learning what really fed your soul, when it was so easy to feed your senses instead.

She felt for him, despite herself. "Franco . . . I have a hunch you're fishing for something you didn't even know you wanted. And you may not want to hear this, but you're using the wrong bait."

He went still. Then he frowned and angled his head abruptly away from her, looked out the window.

Wow. That *profile*. She had to be nuts. It belonged stamped on commemorative medals. What woman wouldn't kill to be her right now, sitting across from *the* Franco Francone?

A woman who knew how lucky she was, that's who.

"Just be who you are, Franco," she hazarded gently, albeit somewhat impatiently. "When you take away the words and the people and the car and all the money and all that. Whatever's left, that's who you are. Whoever that guy is . . . well, some woman might think he's worth passing up a so-called lifetime opportunity for him."

He turned toward her, his mouth quirked bitterly. "What's that? A little backwoods wisdom?"

His feelings—or his ego—or both, were wounded.

"Yeah," she said evenly. "A little backwoods wisdom."

For better or worse, she knew who *she* was.

And every decision she made from now on would pivot on that knowledge. Which, as far as she was concerned, made her much luckier than Franco Francone.

"I want you to know . . ." She took in a deep breath. "That making this decision was easy for me. It's pretty hard not to like you. The only thing I'm sure of is that if I go with you to Napa, I'll lose him forever. And when it came down to losing him forever or meeting Wyatt Congdon . . . well, I guess I should thank you for clarifying my whole life for me."

Franco's expression had gone dark and mostly unreadable. But there was a hint of sulky incredulity in the knit of his brows.

She sighed. And slid her chair back.

"But thank you for the invitation," she said politely. "I hope you have a nice time in Napa." She left a couple of dollars next to her coffee cup and paused. "And if the spirit so moves you, give my regards to Wyatt Congdon.

Because one way or another, he's going to know who I am one day."

And she didn't so much walk out the cafe as strut, with a little swing in her hips.

Just to give Franco a little something to remember her by.

CHAPTER 18

Not ten minutes after Glory got home from improbably blowing off Franco Francone, her sister called desperate for a babysitter, and her mom was out doing some work for Gary Shaw.

So Glory headed over to Michelle's to look after her two oldest, who were five and seven years old and perpetual mess-and-motion machines, while her sister took the youngest to a doctor's appointment and then did some shopping. Glory didn't make it back to her own home again until well after dinnertime. Which didn't leave her any time for self-reflection or recrimination or noodling on her guitar as she mulled over what to do next that she'd originally scheduled for today.

Eli was an all or nothing guy.

What she did next would determine what her forever looked like.

She thought she'd have a quick lie-down when she got home.

But next thing she knew she was opening her eyes with a start; pale morning light had squeezed under her blinds and touched her eyelids. She moved experimentally, surprised to find herself completely clothed underneath an old quilt her grandmother had made from scraps of worn-out clothes she'd saved, so it was like being covered in generations of Greenleafs. She wiggled her toes, bemused; her boots were off but her socks were still on.

She must have just crashed when she got home yesterday; clearly all her emotional reserves had been spent and she'd been running on auxiliary without knowing it. Her mom must have tiptoed in with the comforter at some point, covered her up, and managed to get her boots off with the inimitable delicacy and finesse of moms everywhere.

Glory smiled sleepily, feeling loved, and peered at her alarm clock. It was seven-thirty.

Holy crap!

She had to be at work at eight.

She sat bolt upright and hurtled out of bed, shedding the comforter and bolting down the hall so fast she went into a skid in her socks and nearly wiped out as she rounded the corner to the kitchen. She yanked open the freezer on a hunch.

Her mom must be feeling pretty optimistic about Gary Shaw, because she'd sprung for slightly better coffee. And it was all ground up, too.

With lightning speed she put the water on to boil, shoveled a liberal helping of coffee into the French press, whipped off her shirt, darted into the living room wearing only her bra, and threw on a t-shirt she found folded in the laundry pile on the sofa. It unfurled almost down to her knees. Damn! It was John-Mark's. Shit shit shit. She pivoted to press the plunger on the French press like she was detonating a building and, like a barbarian, took a hit of coffee straight from the carafe. It tasted marvelous, like ink.

Thank *God* she could drive the truck to work today. Otherwise she'd be insanely late.

She paused for a millisecond and listened.

She could hear her mom snoring softly in her bedroom. She listened harder.

Only one warm body in there breathing, though. She stood on her toes and peered out the window. No blue Lexus parked out front.

She had a hunch it was only a matter of time, however, before Gary became a fixture.

Or her next stepdad.

She smiled ruefully. She could live with that. Because he'd probably be her *last* stepdad. And John-Mark would probably like him.

That's when she saw the note in the middle of the kitchen table. Speak of the devil. She had another hunch, and it wasn't a good one.

She snatched it up.

Glo—my car broke down last night on the way to work and I had to hitchhike back to town. I had to walk all the way over here to borrow the truck or I'd miss work.

P.S. Then the truck broke down and I missed work anyway. It's out on the highway by the sign that says "TITS."

　　P.P.S. Truck Donegal picked me up when I was hitchhiking. He says to tell you hi.

　　P.P.P.S. I can't miss any more days of work or . . .

And here he'd drawn a little stick figure of a guy getting his throat cut. Complete with "X"s over its eyes and arterial spray.

ARRRRGH. She squeezed her eyes closed and swore blackly under her breath.

God only knew punctuality was about the best she had to offer Sherrie and Glenn, at least as a waitress, and they deserved at least that much.

She was going to have to run—literally run—to work.

Still, she drew a smiling stick figure of a guy dangling from a noose, and wrote:

Hang in there, John-Mark.
   Xoxo Glory

And even though he hadn't drawn a rectangle, she left him twenty bucks and twelve cents. It was what she had left after she'd given Monroe twenty-five bucks and Giorgio ten bucks, and she'd given her sister forty bucks to help pay for the glasses the baby was going to need. Still, there was no question that having any money at all she could give away made her feel richer.

And then she crammed her feet into the old Skechers slides she kept by the front door, grabbed her keys, and bolted.

She ran the way she used to run as a kid, long breakneck strides, thundering down the dirt road, crashing through the long grass, dragging a hand for good luck on that elm tree, which by rights ought to have been scorched from the heat she and Eli had thrown off Tuesday, and then she practically hurdled the old white fence. She paused here to rope her hair into a sloppy knot of sorts on the nape of her neck and take a few gulping breaths. And then she ran all the way down Main Street the way Boomer Clark had that time he was drunk and had run screaming down the street claiming Bigfoot was chasing him, only it turned out just to be Lloyd Sunnergren's big black Lab-Newfoundland mix, Hamburger, who was harmless and ecstatic to have someone to run with. When you met Hamburger, however, it was easy to see how Boomer might have gotten confused.

She paused on Main Street to breathe for about three seconds, then pushed open the door of the Misty Cat so hard the bells leaped like a cat o' nine tails and almost lashed her in the tush. She looked about wildly, saw the broom, seized it, and began sweeping like a dervish to make up for being ten minutes late.

Sherrie had already pulled all the chairs down and she was wiping a table. She paused and watched Glory for a bemused moment. Then her mouth twitched.

"What does the nine stand for?"

"The wha . . ." She looked down. There was indeed a big number nine on the t-shirt she'd snagged off the sofa. Damned if she knew what that meant off the top of her head. Boys and their clothes.

"I thought a ten might be a little too conceited," she improvised. Rather than confess she'd gotten dressed in six seconds in the middle of her living room about ten minutes ago.

Over from behind the grill, Giorgio shook his head to and fro, as if this was the saddest thing he'd ever heard.

Glory shot him a black look and lashed the floor with the broom.

Suddenly Glenn burst in from the back room and beckoned Sherrie over to him near the stage with urgent scoops of his hand.

She joined him. Whereupon they engaged in what sounded like an impassioned murmured conversation, interspersed with darted looks right at Glory.

Uh-oh.

Finally their little scrum broke apart and Sherrie called brightly, "Glory, can we have a quick word?"

Shit, shit, shit.

"Um . . . Of course." She propped the broom against the wall and approached with slow, steady dignity. Like a penitent, or someone headed to the gallows.

In keeping with the thrills and chills and spills of the last couple of weeks, she wouldn't be surprised to be fired. Or promoted. Or to be told the restaurant was closing for a month in order to bolt the stools and chairs to the floor so they could neither be projectiles nor drums.

Glenn got right into it. "Listen, Glory, I just got off the phone with your friend Franco Francone. Wyatt Congdon is going to be passing through Hellcat Canyon tomorrow and he'd like to hear you sing while he's here."

Whoosh! Her heart launched right into her throat. And lodged there.

For a moment she felt a delicious weightlessness, as though she'd literally been fired into space—she couldn't feel her limbs.

It felt like a full minute before she could speak. And all the while the two of them were beaming at her so broadly she almost needed a visor for the glare.

"Wyatt Congdon is just going to be 'passing through' Hellcat Canyon?" Her voice was two octaves higher than usual and sounded like she swallowed a moth.

She cleared her throat.

"Who knows what the hell these music people do?" Glenn asked. "Maybe he had a few minutes in between gilding his toilet and polishing his Grammys, and he feels like taking a drive in the country. He can give you fifteen minutes around seven in the morning tomorrow. According to your friend Mr. Francone." Glenn was practically twinkling.

Sherrie chimed in. "I'll unlock the front door and let him in and then Glenn and I will skedaddle until eight. We'll be down at Eden's flower shop if you need us for anything."

This is what they'd been planning in murmurs. They were so much nicer to her than she probably deserved.

Glory gave a short, stunned laugh.

But . . . wait. There was something she needed to know.

"Where will . . . um . . . Mr. Francone be while this is happening? Did he say?"

"He's in Napa for a few weeks, then I think he said L.A., and then he'll be back in Hellcat Canyon to film a few scenes with J.T. McCord. Oh! He was pretty adamant that I write something down to tell you." Glenn scrabbled his reading glasses from his shirt pocket and pushed them onto his face but still held the order pad at arm's length. "'Tell Glory it's a thank-you for backwoods wisdom. And tell her we're square. And good luck with that macho jerk.'"

Glory smiled slowly. She was pretty sure the "we're square" was Franco Francone's way of telling her she didn't owe him a thing. She had indeed schooled him.

"I take it you know what that means? Is Wyatt Congdon a macho jerk?" Glenn wanted to know. "Wouldn't surprise me."

The jerk in question was, of course, Eli. At least as far

as Franco was concerned. "If Congdon is a jerk, I'm sure I can manage him."

"Oh, honey, if anyone can, it's you," Sherrie said.

They all smiled so hard and brightly at each other that Giorgio forgot himself for a moment and smiled, too.

Just *look* at what happened when you did the true, right thing, Glory thought, bemused.

In an indirect way, this was all Eli's doing.

"Mr. Francone's a nice boy, isn't he?" Sherrie prompted. "Is there anything . . . you know, there, with you two?"

"Nope," Glory said firmly. "Let's just say he kind of wagered on something and he lost. And this is his way of making good on his bet."

Oddly enough, Sherrie and Glenn shot each other relieved looks. Funny to think they might actually have an opinion about her love life.

The door jangled then. Sherrie and Glenn turned in tandem to the sound. Glory had her calling, and the Misty Cat was theirs.

"You can say you knew us when, hon." Sherrie patted her arm, one step toward the day's first customer already.

"And the sooner I say that, the better, right?" Glory teased.

Both Sherrie and Glenn laughed a little too loudly at that.

Glory got home around four p.m, to find Gary Shaw and her mom were sitting at the kitchen table, absorbed in some paperwork and each other. She could practically *see* the little insular bubble of happiness surrounding them.

Glory sneaked past them, scooped up their old beige landline phone from the hallway, dragged it into her bedroom and shut the door. Just like when she was a teenager burbling on about God knows what—she couldn't remember now—to Mick Macklemore.

She picked up the receiver, raised her hand to punch buttons and froze.

It only just occurred to her that she didn't have Eli's cell phone number.

But her fingers knew the number pattern of his landline the way they knew where to go on her guitar strings when she was playing a familiar song.

She was pretty sure he wouldn't be home. But she wanted to hear his voice.

The greeting was typically minimalist:

"Leave a message for Eli." BEEEEEP.

Her heart gave a pleasant stab as his baritone washed over her.

She hung up quickly, lest she sound like a perv breathing into the line.

For privacy reasons, he didn't have a Facebook page. She knew a lot of law enforcement personnel didn't. She didn't know his e-mail address, either.

She supposed the two of them had . . . always just actually talked to each other, mostly. Like a couple of Luddites. Had always taken for granted that they'd see each other.

So she called his office. The cop shop was pretty small in Hellcat Canyon, so odds were pretty good one of the deputies would answer the phone when someone called the main number rather than 911, especially if the receptionist on duty was in the bathroom.

She exhaled, realizing her heart was hammering like a fourteen-year-old calling her first crush.

That wasn't far from the truth, actually.

"May I speak to Deputy Barlow, please?"

"Oh, Eli is out of the office for a few days, Glory," Deputy Owen Haggerty told her over the phone.

Crap! He'd recognized her voice!

"He's in court all day today and he's going up to county tomorrow morning. Something I can do for you?"

"Er—No, thank you, Owen. No message! Everything's great!"

Click.

Her heart was hammering. For heaven's sake, she needed to get a grip.

She put the phone gently down in its cradle. And mulled.

It was just that it still wouldn't feel entirely real until she told him. And when she did tell him, this remarkable, miraculous thing would become even better. And a million things could happen between now and seven a.m. Tomorrow. From now until then, until she actually saw Wyatt Congdon in person, it would feel like that dream she'd had once where she was trying to cross Main Street downtown, but the street just kept getting wider and wider as she walked and no matter how fast she walked she could never get across until she woke up, sweating.

And yet telling Eli about Congdon would mean telling him about what had transpired between her and Franco, and that would be part of a conversation that could well determine the rest of her life. And though she knew Eli was likely losing sleep waiting to hear from her, she didn't want to have that conversation over the phone.

Maybe it was all for the best this way.

She sucked in deep breath, and released it slowly. And took the phone back to its perch in the hallway.

"Oh, Glory, honey, when did you get in? What on earth are you . . . Is that your brother's shirt?"

"Hi, Mom. Hi, Gary. Yep. Found it in the laundry pile this morning and I was a little desperate. Thanks for covering me up last night, by the way. I didn't even hear you come in. I must have been zonked."

"You really were out like a light, honey." She paused. "But you did stir and mumble a little when I put the comforter over you."

Glory was amused, and a little worried, hoping she hadn't said anything too profane. She'd probably said "Freebird!" Or "show us your tits!" God only knew she'd heard that often enough. "What did I say?"

Her mom hesitated. "You said, 'Eli.'"

Glory froze like a criminal in the beam of an overhead helicopter.

And for an instant the silence was total apart from the refrigerator humming in the next room.

"I miss him, too, honey," her mom said finally, softly.

Gary Shaw was taking all of this in with the sympathetic air of a man who had already heard *everything* about the Greenleafs, and not only could handle every bit of it, but rather liked it.

And now Glory realized they didn't talk about Eli or Jonah in the house because her mom understood how Glory felt about it. Her mom had been honoring *Glory's* feelings.

Glory was a little abashed she'd been found out. But it was useful to know she'd muttered his name in her sleep. Because she supposed the word that popped out when your mind was shut off and your heart was unfettered by analysis, when you were at your most surrendered . . . well, that must be the truest word you knew.

Eli was proud of how well he seemed to be holding it together, admirably, even, in the absence of a phone call or any word from Glory since that day. He'd said his piece, she'd said hers, and there was peace in that. *Piece* and *peace* reminded him of that dip Macklemore's misspelled tattoo, and then he thought about Francone, and even though he knew Glory, at heart, was made of integrity, he knew she was also made of ambition. And the effort it took not to analyze or extrapolate what might come next was like balancing on the top rail of that old whitewashed fence out near that pasture by the elm tree.

He'd spent a long but satisfying day testifying in court yesterday and he was going to work a short shift before he headed out to Sacramento for his meeting with Leigh, armed with an impressive PowerPoint presentation regarding a proposed ten-year plan for his life on his laptop.

Deputy Owen Haggerty was at the front desk when Eli checked in.

"Morning, chief. You're heading up to county today, right? Nothing's really happening yet. Glory Greenleaf called here yesterday looking for you, though. She said it was *WHOA*."

Eli lunged at Owen and clutched his shirt like someone in a melodramatic 1930s gangster movie.

"What do you mean 'whoa'? What the hell? What's wrong? Is she okay? *Owen, what the hell?*"

Owen's eyes got huge. "She's fine! She said it was nothing. Didn't leave a message. The *WHOA* was for your face."

Eli released his deputy, thoroughly amazed to realize he hadn't actually been keeping it together all that well.

"What's wrong my face?" His hands went up to explore it.

Owen stood back and smoothed his shirt and appeared to give some good thought to this question. "Well, when I said the words *Glory Greenleaf* your expression was kind of like you got hit with a shovel. You know, sort of dazed? But also as if getting hit with the shovel somehow adjusted your internal lighting and you were about five times brighter."

They stared at each other.

Owen's eyes were glinting.

Eli willed a flush not to happen. Judging from his skin temperature, he hadn't completely succeeded.

"Very observant. Good use of detail, Owen," Eli said finally. "Anyone ever tell you that you should go into law enforcement?"

Owen was studying him curiously, his eyes still shining.

And Eli was going to have to stand there and watch realization dawning in his deputy's eyes, because Eli couldn't not say what he said next. He cleared his throat. "If Glory calls again . . . give her my cell phone number. And make sure I know about it *right away.*"

"*Ooo*ohhhh!" Owen was all insinuating realization. "It's like that, huh?" Owen began to purse his lips.

"So help me, God, if you make a kissy noise, Owen, I will shoot you."

Owen relaxed his lips obediently.

But they only wavered and curled up again into a grin.

Eli made an irritated noise and a little chopping gesture with his hand. "*Bye*, Deputy."

"Have a safe trip, Eli. Give my best to Devlin. Be safe out there." Owen's voice was still suffused with amusement.

Eli grunted and stalked out to his cruiser, hurled his packed overnight bag into the backseat.

He sat for a moment. But *why* had Glory called? Had she come to some kind of conclusion? To say good-bye? To say I'm coming over, please be naked when I get there? To say Franco proposed and it's on YouTube?

He backed out of the parking lot a little too emphatically, maybe, then took a breath and forcibly steadied himself, because he was the law, not a stroppy teenager, and he could manage this without acting out.

He took in a deep breath. Whatever she had to say, he would hear it. As long as she was okay, he could wait.

It was that tender hour of the morning when pale gold light was just creeping up over the mountain, and Main Street was still metaphorically yawning and stretching. A few awnings were being unfurled, blinds on storefronts cast upward, flowers and fruit set out in front of their markets.

"Hey, Eli?" Owen's voice came over the radio suddenly.

Eli gritted his teeth and seized the radio. "Yeah, Owen?"

"Got a call that the burglar alarm at the Misty Cat was tripped. Little early for them to be open, isn't it?"

He was relieved not to be teased. "Yeah. It's probably nothing, but I'll check it out."

He reached the foot of Main, where the Misty Cat sat (it had been built at the foot of the hill right above the original mining camp, so inebriated miners could stumble out the door and roll right back down into camp, or so legend had it). He pulled to the curb and cut the engine. He knew this beat, the Harwoods, and the Misty Cat so well, and not once since Eli had worked in Hellcat Canyon had they forgotten to disarm the alarm when they did open.

There was a first time for everything, he supposed. It could be a malfunction.

Still, he put his hand on his gun as he approached the window to peer in.

Two men he'd never seen before were sitting at a table near the stage. His senses went on high alert.

But none of the other chairs had been pulled down from the tables yet, and they formed an obscuring forest of chair backs. He couldn't get a clear look at them.

He pushed the door gently; it was unlocked. He slowly, slowly pushed it open to try to avoid jangling the bells, slipped inside, and moved toward them quietly.

They turned toward him, faces expectant but not surprised. And then they both went taut with a sort of irritation.

Oh yeah. These two were definitely not burglars.

One was older and slim and fit in that sleek, yoga-and-personal-trainer Los Angeles way. His clothes, his skin, everything about him had that polished look that a particular sort of wealthy person had, the kind who mostly moved between air-conditioned limos and planes and air-conditioned buildings and mansions and ate only wheat-grass and chickens who ranged free and the like. And he had an air of detached absorption and the sort of charisma conferred by power and utter certainty.

Eli knew a few powerful people. That particular air was cumulative, something that developed over time, and it was earned.

Across from him sat a younger Asian guy, just as wiry slim and fit but a little taller, wearing what Eli thought of as a groovy Franco Francone–esque shirt. He had an expensive-looking haircut and an array of electronics—a phone, an iPad, and so forth were spread out on the table in front of him.

"Good morning, Officer," the older guy drawled, not sounding the least surprised. He didn't move or rise. "You don't look like Glory Greenleaf."

Eli frowned, bemused. And then with a blast of clarity he knew who this guy was.

Hooooooooly shit.

"Good morning. The alarm was triggered and I stopped in to investigate. You two planning to rob the place?"

"No crime occurring here," the old man informed him. "Unless you want to arrest Miss Greenleaf for the crime of wasting my time."

The only thing that got arrested was the assistant's chuckle. By a hard glare from Eli.

"You're Wyatt Congdon," Eli guessed, keeping his tone pleasant.

"My reputation precedes me, eh?" Congdon smiled faintly.

"Something like that." Eli didn't quite smile. Where the hell was Glory? She was never late. And she would definitely never be late for this.

"And you are?" Congdon prompted.

"Deputy Sheriff Eli Barlow."

It seemed as though, for whatever reason, Francone had coaxed Congdon to Hellcat Canyon. He'd brought the mountain to Muhammad, so to speak, instead of luring Glory to Napa. Which could mean Francone was stepping up his campaign to nail Glory. Or that she had done something, said something to Francone to make this happen.

And Eli had no idea where he stood.

And suddenly he realized it didn't matter.

All he knew was that Glory wasn't here. And if she wasn't here, that meant something was wrong.

And Eli would move a mountain to *get* her here, if that's what it took. No matter what happened. No matter what she decided.

"I'm Justin Chen. Junior vice president of Stellium Records," the young guy suddenly volunteered.

"Nobody cares, Justin," Congdon explained patiently.

"Pleasure to meet you, Mr. Chen," Eli said. Pointedly. "If you wouldn't mind, gentlemen, letting me in on exactly why you happen to be sitting in the Misty Cat before opening time, and why you hoped I was Glory Greenleaf? Seems the alarm was tripped, and I'll need to put it in my report."

Congdon sighed. "Certainly, Officer. Our apologies about tripping the alarm, by the way." Congdon shot a look at Mr. Chen, who was clearly going to be assigned blame. "I'm here as a favor to Franco Francone. His father was my college roommate. He's my godson. And he knows me well enough not to waste one particle of my time. But he was sufficiently persuasive with regards to Miss Greenleaf's talents to get me to drive two hours to this little . . ." He waved a manicured hand vaguely, irritably, to indicate the whole of Hellcat Canyon.

Oh, how sweet. Congdon clearly wanted to use a word like *backwater* or *bumfuck* but he was being sensitive to Eli's feelings.

"It would take a nuclear holocaust to keep Glory Greenleaf from a meeting with you," Eli said, and he was impressed by how natural the words sounded because inwardly his nerves felt pulled back like a slingshot. "I've known her all my life and I would swear to that in court. Something must have held her up. A flat tire, maybe. The roads out here can be a little tricky."

Eli sensed these words were basically a drop trickled into the ocean of Congdon's indifference.

"I guess that would make this Miss Greenleaf's Hiroshima, then." Congdon was amused, albeit in a detached and cynical way. Glory was nothing to him.

It was one of the more discordant moments of Eli's life. It was inconceivable that anyone should experience Glory as nothing, when she was in fact everything.

"Call her cell?" the assistant offered, nervously, placatingly into the chilly silence.

"She doesn't currently have one," Eli said.

He shouldn't have said that.

Or maybe it was exactly the right thing to say.

Because the two men, who had seemed to be restlessly rustling their flight feathers when he'd entered the restaurant, went still. It was clear that whereas Glory was just an irritant before, she'd now become faintly interesting, albeit in a circus-freak way, to these men. Because in their world, not having a cell phone was akin to not having a head.

"I'll get her here inside of fifteen minutes," Eli said abruptly.

"How are you going to manage that, Deputy? Are you going to put out an APB?"

He actually didn't know. All he knew was that he would. Eli's faint, bland cop smile betrayed absolutely nothing of his turmoil.

"It's possible, Mr. Congdon, that you watch too many cop shows."

"Just the one. *Blood Brothers*."

"Of course," Eli said neutrally. "You're *certain* Glory knows she's supposed to meet you here?"

"I'm told Francone managed to convey the particulars of this meeting to her. Justin found the time in my schedule, after considerable juggling, I might add."

Justin nodded vigorously.

"And now that son of a bitch Franco is lounging on my estate while I'm sitting here waiting for the flaky Miss Greenleaf." Congdon sounded amused by this. Clearly he was fond of Francone, and God only knew why.

"Fifteen minutes, Mr. Congdon," Eli repeated. And now his heart was racing. "She is not a flake."

Congdon stared at him curiously. "Listen . . . Deputy?" Congdon issued the title gingerly, as if Eli was yet another actor playing a part. "I didn't really have the ten minutes I just wasted waiting for this person. I don't have the two minutes I'm using now to discuss this with you. When you see Glory Greenleaf, you can tell her she fucked up her shot, and well, when you fuck up your shot . . ."

Congdon didn't need to tell Eli about fucking up a shot. He was about to fuck up his own, if he didn't leave for Sacramento in the next hour.

"Mr. Congdon, this woman is unforgettable," he said swiftly.

It might have been a tactical mistake. He'd failed to keep all of the emotion from his voice.

And even as he said it he knew precisely how it sounded: some rube was deigning to offer an opinion to Wyatt "King" Congdon. Like some rube who was probably doing the woman in question.

"I won't forget that she wasted my time, if that's what you mean." Congdon said this with a sinister sort of vagueness. His thoughts were already somewhere else entirely.

And then Congdon put his hands on his chair arms and leaned forward, preparing to get up out of his chair.

Like a mirror reflection, Chen did the same thing.

In one swift movement Eli whipped his handcuffs out and slapped one of them on Congdon and the other to the chair. *Click.*

Justin Chen sat back down hard in shock.

"What. The *fuck* . . ." Congdon yanked his arm upward. He wasn't going anywhere.

He turned to Eli, his face white with the kind of fury that could curl and blacken the leaves on the trees for miles around.

Didn't even singe Eli, however. He was made of stronger stuff.

"You'll thank me later" was all he said.

CHAPTER 19

Before he got in his car, he'd dragged the cement planter outside and pushed it up against the door, then darted around back and did the same thing. Congdon and his assistant weren't going anywhere.

"False alarm at the Misty Cat," he calmly radioed Owen. "No need to respond to any other calls from there. I repeat: no need to respond to any calls there."

Owen was quiet a moment. "Um . . . Eli? Everything okay?"

"I've got this, Owen," he said tersely. "Just assume that I've got this."

There was a beat of silence.

"Okeydoke, chief," Owen said. "Good luck."

Bases covered, Eli actually switched the siren on.

It occurred to him that what he'd just done was as melodramatically asinine as anything out of *Blood Brothers*. Irony of ironies. He could lose his job over this. He could lose his whole career over this.

There were a lot of *coulds*.

They were unimportant at the moment. Because *his* superpower was staring straight into the heart of a situation.

If he'd let Congdon walk away, he'd have to live out his life with the knowledge that he hadn't done a thing to make sure Glory didn't miss this moment. And that was inconceivable.

If he didn't find Glory within the next fifteen minutes, he'd go back and free the man and deal with the consequences then.

He floored it, siren wailing. He practically took the three turns between the Misty Cat and the Greenleaf house on two wheels, at speeds that would have made Franco Francone's Porsche look like his old Fiero. In seven minutes rather than the seventeen it ought to have taken, he came to a screeching halt on the dirt road in front of it. He leaped out of the car, running past a gaping Mrs. Binkley holding a trowel in one hand, and hurdled the picket fence.

Law enforcement leaping out of cars in front of the Greenleaf house: Nothing their neighbors hadn't seen before.

He thumped a fist three times on the door. "GLORY!"

He stepped back and waited.

It felt like his heart was pounding just that hard on the wall of his chest.

No response. He put his ear to the door.

The whole house seemed inordinately still. It was as if the wind had agreed not to stir a single blade of grass or leaf on a tree. Like the house was enclosed in some kind of dome.

His heart flopped over hard in his chest with dread.

He tried the door handle. "Glory?"

The door was unlocked.

He put his hand on his gun, and pushed it open slowly, right into their living room.

He almost didn't notice her, because she was standing in the middle of the room, as motionless as the sofa. Striped in diagonal light and shadow from the vertical blinds.

She looked indescribably pretty: hair brushed to a sheen and hanging down her back, a top he knew she'd chosen because it was blue and had little frills at the arm holes and fit her like a corset. She was wearing a lot more makeup than he'd ever seen her use, all carefully applied.

"Honey . . ."

The word slipped out.

Something was really, really wrong.

He realized then that the reason he'd noticed the makeup at all was that she was stark white.

"What are you doing, Glory?" he said gently, reasonable as a hostage negotiator. "You need to grab your guitar and go. Wyatt Congdon is waiting for you at the Misty Cat."

She swallowed audibly. "Can't." Her voice was a sandpapery whisper.

"You can't . . . what?"

"Grab my *guitar.*" Now her voice was louder than it ought to be. As if she'd lost her ability to calibrate. She sounded almost blackly amused. "It's gone."

Shit.

"Glory Hallelujah Greenleaf, look at me."

She obeyed. Reluctantly.

Her eyes were red-rimmed. The mascara she'd carefully applied was smudging beneath her eyes. Water resistant. Not water*proof.*

God *help* the person who had made her cry. When he found out who it was, they were done for.

"Glory. From the beginning."

She took a breath and exhaled. "Okay. Eli, I told Franco I wouldn't go with him to Napa. Not ever. He apparently set this up because he's not a complete dick and I schooled him. Long story."

"If you say so," Eli encouraged her. But a huge dark weight he hadn't been fully aware was there lifted and sailed away, and suddenly he felt made of light.

"I got up really early and I ironed my shirt. I was alone in the house. Mama has that job with Gary Shaw now? Well, she got up early and she's out showing a house. I took a shower and did my makeup and then I said a little prayer . . . and I guess that's not relevant, but that's what I did. And when went back to my room to get my guitar . . . It's always leaning next to my dresser in its case. Last thing I see at night, first thing I see in the morning. It was gone. I found this, though."

She handed Eli a note.

Glory—I took your dad's guitar to see if I could
pawn it to pay for my carburetor. I should be able
to get at least a couple hundred bucks for it. I'll get
it back to you, I swear, inside a month.

P.S. Sorry sorry sorry sorry sorry sorry

Eli swore so blackly and vulgarly Glory's eyes went wide and a little real color flowed into her pale face.

"Eli, do you think it's a sign?" she said desperately.

"A sign your dumbfuck younger brother took it and pawned it. Yeah."

And now he realized he'd never really been angry before. What he felt now was a whole new emotion. A rage so transcendent it was almost holy. This must be how crusades began.

"I think he just panicked. I mean, we've *all* felt desperate. And technically it *is* Dad's guitar. It's not like it was willed to me or anything. I don't think John-Mark knows what it's actually worth. Four thousand dollars, Eli."

There was a beat of silence.

"Holy *shit*," he breathed.

"It's a classic," she said dryly. Her voice cracked. "The one lucky break my dad got. I'm starting to think destiny does *not* want me to leave Hellcat Canyon. Because *come on*. What are the odds here?"

Eli swiftly counted to ten to get a grip on his temper.

"Listen. That's bullshit. Glory, it's time to decide whether loyalty to your family is going to keep you from soaring the way you know you can. The way everyone in Hellcat Canyon knows you can. The way you want to and know deep down you *need to* or you will just die. They just don't get it, or he would never have done this to you. This is a sign that you need to realize that *you matter*, Glory. You and your hopes and your dreams and what you want. Fuck John-Mark. For now, anyway. You are going to the Misty Cat, guitar or no guitar."

Her hands went up to her face. Then she brought them down and filled her lungs with a deep breath.

He was getting through.

He took a step closer to her, the words coming in a rush.

"I know you think I broke your heart, Glory, with the whole Jonah thing. Maybe that's even true. But here's the thing: I will be damned if anyone *else* breaks your heart, and I don't care whether they're related to you or not. You are going to the Misty Cat. Now. If I have to drag you there in handcuffs. You've got to the count of three. One. Two. Th—"

But even as he counted, a smile grew softly, gradually, until she was clearly radiantly amused.

"Okay, I'll come, Eli," she said mildly. She was glowing now, with a light that he felt clean down to his soles. "You don't have to resort to bondage."

He was heartened by that little bit of wickedness. He pivoted and threw the front door open. "Then run," he said.

And she did.

Eli had the engine started before she got the door of his squad car shut.

"I always knew you'd end up in a police car," Mrs. Binkley crowed after her.

"Damn straight!" Glory shouted gleefully out the window.

And then because Mrs. Binkley would both hate and expect it, Glory levered her torso halfway out the window and hollered "Yeeeee*HAAAAW*!" when Eli hit the gas with a force that threw them both back in their seat.

She'd never said *yeehaw!* in her entire life.

He ran two stoplights, wove around two cars, nimbly dodged three deer nonchalantly traipsing across the road, and with a screech of brakes, halted in front of the Misty Cat.

He drove the two of them so fast he wouldn't be surprised if he'd obliterated the laws of physics and arrived at the Misty Cat five minutes before he actually left.

There was a split second of loaded silence.

He didn't offer to come in.

She didn't ask him to.

They both knew she needed to do this on her own.

She smiled at him and no matter what happened next in his life, he'd given her this moment and that smile and just those two things right there seemed the entire point of his life.

"I almost forgot, Glory . . . you're going to need this."

And he pressed the key to his handcuffs into her palm.

Wow.

Power almost has a scent, Glory thought. Because the air in the Misty Cat felt oddly like the air before a snowstorm. Portentous. Charged. Icy.

Her senses were so raw and alert she could almost sense the molecules inside that familiar space had shifted somehow to accommodate the sheer volume of Congdon's legend and ego.

Two men were actually sitting there. They were as silent as if they'd never spoken a word in their lives. The blinds were slit and they were striped like prisoners in shadows and morning sunlight.

Congdon looked up at her. His eyes were the sort of cool, clear blue-gray of old flashbulbs.

If she'd held her hand near him, she was pretty sure she would have pulled it back dripping with icicles.

Her second impression was that Wyatt "King" Congdon was a surprisingly slight man for someone who possessed terrifying power. He was that Los Angeles sort of skinny, and his complexion so alight with health and tending, he radiated in the Misty Cat like a parking lamp. He hadn't a visible line on his face and only a few visible hairs on his head.

Sitting with him was a very good-looking young Asian guy with the hippest haircut she'd ever seen.

They didn't do any of the things men usually did: they didn't lean farther back in their chairs to give themselves a full-length view of her, they didn't shoot to their feet and fall over themselves to impress, their pupils didn't flare to the size of quarters.

Pretty women with excellent racks were as common in their world as trees were in Hellcat Canyon, and came in as many varieties.

"I'm terribly sorry to keep you waiting."

Her voice sounded strange in her own ears. Like she was hearing it through a pillow.

Whoosh. Whoosh. Whoosh. Her pounding heart was sending blood to her ears, that was why. Rhythm. Everything about the body was a rhythm, she realized then. It was an oddly comforting thought.

"If I'd had a choice," he said tersely. "I wouldn't have, Miss Greenleaf."

He gave an illustrative tug.

He was handcuffed to the chair! Holy crap. That might be the hottest thing Eli had ever done.

Pushing the planter up against the Misty Cat door so they couldn't get out was the second hottest.

Congdon's voice was pleasant and even and scary as hell.

Boy, was he was pissed. So pissed he didn't bother to introduce himself or the man sitting with him.

It could already be over, as far as she knew. Given the handcuffs and her tardiness. But she'd made bravado a way of life, and everything up until now had been a mere practice run for this moment.

"I won't keep you waiting any longer, then." She drew in a long breath.

And she turned away from them and slowly walked

toward the stage. In her current condition, the few feet seemed to elongate as if she were standing before a fun-house mirror.

And she put a little bit more swing into her hips, just because.

She pivoted.

The temperature in the room had changed ever so slightly.

They'd liked the back view quite a bit.

And she knew she could do this. She would charm them to the soles of their feet. She would win their cyni-cal little dollar-sign shaped hearts. She would make them genuinely *love* her. Love *her*. She would make them forget themselves and everything else but her voice, and for the next three minutes, she would pull them into the world of her song, a world in which she was the empress and they were the minions.

She knew how to do it, too, with a guy like Congdon:

She would take control.

"If you would be so kind as to give me a beat." She slapped her hand on the table near the stage in an undulat-ing, martial rhythm. "Bass, SNARE, bass bass SNARE. You know how to do that, right?"

Congdon froze. Then he nodded irritably to the other guy.

Who did as ordered.

He slapped his hand down on the table. Bass, SNARE bass bass SNARE. He had good rhythm.

She moved her shoulders into the beat, and then her hips, and she heard the music in her head as plainly as if her whole body was an orchestra.

And opened her mouth to sing.

She loved the acoustics in that room and today they really loved her back more than ever.

She sang to those two men as if they'd broken her heart and won it all over again. She sang her songs to them as if Eli himself were standing there, and she knew in that moment of pure epiphany that he might as well have been, because he seemed to be with her all the time, anyway. She understood now that his love was the filter through which she saw and felt everything.

Her voice all raw emotion, turning notes into playthings, leaping octaves as effortlessly as she and Jonah and Eli used to skip the stones over Whiskey Creek.

And the sound of her own voice rising in that room seemed to fill her soul like a sail.

She felt invincible and euphoric and utterly peaceful.

And for the duration, those two men did not so much as twitch a hair.

She recognized thrall when she saw it. It meant they wanted to absorb every single particle of sound.

And she released the last word of the song like a sigh, which trailed into vapor on an impossibly high note.

It rang in the room.

She closed her eyes briefly. And when she opened them, like a fragment from a dream, Giorgio emerged from the kitchen and casually handed her a guitar and slipped back into the shadows.

I'll be damned, she thought. It was the Alvarez acoustic Dion had been repairing.

Eli must have coordinated that little loan from behind the wheel of his squad car. And somehow gotten word from Dion to Giorgio before Giorgio left his apartment above the music store for work.

You are never *alone,* Eli had said to her.

She realized the two men hadn't said a word yet.

She slung the strap of that guitar around her neck as tenderly as if it were a lover's arm, and in a way it might as well have been Eli's. Both of those men shifted in their chairs and Wyatt Congdon actually reached with his free hand to touch the back of his own neck as if he could feel her hand on him.

She looked at them in silence for a moment.

Congdon's pale eyes thoughtful, his assistant's fixed and stunned. In a good way.

But there was something she needed to do.

She stepped down from the stage. In the silence, her boot heels rang like gunshots as she moved toward them.

And she slipped the handcuff key from her pocket and laid it down in front of Wyatt Congdon.

In the silence of the Misty Cat, the little metallic clink echoed as if she were betting her last dime.

He stared down at the key.

Then up at her, thoughtfully.

His eyes were gray. A gold fleck, like a pirate doubloon, floated in the iris of one of them.

"You wrote that song?"

"Yes, sir."

She saw evidence of a real thaw in the way his face subtly softened and lit.

"Sing another." He made it sound like a suggestion. His voice had gone gentle, almost abstracted. Something thrummed in it. If he'd been a mere mortal, she might have called it glee.

"Yes, sir."

She turned around. And she put just a hint more swing

in her hips on her way back to the stage. Let them enjoy that view again.

Justin Chen leaned across to Congdon and whispered, "Your flight is . . . and should I . . . do you want me to . . ." He gestured to the handcuff key.

"I'll flap my own arms and fly there on my own if I have to," Congdon said peacefully. "And this isn't the first time I've been handcuffed."

Alarming the young ones in this business never got old. He leaned back. "Kinda like it, in fact."

He hadn't felt this happy possibly ever.

But it felt like that every time he discovered someone magnificent.

Glory dragged her pick down over the strings and obeyed.

She sang another.

"**S**ing another," Wyatt Congdon said softly, when she was done.

She did.

"Sing another," he said after that.

Five times he'd said this.

Like a child entranced by a magician's trick, he wanted to see her do it again and again.

And finally he stopped. And she remained motionless.

All was silence once more.

"Miss Greenleaf . . ."

Her breathing arrested then. Time was suddenly an echoing chasm.

The next words of out of his mouth could very well be the bridge between her old life and the rest of her life.

". . . I think you have something very, very special."

Every single moving part inside her body seemed to pause, waiting.

For a *but* or an *unfortunately*.

And then she knew they weren't going to come.

"And you *know* you have something special, don't you?"

And then Wyatt "King" Congdon grinned.

He looked like a boy who'd unwrapped the very Christmas present he'd yearned for but had given up hope of ever receiving. And Glory saw him now not just as a cold-faced vehicle to her dreams—though he was indeed that—but like a human who had a tough job he loved, a human who had absorbed countless disappointments in search of the needle in the haystack, the diamond in the junkyard.

As a human who was relaxed now. Because he knew what to do next. There was a drill, and he knew that drill, because he'd all but invented it.

The thing he and Glory had in common was hope. And love.

Whether it was love of music or money or both didn't matter. She could work with love.

Because she knew exactly who *she* was.

She smiled back at him. "Call me Glory."

A now un-handcuffed Congdon all but walked on air down Hellcat Canyon's Main Street at a speed that had Justin Chen scrambling to keep up with him because there was still a chance he could make his New York flight. Congdon *always* walked like he was fleeing the scene of a crime. He was pushing seventy years old and he'd taken advantage of nearly every available mind-altering substance back in the sixties and seventies because that's what everyone did and hell why not, but after one heart episode in his fifties, he was now aggressively fit. Congdon never did anything by halves.

"Holy crap, Justin . . . that voice . . . it's like if Adele had the twang of a Carrie Underwood, but this girl has something raw all her own. Not too many women have that smoky thing going, that depth, with that kind of power or range. And the emotion, the maturity, the expression. Christ almighty. And she's beautiful, almost elegant, in a raw way. Like . . . oh, Shania, only dangerous. Bobbie Gentry. Hotter than Crystal Gayle. She'll be a fun interview, too."

"Wait . . . Crystal Who? And remind me who Bobbie Gentry is again?" Justin was embarrassed that he was starting to sweat to keep up.

"How old *are* you, Justin? Do your homework. My uncle had a Crystal Gayle poster in his room. She was my first crush. Hair way down past her ass. Gorgeous, gorgeous woman."

They spent a moment in reverie about the wonders of getting lost in long hair.

"Pays to know your history in this business, Justin, if you want to survive. We're about to make some more history."

"She doesn't have a cell phone."

"You can e-mail her. She can tell that story later. About how she was once so poor she didn't have a cell phone and had to audition without her guitar because it was stolen. To Jimmy Fallon, on *The Tonight Show*. Next year, maybe. Soon though."

CHAPTER 20

So disappointed not to see you today, Eli.

Never had one eight-word sentence from Leigh contained so many dimensions of admonishment. He *was* genuinely disappointed. Possibly even hurt.

Eli had felt the shame of it flushing his skin as he held his phone and stared at that text.

After he'd dropped Glory off at the Misty Cat this morning, he'd texted Leigh heartfelt apologies and told him that he'd had a personal emergency to attend to and would be unable to make the meeting in Sacramento.

Which was basically true.

The vague nature of the message told Devlin that it was a "personal" emergency indeed—if his mom or his sister was in some kind of jeopardy, Eli would have said exactly that, because Leigh knew both of them.

Still, Eli's job wasn't in jeopardy.

Probably.

Then again, he also probably wasn't in any immediate danger of a promotion.

He'd take his lumps and call Leigh and see if there was

some way he could explain what he'd done today in a way that didn't make him sound callow or irresponsible, or worst of all, purely crazy.

He had, at least, been engaged in police work all today.

Very specific police work. Even if he wasn't officially on duty. And Leigh was a music fan. So maybe he had some leverage there.

The only thing that mattered at the moment was that Eli had accomplished his mission, and he'd returned home only a little while ago. He'd thrown his body down onto the sofa and tipped his head back, and the relief and triumph of accomplishing what he'd set out to do today went a long way to offseting the idea of Leigh's censure.

No sign or word from Glory, though. No message on either phone.

He suppose there was a possibility that Wyatt Congdon had installed her in a limo and efficiently, immediately whisked her off to Los Angeles or to wherever stars were incubated and that would be that.

He just didn't know. And as day was fading to twilight, he dozed off right where he was sitting, feet up on the coffee table, phone on his lap, thinking of her smile today, and he began to dream of a woodpecker, of all things, outside his window.

Tap tap. Tap Tap tap.

"Damn woodpecker," Eli murmured, grumpily, in his sleep.

Then his eyes flew open. And then he shot to his feet. His phone clunked to the floor.

He was upright before he was fully awake.

He could feel the nip of the evening breeze in the house. He'd left the front door ajar; the screen door was filtering in fresh air.

And Glory was standing outside in the little golden pool of his porch light.

She'd been tapping on his door frame.

He moved toward her slowly, hesitantly, unconvinced he wasn't still dreaming. It never occurred to him to turn on the light first.

She seemed to belong in that spotlight.

He didn't think he could speak just yet. He was far too full of emotion to get a word out.

"It started raining on my way here," she said, by way of greeting. "First rain of the season."

He pulled the screen door open silently and held it open for her.

She hesitated.

And then she stepped inside.

As if on cue, the sky opened up and the rain came down in noisy buckets, casting that wonderful dirt smell on the air, banging a variety of notes on his roof and windows and gutters.

"I saw your truck out front. I hope it's okay that I just stopped by."

He smiled at the absurdity of that.

She seemed almost shy. Radiant as the moon standing there in his shadowy living room with news he was certain he already knew. Whatever happened, he was just unutterably grateful he was here to witness this moment. And that she had come to him with it.

Finally she got the words out.

"They loved me, Eli."

She sounded not so much disbelieving, as dazed and enchanted.

A torrent of love and pride flooded his circuits. For a moment he simply couldn't speak.

She knew.

She waited.

"I know," he said simply, softly.

"How did you know?" She was genuinely surprised.

They were both whispering, for some reason, like conspirators or symphony goers who don't want to interrupt the music. And with every word they were drifting closer to each other, because that's what magnets did.

And now he could smell the rain on her, and see that her shirt was clinging to her from it.

"The sun rises in the east, the earth revolves around the sun, you can see the Big Dipper if you stand out on the big rock near Whiskey Creek. That's how I know. It was inconceivable that it would be otherwise."

She smiled slowly, hugely. "You always were pretty damn sure of yourself."

"Said the pot to the kettle."

"And you're always so bossy, too," she added, almost hopefully.

And as they were close enough to blend right into each other, she addressed these words practically to his chin.

"I know," he said on a rueful, sympathetic hush. "For instance, I insist we get you out of that wet shirt."

He reached for the top button. And worked it open, slowly, deftly.

Her breathing was swifter, a counterpoint to the rush of the rain outside.

His fingers slid down to the next button and freed that, too.

And the next.

"Eli—" she whispered, but she didn't finish the word because he stopped it with his mouth and kissed her.

And as her shirt slipped open, he pushed it away from her shoulders and used its sleeves to tug her tightly into his body. He kept her in that sensual little straightjacket for a moment as he trailed his lips, his tongue, to her throat, where he savored her pounding pulse, to her ear, where he traced it and heard the catch in her breath as bonfire after bonfire of sensation lit all over her body, and where he breathed, "no quarter."

The title of one of their mutual favorite Led Zeppelin songs, as it so happened.

"Bring it," she whispered.

He eased her away from him, peeling her shirt the rest of the way off her shoulders, and she gave a little half shimmy to send it fluttering all the way to the floor.

He paused for perhaps a heartbeat to feast his eyes. "Pretty," he murmured of her teal-blue lace demi-cup push-up bra.

"Got it at Target," she said.

He gave a short laugh. He unclipped the center clip with a sort of leisurely ceremony, even though he could have gotten it open like a ninja.

His hands were shaking a little.

Later the two of them would think of that click as one of their favorite sounds in the world.

When her breasts sprang free, he fervently muttered "Christ," a prayer of thanksgiving if she'd ever heard one, and he filled his hands and sighed like a man crawling through a desert who'd just reached an oasis. He dragged his thumbs over her nipples, already hard as beads.

She made a sound she didn't know she was capable of making. A purely animal sound of pleasure, and Eli pounced on that as though it were a mating call.

His hands were everywhere on her, hot and claiming, sliding over her bare skin, slipping into her waistband, cupping her ass, and they joined in a kiss that was just as demanding and thorough.

She plucked at his shirt and he got the message. He took his hands away from her long enough to reach for the hem and yank it off over his head. There was a terrible moment that lasted approximately three seconds but felt like an eternity where he appeared to be trapped in it. Working as a team they finally got it off and he all but hurled it across the room as if it had purposely attacked him.

Her head went balloon light when she saw him bare from the torso up, from the hard wedge of his shoulders tapering down to his waist and that lovely ferny trail of hair that disappeared into the jeans that clung to his hips and pointed to that fantastic bulge in those jeans.

He *was* a wall. Maybe a fortress.

All safety and danger wrapped up in one.

They all but collided again, the shocking pleasure of skin on skin made her feel drunk and wild. She traced those delicious little gullies between quadrants of muscle first with her fingertips, then lightly with her nails, then her tongue, rewarded with his sucked-in breath of pleasure. She continued to follow the little fingertip trails she'd drawn with her lips and her tongue and let her hands skate down that taut waist into his jeans where the scoops of muscle on either side of his butt seemed to have been designed for her hands.

He reached for the button on her jeans. He popped it dexterously open. And then with ceremony, he dragged her zipper: *zzzzzttt.*

Another excellent sound.

She was shivering with hunger for him, and with anticipation for what was to come.

Together they pushed her jeans off down her hips, and she did a sort of hula hoop shimmy to get them off. She stepped out of them.

And he reached for her again.

She could feel the hunger in him.

She bit his chest very softly because he was beautiful and smooth and because she'd always wanted to.

"Ow," he gasped, sounding thoroughly pleased.

He scooped his hands under her butt and she locked her legs around his waist, and he carried her a few feet and dumped her, albeit somewhat gently, on his couch, like prey he intended to devour.

He dropped to his knees next to her and touched his tongue to her nipple and got a little fancy with it there, then slid his hand over her rib cage, down, down, into the waistband of her underwear, where it vanished between her legs, which fell open to allow him access. He knew exactly what to do when he found her hot and wet. He teased and stroked, circling, finding a languid friction that was going to make her permanently lose her mind.

Waves of electric heat swept up and out through her body until she was all but incandescent with need. Wild and arcing with it.

"You *motherf . . .* oh my God . . . *Please . . .*"

His tongue traced what felt like the alphabet over her nipples and fresh zaps of pleasure had her whimpering now. She was indeed begging.

He peeled her blue lace undies down her legs and threw them God knew where.

Enough begging. Time to demand.

"Eli, *now*. I mean it."

"Talk about bossy."

And then he was bridging her, propped on his arms. She arched up to lock her legs around his waist and he guided himself into her. And he smiled down at her and she smiled up at him, both of them amazed, savoring the feeling of being joined. Their smiles faded, and all was serious and intent and pretty soon out of their control completely. She locked her feet around his back and clung to his shoulders as his hips drummed.

"Glory . . . my God . . ."

Their bodies arched and met and collided, hard, the roar of their breath mingling, the leather sofa making soft farting noises as they slammed the devil out of it.

Her head thrashed back and she heard a moan that may have come from him or from her—it was impossible to tell. It was the sound of almost unbearable pleasure. She was nearly there, nearly there.

And her skin was made of cinders and then release bowed violently upward and shook her.

"Glory . . ." His voice was a rasp. "Jesus . . ."

How convenient that she'd been given a name that already sounded like a hosannah.

She heard her own voice call his name from far, far away, like some distant signal of a distant song in space. She was floating overhead. She was comprised of nothing but bliss molecules. It would take a while to reassemble.

He came with a cry that was almost wild. And she held on to him as he shook, triumphant, replete.

"I have a bed." He sounded drowsily surprised. As if he'd suddenly remembered.

They'd both somehow returned to full consciousness and their bodies.

"Yes, but it's so far away." She loved being mashed together with him, limbs entangled, sweat drying on their bodies. The house was pitch dark now, apart from various little electronic eyes shining at them from the dark: the microwave clock. The burglar alarm.

He chuckled groggily. "More room for shenanigans on the bed. A blank canvas just waiting for us. Plus, I'm told my sheets are 1200 thread count. I wouldn't want that job in the sheet factory. Counting all those threads."

She laughed. "More threads is better. You don't want sheets that can exfoliate you."

He sighed happily. And then, pulling another ninja move, he rolled off the couch into a crouch, draped her over his shoulder and stood and hauled her off, like a fireman rescuing her from a burning building.

"Show off," she gasped. She hadn't even had time to give a little shriek.

"All that practice carrying sacks of flour. I've got something to show you in there."

"Does it involve your handcuffs? I brought them back with me. They're in my purse."

"Nope. But hold that thought."

He laid her down gently on the side of the bed with the un-dented pillow, and she burrowed in as if it were home.

And suddenly he couldn't breathe for how right all of this felt.

As if the jigsaw puzzle of his life had been missing just that moment, a sore place that air blew through, and here it was finally. Her head on that pillow.

"Here."

The "throw" his sister had sent him last Christmas, as though she thought he spent his evenings curled up with a cozy English mystery set in the Cotswolds and a cup of chamomile tea and a faux fur draped over his knees. He kept it folded at the foot of his bed, and he tossed it to Glory. She seized it with a happy exclamation and pulled it up over her, all but purring over its softness.

She looked like a czarina.

He went still. Held in thrall.

You're beautiful, he almost said. *I love you*, he almost said.

She read the first in his face. She smiled back at him, receiving the tribute like a czarina.

And his next words were tantamount to the second.

"Look over there in the corner, Glory. By the window."

She sat up, letting the fur fall indolently down to expose one pale shoulder and a breast, and his head went light.

Just looking at her body was a little like having a hand permanently on his cock. The nipped-in waist and that swelling curve of her ass, and those heavenly, full, up-tilted breasts were as erotic as it got.

She peered where he was pointing.

He was going to savor the expression on her face forever.

"Eli . . . is that . . . is that my *guitar*?"

He took it out of the case and brought it over to her. She

reached up for it as if she were Moses reaching up for the commandments.

She held it in her arms.

She was suspiciously quiet.

She didn't look up, either.

"Are you going to cry again?" he teased softly. "You are *such* a girl."

She laughed. And sniffed.

Then looked up at him.

She didn't have to say thank-you. He'd remember that look, too, for the rest of his life.

She ran her hands over it, as if to check for broken bones. "How did you find it?"

"Put out a bulletin on John-Mark's car. A deputy friend of mine pulled him over on his way to Black Oak for a minor infraction. She called me and held him there until I showed up. Guitar was in the backseat. I took it from him and he knows why. He felt so guilty, Glory. He almost cried. He was so scared of Cameron—she can be tough, believe me—that by the time I got there he just looked like a skinny, quivering kid. I tore him a new one, anyway, one he isn't going to forget. I told him if he needed money he could get himself some better skills and a better damn job. I'll see about helping him however I can. I think he has it in him to make it."

Glory was listening to this as if it was now her favorite bedtime story. "But . . . wait. Didn't you have to be some-where today, Eli? I called your office yesterday. They said you were going to be gone all day."

He didn't even hesitate. "I had to be here with you."

She stared at him and frowned a little, but he met her gaze evenly.

It was only the truth. Or at least one part of it. He didn't need to burden her with the rest.

"Want me to put it back in its case?" he asked. "We wouldn't want to jounce it off the bed."

"If you would."

He settled it tenderly back in and locked it up. And he sat down across from her.

"You look like a czarina," he said softly.

"In all the excitement earlier, I may have forgotten to tell you how hard and thoroughly I blew off Franco Francone."

"So I gathered," Eli murmured. "But say it again, because it's making me hard."

She laughed.

He leaned forward and kissed her softly. Then traced her lips delicately with his tongue. Then parted her mouth with his lips, and took that kiss to dizzying, spiraling depths, savoring the sweet hot satin of her mouth. He slipped the furry throw down from her other shoulder and dragged the fur lightly, deliberately, to and fro over her nipples.

She moaned softly against his mouth. "You are a mad genius," she whispered.

"You have no idea what I know," he whispered by way of reply. "In my hands, everything is a sex toy."

"Even me?"

"Especially you."

She wrapped another little section of the fur throw around the head of his cock and stroked hard, letting her fingernails drag lightly behind to cup his balls.

She did it again.

He hissed in a breath.

"I'm a quick learner," she said.

"Holy . . ." he breathed, impressed. "Don't stop."

She did it again, then bent to close her mouth over the head and suck.

He groaned, and threaded his hands in her hair.

"Don't stop . . ."

She dragged her tongue up the shaft, then closed her hands over it and stroked hard, and leisurely and skillfully, and sat up again to cover his lips with hers.

Vixen.

"I can't decide," she murmured, "if I want to sit forward or backward when I ride you."

In a couple of swift moves he'd folded her into his arms and rolled her over onto her stomach and pulled her upward onto her knees.

"I decided for you."

He dragged his hands along her spine, tracing the lyrical curve of her with his hands, her torso, the nip of her waist, the swell of her hips, so like a guitar. He dragged his palm over the satin coolness of her ass and pulled her closer into him.

Then eased into the slick, satiny wetness. And withdrew.

And thrust again, teasing both of them.

She moaned softly, a low keening sound of pleasure. "Eli . . ."

How many of his dreams had included her moaning his name?

Suddenly it seemed all of his dreams had. He couldn't imagine wasting all that precious time thinking of anything else.

He moved again, teasing her cleft, and she made a sound that was nearly a growl of pleasure.

It went to his head like a belt of Everclear. Every cell in his body was electrified.

He moved again and again, almost languid, but pleasure had claws and they were sinking in deeper and deeper.

He watched her crimson nails curl into the white fur of the throw, and her black hair whipped like a storm cloud as her head thrashed.

Her body swayed with her swift breathing. "Eli . . . so *good* . . ."

He could hear the roar of his breath and hers, and feel the sweat beading on his body as he slid inch by slow inch in again, savoring the hot, silken cling of her, and she arched upward to meet him.

And again.

She writhed as pleasure surged and built in her, and her pleasure rippled through him, and then the madness won out over control and he let go.

His hips drummed swiftly as he gripped her, pulling her into him to take her deeply. The primal smack of their bodies and the tattered roar of their breathing and the moans ripped from each of them were all of a piece; all of it made them wilder still. And then her body arced upward and he heard his name in a hoarse cry, as if from a distance, as pleasure all but tore him from his body and cast him like stardust into the ether.

They collapsed together, brainless and boneless, sated and sweaty, sex-drunk and peaceful.

She sighed and he wrapped his arms around her, and she flung a leg over the top of him, and he cupped the back of her head, and they both fell asleep as hard as if they'd killed each other.

He woke up when his leg was asleep and they were both

chilly, and they communicated in murmurs and grunts like forest creatures, and got under the covers, claimed separate pillows, entwined their limbs, and then slept a dreamless sleep, because all their dreams had just come true.

CHAPTER 21

It was the silence that woke him up. The rain had come down pretty hard all night, and the sound of it, and Glory's breathing, had been like a lullaby.

He reached over and the sheets were still warm. He smiled with manly satisfaction and peered out his bedroom's French doors.

She'd pulled the throw from his bed, wrapped herself in it like a coronation cape and trailed it out.

She was on the back deck, head tipped up, looking out at the dawn. No color in the sky yet. Just a sort of shimmering silver on the edge of the canyon.

She didn't turn around, but she knew he was there.

"*That's* about what color your eyes are."

As if it was a question that had haunted her for ages. He supposed she meant the gray of the dawn sky.

He smiled. "Can I get in on this throw?"

She opened it like a flasher and let him inside. He wrapped his arms around her from behind and she burrowed into his still-warm-from-the-bed body and clasped it shut in her fingers.

They were quiet for a long time. This was new and

beautiful: each other and the dawn. They'd known each other forever but so many new and beautiful moments could lie ahead.

"They want me to fly to Los Angeles," she said finally.

"Yeah?" he answered softly.

"I've never flown. Let alone *alone*."

"You'll love it. You'll love all of it. You were made for it."

"They said words like *agent* and *producer* and *publicist* and *stylist*. Though they kinda like my style."

"Who wouldn't? I like what you're wearing now, for instance."

She smiled again.

They were quiet. He savored small things: how her head fit snugly beneath his chin, how it felt to breathe with her.

The stars retreating, giving way to the sun.

The silence with her in it.

He broke the silence.

"I love you," he said softly.

He hadn't fully known he was going to say those words then. They'd just sort of emerged as naturally as a breath. Part of the moment.

But he knew why he'd said it then when the words rang in the morning calm like a tolled bell. Or a chanted prayer.

He felt her breath catch.

He added softly, "I know you probably already know that. And before you say anything, Glory . . . I don't ever want to be a reason you feel obligated to stay in Hellcat Canyon. I don't ever want to be the reason your world feels smaller or constricted. What I want is for you to have whatever you want. Always."

She burrowed more closely into him. She obeyed him: she was silent.

"Okay. I understand. But Eli . . . before I say anything . . . I have to show you something."

"Does it involve the handcuffs?" he teased.

"Nope."

"A tattoo I might have missed in my explorations?"

"Nope."

Now she sounded nervous. And a little somber.

Which made *him* a little nervous.

"Not yet, though, okay?" she said. "It's not here. We have to go to it at a specific time. Let's sit out here and watch the sun rise."

This was very mysterious. But he didn't hate mysteries.

"Okay, let's move to the chaise."

They shuffled on over to his padded deck chaise and curled up, cocooned in his throw. She snuggled back against his chest, her head leaning on his shoulder.

They watched the gold arc of the sun nudge its way up.

And then she turned her head up in an invitation, and he angled his, and their lips met softly.

For a while they fell in to nearly chaste kisses, leisurely but seductive, reveling in the decadent, delicate discovery of the pleasure that could be had from lips alone. The promise of untold pleasure that lay ahead of them.

And inevitably his hands began to roam, languidly. Less starved, more leisurely, more luxuriating. He stroked her breasts, and she rippled into his touch. Her shuddering, ragged breath as desire overtook her was the most erotic sound he'd ever heard.

She turned around, slowly, gracefully, and straddled him, stroking his cock, then sliding down over it. And the hiss of breath, his head going back hard, was the most erotic thing she'd ever heard. She looped her arms around his neck and kissed him, moving over him slowly, slowly, even as his hands slid to her hips to urge her on. But no, it was her turn to tease. To watch his eyes go black and intent. To see the cords of his neck go taut. To make him sigh softly, and then beg her just as softly, using her name, as she traced his ear with her tongue and teased herself with the slow rise and fall of her body over him. Slowly taking him into her, then sliding up and away, then slowly easing down again.

His breath was sawing now, and her nipples chafing his bare chest made her ever more lust crazed, and that feeling of soft fire over her skin spread, and she knew she was close.

"Christ . . . love . . . I am *dying* . . . *please* . . ." His words were broken gasps.

He arched up, groaning. Begging.

But she had all the control. She laughed softly, sadist that she was.

"You want it, Eli?"

"Yes."

"How *bad* do you want it?"

"Fucking essay questions *now*?" he moaned.

She laughed a sorceress's laugh. And then she showed mercy to both of them. He held her fast, arms locked around her, bucking his hips up to meet her as she came down over him, ever more swiftly, ever harder, until she was whimpering, and then her head fell back on a raw soundless scream as she came, wracked with wave after wave of white-hot bliss, and she felt him shaking in her arms, coming just as hard.

They showered happily and quickly together.

And then all at once she was in a mad rush. "Eep! We have to go *now*, Eli."

He threw on a pair of jeans and a sweatshirt and hiking boots.

And then, his heart accelerating to Porsche speed, he hesitated only briefly. And he slid open his nightstand drawer, took something out, and pocketed it.

Since it was only just past dawn and chilly, he tossed Glory one of his sweatshirts and one of his old jackets, both of which engulfed her. Her hands disappeared. The effect was pretty comical.

"I think you should hire me as your stylist," he said.

She laughed. "Come *on*. We have to be there at a certain time."

"Okay, jeez. You're not taking me to the dentist, are you? We don't have an appointment somewhere?"

"Nope. Shhh," she ordered.

Bossy thing.

As it turned out, they were going on a hike.

She was still nervy. Her hair was a shambles, but he didn't tell her, because he liked knowing it was because she'd slept in his bed and because his hands had been rummaging around in it.

She held his hand the whole way.

Hellcat Canyon, Whiskey Creek, Coyote Creek. All of it apart from the creatures who made their homes in the trees and shrubs and burrows was still pretty asleep.

They were both pretty sleepy and a little bit sore from all the vigorous lovemaking, and it was a pleasant and dreamlike walk. Leisurely and familiar. Not in fact, unlike actual dreams they'd had about each other over the years, except now they finally got to hold each other's hands.

She led him through the old pasture, and past that elm, just as dawn's light tickled the tips of the long grass there. She cut across Whiskey Creek to the secret shortcut up to the Full Moon Falls trail that every kid who grew up there knew about.

From there, it was a pretty decent long hike, with plenty of rises, but they were both used to walking. They startled deer on the trail. A chorus of birdsong, a half dozen varieties, had started up, and they enjoyed that as a soundtrack as they walked.

He'd seen this trail in nearly every light, in every season, and he never tired of it because if you were born in the country you grew to appreciate the subtleties: when the Indian paintbrush and Scotch broom and wildflowers bloomed, which trees leafed out when, which ones were bound to put on the biggest fall show.

And suddenly he knew where they were going.

He just wasn't entirely sure why *she* was leading him here.

They stood in front of the vast, ancient tree known locally as the Eternity Oak.

"Okay, Eli. You know how you told me not to say anything, right? I'm going to answer you now. But my answer is illustrated."

She led him over to the tree, and ducked behind the vast trunk to one of the branches that reached out toward the fall.

And a shaft of morning light lit them up:

GHG + ELB

His breath left him in a gust. "Glory . . ."

She turned to study the effect of this on him, and her smile was huge.

"I carved them there early in the morning the day after your seventeenth birthday. Remember that knife Jonah gave to me one Christmas, that cheap little pocketknife? It was the day after I played that song for you. After the party, I had to do something. I think I always knew, Eli. I just didn't know what to call what I felt. And then I did. And this is what I did about it. You know me—I go all in. It's okay to cry now."

"I'm not crying."

That was actually a little bit of a lie.

"So what I'm saying, Eli, is it's impossible for you to ever be the reason the world feels smaller to me. You have to know that *you* kind of already gave the whole world to me. And by that I mean that I feel free and safe and brave when I'm with you."

He swallowed.

"So if you think you're doing me any favors by deciding you'd better, oh, let me go, shooing me off like some wild bird that you've raised, or something . . . well that's too bad. You're stuck with me. I am music, I guess, and music is me, but as long as I have you, everything else in my life is a grace note. Life doesn't make sense without you. Eli . . . you should know that *you* are all my songs. And all my songs are you. One way or another. I don't see that ever changing."

He gave a stunned laugh.

Next to "I love you," it was the best thing anyone had ever said to him.

He stroked her hair away from her face. Looked down into those midnight-blue eyes.

"Wanna hear something funny?" he asked her.

"Always."

"It's quite a coincidence," he warned.

He saw in her face that she anticipated what he was about to do.

"Come over here, Glory. I'm going to have to give you a boost. " He knelt and hoisted her up by the waist as if they were figure skaters performing a routine.

"Hurry. I'm strong but you're not a feather. Run your hand along that branch there. Then look at it."

She did.

He felt her go still.

And he saw her face light up like a sunrise. She laughed. "Eli . . . Oh my God."

He lowered her into his arms again.

She knocked tears from her eyes, and said, "I think it might be raining again."

"You beat me to the tree by a few hours that day, but isn't that just like you? I carved them there the day after my seventeenth birthday. I felt like you'd gone and carved them right on my soul that night anyway. I had to do something about it. Me and the tree. We kept that secret for a long time. I felt like I was alone with it."

Dawn was bathing them in a cloud of filtered light and the tree's fall wardrobe made it look like it was wearing leaves of gold.

"Glory . . . ?"

And now his voice had gone husky, and he felt like the pounding of his heart could have drowned out a stadium's worth of cheers.

She looked up, eyes wider. Alerted by his tone.

"I kind of feel like I need to do something about *this* moment, too."

He fished his grandmother's ring out of his pocket. He kissed the palm of her hand, laced his fingers through hers. "Will you—"

"Yes," she said eagerly.

". . . marry . . ."

"Yes!"

"Me?" he said softly, determinedly.

"Who, you?" She looped her arms around his neck and stood on her toes and whispered in his ear, as if confiding the secret of the universe. "Yes."

And then he slipped the elegant old ring that once belonged to his rather patrician grandmother onto her slim, tough-tipped, rock-and-roll hand, and it surprised neither of them that it fit perfectly.

CHAPTER 22

"Eli?"

His mom's voice was cheerful but just a little taut. She always answered on the first ring. He knew she tried to disguise the anxiety, but it was there.

"Everything's great, Mom."

He always said this first. And then she would relax.

"What's going on, honey?"

"Well, Mom . . . I gave Grandma's ring away."

There was a beat of silence as the meaning of this settled in.

"You're getting *married*?" she breathed. Pure joy. She made the word *married* about four syllables long.

"Yep." He grinned.

"Who is it?"

He paused.

And then the pause kind of stretched.

And in that pause, she guessed.

"You're going to marry her, huh?" She sounded cautiously bemused.

He gave a short laugh. "Glory Greenleaf. Yeah."

Glory Hallelujah Greenleaf Barlow. He loved the sound of that.

"Well . . . goodness!" Her brightness was a trifle strained.

Eli stifled a laugh. He wasn't surprised.

"So, honey, how did it come about?"

He gave her a very broad outline—ran into her again at a party in Hellcat Canyon, things kind of took off from there. And he told her about Wyatt "King" Congdon and the discovery that took place in the Misty Cat and what was next for Glory.

His mom was struggling more than a little with this news. She knew the history of the Greenleafs, and how what had happened with Jonah had actually broken Eli's heart.

"Well, I'm incredibly happy for her. She's wonderfully talented. And I'm so happy the world will have a chance to hear her. Oh, but, honey . . ."

"Yeah, Mom?"

"If she's really successful at this . . . she'll be touring and recording and doing interviews and shows and Eli . . . the kinds of publicity involved . . . your life could become a zoo. You'll be away from each other so much. It could be so hard on a couple. And hard on a family, if you have kids. It could be so *lonely*. And I want so much for you to be happy. I do. Sweetie, you deserve to be *happy*."

He'd expected her to say exactly this.

She was just reciting stuff that both he and Glory already knew. And he knew his mom was worried.

He waited it out, listening patiently.

And then he waited another moment after his mom stopped talking.

"Was it easy?" he asked gently. "Being married to Dad?"

She was silent.

"Even if you still knew how it all would end, Mom,

would you do it again? Marry him? Make a life with him?"

He was going to make his tough mom cry, but he needed her to understand.

"One minute with her . . ."

He didn't finish. His mom understood the rest: . . . *is better than a lifetime with anyone else.*

And she did understand.

In that silence, she made that leap on her own.

"I'm so happy you found someone to love like that, Eli." Her voice was thrumming with love and tears.

"I learned how to love like that from you."

A moment passed and neither of them spoke.

He heard her sniffling. But she pulled it together.

"She loves you, too, you know, Eli. Glory does." She sounded like she was reassuring herself when she said it.

"Oh, I know." He was smiling faintly, triumphantly. "But what makes you say that?"

"That night when she played that song . . . that beautiful song . . ."

"'Songbird.'"

"Yeah. She was singing it to you. I don't know if you could tell. But I could. Back then, even back then, I knew. She's so gifted."

They sat in a moment of sort of radiant silence that they could both feel even over the phone. Smiling through tears.

"She's some girl," his mom said, finally, in a more normal voice. Processing this. Coming around to the idea, albeit cautiously. He heard the humor in her voice. After all, she'd known Glory her whole life. Caution was a reasonable reaction.

Eli's smile grew into a grin. "She is, at that."

"You two will have the *prettiest* babies. I can't wait to hold them."

"Yikes. First things first, Mom."

H e sat on one side of the glass.
      Jonah sat on the other.

And he still looked like Jonah. Handsome devil, a lot like his sister, lucky with the ladies, particularly fond of bad girls. There wasn't a single ugly Greenleaf, that was for sure.

He looked like Jonah, but he was a little pasty and hollow-eyed, and prison-buff.

Jonah, expressionless, bemused, picked up the phone.

And then Eli saw his hands were shaking. "Hey, man," Jonah said.

"Orange isn't your color, man."

Jonah snorted softly. "Since when do you care about color?"

"Went on a couple of dates with a makeup artist a while ago. Did you know your eyebrow isn't supposed to go any farther than past here?" Eli pointed to that spot.

"No shit?" Jonah was genuinely interested. He touched his own eyebrow.

It was such a stupid thing. But the fact that they could instantly fall into talking about whatever, that Jonah was feeling his own eyebrow made Eli miss him like mad. Because he was curious about everything. He didn't really judge anything. He could make anything funny.

Eli knew a swift surge of frustrated anger, but it evaporated pretty quickly.

Things were how they were.

Neither of them had apologized to each other for how things had gone down. It was sort of implicitly understood how it had happened. And Jonah, unlike his stubborn sister, really didn't quite have it in him to hold grudges.

They were silent a moment. Kind of just happy to be sitting near each other again.

Jonah cleared his throat. "Hey, check this out, Eli. I'm learning Spanish."

"Yeah, I'll just bet you are."

"No, man. For real. Not just the filthy words. Learning Portuguese, too. Gorgeous language. They started me in on French. Next up is the fancy stuff, Chinese and Farsi. Tagalog, probably. Damned if I'm not actually good at this stuff."

Jonah did have that kind of mind. Quick and absorbent. There were easily about fifty things Jonah could have done for a living. If he'd had flawless grades or a family with money or the patience or focus or . . .

There was really no point in thinking about the "what-ifs."

Ironically, being confined to one place was about the only way Jonah would have ever channeled his endless energy and cleverness.

"Yeah, I can see how that might be true. Damn, Jonah. You can make a living as a translator, you know. Something like that. When the . . . time comes."

Government agencies were hardly eager to hire felons. But Eli knew he'd pull strings and move heaven and earth to get Jonah a job like that, if it helped.

What Jonah did after that was out of Eli's control.

But Eli realized now that it didn't matter. He was essentially family. Had always been family.

He was stuck with him.

And if he pulled any shit like that again, Eli would arrest him again.

Jonah was staring at him shrewdly.

"You got something on your mind, Barlow. You're not just here to soak up the ambience. Or my pretty face."

Eli figured he might as well come out with it.

"Yeah. I came to tell you I'm in love with your sister."

Jonah went perfectly still. Oddly, his expression didn't change.

"You mean Glory," he said neutrally. Finally.

"Yeah. I mean Glory."

He was silent for a long time.

"Well, yeah, I knew that." Jonah sounded faintly puzzled.

"What do you mean?"

"I mean, the sun rises in the east, the earth revolves around the sun, and you're in love with Glory. I think I've known that for at least as long as you've known it. Not consciously, but it was just sort of always there. I just didn't know if you'd ever find the right time to do something about it."

Eli didn't know what to say.

"Shit," Eli finally said, eloquently, in surprise.

Jonah laughed.

"Better you than that dip Mick Macklemore."

"Flattered."

"She loves me, too, by the way," he added, a moment later.

"Yeah. I guess I kind of knew that, too."

Jonah was smiling at him.

Eli felt himself blush. In a prison, and he was blushing. "I guess I wanted you to know. I'm going to marry her."

Jonah went still again. And then he drew in a long, long breath, and released it. He nodded.

They didn't bother saying all the stuff that was understood: that Jonah would miss the wedding. Would miss a lot of very important things, in fact.

"Congratulations, then, buddy," Jonah finally said. Quietly.

"Thanks," Eli said gruffly.

They were quiet a moment.

Jonah quirked the corner of his mouth. "Hey, I hear some movie star bought my old house."

"Yeah. John Tennessee McCord. Good guy."

"My mom visits. Tells me these things. Sometimes she hauls John-Mark or Michelle in with her. I see my nieces and nephews sometimes. Not Glory, though." Jonah's voice had gotten a little frayed. "Never Glory."

"I know," Eli said softly.

"She . . . took it hard."

That was an understatement.

"I think because she loves you best, Jonah."

Jonah's eyes slowly reddened. His breathing was audible now, as he tried to get a grip on his emotions.

And then he swallowed. "Yeah. I get it, man."

They sat together in silence a moment.

Jonah took in another deep breath. "Will you tell her I love her? And miss her?"

"Yeah. Of course," Eli said softly.

"Miss you, too, bro."

"Yeah. Me, too."

He didn't know whether, when Jonah got out in about four years, his sister might be at the top of the charts. Or he might be an uncle to a baby or two.

He did know he'd probably be glad to see him, no matter what.

"I'll talk to you again soon?" Jonah said, softly.

"Sure."

They fist-bumped each other through the glass.

And Eli turned and walked away.

"Can you get those off easily? Because they're going to want you to take them off."

Eli was peering down at Glory's cowboy boots. Above them, jets were roaring into the sky, and travelers were dragging vertical stacks of luggage toward the automatic doors.

"Don't worry. They're boots. I know you like it when I keep them on sometimes, Eli, but I can get these off quickly enough."

"Okay. Ask questions anytime you're confused. Don't argue with the security. They're your friends. They might feel you up a little extra after you walk through the X-ray machine, but they feel a lot of people up. It's random. Mostly."

"Would you blame them?" She swept a hand down her own sweet self.

"Not one bit," he said sincerely. "Not every day you get to touch a work of art. Okay, what else . . . Check the boards to see if your flight changes. Or check your phone." Eli had bought her a new cell phone; they were living together at his house now. "Britt Langley says she'll be in L.A. for another week and she'll meet you at your hotel and you can have dinner with her and J.T., and when you come back, you can come back with them. If you have any questions or worries about what's going on at the record label, J.T. will hook you up with the right people, just not Francone and . . . what?"

She was grinning at him. "I love you, too, Eli. So much."

He smiled back at her. "Yeah, I know. You got this. You scared?"

"Nope."

"In other words, yep."

"Oh, nervous. A little. We'll take things as it comes."

She used *we* a lot these days. As often as she possibly could. She liked it.

My was another word they both liked.

As in "My husband, Eli."

"My wife, Glory."

She held out her hand, where Eli's grandmother's old ruby and diamond ring and her own slim vintage diamond wedding band caught and shot little sparks in the sun. They'd gone and done it one afternoon at the courthouse and decided they'd have a big party when she got back from Los Angeles, invite everyone they knew, hell, even Mrs. Adler. Eli didn't think the diamonds were anywhere near as dazzling as the woman who wore them proudly, but she loved sparkle, and he caught her admiring them a lot in a lot of different lights.

"I'll miss you a lot," he said. Gruffly.

"We can talk dirty to each other on Skype. I want to hear all the non-dirty stuff, too."

"I'll save it all up for you."

He kissed her. Hard, and then soft. She hung on to him extra tightly a moment. Because she needed it, and she knew he did, too. Because she knew that his life could be pornographic garden gnomes one minute and a gun wielding meth addict the next. Because they would never get enough of holding each other, no matter what.

He kissed her fiercely one more time and then whispered, "Go get 'em, tiger."

She finally let go. And walked backward, blowing him a kiss.

He caught a glint of something else sparkling in the corner of her eye. She brushed at it.

She looped her hand around her new bright red carry-on case, in which she'd packed, among things like her favorite blue bra and faded jeans, a box of the cassettes she'd recorded over the years and her stuffed tiger, so she could finally say, "See? Told you we'd see the world."

And when she finally turned around and walked away, she put a little more swing into it.

Just for him.

EPILOGUE

One year later . . .

E li leaned back against the bar at the Misty Cat
Cavern in the "V.I.P. section," his arms wrapped
around his wife, who was snuggled up against
him, head tucked under his chin. It was both an em-
brace, and kind of a way to hold each other up. They
were both a little dizzied by what they'd learned before
they set out for Glory's show at the Misty Cat this evening. They both felt as if they'd belted down a bottle of
champagne each. Champagne made solely of bubbles,
maybe.

Glory finally looked up when the house lights dipped
portentously. It was her cue to get a move on.

And then she froze. "Omigosh! Eli don't move. You
have a spider on your neck."

"Holy—! Get it . . ."

Glory reached up and plucked it off.

Ah, country girls. Not afraid of a damn thing.

They peered down at it in her palm. "Oh!" She was
bemused. "It's not a spider. It's one of my fake eyelashes."

Eli laughed.

A pit crew of uniquely skilled women had just spent a couple hours on her makeup to make it look like she wasn't wearing any makeup. And then they'd worked on her hair for about an hour to make it look as though she had just rolled out of bed. As part of this routine, a fluffy row of fake eyelashes was glued to each of her eyelids.

Those women were watching her nervously now, suspecting their good work was being undone.

They'd let Glory wear her own jeans and her own white lacy shirt on stage, at least.

She wouldn't be fitting into either of those for much longer.

She and Eli kept having thoughts like that. They now saw all the little details of their world, the mundane and the profound, through the lens of their news. Each new realization was like a fresh rush of intoxication.

"I better go let them fix me." Glory gestured with the eyelash. "I'm supposed to be on in ten."

He gave her behind a pat as she turned and tossed him a minxy look over her shoulder.

He exhaled, happy he had something to lean against, because damned if she didn't make his knees weak.

He was kind of wishing he could be alone with her now.

But also knew that this was a night destined to be unforgettable in their family's history.

And that they were never really going to be alone together again, anyway.

Funny how things suddenly became very clear. Even though Leigh Devlin had been pretty understanding, ultimately, and the undersheriff position wasn't off the table for Eli, something about watching her walk away at the airport had prompted him to research what it would take to start his own private security firm. It would be a juicy tactical challenge requiring all of his law enforcement training and skills as a leader, with perhaps a little adjunct training. At some point Glory was going to need a bodyguard. He was that guy. And what mattered, he'd realized in a heartbeat a few short hours ago, was that his family remain together, and all other choices would hinge on that. It would be the one defining law of his life from now on.

Tonight was in fact a culmination of that moment when she'd left for Los Angeles to meet with Congdon and his Stellium staff about a year ago.

In that first meeting, the efficient, seen-everything people at Stellium Records didn't so much as hike a brow when Glory told them she'd never professionally, let alone *digitally*, recorded anything.

"All I have are these." And she produced the shoebox full of cassette tapes she'd recorded in her bedroom.

Wyatt Congdon had stared at that box, frowning. And then the frown tipped up into an enigmatic, private little smile that sent surreptitious nervously excited looks ricocheting among his staff.

He'd made them sit with him at a huge conference table and listen to all of those tapes—original songs, covers, fragments of songs interrupted by Glory yelling at John-Mark to get out of her room, random noodling, dogs barking in the background—which took about fifteen hours, all told.

And then a sort of slow-dawning glow spread over his face. It was like watching spring taking over the land. Only maybe slightly more wicked.

His underlings knew that look. They hadn't seen it in what felt like too long. If they'd had to call it something, it might have been *eureka* or *money*.

He was about to do the thing that made him magnificent. See the magic in the seemingly mundane.

Stellium chose ten of Glory's taped songs, digitally remastered them with a light and skillful hand so that every breath, bird chirp, and door squeak was included (but no yelling at her brother), sneaked them out online as *Glory Greenleaf: Live from My Bedroom*. The cover artwork just a photo of an old cassette tape labeled with Glory's handwriting.

And like a match to tinder, reviews, word of mouth, blogs, Twitter, Facebook made downloads treble by the week. People couldn't get enough of the soulful, hushed intimacy of those stripped-down songs. Her voice as immediate and erotic as a breath in your ear. More than a few babies were conceived to them, and guys who really wanted to impress a girl claimed they were into Glory Greenleaf.

Stellium had barely done a damn thing, let alone spent a damn thing, compared at least to the usual promotional circus for a new artist. They really just wanted to get a brushfire started. To prep the world for the conflagration that would be Glory Greenleaf's career.

They hadn't really anticipated *Live from My Bedroom* . . . charting.

Let alone at number *twenty-five*.

And "Featherbed" charted as a single at thirty-two.

And then they both began to slide a little.

No worries: It would skyrocket right back up there when *Glory Greenleaf: Live at the Misty Cat* was released in six months' time. *Live from My Bedroom* was the aperitif.

Live, Wyatt Congdon had decided, was the best way to experience Glory Greenleaf.

As it turned out, thanks to experience hashing out shoe-string budgets with her mom over the years, Glory was a calmly ruthless and practical negotiator, and armed with a husband who had a law degree and a charmingly cut-throat new agent named Nafisa Patel, whom she'd found with the help of J.T. McCord, they all had an invigorat-ingly good time hashing out contract terms that favored her immensely. She wasn't going to get rich overnight, and she didn't care. She and Eli had taken this opportu-nity to craft a plan that would let them have the life they wanted and take care of the people they loved, within reason.

Of course, life had a way of chucking monkey wrenches in.

Life had in fact just chucked the sweetest sort of monkey wrench in.

She was aglow with her secret as she submitted to a quick re-glue of her eyelashes and a refreshing of her lip-stick. Then she gave the waiting Monroe Porter, whom she'd insisted on hiring for tonight and whose heart was still with death metal but was a Glory Greenleaf fan, a little high five.

She lifted her guitar gently from its stand, where Gior-gio had settled it, perfectly tuned.

A couple hundred people, a compact but fancy sound-board, and a film crew of two had been shoehorned into the Misty Cat Cavern for two nights of sold-out shows, the first time, in fact, the Misty Cat Cavern had pre-sold tickets. All of this was Glory's idea, seconded by Wyatt, and approved by Glenn and Sherrie, given that it was sort of the fulfillment of a promise and a reward for having faith in, and suffering through, an abysmal waitress.

Glenn, a born emcee, stepped in front of the mic to do the honors.

"Ladies and gentlemen, thank you all so much for joining us on this special night. This is the first night in a pair of shows that I'm certain will become music history legend. Hellcat Canyon and the Misty Cat Cavern are proud and pleased to welcome our own . . . Glory Greenleaf."

The applause and cheers were thunderous.

She smiled through it.

"Sorry we're running just a little behind, but my pit crew had to re-do my lipstick because I was kissing my man."

The audience laughed and *wooooo*'d at this.

"Have you *seen* him? Can you blame me?" She swept a hand toward him, and the stones on her wedding ring glinted and sparked in the little spotlight. One of the sound guys attempted to swing the light in Eli's direction. Eli nodded and gamely raised a hand in greeting, accepting the tribute and that little chorus of *wooooos* with dignified aplomb. Yep, she's mine, I'm hers. We kiss a lot. You try anything, boys, and, well, I'm six foot five. It won't go well for you.

He was glad the spotlight only managed to swipe him across the neck, and missed his face because he didn't quite trust his eyes. They might still be a little on the shiny side.

The last thing she'd whispered to him before she'd found her eyelash on his neck was "We'll name him after your dad."

"Boys and girls," she said, as she slung her guitar over her neck. "Never waste a chance to mess your lipstick up on someone you love. You can always just touch it up again, and I've learned you don't always get do-overs. Life is short. Love and music make it worth living."

As Franco Francone would have said, *a little backwoods wisdom*.

She almost snorted at herself, though.

Like she knew anything at all.

Despite the major contract, the buzz, and the slew of people devoted to making her career take off, she still kind of felt like she was making it all up on the fly. Though now that she had Eli and her music—everything she'd ever wanted—forming the backbeat of her life, riffing on everything else was a lot easier.

Still, it was like every bit of wisdom she'd ever acquired needed to be re-assessed. Funny how the prospect of becoming a mother could make her feel as blank, as open, as a newborn.

She took her place in front of the mic stand, her guitar protectively warm against her belly, and looked out into the audience. Sprinkled throughout were so many people she loved, either because she actually loved them or because she'd learned to love them because they'd been a part of her life for nearly as long as she could remember and so, by virtue of that, were part of who she was. Her mom was now Mrs. Gary Shaw—they'd gotten married at the Black Oak Country Club, possibly the fanciest thing a Greenleaf had yet done. And they were living in the old Greenleaf house for the time being; her brother John-Mark, thanks to Eli, now had a part-time clerk's job at the sheriff's department and was doing well and impressing everyone, though it no doubt helped that he had the eyes of all the deputies on him all day long. Her harried sister, Michelle, was even there. They'd found a sitter for her kids: Rosemary, who ran the Angel's Nest Bed and Breakfast and loved kids and so longed to adopt kids of her own.

And when she slung her guitar over her neck, it kind of felt like her dad was there, too.

It occurred to her in a flash that her guitar wasn't going to lie flat like that against her for too much longer, and her heart gave a stabbing, joyous leap.

And Jonah . . . was always present by virtue of how profound his absence was.

Only yesterday she'd been ambivalent about going to see him. Still nursing vestiges of sizzling anger and hurt.

Today, all of that had been completely erased by joy. Grudges were such a waste of time when you could just love someone instead.

She straightened her harmonica strap and gave her hair a flip over her shoulder that little Annelise, out there in the audience, unconsciously immediately mimicked.

She was there with her mom, Eden, and Sherrie and Glenn. There was Casey Carson and Kayla Benoit, best friends from way back, even if Truck Donegal got between them now and again, and there was Truck, helping Glenn to keep an eye on things. Even Britt Langley and John Tennessee McCord, such lovely people and now counted as good friends of hers and Eli's, were back from Los Angeles and tucked into a corner so no stranger in the crowd could have a conniption about the presence of a celebrity like J.T. Hellcat Canyon was their permanent home.

Giorgio was up at the mixing board. Turns out he was just as much a savant at mixing sound as he was at conducting the grill. Giorgio understood balance, timing, rhythm, and order. Glory understood that surly guy felt the world kind of like she did: in terms of rhythm and sound. There was more to him than met the eye.

He gave her the thumbs-up.

Justin Chen was there, but not Wyatt Congdon, who was in New York being Wyatt Congdon. He hoped to fly in tomorrow. Casey Carson, Glory had noticed, was eyeing Justin and was getting eyed in return.

The actual The Baby Owls were there, too. She'd met the three of them in Los Angeles: Clement(!)—she couldn't wait to suggest *Clement* as a middle name for the baby, just to see Eli's expression—Stephen, and Billy were sitting out there, blending in pretty well with some of the other bearded types who'd shown up. They were happy to be a part of the story of Glory Greenleaf's meteoric rise, especially since they got a song out of it ("One Night in Bumfuck," a song from their next record, sanitized for commercial airplay as "One Night in Nowhere," was a big hit), and they were mentioned in practically every article about her to date.

She didn't mention Franco Francone, though. And neither did Wyatt Congdon or any of Stellium's publicists—who would have taken that connection and run with it—since she'd made that a condition of their contract.

Franco didn't actually mind. He apparently figured that someday when Glory Greenleaf was sixty and dictating her autobiography to a ghostwriter she could mention that she'd passed up an opportunity to have sex with Franco Francone, and he'd been so stunned he'd sent Wyatt Congdon to her instead. He had a feeling he'd cross paths with

Glory again, regardless. He wasn't eager to cross paths with her husband.

Mainly, right now, Glory was struck by all the new faces in front of her. This would be the shape of her life from now on: more new faces than old. People who'd seen her at The Baby Owls' show, and spread word of her with evangelical zeal. A couple of people who won tickets to see her in fought-over online contests and were now aiming their eyes at her with shining awe and adulation and anticipation. Glory was suffused with a humble shock: she was doing what she loved, and it made people happy. Did it get any better than that?

These were the first people to see Glory Greenleaf live, apart from the Hellcat Canyon regulars.

They were present for a moment in history.

"Freebird!" someone shouted, predictably.

She laughed. "Careful what you ask for, darlin'."

And she sang the opening line of that song in public for the first time.

The crowd howled and clapped in amused approval.

One day she *would* do the whole song.

Maybe . . . even tomorrow night.

If the Stellium Records people had come into this with ideas about keeping this show predictable or in line, they were in for a few surprises. She was Glory Greenleaf Barlow and they were in Hellcat Canyon, after all, where it seemed just about anything could happen.

She looked up at Eli and told herself she would not cry because the eyelash would end up skittering down her face.

He was just going to have to do the misty-eyed bit for both of them. And she'd play "Songbird," just to tip him right over that edge.

She rocked that crowd, as if they were in her own cradle. As if they were in their own private stadium.

And by the time she wrapped it all up with a tender version of "Permanently Blue," Marvin Wade slipped whatever internal mental tether had kept him sedately seated for the show and got up to dance, twirling gently around the small expanse of floor like a dandelion set free into the wind. And no one stopped him, because he was just doing what they were all doing inside anyway. Maybe in particular what Glory's and Eli's hearts were doing.

And eight months later—on the same day that Eli and Glory first held Zachary Henry Barlow, who surprised no one by entering the world yelling at the top of his lungs and sporting a thick shock of dark hair—the rest of the world was introduced to the first video from *Glory Greenleaf: Live at the Misty Cat.*

It was just Glory and her guitar on stage alone at the Misty Cat Cavern, suffused in dusty golden morning light, while Marvin Wade danced his slow, swirly dance, going around and around and around.

REL 1216

*G*ive in to your Impulses!

These unforgettable stories only take a second to buy and give you hours of reading pleasure!

Go to *www.AvonImpulse.com* and see what we have to offer.

Available wherever e-books are sold.

AVONIMPULSE